Jennifer, Inc.

By Russ Haywood

RUSSELL HAYWOOD, December 2017

Copyright © 2017 by Russ Haywood

eBook also available on Amazon Kindle and Google Play

Science fiction. Alternative history. Dark comedy. Politics.

ISBN-10: 0-692-04790-5
ISBN-13: 978-0-692-04790-3

Cover art by Suzana Stankovic

Author photograph © Russ Haywood

www.russhaywood.com

Negative freedom, or the "freedom from" traditional authorities and cultural/social restraints, and the positive "freedom to" live authentically and realize one's true individual self. If one is granted negative freedom without positive freedom, and thus left uncertain, alone and powerless, he or she may be inclined to escape from freedom and submit to a higher authority. An analogy would be the urge that many adults have felt at least once in their life to return to their mother's womb, where one is deprived of freedom, but safe from the dangerous and chaotic outside world.

Will Americans submit to despotism in an urge to "escape from freedom"? Erich Fromm saw it coming.
By Conor Lynch. February 2017. Salon Media Group, Inc.

FORWARD—MEMO

Eddie. October 2027

"Heya, Sara. I'd still love your feedback. Haven't heard from you in a few days, haha… Totally get you're busy, just want you to know I'm taking these proposed System adjustments seriously. What do ya think of my draft note below? It's probably my suicide note. I'd like it to be really good. lol"

MEMO TO: All employees, All Contractors, All Customers
FROM: Ed, System Admin
DATE: 10/19/2027 (draft)
SUBJECT: Emergency! Jennifer is a psychopathic black hole of death

Team—

If you're reading this, I'm probably dead. My "Plan A" failed and this is my resignation/obituary. Farewell. Please see the attached file summaries on Jennifer being a psychopathic black hole of death.

If you've never received a direct message from me: Hi. My name is, or was, Eddie. Jennifer's System Administrator and Technology Architect. I've been with Jennifer since the beginning—the first literal Insider. (Ha!) I helped build, manage, and facilitate much of what Jennifer did. Know this: In my dreams, I wanted our world to be free and independent, where we could easily laugh at my story with detached amusement as the 'shit show' that never was—an entertaining nightmare from a parallel world forgotten once we wake. I had no idea this darkness could come so close and be so real.

If you're reading this? Fuck. I really screwed up and it's probably too late. Escape. Find a way however you can. Join nomads in the most remote corners of the Earth for a generation or two. Escape even if it kills you like it did me. Honestly, I doubt any of you will be Outsiders or see real daylight again.

I'm partly responsible for Jennifer's all-consuming acquisitions. The "disappearance" of millions. The pending death of billions. The wholesale destruction of cities through the economic collapse and the violence of unchecked poverty. I ignored her warped quasi-truths and enabled Jennifer's world. I didn't realize our end would be so much worse than I ever could imagine.

But how can anyone imagine the unimaginable? I assumed business managers earning more and more, and workers less and less, would remain within natural limits of decency. I thought the market would self-correct! I thought I was making us all great by looking out for myself.

I know the economy sucks. We all feel it. I get *why* some of you think she's going to help you. I was tired of being a Temp. Was tired of slapping my face on the hard desk of life, going nowhere. Sure, my once friend and co-worker *is* cute. She's smart, strong, and an intense success. But her success is only for her—*always for her and no one else!* Inside she's rotten. She lusts violently for a crueler darker world than any monster from fact, fiction, or nightmare that I've ever seen. You need to permanently remove any delusion that Jennifer will save you. Do *not* toss your life away as a hostage to your own destruction. Please don't.

I played a complicit part in my own destruction. I loved her. Don't follow my path. Run.

Best of luck and goodbye,
Ed

CHAPTER 1—WORKPLACE INTRODUCTION

Eddie. February 2022

My day starts at 7:20 a.m. I can't tell if I've shaved this morning. I *could* move my hand to check my face but am undecided if I feel too depressed or too tired to try. There's not enough Coffee Flave™ in the world to track call yields at 7:23 a.m. And worse, Tad is three minutes late for his morning Walk-By™.

Tad "Action" Jackson is my washed-out quarterback of a supervisor at TempGrace: *San Antonio's Finest Temp Lease Wranglers.* Every Tuesday he Walks-By™ to share the fresh motivational insights of a single TempCollege course in Athletic Performance Management mixed with the part-time inspiration of a cheap consultant distracted by his next golf appointment.

I listen to the quiet murmur of hundreds of phone calls and interviews around me. Nine years of part-time TempCollege and two full-time TempShifts™ each day compose one beautiful symphony of a career. The buzz of our inefficient lighting harmonizing with the HVAC system entertains my ear until Tad's new training assignment arrives.

I softly tap a syncopating set of triplets on the desk, alternating knuckles of my right and left hands. *Zero time for jazz,* I frown. All I can do is hum lines on my walks to work or compose to the drone of the drones sitting around me.

Earn enough working to start a band I need to pull my life together, I rub my temples with meek despair. *No band, no savings, no girl. And I smell funny,* I sniff my armpit, *like cheese. Am I fermenting? I can't afford cheese and I'm unsure how that chemistry works. I can barely afford showers, at least not with water at $3.15 a gallon. Fuck! I remember the days when it was only $1.79. Being culprit to my own odor is an unfortunate possibility. Maybe it's someone on the other side of my row?* I lean over to look at the endless grey Office Cubes™ around me, but can't see smell.

I glance at the time as I plop into my thinly padded chair. 7:26 a.m. *God, I'm exhausted. I hope this trainee isn't a chick,* I suddenly worry. *That could really screw my System Score™.* I scan Tad's email. *Yup.* He wrote 'she' and 'her.' *Shit. Can't stray far from my work game only two years from Management Consideration Status™. They only hire hot ones into this level, and it's not like we have a lot of personal space in our cube rows. Working next to each other might make my Consideration tougher. Are they setting me up to fail with this chick so they can use her distraction as an excuse to slow me down?* I glance irritatedly at the sad grey carpet of the narrow row between our shallow Temp Cubes™.

I've noticed the personal space allowed each worker has dramatically shrunk the past few years. *But hey, whatever keeps the lights humming and the paychecks moving,* I muse. *A great bottom line for the company is good for us all.* Further minimization of the workforce remains a casual worry of mine. I can't help but glue my eyes to the scare articles always showing up in *TempLife Magazine* scattered around the office: "47% of current American jobs are at high risk of being automated over the next ten years! Software like The System™ cheaply provides automated financial advice and management to the work of accountants and stock traders, and replaces the work of many TempsQuants™. As a benefit, The System expands the number of TempCoders™ and the people getting cheap financial advice and investment products. A net positive! Worry not. The hardest workers will always enjoy TempWork™."

However, I remember a lady in one of my TempCollege classes a few years back who worked at a big bank's electronic-trading desks from 2003 until the 2008 Collapse. She said the company only needed one TempCoder for *ten* of the old-school traders and TempQuants who lost their jobs. Worse, she said, that TempCoder was eventually outsourced to India.

I scratch my chin, *What if the TempLife article was wrong?* I've seen so many signs of the workforce shrinking smaller and smaller in my TempConnect™ calls. More and more, I'm recruiting temps for entry-level and low-paying jobs that serve the wealthy elite. Roles like cleaners, personal trainers, and baristas; programmers, architects, and manager roles seem rarer by the day.

If technology's coming for us all. Fine. I smirk. *I have a plan: work as hard as possible, even if that means I'm John Henry against the steam shovel. I make my own success. I'll never be a*

'Handout-Lout' like the hundreds of the lazy poor I see on my walk to work.

I bend a paperclip into a straight line on my desk hoping to break my depressed funk. No luck. Tad's footsteps finally approach my cube at 7:42 a.m. "Twenty-two minutes late," I mutter turning to welcome a pair of smiles.

One smile holds Tad's gold tooth, implanted after the 2012 Hobo Riots™, framed by his square jaw and slick brown hair. His smile is always so proud because, "this tooth alone makes my net worth ten times bigger than yours, Ed. So, listen up." His attitude makes him seem forty feet tall. Which makes sense, as he's probably paid six times more than me.

The other smile is radiantly feminine. Feminine in the way your whole body disregards all common sense—like looking for traffic crossing a street—and stumbling closer in amazement. Her skin is perfect. Her chin gracefully drops from delicate cheekbones that mantle black eyelashes and piercing blue eyes. The young woman's dark hair gently curls past her shoulders around a low-cut dress shirt that sculpts two of the perkiest breasts man has seen since Eve. If I were walking, it's at this point along her curvy highway I'd stumble and smear out my life with a dumb grin.

Other workers stop and drool at her like pathetic comets falling into the sun. *Zero guesses why the Temp agency hires only the hottest temps for themselves?* I darkly snort to myself. Don't need much to imagine what sort of Prospect Engagement Process™ the management team used to interview their hundreds of thousands of applicants. I'm always grateful to outlive the three-month work-life of a hottie-gadfly, like this dumb piece of hot ass. *She'll be lucky to last two weeks,* I sit up, set on playing it cool.

"Ed, this is Jennifer, our new Associate Recruiting Temp," Tad pats her shoulder a half-dozen unwanted times. "Walk her through the call schedules and help TempGrace Score™," he punches my arm, smelling like coffee and a stale fart.

I stand and shake her hand like a moron, my detached cool instantly melting on approach. "Uh. Hi, Jennifer. Great to meet you."

Why did I pick such frumpy clothing this morning? She looks to be in her early twenties, like a rich girl whose next appointment is to remove chewing gum from her hair. *But holy shit. The pull of her gravity is intense.* Workers in our row keep leaning slyly over their desks to check her out.

How long before she's on her back in Tad's office, or smearing her tits across the desk of James, our CEO? I wonder. The end of the day? I remember my TempBusiness™ textbook: Since repealing restrictive labor laws that ruined our economy, TempScience found that on the job fornication considerably helps job creators relax from their responsibilities and bring clarity of vision to potential profit opportunities. I don't always like the exploitive behavior Temp culture produces, but also can't judge the management team *too* harshly for improving the scenery.

"Jen-ten, this is your cube across from Edster," Tad offers the vacant desk across the narrow hallway from me. "Settle in and we'll see you at the ten o'clock TeamBreak™. Pound it, y'all." After a pointless fist bump, Tad leaves with a sly stare at neither mine nor Jen's eyes.

Tad already gave her a nickname: *Jen-ten.*

I imagine this poor girl's next few months until she's dismissed for getting pregnant or "promoted" to a receptionist desk in the Slut Bin. I bet the worst is the nicknames. "Jen-ten-errater, generate ten copies of this email archive. Jen-o-rate some nice cleavage for the clients, please? We need a distraction to switch the contract." *The bimbo is in for hell and that little brain behind her dumb smile has no idea.*

"Hi, Jennifer. Sorry you got put here," I sheepishly console her as Tad's footsteps fade safely away. "He's not too bad after the second spray of mace, and sometimes a real job *does* come through for us Temps. We actually can escape," I say, smoothing my shirt. "I see it once or twice a year. Alright," I instruct her, "First, you log into the System by—"

"—Oh, no worries. I worked here last year, Eddie." Jennifer places her bags on the ratty floor with a grin and settles into the spinning chair, looking at me. "I quit last January to review other Temp Agencies around the country," she waves off the topic. "It's good to be back," she then leans to absently flips on the computer and opens an Assignment Sheet™ like a pro.

"Huh?" I ask, scratching the back of my head, walking to her screen. "Yeah, those are your assignments." I pointlessly instruct. "And yeah, those are your tasks."

"Yup. I know," Jen politely nods.

"Oh, okay. Uh. Why the hell did you come back to this shithole?" I inquire in a confused and serious whisper.

Even for hotties, Temp World holds one-way contracts out of the industry: Do your job or never come back. This minimizes workers' ability to transfer trade secrets, instills a healthy moral hazard, and keeps salaries low. The key is to loyally follow TempGrace's drum to avoid the TempBlacklist™, because there's no fucking second chances in a world of 46% unemployment. We have enough problems without morons in Congress trying to raise the corporate and high-income tax rates to 3.1%. High taxes are how we got into this economic mess and the middle-class will remain a buried fossil like it has since 2009.

"I wanted to see how other temp agencies worked," Jen continues, looking at her objectives and typing as she talks. "Which was fascinating, and depressing," she shakes her head. "I like Texas. Guys like you are nice here," she smiles up at me and touches my arm, "and Texas is the most pro-business and anti-worker environment in the Southern United States." She distractedly adds, typing away at her next assignment. "I read a book called *The Super-Americans* that says Texas is a place where 'Americans see themselves reflected, not life-size, but bigger than life.' I liked that a lot. Fits my style."

"Uh, that's great. We'd like to see that too," I nod.

Her eyes scan more spreadsheets and then she opens new tabs in the System. "Perfect," she grins, and then scowls as her password fails to open the new page.

"Oh, that's not an area you have access to…"

She looks up with large eager eyes, "Can you please log me in here?"

I nervously swallow, "Uh, sure," and lean forward to type. "Probably shouldn't do this…" I bury my nervousness.

"Thanks," she cheers. "They're opportunities to make it *huge* out there," Jen nods, taking control of the computer again. "I'm hoping this office works best going forward."

"That's cool," I awkwardly chuckle in wary amazement. *But one thing doesn't make sense.* After a second of thought, and not wanting to leave her and return to work, I ask, "How'd you get back into the office pool? There's 'no grace for the disloyal at TempGrace'." I finish with a mock scowl, which I hush as I realize I'm speaking too loud. I've seen people fired for less.

Her face bursts with amusement. "I might have to keep you around. You're funny and handsome. A rare catch," Jen's glimmering smile teases.

Co-worker's heads turn to us like flowers seeking the energy of her sun. I feel embarrassment bloom into a shade of Moron Maroon. Yet her laughter is the most beautiful sound in the world, and a song I refuse to hush. That'd be like smothering the one bird who flutters into a dark prison to chirp and sing. Some days you need to hear something beautiful, even for a little while, even when you know the other prisoners are going to kill it, pluck it, and eat it for dinner. Her song's easy and free, and lifts my heart.

"Look. Ed." Her eyes lock onto mine. She lays two hands on my arm and shakes me.

—*Wow.* Her touch seers a bolt up my arm into my heart.

"They had me back because I wanted to be back," she casually adds.

I love how her eyes twinkle. Do only young birds have this much enthusiasm for life?

"Wait," my brain barely recovers from the dopamine rush of her attention. "But how'd they accept your re-employment?" I whisper in sudden confusion, "If you couldn't work in this temp office, *no* office had you. The whole world's Temps. A bad reputation with one firm is a permanent economic death. I spent six years in TempTraining to even be *eligible* for TempGrace."

A solid TempRecord™ motivates workers to appreciate their one chance to temp for an office like TempGrace.

She chuckles casually at the question. "You really believe that? Ha. You're awfully easy to brainwash, eh? If a girl has powers, it's only fair she uses them, right?" she asks. "Shouldn't let society hold hard work and ambition back with silly norms?" She touches my arm again, this time gently. With a soft, "You're kind to worry. I love your energy. We'll need to keep talking," she becomes busy at the workstation.

Turning away, her legs sculpt a masterpiece into her dress pants as her tush overhangs the luckiest chair in the world.

"I'd love to help you as much as possible," I dumbly beam to her back. "I'm on deck for anything you ask."

God you're so gorgeous. I'll do anything for you. Rub your back. Take out your garbage? Wash your dishes? Fuck you in the mouth?

Jen, name it.

Today's going to be a distracting day. With half my thoughts on her and half trying to make myself not appear too much like a dip-shit; that doesn't leave much time for work. I officially worry my numbers this week are screwed. Our row of cubes is for Senior Long-Term Temps™. Hotties don't last long, nor do the guys who flirt with them. I quickly turn to my workstation.

CHAPTER 2—EMPRESS OF WILMINGTON, ILLINOIS

Jennifer. April 2012

I could live in this garden forever, I whisper the dream to a spring breeze. Lazy white clouds float beyond budding tree branches. I study, lounging in our small backyard garden. Mom finished my home-school lessons early so she could work on church things. I'm alone to enjoy myself. *As it damn well should be.* To thrive, I've always needed the whole world to myself. I need my space.

No judgment or shame. No other expectations. Me being me.

I turn my head from the beautiful corner of the cramped yard, and my dream breaks. *Our house sucks.* It's pathetic. Shingles are worn. Siding rotten. *The little corner garden is our only nice thing.* I frown, comparing our crummy two-bedroom home to the large two-story house next door with the perfect lawn. A double lot. *A large front porch that is never used?! We don't even have a paved driveway,* I mutter, glaring at our shabby carport. *Not that our car works.*

I pound my book against my thigh in frustration. *Worst part is Mom and Dad make okay money. They give their salaries away!* I try to ignore our self-imposed poverty and refocus on the small beautiful corner garden of our yard, so I can feel more like me. *Supreme.*

I have a strong personality. I've learned to hide myself. I'm always pretending. Not being me. Being a chameleon is exhausting. Being 'nice' is exhausting. In this slice of garden, I don't pretend. *A Goddess amongst weeds and roses,* I smile.

Fuck, it's nice out, I grin at the sky and relax. First day warm since September. The sun bakes our yard to over 70 degrees. *Mom and Dad never allowed our heat to be above 61 degrees this winter.* I shudder, recalling our pointless chill.

I glance down at a trickle of sweat, pleased last year's bikini barely fits. *Barely fits in a good way. Fuck yeah, bitches!* Derek, the neighbor guy in the even shittier house next door, can't help but look. *He always finds time for chores when I'm outside,* I smile, slyly noting his drooling glances behind my sunglasses. He pretends to rake dead grass and pick mushy leaves. Pretends to not smother the shabby tulips his wife planted a few years ago. *I never fantasize about him in that way, but it feels nice and warm when he pretends to 'look at me without looking' like most guys do. I love those looks. Even guys holding hands with their girlfriends will turn their heads at me. Haven't caused any car accidents, yet I'd love to ruin some dude's life because he needed another glimpse. But stay away. I hate when guys try and talk with me. Just your worship is fine, boys. Thanks.* I'd be terrified to lose my power to turn heads.

The mere thought of Derek's secret attention casually sends a finger deep into my warm belly button.

Mmm, yum. The pressure feels nice. Powerful. Carnivorous.

Since age seven or eight, I've noticed a thing for belly buttons. I liked the look of mine and other girl's soft navels. I get a warm, nice, tingling feeling. A feeling only now I understand is what most people feel during sex. I love things in my belly—real or imagined. Most people who noticed thought I was weird, or had a problem, until I learned to hide the thrill. Now, I hide many of my thrills.

Adjusting my headphones, I hear Mom and Dad fighting through a cracked window with a plastic bag taped across it. I pause the next song to hear what the argument is this time.

Usually, it's about money.

"Kissing me isn't cheating on God, Megan. *I'm your husband.* Look at this ring. Look. We're married."

"Tom. We knew this marriage would be hard. God comes first. You're second. That was always the deal," she sternly whispers. "I won't deny the Holy Spirit's grip on me."

"So, I can't ask for a kiss when I get home?"

"No. We're here for Jennifer, to show her how to submit to the love and will of Jesus Christ. You, me, her." She says through a long slow breath. "We're servants of God first. Jen second. And each other last."

"But *I* love you, Megan. *I'm* right here. How can you lavish love across the whole of humanity yet put me in hell every day you deny an ounce of even basic attention? Whatever. He can be in your spiritual heart. Let me be in your physical one. The denial fucking hurts."

"Look. If you calm down and repent for being so perverted, I'll consider letting you rub my feet tonight."

I casually stretch, bending wide left and wide right to sweep a glance through the patio doors into the living room.

A sigh escapes Dad's lungs as he settles on the couch, "Of course, Megan. You know I miss that."

"Thanks, luv," Mom bends down, kisses Dad high on the forehead and walks out of the room. Dad sits, his shoulders hunched, staring at the floor.

He looks so handsome, I admire.

I know they're stupid sometimes, but I feel giddy about the suffering my parents go through to love me. If you're unwilling to greatly suffer for someone, how do they know you *really* love them? I melt into the sun and match it's golden grin. *Everyone should suffer for me. Everyone should love me.*

I return to my lesson: *The Holy History of Jerusalem.*

Ugh. Dad's a way better teacher than Mom. His topics are challenging. I like feeling smarter. I feel stronger than others. With Dad, if I get too bored, we talk about any more interesting topic I want. He promises to teach more eleventh-grade subjects next fall. *About fucking time.* I'm pissed he can't focus on me 100%. He's tutoring those other fucking kids.

Dad's been out of work for two years. The deadbeat State of Illinois pulled the plug on the whole public college system. Not much paying work for a Women's Studies Professor beyond general tutoring. As one of the Nation's top Feminist scholars, Dad gets invited to speak at conferences once or twice a year, but they won't pay. Everyone in academia is so fucking poor since the government canceled all public student loan support and student admissions dropped 85%!

Dad *really* hates President Ron Paul for that.

Mom wouldn't let us move to Palo Alto when Stanford offered Dad to chair the Feminist Studies program. I would love being a California 10! But no. Tiny Wilmington, Illinois was the first place Mom found a congregation looking to embrace the words of Jesus Christ as she read them, and not just dance to rock music worrying about The Gays. I secretly think Mom really likes telling people what to do and believe, and no California congregation would let her do that like Wilmington's Free Church of the Ascension does here.

Alright. I snap the book shut, sick of Old Jerusalem. *King David can suck my dick. The Hellenistic Kingdoms too.* I lay the book on the deck and stand and stretch for real. I wave at Derek, who startles awkwardly at my acknowledgement, foolishly thinking I never noticed him. *Dummy.* I slide the patio door open with a gentle whoosh.

"Hey, Daddy." His face genuinely lightens when I walk in. I give him a kiss on the forehead where Mom did.

"How's your day, sweetheart?" he beams, standing to wrap me in a solid hug. "Whoa. You're warm." He gently pats my arms.

"Yeah, it's beautiful out."

"Glad you're enjoying it. Past time we got sun."

"No kidding. I even got thirsty. Hey… What were you and Mom fighting about? I couldn't hear," I ask.

"Um, just chores," he says. "I was wondering if Mom could clean the bathroom this week, or if we could at least use gentler cleaners. That hard stuff makes me woozy. She thinks it cleans better," he shrugs, looking away.

"M'kay. Oooh, I hope we have lemonade?" I stroll past his lies to the kitchen for a glass, fill it from a container in the fridge, grab a beach towel from the closet, and return outside. I gently set my cup on the pavers between the lawn and the sprouting flower bed. The humidity fogging the outside of the glass. I spread the towel over the grass to face my favorite view of the garden. Surrounded by beauty, I lay on my belly, and skip to chapter nine, *Roman Aelia Capitolina Period.*

I read for another hour. Roman Emperor Hadrian was one badass! After killing a half-million people, he locked a whole culture out of their own city for decades, giving them one pitiful day a year to glimpse their old lives.

I would love to be an Empress. Millions of underlings courting my favor, terrified of displeasing me. Unquestioned obedience to my whims and wants. I feel such a rush that I stop reading and set the book aside to enjoy my own fantasy.

Lying face down on the towel, I close my eyes…

I'm right here with Hadrian. He sprawls heroically on his own towel next to mine. No guards. No weapons. He loves me more than air. I grin and jump to straddle him aggressively. His strong biceps wrap around me. He adores my playful energy and rewards it with kisses. I push him down hard with my weight, holding his face close to my heart. I feel incredible. He's so strong. His kisses are light across my chest. He clutches me tight as I feel a sudden rush. I'm absorbing his energy, his power, his life. He's slowly disappearing and doesn't even realize until it's too late. Suddenly, he struggles. But I'm the strong one now. He's getting smaller, gasping for oxygen as he disappears completely under me. I spread my arms and legs to fully welcome the feeling of his insignificance under my heart. Soon, I don't feel him at all. I know he's gone.

I'm the Empress now.

Mmmm.... I open my eyes to watch the world sparkle. *My realm is beautiful. A place I see all and know it's mine. Plants fight for my light, strain for my attention. I choose to weed the weak and prune the overgrown.*

As the bliss fades, I reach to my lemonade to cool off. Lifting the glass, I notice two ants struggling on the last ice cube. I pause, entranced by their helplessness. I imagine them looking up at me. How unknowable I must be. *I am your god,* I smile softly down to them and bring the glass to my lips. I swallow and swallow until I'm sure half the lemonade and the two ants are gone. All of their dreams, all their plans for the day, all their hard work—are consumed as part of a sudden cool rush that floods my belly. *I didn't even notice them!* The thought forces me to immediately clench at a searing warmth exploding between my legs. Ripping at the grass, I sigh again with quiet pleasure.

CHAPTER 3—BRIGHT NEW DAY

Eddie. February 2022

I wake the next morning surprised that for the first time in my life, I am genuinely excited for work. *I get to talk with Jennifer!* The thought cracks a smile across my young frown lines. I turn on the lamp I rescued from a dumpster. I plan several sets of questions and conversations to ask Jen while brushing my teeth in a small kitchen sink.

With a coin purse around my neck and a shabby towel in hand, I whistle a jazzy tune walking to the communal bathroom. My apartment building is a converted truck stop with fifteen small rooms that share the old truck stop bathrooms and showers. When the cargo industry downsized from the commercialization of Arbrims Theory, nearly all semi drivers were laid off and replaced with bicycle carriers and economy cars that didn't need truck stops. All the tech blogs were excited by the Scale Symmetry Theory discovery—that the size and weight of matter can be adjusted in the 7th dimension by a few forgettable sounding "ieum" elements energized with agravity—and all that. They wrote how it would revolutionize transportation and the movement of people. All Logistical Shrinking™ really seemed to do was make us Temp Recruiters busy sorting unemployed truck drivers.

"Fuck," I grimace. The only available shower pen didn't return accurate change. "Funny how the landlord doesn't rush to fix that, eh?" I say to a frumpy old guy in line.

He grunts, "We'd bathe in shit if it saved them a dollar."

"Well. That's business," I nod with a smile.

The guy grunts, not wanting our conversation to continue. *I'm so lonely.*

I'm low on time and can't wait in line for the cheaper shower pens. I suck up the $4.00 per shower for a gallon of warm water, soaping up trying to ignore an hour of my salary is swirling down the drain. *It was good when Texas privatized water,* I remind myself, rinsing suds out of my hair. *Old socialist Texas stopped wasting so damn much and let the market fight for what little water was left.*

Fifteen gallons of cheap water a day for basic needs was nice—but everyone loves a handout. That's how our old world collapsed.

I live two miles from work, but the walk takes over an hour depending who's on the corners and who is or isn't drunk. *God, I hate how many lazy unemployed bums there are.* I frown at their sorry sights. *Motivation for my calls.* In the morning chill, I recall becoming an hour late because police busted up a possible Collective gathered in an abandoned warehouse for shelter and "community." *Lazy fucks,* I spit at the street corner where I saw it all happen. *The police almost hauled me away too as I stumbled on the scene! Once they called Tad to verify my employment, they all started calling me "Sir,"* I remember with pride. *Ha, the captain himself even drove me to our office as an apology, and to minimize TempGrace's wrath.*

I hold my head high, walking along abandoned smoke stacks and warehouses whose carcasses silhouette the dusty red sky of a new day like dinosaur bones from an ancient era. The only active facility is a repossession warehouse. Every day I watch bike couriers pedal up to a grimy receiving dock with reclaimed property from schmucks not responsible enough to pay their bills. The curriers open their satchels and place miniature boats, cars, pieces of furniture, and other two-inch-tall items on a plastic card table and fill in repo paperwork. *Arbrim's Theory at it again, greasing the movement of resources on a more efficient level than ever seen before,* I smile in wonder how the new shrinking technology is strengthening the economy. *Take from the slow and weak; and give to the agile and strong.*

After waiting thirty minutes in the Secure Work Check™ line, once inside TempGrace, I stroll down my row of cubes. Seeing Jennifer feels like someone installed a whole set of skylights in our row.

"Morning, Jen," I say. It's 7:09 a.m.

She turns her dark soft hair towards me and smiles, "Hey, Eddie. How was your night?"

"Can't complain." Actually, I could. A load of pre-teens broke into my two-hundred square foot apartment for the seventh time in the past two weeks to steal my food and shampoo. I can't afford locks, so I wedge the door shut with a stool and coat hanger. Once, I had the witty plan to place a bucket of stale piss and shit above the door as a booby-trap. But my witty plan had me instead vomiting in the hallway, buckling at the knees, covered in my own excrement when I forgot I put it there. *All the things I do just seem to get me covered in shit.* Ugh.

Her smile and eyes linger on me, "Of course *you* don't have any complaints. One day I'll have your energy and confidence," she says.

"Hey, you'll get there," I smartly sit and fold my hands. *Play it smooth today.* Seeing Jen's eye return to her screen, I reluctantly turn to wake the computer, my chair still warm from the night-shift guy. *Maybe that's where the cheese smell comes from?*

Once I sense Jen deep in work, I bend and pretend to retie my shoelaces for no reason other than sneak a look at her. She has a tight knee-length skirt on today. My eyes widen. *Of course she looks fabulous, dummy.* Jen suddenly shifts sideways and cross her fantastic legs. My heart nearly explodes. *How perfect was that? Oh my god, I couldn't have timed that glance any better.*

Half regretting my peek, I sit up, realizing my thoughts are guaranteed to be all over her today. I steel my resolve. *No distractions today.*

9:30 a.m. is our Standing Team Meeting™. The Senior Temps, plus Jen, about forty of us, meet with Tad at the end of our rows with our printed WorkScore Analytics™: a simple large font percentage in black ink on white paper with a timestamp spit by the System software that summarizes our profitability performance of the day before. This allows managers to set impossible goals while measuring all aspects and limits of a worker's productivity. A 70% or above rating and you are fine. Nothing good happens at 100% except next week that same level of work seems to be worth only 80%; only noobs aim for 100% their first few days before they either crack or get harassed by other employees. Those who score well are rewarded with the privilege of continued employment. Those who resist sacrificing their personal lives for work are quickly discarded. In the 60% area, you earn a meeting with James the CEO, expanded daily supervision, and random work inspections.

A WorkScore™ below 60% is an automatic dismissal—you aren't a go-forward option anymore, and your personal TempReport™ is fucked. No agency will hire you. You're actually double-fucked, because your WorkScore is often used for loans, bank transfers, setting rent and all sorts of financial stuff. Essentially, if you break trust in one place, restrictions are instantly imposed across the entire Temp society.

A simplistic system, but one that frees managers' valuable time to think strategically, rather wasting time motivating lazy employees. There's no room to hide from work with the System keeping workers accountable.

WorkScores allow us to produce so much economic surplus, that I'm betting once this depression is over we can afford to liberate all of humanity from work and want! My dream is when computers and technology *do* really start performing more and more of the work, we'll be free to create, learn, or start new businesses in an economy no longer forced to subside on the gruel of daily labor in a shitty warehouse with shitty lighting.

I itch my fingers and remember the ten years of clarinet lessons I've abandoned. *I can start a Jazz House?* Standing, waiting for Tad, I wonder why this economic progress is taking so long. *Ah,* I put the thought aside, *here comes our manager checking our profitability scores.* Tad passes me with a nod, half-noticing my number, and then sharply stops with a grimace in front of Jen.

Jesus! Jen's score from yesterday was 17%. Fuck fuck, no! Why didn't she ask for help? I panic. I watch Tad pissing himself too. *He'll have to dismiss Jen from the office before he can dip his cock in her.*

"Jennifer. Ed." Tad slowly approaches with clenched teeth. "I thought we spoke about getting properly oriented how things work here…"

Tad raises both his hands specifically at me as if to say, *C*ome on. Help a brother get some.

My mouth goes dry. "Hey, Tad. Yeah, you're right," I say. "I was there all day to help. She didn't ask. I didn't know. I swear."

I really hope I'm not screwed. I feel I'm about to faint. *My luck to play it cool and trust a pretty face!* My anger boils. *If she gets me demoted I'll need* years *to get to where I already am.*

My fist clenches tight. *Goddamn it! I hate how such a simple thing can totally fuck my life.*

Tad looks genuinely disappointedly at Jen and me.

"Well. Jen, what happened here?" He crosses his arms.

"Nope. We're not doing it this way," she says, crossing her arms. "I spent eight hours working on something else."

"Okay. Um, well, 'something else' ain't what we pay ya' for." Tad sighs. There's no way he can hide her results from the omniscience of the System. "Jen, we'll need to—"

Jen stops him with her hand. "—Listen. Tad. I get it. You can *pay* me for whatever you want," she says, her eyes twinkling. "Let me explain my ideas to the managers and I'll put out 110%. Anytime you ask."

Thank god, I relieve. *She's smart enough to play the game.*

Tad's mood lightens at the fair excuse to deliver her to the managers for a performance review, where they can all measure her Go Forward Opportunities™.

"Alright, fine," Tad says, adjusting his collar to breathe. "Sure. Maybe we can pursue some remedial training, after work?" he adds, pleased with his new mentoring opportunity. He pats Jen on the shoulder with both hands and moves to Jerry, Sam, and Jose who have 80%.

Turning to acknowledge us all, Tad says "We know this depression is hard on folks. Their voices get desperate and they say stupid things. Remain professional. Remember to not over-communicate salary terms in the contracts if you don't need to. We are paid on Time-to-Fill, not on being best friends with our prospects. Our clients want their Temps paid a diminishing variable salary. Also! This winter heat wave has made air conditioning an unexpectedly large expense this month. We'll continue to maintain air conditioning at ninety-degrees until this abnormal cycle breaks. I know we're sacrificing and working hard. Keep up the great work. But, this *does* mean your emergency electricity surcharge will continue to variably impact your salary, until probably the end of summer."

There are a few groans. It's cooler here than my apartment, so I didn't mind much beyond a shrug. *At least during serious scorchers, the company has paramedics on standby to revive workers overcome by heat.* I remember one guy saying he 'never felt more like a truer turd in any other TempWarehouse™ than this one.' He was laid-off a month later. *I'm still here.* I raise my shoulders. *Goes to show the advantages of my attitude over his. I'll swim in shit if the company needs me.*

"Y'all got questions?" Tad asks.

There were the two traditional time wasters from the idiots in the group. Then Jen raises her hand.

"When was the last time the air-conditioners were inspected? Old units can be two or three times more efficient with a tune up. Maybe they need more Freon?" she asks, briefly fanning herself.

Our co-workers turn their faces from bored to frozen. Tad tilts his head almost sideways. If you want a job here, you keep your mouth shut. Jen doesn't give two fucks about her awkward statements and keeps talking.

"TempGrace seems way behind on technology. There are tools out there that can *really* cut costs. So. Let's maybe take off our blinders and pay attention, hm?" she asks. "I looked up our light bulbs here, did a count in the TempWarehouse, and found a simple investment of $20,000 in LEDs would save us $900 a month for this warehouse alone. I already called a vendor and got a 15% discount on a bulk deal—if the managers are interested," she says, holding up a paper.

Tad's so annoyed I worry he'll puke.

Jen, no one cares about your opinions!

"I have a juicy business case, Tad, right here…" she dangles a short memo from her fingers, rolls her eyes, and walks away.

A monkey falling from the ceiling would have been less surprising here. Not knowing what else to do, the rest of our team drifts away as Tad's thundering thoughts condense. I watch Jen's ass as long as I safely can, trying to memorize her curves. *Damn. I wish I'd gotten a lot closer to that,* I marvel before Tad blocks the scene to blacklist her insubordination. *Well damn,* I mutter, *that's the last of her.* I feel the oxygen has been sucked out of my lungs as I slug back to work.

The rest of my morning basically sucks. I knew our pretty bird flying away was inevitable. I loved the gravity such a beautiful creature held on me. Even though this wild bird lived a different life in a different world I already thought of her as my intimate friend and on the path to being incredibly close. The reality of her dismissal was a jarring disappointment.

I call Jack in Cleveland about a new opening for a welding temp job in a Greensboro steel works. I call Jake in Montgomery about a temp mechanic role in Tallahassee. I call Jana in Kansas City about a nanny temp job for a wealthy family in Dallas. They can all enjoy the privilege of temporary employment if willing to work off the costs of their transportation and accommodations, *and* if they're willing to work the first trial months for free, I cautiously add. Obviously, the best way to get in the door at corporations is working *entirely* for free. What manager doesn't love free labor?! But then, we at TempGrace wouldn't get a percentage of the earnings beyond a finder's fee, so the Temp Industry has gently pushed back against the increasingly common practice of Fulltime Free Labor™.

Three calls in a row cheer yes with tearful relief. I feel good helping those willing to work. Being helpful is my favorite part of my job. TempGrace gets a large slice of their income, and everyone wins. The market works.

After more successful calls, I earn my System approved break when the blue TempBreak Light™ illuminates above my desk. I stand, crack a few knuckles, and behold the endless gray rows of our TempWarehouse stretching two hundred feet in four directions. I marvel at the symphony of the industry around me. A thousand men, and a few women, at all stages of life singing a chorus to lull a hundred million unemployed Americans off their butts and back to work. A challenge for sure.

My chest swells with gratitude. I'm a full-time temp helping the industry change people's lives for the better.

I finger a random arrangement of classical notes on my arm as the music floats into my ears. I finger a page of Mozart's Clarinet Concerto on the buttons of my shirt. The steady hum of the lights set my tempo and tone and threads my imaginary melody into the air. Soon, the murmur of calls and the hum of the lights mix, and my mood randomly ruins. I stop my music and return the lighting's harshness with a glare of my own.

These shitty lights destroyed a beautiful waxed-wing bird who flew too high too soon.

I eat some TempChip™, stretch my neck, and return to the "Ja-" names as my TempBreak Light™ blinks out. I call a Jacquelyn in Nashville about a temp job as a janitor in Charlotte. She says no! "Wise on the fact" our client was "never going to allow wages to rise above living costs. I'd never escape the perpetual debt for 'the privilege of employment'!"

I shake my head and bite my tongue to prevent myself from responding rudely to her tone. *I am a professional,* I remind myself. Research shows human brains think of companies like TempGrace not as objects, but as people. I need to represent the caring and mentoring aspect of TempGrace's personality. I advise my poor client: "Dear. Let me give you a helpful hint. What's good for business is good for us all. True professionals submit their personal wants under greater corporate needs—not their selfish wants as workers. That's what I do at TempGrace, and what our clients deserve from their prospects. I'm sorry you feel so entitled. Good luck and goodbye."

I hang up and cross Jacquelyn off the Global Prospective Temp List. *Bye.*

It's finally lunchtime. I've discovered the highest calorie-to-dollar meal is a bulk-pack of vanilla protein bars. I'm all about the calories to dollar ratio! Protein bars are clean, have a fair nutritional value, and can sit in a desk drawer with a lower likelihood than a fresh sandwich to get stolen or moldy. I open my drawer and munch on a bar. *Walking to work and eating healthy: I take responsibility for my health until fate deals me a hand that sends me into the ditch to starve and quickly die. That's how life works. No idea why the socialists care so much about health care? I live fine making my own decisions and being responsible for myself; and have zero desire to subsidize someone else's poor lifestyle choices.*

Tad and Jen walk down our row laughing together, "Thanks for lunch." Jen smiles and touches his arm.

"Hey, no problem. Nice work today. We need to talk more about Chile later. Hey, Eddie," Tad half-acknowledges as he leaves.

Jen stands at her desk poking at a folder of papers and a few graphs. A half-chewed protein bar half-sits in my mouth, as a fiery flush burns along the dry skin of my neck.

"Ah, hi? Jen?" I finally swallow.

She turns and notes my lunch with a frown, "Hey. What you got there?"

"Protein bar. Has the best—*Wait.* Wait. Whoa," I try to collect my mind. "Um. *How the hell did you not just get fired?* Jen. Seriously, I thought you were toast." I stand and sternly cross my arms, "I mean, thank god. *But holy fuck.* You can't just say things here."

She shrugs, sets her papers down and leans up against the desk with a quiet smile. Her look is almost too direct on me.

"Easy. I walked into James's office to show him a report 'that Tad asked me to write.' By the time Tad stormed in, James already thought it was a good idea. Told us nice work with those pearly whites and strong black face of his. Tad had a really *fantastic* 'Oh shit face' when James said just yesterday our light bulb contract was up for renewal. They took me out to lunch!"

Fucking Hell. These guys are pros, I marvel. *Why do all the cute girls fall for the Player's Game and not the nice guys like me?* I bitterly wonder.

"Jen. It's a *game*," I whisper. "They're stringing you along to see how much you'll *do* for them. And I don't mean work projects."

"Naw. Money talks and incandescent light bulbs suck old-school. What a waste of heat." She wrinkles her eyebrows with annoyance, "No wonder air conditioners are working so hard." She looks up, "I swear it's like 'Welcome to 2005' here. Should we all frost the tips of our hair while talking on flip phones?"

"Jen. I could never, *never,* have done that. Jesus." I shrug with wary amazement, "Awesome." I didn't want to add how 'awesome' it must be to have a fantastic pair of tits jiggle open the doors of the world.

"Yup." She smiles, "Going to cut a purchase order tomorrow. I just need to review the vendor contract with James after work tonight," Jen says.

Ha. James must have been caught unprepared and probably humored her while winking a secret code to Tad how, 'This hot one gonna give us some fun,' and Jen was too dumb to notice.

"Oh. Great," I suspiciously nod.

No one gives a shit about your light bulbs, Jen.

I feel a rush of jealousy—for all I know she was probably on her hands and knees the whole time she was 'getting things done' this morning. On the bright side, I'll get to look at her for maybe another week before she's 'promoted' into a small role closer to the executives.

Jen, there's a reason we're all men in the Senior Full Time Temp Area: Sexual harassment doesn't make us pregnant. Thus, my dear, we men stay around.

"Uh. Yeah. Wish I had your confidence, Jen. I'm pretty sure they'd never listen to a thing from *me*," I say. "What's your secret?" I mock-glance at her figure more sarcastically then I intend, and instantly regret my tone.

Her response is gracious. "Don't knock yourself for being timid, Eddie. That's useful too," she smiles, rubbing a spot behind her neck. "We all have skills and strategies available to us. My *assets*," she says with a sly smirk, "only help so much. If you *really* want to know the secret to confidence," she straightens into a distant look, "it's looking at the world like it's full of ants. The managers.

The great Lords of Wall Street. All of them can and will be set aside. Especially you temps."

She looks coolly at me.

"God, I love the potential here," Jen says. "Like, wow. You'll see so many incredible things once I pull us together."

"Yeah. Sure, cool," I shrug. Feeling self-conscious of my criticisms I try to rebalance the ideal five to one complement ratio. "You're really smart and stuff. I think that's great. You got initiative. You'll figure it all out," I reluctantly cheer.

Jen's face lights up. "Careful with that brown-nosing, Ed. My ass will eat you alive," she says.

"Hah," I chuckle at her crudeness. My eyes return eventually to work as Jen returns to her fantasy world. *I consider myself a respectful guy with women and all. I'm not going to just grab her and take a slice, but god, will you just let me fuck you, Jen. Please? Like right now would be fine.*

Five days later, I walk into the office and immediately notice my shadows are different. They have sharp edges. *Odd, I've never seen a shadow with a sharp edge.* I hold my hand to it and trace the light beam up to the source: a bright new light-bulb. I see Building Maintenance on a ladder installing the last of several hundred LED light bulbs. It's 7:19 a.m.

CHAPTER 4—SERVICE SUNDAY

Jennifer. June 2012

On Sundays, Dad and I walk the five blocks along River Street to Mom's Free Church. We're both expected at the 9:30 a.m. service, even though we both expect not to interact with anyone, and we both expect our presence is as pointless as Mom's ceremony and her prayers. Not that anyone talks in church anyways. We're to listen quietly to Mom, believe what she wants us to believe, and sing what she wants us to sing.

It's funny; sit and shush because someone "important" is talking. Who cares? No one's that important and no one's as smart as they think they are. Mom was *furious* when I was expelled from her own Youth Confirmation program. The teachers refused to have me around. I knew the stories better than they did, added the details they missed, and made sure the class knew I knew. Might be awkward to see Ms. Thomas today. Well, awkward for her, I don't care. Same thing happened with the public-school teachers; only there I used a gaggle of boys to carry my books. They all wanted to kiss me. I wanted them to follow me. A cute arrangement. I miss that…

I crave any ping of excitement I can get in this dumb town.

I hear people call Wilmington a cute town with cute little houses. Mostly tourists from Chicago or the hard-core joyriders traveling Route 66 for some pointless reason. *Who cares about the old road west? This town is dumb.* They love Nelly's Diner, Lickety Split Ice Cream Shoppe, and getting their picture taken with the Gemini Giant. *Whatever guys, yes, there is a world of barely intelligent life outside Chicago. Yay, you've discovered it. Here's a gold star.*

Less cute are the skeletons of unfinished suburban homes outside of town, rotting in the mud. Not cute is the closed DOW Chemical and Cold Storage facilities emptying half the town's wallets.

Though, I do love the rivers and streams. The Kankakee River tries its best to wash this dull place clean, and Jon Stein got my first kiss on a sandbar of Forked Creek two summers ago. We'd been friends since elementary school. He moved away this spring. *From heartbreak about me,* I assume, adding a grin and a skip to my step. We'd play army with little green plastic soldiers in the sandbox. Jon would get mad when I always broke the rules. I'd turn into Godzilla, step over all his defenses and finish his forces off with the overwhelming crush of my foot. There's nothing he could do! I loved it so much.

Ha! My first memory of getting in trouble was with Jon, I playfully twirl my hair. We were four, and had been playing with toys all afternoon in my room. Mom walked in with cookies and milk, and saw me sitting on my toy chest coloring.

"Where's Jon?" She asked, confused. "Was he picked up?"

"No…" I continued coloring with a big grin.

"Where is he?" she asked.

"Hiding!" I giggled.

A muffled, *thunk, thunk, thunk,* vibrated nicely under my bum.

Mom stopped smiling, "Jen. Why is Jon in your toy chest?"

"Because he's my toy!" I laughed, "I'm playing like grandpa."

Mom angrily slammed the cookies and milk to the floor, yanked me off the chest, and opened it to free a very red-faced Jon, gasping for air.

"Jen! Not okay! Time out," she violently jabbed to the corner of the room.

"No!" I screamed and stomped my foot.

"Jon," she lifts him from the chest. "Don't *ever* let Jen do that again. Go home," she escorts him out the door.

I was in time out for two hours, completely unperturbed, until Mom was dismayed with its total lack of effect. *Duh, punishments have no effect on me,* I smile. I spent the two hours thinking how great it felt to have Jon locked under me. I knew it was wrong, but I didn't care. I just wanted the pleasure.

Jon always forgave me and adored me for years. I strung him along until he was so pathetic I couldn't resist. He offered to clean my room and do my laundry for a month—for only a kiss! *How could I say no to such a gentleman?* To this day I swoon at the memory: sneaking him home when my parents weren't around so he'd do all my chores. Finally, after weeks of his begging, I rewarded him with a quick meaningless peck on the lips and walked away.

He wanted our moment to be tender and special. He wanted his hard work to be rewarded with an equal compensation of my love. *No. I don't get manipulated like that, boys. Sorry.* After the shock of his nonexistence with me wore off, he got really upset and didn't talk to me for a year, then his family moved away.

His loss.

I guess I don't do well with friends.

Boys, girls—even some adults—latch onto my shadow looking for something great until they realize I'm not on their level, not even close. *I'm on nobody's level.* They eventually feel themselves shrivel up and char; realizing the heat of my will is so strong they must detach in wounded self-preservation. *Crawl in my hole and die, fuckers.*

But not Dad. I'm walking arm in arm with him. He's been talking about the three-generational migration habits of the monarch butterfly this whole walk. We've seen three Monarchs! But he worries they'll probably go extinct in twenty years because no one really cares to spend a few hundred bucks on habitat for them.

Dad's strength is his egolessness. He bends so easily he can never break. Which is amazing. I could never be that flexible. I have my wants and they are *mine*. I could never give up My Way. He's so much stronger than I'll ever be. I worry my life is one huge insecurity, while his submission to the whims of the world is the ultimate confidence and strength. He and I are the perfect pair.

The Free Church's Welcome Crew paints their hollow warm smiles around us as we climb the concrete steps through the white wooden doors. We receive a yellow service program with a soft picture of a haloed Jesus playing with children. Nancy Costello gives Dad a hug and sends me a compliment of how pretty my dress is. *Duh.* I smile a nice thank you at her. Church people are only nice with us because Mom's the head preacher. When we first moved here eight years ago, it was a *huge* scandal Mom was married to practically an Atheist! Mom already had the job; it took Dad a long time to fit in after that.

Dad's passive confidence keeps The Churchies chill and less annoying about life and scripture than I bet most church people normally are. His regular presence reminds the congregation they are supposed to be about love first and judgment last. And when *he* volunteered to coordinate many of the community Social Justice programs in the 2009 Collapse, the whole congregation and the eleven other churches in Wilmington knitted together to help! They weren't about to get 'out-Jesused' by an Atheist who didn't give a shit where their beliefs came from, as long as they were helping people.

The electric organ paints joyful spiritual colors that I reluctantly admit, lift my mood. Everyone's happy. Mom's inspiring her flock in the pews near the front of the congregation. Dad and I sit in the back to ceremonially watch. James Baker greets me and "Professor *Díaz*," and asks about Dad's various job opportunities. I sense a subtle jab but it rolls off Dad like water on a duck's back.

A deep, final tonic G chord vibrates our bench. Silence tightens the room as Mom walks to the pulpit, bows to the cross, and turns to greet us.

She announces the Summer Potluck. We sing. We witness. We sing. We enjoy Mom's sermon:

"When churches use ceremony, hand holding, and kumbaya—we embrace a great and necessary mechanism of comfort and tradition. Yet, with this comfort, we need to be wary that the words of Jesus Christ—and what they truly mean—can get lost. At Free Ascension, our church is about the uncomfortable integrity to the truth and love of our Lord and Savior, Jesus Christ; and to the truth of a man who loved the world so much, he sacrificed his life. Through Christ, we learn our lives are *not* about becoming rich or powerful, but submitting to the totality of God's love. That Love is our dictator and our tyrant.

"Without His love, we fail to blossom into true spiritual beings. From ancient Rome to modern Washington, we find that it is the most privileged of us who are the most loveless of us. Luke 12:48 teaches 'to whom much has been given, much is also required.' Much will be expected from the one who has been given much, and the more a man is trusted, the more people will expect of him.

"The False Masters of Washington and Wall Street, servants who pretend to be masters, work to fill the gaping hole in their souls with more money and more power—yet do the least to mend the poverty of their own hearts and of others. The false masters forget, or worse yet, have never learned, that *only the service to the love and truth of Jesus Christ, and service to his creation, will fill the empty pit in their hearts.* Without unconditionally accepting God's love, we might as well cast ourselves directly into this pit to become closer to our inevitable Hell.

"Being a part of God's kingdom means stepping away from the dark selfishness of greed, and understanding that we are servants in God's house. Jesus wants us to serve all of God's children: the poor, the blind, the heathen—or simply those fallen from the path."

Mom looks at Dad and I before continuing.

"Jesus wants us to understand the love of God is an all encompassing totality. A totality that demands the surrender of our wealth, the surrender of our ego, and the surrender of our souls to his crusade of Love. The true Christ-like *Christian* follows the example of Christ's sacrifice with her own acts of sacrifice. Love is suffering for other people."

Mom nods at the ushers, who move down the rows with a gentle clink of their donation collection plates.

"The more we give, the more we receive. Do this and witness an early glimpse of Heaven on Earth. The strife and destitution of our neighboring cities like Joliet and Bourbonnais, has spared Wilmington. Our entire community has answered God's call. The eleven houses of worship in Wilmington form a true Christian-led spine of compassion in our community. Our message of Luke 12:48 today is being repeated in Wilmington's Church of the Nazarene, Grace Lutheran, Saint Rose, First United Methodist, Church of Christ, and First Presbyterian.

"Collectively, your community of Christ has opened the Baltimore Street Food Bank, established the Chore Share Program, and flooded the holes with compassion that the State has callously dug—with love and kindness. In sharing God's love with selfless, egoless, sacrifice, we've created an oasis of nurturing love and cooperation within harsh economic disaster. An oasis even Senator Obama regularly touts on the national stage as a model! Our community does this because we know that in carrying those uprooted and suffering, we carry *ourselves* into the Grace of God. Hallelujah. Amen."

Mom always gets applause. We stand. We sing again. We shake our neighbors' hands saying, "Pcacc bc with you." And we smile.

"Pass the peas, please?" Mom asks over the soft clink of silverware in our small kitchen. Sunday night is always pot roast dinner.

"Of course," Dad moves with a dramatic reach to elbow me playfully in the forehead.

I smile, pushing his arm away.

"Thanks," Mom says, scooping two large spoonfuls and turning to me. "Peggy was asking about you after the eleven o'clock service."

"Yeah?" I duly muse. *Ugh. Peggy.* She lives five blocks away and is the most boring girl in the world. I'd pretend to be sick when she comes over, but then she would return with soup! A lesson learned the hard way.

"She wanted to hear what you were up to," Mom continues.

"Yeah?" I answer with a noncommittal shrug.

"I think she misses you. Ha. Remember when you two were so inseparable, everyone called you JPeg?" Mom laughs.

"Eh. Yeah." We *used* to be best friends, but then she got fat and dumb and I deserved better. Mostly, she was so fucking annoying and nice.

"Jen. Dear. I worry you're going to burn through friends and no one will come to your graduation party. What will people think? There's only 5,000 people in this town. You're running out of opportunities. We don't get unlimited chances for a happy, fun life."

"Eh. Yeah." My mood spoils. *Shut up, Mom.*

"So a happy, fun life doesn't matter to you?" She asks, concerned.

"Eh," I cut into my roast. *Shut up, Mom.*

"—Megan. Jen will figure it out." Dad says. "She's a strong smart butterfly on her own path."

"Oh, she's strong and smart. No doubt about that," Mom snaps with a glare. "Honey," she levels to me, "your friends are worried about you. They love you. Whatever happened, they forgive you. I'm worried you've locked your heart away in a freezer. I know how much that hurts. I was like that too. When I look back at how much time I wasted, I feel ashamed how much I lost. Ashamed. I don't want you taking as long as I did to learn about love. High school is starting. College too. It's easy for boys to like you."

"Mom!" I shout with embarrassment, slamming my fork down and crossing my arms. "I don't want to talk boys with you!"

"Honey. What I *mean* is this life is short. I want you to be ready for it—as smart and far ahead as you are in school, your friendship skills are *way* behind. Like grade F," Mom moves a consoling hand towards me.

"Mom. Please." I feel my face getting red and my back hot and sweaty. *Mom, I'm two seconds away from stabbing you in the neck with my fork.*

"You're almost sixteen. Most girls your age *only* care about friends and boys. I almost want to take away your books and force you to go to the mall and talk to people. Make friends. Jen. Live. It's summertime now, classes are done, and all you do is read."

"Megan, I know Jen will figure it out. Teen years take time," Dad says.

"Yeah, but if you don't learn some things young, you don't learn them ever," Mom scolds us. "Last week, you were reading about Genghis Khan all night. Who is it this week?"

"King Leopold the second, of Belgium…" I huff.

"What kind of friends are those? I'm gonna want grandchildren one day."

"Mom," I glare. "What I do with my special books is *my* business—no one else's."

"Well, Uncle Greg won't be much help." Mom teases me, trying to lighten the tense argument.

"He and Ben might adopt?" Dad playfully interjects with a sharp laugh.

"Not the same!" Mom dismisses, "And they're too far away."

"And too Libertarian," Dad says. "Libertarians are terrible parents."

"Hm?" Mom asks, annoyed and firmly clicking her fork against her plate.

"Hmmm?" Dad playfully returns, "Their sense of 'development' requires financial incentives! As if all relationships in life merit a financial compensation. When was he coming up? July 2nd?" Dad asks.

"I think the 14th," Mom says.

"So not the 4th? No fireworks? Too busy stealing land and plowing rainforests?"

"Hm?" Mom asserts with half a smile.

"Hmmmmmmmmm?" Dad goofily contorts his face.

"He says locals are fairly compensated," she finally bursts with a laugh.

"Yeah? Beads? Blankets?" Dad asks, tilting his head quizzically.

"Tom," Mom folds her hands on the table.

"I like him. But he's a huge ass." He says with a smile, "Like ginormous."

"Tom." Mom laughs, "Be nice."

"Hey. *I'm* not subjugating poor and developing areas with exploitive infrastructure contracts. Tell *him* to be nice."

"Chile today has lower unemployment, less crime, and more stability than Illinois," Mom says.

"Yes, but, Illinois is also a democracy, at least for now...no promises," he jabs a finger at me with a wink. "Jen. Did you know that over a quarter of the world's democracies have disappeared or relapsed the past thirty years?"

I shrug. *I don't care.*

"It's true." His brow wrinkles. "An article in the *Journal of Democracy* measured a terrifying decline in support for democracy in the West. In the U.S., the number 'of people saying it would be good or very good for the 'Army to rule' rose 240% from 1995 to 2012.' Most worrying," Dad looks at his roast, "the trend is strongest among the young," he looks at me. "Who knows if your generation will save democracy, or end it. Or, maybe, it doesn't matter," he smiles at Mom's bored face. "Maybe we've already lost our republic? Researchers at Princeton and Northwestern discovered 'U.S. policies are formed more by special interest groups than by politicians representing the will of the general people' and that 'average citizens have little or no independent influence.' Cool, eh?" he sarcastically cheers with his milk.

I shrug. *I don't care.*

"And, funny story: researchers say the US is *already* an oligarchy, only pretending to be a democracy." He spreads his arms wide to address society, "The 'democracy' we have is an illusion tricking submission of the public to the elites." He smiles.

Fine whatever, I shrug. *I don't care.*

"Tom, you need to spend more time with Jack McHardy, and put this talk in a better place than dinner. Oh, Jen," Mom switches gears, "Uncle Greg is going to take over your room. Hope that's okay. You can have Dad's cot next to my bed for the week. Or the couch? Your choice."

Dad fidgets, looking at his food.

"Mom!" I glare in frustration. "This dinner is terrible. I'm so over not having a say in my own life!" I drink my milk, hoping it's a magical potion that can turn me into a huge hulk who busts out of this house and into a bank vault to live happily ever after. *No luck.*

"So. I have to ask," Dad smirks, "Are we going to charge Greg market-based rent?"

"No. He's our guest!" Mom shakes her head incredulously, "Why would I do that?"

"Um. Have you spent five minutes with your brother?" he laughs. "Nothing like a Libertarian to be a bad house guest: All independent when it comes to profit and ignoring the community supporting him. I have zero problem turning the tables. Charge water by the ounce. Every flush: 'That's $0.63 please, Greg.'" Dad playfully holds out a *Gimme* hand, "Every sip: 'That's $0.07 please, Greg.' He wants us to live under Ron Paul's total free market insanity. Let's take away the abstraction; let's paint a vivid picture what it means to be consumed by an all-encompassing free market. Eh, eh, eh?" He asks.

"No. That's final." Mom's firm smile drills Dad.

"I hate giving Greg a free pass. He assumes 'the state is the only source of coercive power.' Wrong. History's clear private organizations are plenty corrupt and destructive to the economy and the public. Pennsylvania Coal and Iron ran their own authoritarian state for decades," he lists on his fingers. "Rubber Barons enslaved entire regions in South America and Africa. The 'feeble government' libertarians lust after is fertile soil for privatized goons to fill the power vacuum and do whatever they want."

I wish I could do whatever I want, I muse. *Like getting the fuck out of this dinner and out of this house.*

Mom looks at him hard and the table is quiet.

"Okay. Yes, dear. I'll hush now." Dad innocently complies with comical kissy lips.

"Hey. Can it, mister," she laughs at him. "Okay, you *two* clean up," she says.

It was decreed dinner was finished, and it was so.

CHAPTER 5—PROJECT

Eddie. April 2022

The crisp snap of a fresh vegetable behind my neck startles my focus. I twist to see Jen staring oddly at me, only six inches away, chewing a carrot. She's holding a stack of paper with her non-vegetable holding hand.

"What's happening?" she asks behind a mouthful of carrot, and takes another bite.

"Gross," I frown. "Didn't your parents teach you not to talk with your mouth full?"

"Mm," Jen nods and opens her lips wide and brings her mouth down and close, showing off a large slimy pile of orange pulp. "Yes, they did," she mumbles, chomps a few more bites in my face, and moves even closer before she forces a predatory swallow. "They taught me a lot. A lot about rules and 'shoulds.'"

She looks over me, her legs touching my chair. My mouth forces a dry gulp. She's wearing black stilettos with black nylons, a dark green dress, and glasses. Today, it's the Sexy Librarian look. Yesterday was her Power Suit day.

"Ed. The world doesn't care about rules and shoulds," she plops a heavy hand on my shoulder, shaking it gently. "We just pretend it does so we can feel good. Hey, you need to help me sort these performance reviews," she taps a stack of papers on my head. "You know these people."

"Why are *you* doing that?" I ask, genuinely perplexed, failing to awkwardly preserve my personal space from Jen's invasion. The last thing I need is a boner when I stand up.

"Because, Ed. I'm someone who likes to be in charge. James is thinking about laying off a few Temps to stir the pot. That got me really excited and I wanted to help. He said I could pick ten."

"What? Are you serious? Jesus. What kind of project is this?"

"I want to ID the top performers in the company, pick ten to release, and select another few thousand or to be ready for, uh, downsizing," she says.

"Thousand? James *really* asked you to do this?" I ask.

"Um, yeah, totally," she looks away. "James and I were, uh, talking. He mentioned he was working on cuts. I needed to help and he said 'sure.'"

"Just like that," I hush incredulously waving my hands like a crazy person. "James says *you* get to pick who gets laid off?"

"Yeah. Well, after two blowjobs. One-and-a-half, actually," she laughs mimicking the appropriate motion on the diminished carrot before violently finishing it off.

My face clouds. "Ah, hm. I should really work on my calls…"

"Oh, come on, Ed. Don't you want to work tightly with me?" Her hand clasps the back of my neck with teasing violence. "Or should I ask Rick or Bill? They've been here as long as you, right?" she asks with a cool look. "They could help me."

I hate Bill. Rick always smells like nice cologne. There's an empty desk next to each of them she could have if she liked them more than me.

"Fine, I'll help." I reluctantly stand.

There's no one I hate enough to want laid off. That was like wishing someone dead—and not for fun, for *real*. TempGrace is already an enormously hostile work environment. I'd prefer not adding to the pain. Employees facing tough life moments, like a deadly illness, receive no empathy or time off but demerits for not being focused on work. *But,* I muse, *at least it's better to have a seat at the table than wait clueless in the hallway. I'll influence Jen's process, ensure the good people have a chance. Do good as an insider.*

I follow Jen along the worn gray carpet into the well air-conditioned area where managers have their offices. We talk how expensive lunch is now that farm workers are organizing for back pay, how produce rotting in the fields is disrupting the food chain. She paid $5.00 for that damn carrot! We're both pissed at how some people can't accept the opportunity for hard work without getting greedy or jealous.

"Workers today need to stop the nostalgia for the old days when labor earned a fat $8.00 for a whole hour. A ridiculous rate!" Jen says.

"My Senior Temp role barely makes half that…" I say as Jen slides open the door to an unused small windowless office. A dim light flickers to reveal a tiny table and chair. I center the table and pull the one chair over before looking to scavenge another seat.

"No. That's my chair. You get the floor," Jen interrupts, sliding the door shut.

"Huh? Oh, well, I can just stand," I say.

"No. I don't like it when you're taller than me."

"What?" I laugh. "Oh, come on. It'll just take a second to find another chair," I encourage, reaching past her for the door.

"No. Ed," she firmly keeps the door shut. "Life is much simpler when I make choices for you. I know how this world needs to work." She sternly points to the floor, "So sit."

"Okay…" I roll my eyes at her demeaning tone. *"Bossy, bossy, bossy."*

"Good boy," she dryly teases.

I cross my legs and lean against the wall. "Should we pick the bottom ten?" I ask. "This could be quick. I think those review sheets are sorted high to low by System Scores™. The ones we recommend will probably be all around 60.5% to 61%. Who are they?"

"No, no…" Jen slowly spreads the pages across her small table. "You're so lazy. I was thinking," she says. "Yeah, okay, we mark the bottom three, a few middle, *and* a few top performers to release a fresh thrill of moral hazard in the office," she grins.

"What? Jen, that doesn't seem fair," I say.

"No one cares about 'fair', Ed. The market doesn't care about 'fair.' All it cares about is hard work and profits. It's natural for workers to be lazy. Some learn that because they're a smart middle performer who can float above the cuts, they don't need to work as hard as they *actually* can. Nope. Not in my world. The real world. It's a moral responsibility that I teach you all lessons about what the *real* rules of the market are—not the one we think we have."

"What 'real rules,' Jen?" I open my hands in annoyance. "TempGrace has clear rules and policies on what good work is, and is not. That's how our System Scores are set. You can't just lay off people because you want to," I say, looking up at her.

What the hell is she thinking?

"Ed." She stands upright to look down at me. "This is for everyone's good. Sure, the pain sucks for the individuals, but it makes the corporation stronger. After this, Temps will work so much harder over the next few weeks! It'll be amazing," she leans to study the sheets, her back straightening to force her curves through her dress. "Anyway, the policies are fine," she shrugs, spreading the papers across the desk. "The market *always* wants her efficiencies. *Always*," she declares. "Our defense is innovation; seeing the world change and breaking rules *first,* rather than 'just doing things because you're supposed to.' Besides," she kicks me playfully in the shin, "I have the red marker," she waves it over my head, "and James's cock. So… who, who… gets my ten red marks?" She smiles at the papers on the desk. "Okay, yup, the bottom three are out," she slashes a red marker three times across the last page.

I didn't even see their names.

"That felt amazing. Pages and pages of teeny-tiny lives, all right here." She passes an odd shiver of excitement before leaning over the table. "Hey, here's *your* name, Ed. Wow. 89%?" she winks a gorgeous eye at me, "Hmmm…"

"Ha. Ha. Ha. You're funny," I shrug, irritated at her cavalier tone.

"Ed. I can pick *any* ten Temps," her smile becomes less playful and more severe. More predatory.

My heart tightens as I realize she might be more serious than I thought. "Uh, Jen?"

"Tell me," Jen sits, swiveling her chair toward me, her knees two feet from my nose. "What are you going to do for me, to keep your job? I'd like to know you already respect the power of a free market and don't need a lesson." She crosses a long nyloned leg over her knee to rest hands on her lap.

Huh? My mouth drops open. I'm now eye level with her heel three inches from my face. "Yes," I gulp, not really knowing what to say. "I've been aware of the free market, for some time." Beads of sweat collect on my forehead. "I'm aware of it every day I walk outside. Every minute of the seventy-hours-a-week I work for a $280 paycheck," I say, unsure where I should lay my eyes along her intense figure.

"Mmm, but do you *love* the free market, Ed?" She slightly extends her shoe to slowly rub the side of my face. "Do you *love* how it transforms societies and reallocate trillions of dollars of resources? Do you *love* how desperate labor, matched with excess capital, gets work done with incredible efficiency?"

"Yes. I do," I feel nervous sweat trickle down my back.

She extends her shoe to slowly rub the other side of my face. "I want to know that I can teach you. And that you will obey. If the Market demands it, would you kiss my shoe for money?"

"Um, yes," I unexpectedly crack.

"Would you for a dollar?" Her foot shifts to the other side of my face.

"Yes."

"Her foot moves down my chin. "I want to lead you, Ed, lead you towards riches and wealth. Be your mentor. Would you kiss it for one cent?"

"…Yes."

"Do it," she leans back in restful anticipation, "kiss the heel of a *truly* Free Market."

I smell stale floor dirt and dry foot sweat. I feel dizzy. I slowly kiss the heel of her shoe.

"…Good," Jen sighs.

After a lingering second, she slowly settles both feet on the ground and reaches into her pocket to retrieve a cent, and tosses it at me. She adjusts her hair and calmly returns to the lives waiting her judgment.

I sit in tense silence. I feel small. Hypnotized.

"Okay. Picked seven more," Jen says as a few staccato scratches interrupt the tense quiet of the room. "Thanks, Eddie," Jen stands and collects her papers. "Spared you this round." She grins.

"Who'd you pick?" I ask, emerging from my daze as Jen is halfway to the door.

She spins with an energetic smile, "Don't know. Some random fucks. Later." She disappears beyond the door.

What happened? I wonder, slowly crawling out of the daze Jen shoved me into. *How much are things changing here?*

In a different world, a previous generation of Americans could expect a social compact: You loyally work for company and it would return loyalty to you with a good job and decent retirement. The relationship was balanced. Now, I've learned to work hard and give *more* to the company than the company gives to you is your only hope for happiness. As long as you do more for them than they do for you—you're alright. We have to be givers, and they the takers.

At least I know that. Some old dumb fucks never saw how one sided their relationship really was and got totally screwed when they naively expected an equal return from their managers.

I want all companies to be as successful as possible, even if it hurts individuals. I respect a healthy cutthroat culture where some workers are culled each year. I only want *reasons* for the culling, not blind lust. Is Jennifer changing that?

CHAPTER 6—SUMMER

Jennifer. July 9th, 2012

Die, bugs! I swat five mosquitoes walking to the gas station on the north edge of town.

I'm sick of helping Mom and Dad. *Their house, their problems! Not my responsibility to ready the house for Uncle Greg. No matter how much you nag.* They've been annoying the piss out of me all week, cleaning the house. New coat of paint here, polish the door handles there. I think Mom's embarrassed how plain our simple little two-bedroom house is. I remember he's kinda rich? Good. They should be embarrassed! I'm embarrassed too! Welcome to the team, guys. Greg should visit more often, maybe *then* Mom will break our self-imposed poverty and buy me a car?

It's so humid, I complain, feeling grimy and sticky in the windless heat of summer. But I don't care. I try to be good at not caring. I have more control when I don't care. I don't care about the house. I don't care about Greg. I don't care about school or anyone in this town. I sure as fuck don't care about Mom's and Dad's expectations.

I sweep my eyes along the grassy pavement and crumbling patches of tar for an ant war. *Maybe crushing one of those would boost my mood?* I love offering the conflict a scrap of my lunch so I can watch one colony fight another. I imagine the ant generals commanding their drone warriors through World War I trenches over an exploding No Man's Land of Ant Death; their fighting meaning nothing to the Goddess looming miles beyond their comprehension. I'd watch them, impossibly huge, entirely unrecognizable, and then calmly step my shoe into their midst. Thousands would instantly crush under my foot. I'd stand feeling incredible and step away to behold the lifeless void and confusion. I'd carefully return, savoring each second of each step until all the little ant lives are taken by me.

But I don't find any ants today. *Another day.*

I pray Morgan is working today as the abandoned car dealership next to the gas station comes into view. Mom and Dad *never* buy me snacks. *Too much of an indulgence,* they complain. I'm forbidden from even visiting the Lickety Split Ice Cream Shoppe. *"No empty calories when others have none at all,"* I mock their stupid lecture. I need to use my own allowance to buy snacks! What a fucking joke. Two hours of gardening is only worth $10, and Mom and Dad want me to donate *half* of that to their social church programs? No way. Fuck that. Why do we keep ourselves as poor as possible to make other people happy? The gas station's glass doors slide open like revelers eager to see me and a blast of cold air prickles my skin. *I forget what air conditioning feels like!* I suddenly feel too cold. *Mmmm.*

"Hi, Morgan," I smile at the frumpy lady behind the counter with too much makeup.

"Jen," she says, "How's your afternoon?"

"Hot. Gardening. Wanted ice cream." I tug at my sleeve, a small pile of dirt lands on the sterile white floor.

"Wonderful. Got some new caramel chocolate swirl cones you might like," Morgan impishly tilts her chin towards the waist-high glass freezer in front of the counter.

"Ooooo," I eagerly nod and stride towards the treats with a big grin. "Oh, gee. I'm filthy," I tug at my hair, noticing how dirty I look in the glass reflection.

"Don't worry about that one bit, darlin'. It's summer time. Get dirty. Have *fun*," she winks emphasizing 'fun' for some reason.

Fun? Like Sex? I wonder. *No way. The guys here all blow.*

"No kidding? Right?" I agree anyway. Morgan is awesome. She's always supportive of whatever I want to do. She's a divorced Mom with three kids from three Dads and not much for the church circles. No gossip from her on "how the pastor's daughter got caught buying treats for herself." Morgan even offered to let me "buy cigarettes to hang out with the cool kids" skateboarding in the abandoned lot next door. She's the only parent who doesn't feel like a parent. Her kids must be so lucky. *"Do whatever you want, honey. Don't worry about none of that. You just got to be yourself,"* I grin as her past advice tumbles through my head.

I don't want to feel guilty about buying ice cream.

We talk a bit. I pay her with a few crumpled dollar bills and return into the outside heat to sit on the curb in the hot sun. I peel back the cone's wrapper and enjoy my first bites. *So yum, god!* I amaze at the rich caramel flavor sliding cool and thick across my tongue. I eagerly enjoy more bites and fight an encroaching brain freeze. *Whoa, slow down,* I lean my head against an air compressor and close my eyes. I hear a distant lawn mower. A few birds chirping. I feel a cold drip on my knee. *Fuck!* I quickly reach to wipe away the stain, but realize my gardening pants are filthy enough. *It's fine...* I relax and finish the cone, laying my head back to savor the lingering tastes.

I hear a few cars pass slowly in or out of town. An airplane adjusts its approach to some far-off runway. A warm wind swishes through treetops. Two birds chirp. *It's so peaceful being alone. I don't need anything from anyone. I only want there to be me. Just me.*

A stuttering belching truck enters the station. It gets louder and smellier until it blocks my sun. I open my annoyed eyelids as a saggy beaten pickup truck halts in front of me. The truck's bed is over loaded with furniture and ripped plastic tarps. I see a Michigan license plate caked with dirt next to a torn, "Women belong in the HOUSE ...and the SENATE" bumper sticker. A grandma with a shotgun rises un-announced from a piece of furniture stacked in the back of the truck to lord above her lumpy mess.

"Child." Her voice warbles down, "Edna, give the poor girl some food."

A tired, middle-aged woman with thin blonde hair opens the front driver door and painfully extends down a sleeve of square pale cookies. Something's wrong with her. I'm unsure where her pain is, other than everywhere.

"Oh. Uh..." I look sheepishly at the two of them, but reach out to grab a few cookies once I notice they're my favorite kind. "Thanks!"

The grandma jumps from the bed of the truck to evaluate me.

"Dear, your parents alive?" she leans her shotgun against the truck. "What city they in? We can take you anywhere, as long as that's south or west," she removes her road goggles, exposing bright clean skin around worried eyes.

I nod. "Uh. They live here in town," I say, reaching for a few more cookies before Edna moves them away.

"Are they treating you well? Do you need help?" the grey lady kneels sincerely next to me.

"Um, they're stupid sometimes, yeah. I mean, but I guess I'm fine," I shrug, wrinkling my nose at how annoying my parents are.

"I'm sorry to hear that. We thought this mess would be better down south. Heard Wilmington was a good place. We've heard that all over," the grandma observes, nodding at Edna. "We lost our Emma" her voice tightens, "taking a bad shortcut through Gary, Indiana. We've room if things seriously aren't right, dear."

"Your parents, they aren't using you for—stuff?" Edna the driver darkly asks.

"No. I'm fine. My parents are fine, I guess," I shrug between bites, not caring where my crumbs land. *Who are these weirdos?*

"Oh," the temperature of the conversation chills. "Sorry. We've seen so many lost souls since Detroit. I assumed neglect," the grandma looks awkwardly around the station, stands, and wipes her hands on her ratty trousers. "We've seen children forced do things I couldn't imagine."

"I was gardening with them. Oh! My clothes?" I laugh, cookies crumbs exploding out of my mouth. "No, *I'm not poor.* Geeze," I roll my eyes. "I'm fine. We have a house. And food."

"I see. Well, um, might we use that air pump behind you?" she points. "Emma's patch-job isn't holding as it used to. Old Route 66 here is a hard road. Didn't expect to be back on it but here we are again…"

I awkwardly stand to leave, "Okay. Um, bye." I brush off some crumbs. *And god, take a bath.* I pinch my nose. *Their stuff reeks!*

I walk home through a breeze of lazy cottonwood seeds floating through the sky. This whole street is lined with proud large cottonwood trees. I adore how free their seeds float; their dance making me so happy. I stop moving. The soft cotton brushes past my cheek, I lift up my arms and it feels as if I'm traveling through stars. Floating through the universe. Free. Careless. Like these seeds in the wind.

I never want to be tied down like I am now. No restraints. Not ever.

But I *never* want to be seen with a ratty tarp and a truck of stinky junk. *Gross,* I wrinkle my nose as I continue my walk home. I've never felt so eager to take a shower and wash the poor away.

I go straight home and do just that.

Unlimited freedom has been a throb in my heart for several weeks. Freedom from parents telling me what to do. Freedom from my own chores. I spend the rest of my evening fantasizing the beauty living a *truly* free life would be. No limits.

Mmmm, my body tingles as I remember Jon Stein vacuuming my room without a cent of profit. I was his absolute. His monarch. Absolutely free to do anything and be myself. The tingle feels so nice I look around to see who's watching. Damn it! Mom is there in the kitchen and Dad's been coming in and out of our room to talk with me all night. I hate being unable to make a mess in my own bedroom. Especially when I really want to make my own special kind of mess...

Maybe reading alone will do it again? I grin, eager to learn more. I reach open my book to read about my stud muffin, King Leopold II. *He enjoyed steamy sex with young girls. I might actually have a chance with him? If only he hadn't died 103 years ago! Just my luck. If I could be free to change that for one night...* I trace a finger down my belly and into my belly button, and press into warmth and pleasure.

His long white beard rests against the lace on my neck as we waltz across the Throne Room of the Royal Palace of Brussels. I clutch his tall thin frame close as we dance under neoclassical arches of white and gold. The massive room is alight from the warm soft fires of a dozen chandeliers holding two thousand candles each.

My long gown flutters and flares at each twirl. The evening clearly matching our magnificence.

His voice is strong. Regal. "What future can there be, when the visionaries can't create the world as they see it? What would the world become if great leaders weren't so hamstrung by fear?" Leopold bemoans as we dance, "What is a 'king,' if not allowed to rule? What's even the point?" he confides his sorrow.

"I know. I'm sorry, dear." I look deep into his narrow eyes. "You've freed the heart of Africa. Remember? I admire you so much for that." The room spins around us, but I only care about his hard eyes and strong nose. Leopold really resented the role of king in a constitutional monarchy. His powers in Belgium were tied and bound, but he found his own ingenious way to be free: he held *absolute* power over his Congo Free State.

"Yes, but I am king who cannot be King!" He shames himself.

"The media, the press. They undid you. They embarrassed you," I report. "They made you weak. You should have banned photography and journalists."

"I know. I know. But it isn't that easy," he says. "All the eyes of Europe were watching. I spent a fortune on counter-spin and bribes to maintain the good image of my Congo Free State as long as I did." He shakes his head. "Despite controversy, sweet Jen, I enjoyed success. I had a protection: People shudder and turn away from the scale and reality of my power. They turn their minds off and hand them to me. When subjects see a pitiless and money-crazed king towering toward the sky, they do not even wish to look! They see him not as part of the human race. For He is King. And it hurts their collective instinct to see a King degraded. The masses shrink their psychology and shrink their will against hearing particulars of what His reign truly means and how it came to rise. They shudder, turn away, and even *defend* His total and absolute hold over them. They know His power is derived from an all-knowing god, and that to obey him is to essentially worship god."

"Obey a King means to worship god?" my heart cracks open. "What went wrong? Teach me." I say.

He caresses my cheek, "If I could have hidden my Congo forever from the world, I would have found a thousand times the profit and a thousand times the peace."

I look at him with sympathy and all my love at his clarity. "It could have been your stress-free garden—your Eden. And you, its unquestioned god… What bliss." I drip.

"Indeed. But that's not enough. I feel like so much of my potential has been artificially cut short. Oh, my treasure," he bathes me in adoration. "We only have one night together. I wish this was otherwise, as I am unable to free myself permanently from death. At midnight, I will be gone as forever part of your dreams."

"No." I clutch him tight.

"Shush," he says. "I am an old man. This is the way of life. This is why we love, why we conquer. Because tomorrow will not always come and our mark on the world must live past us." He suddenly interrupts our dance, "Come. Let me show you something." He grabs my hand and we run through the halls. We laugh and whoop and holler with unrestrained joy. Servants scatter and disappear as our laughter approaches and passes. Giggling, we burst into a dark room and fumble for a candle to illuminate our faces, our souls, and the path to the balcony door. A latch unhooks to reveal the warm night of 19th century Brussels sleeping before us.

Beckoning to the soft glow of the city below, he bares his heart. "It pains me this is only partly mine." He waves a hand over the city, "Yes, I loom above them all. Yet, the horses, the factories, and the workers—they stubbornly cause me problems. They *should* be firmly in my pocket, and I chafe they are not!" He turns and embraces me tenderly, "I think this planet is too small a sphere for your exhaustless energy. The world is all parceled out, and what is left of it is divided, conquered, and colonized. But look," he turns my chin to the heavens. "Think of these stars you see at night, these vast worlds which we can never reach. I would have you annex the planets if I could; think of that often, Jennifer. It makes me sad to see them so clear and yet so far beyond your grasp… I know there is strength in you to build a new Free World, one of higher bliss than even my Congo Free State. Think of that. Please, Jen! Dream of that."

He tilts my chin down to move his lips to mine for a tender kiss. As our lips near, I feel the heat of his passion vanish in empty air before we unite. My heart drops. I'm left hollow and alone as the clock tower bells in the small city below strike midnight.

I look down at the city; it's so small beneath me. I feel the imposing power of the palace behind me. I rise higher, like I'm suddenly standing at my true height after a lifetime of slouching. I see the whole region below me, lights strung like the small glowing embers of a scattered fire before just before they are finally stamped out. I stand again and now see all of Europe below me, the Old World's dark edges cut into the glittering moonlight of the reflected sea. I reach higher again, and see the whole Earth spinning quietly below, its clouds swirling like a dark marble. *My marble.* I pick the planet from space and hold it between my fingers. It's so tiny in my hand, yet its weight so real. I hide it in my breast pocket with a blissful smile, and sigh myself pleasurably to sleep.

CHAPTER 7—COFFEE BREAK

Eddie. May 2022

The happiest day of my life begins at 10:12 a.m.

We finished our Standing Team Meeting not more than thirty minutes ago, which, for reasons obvious to me and my co-workers, Jennifer no longer presented her System Report. Instead, Jen met directly with James and the other top managers for a half hour.

I was on spreadsheet seven, with my chin heavily leaning on my hand, feeling depressed. *This isn't getting me closer to buying a clarinet.*

Suddenly, two firm tits land on the crown of my head as a pair of warm hands cover my eyes in a wonderful darkness.

"Guess who?" Jen's voice scalds in the dark.

My heart throttles in amazement. *Holy shit this isn't real. This can't be happening.* "Um, Napoleon?" I ask.

"Haha, close. Good guess," she says. "Try again."

I want this moment to last forever. I want to turn to dust before she ever lets go of me, "Huck Finn?"

"He's not even real." She releases her grip and knocks me on the head.

Damn. She got wise, I ache at the coolness of her absence and twist to look at her. She remains totally in my space, not bothering to step back. I feel a strong blush rise in my cheeks. I lean to stay polite and so my face isn't totally in her breasts.

In reality, I ache to kiss every inch of her, seen and unseen. Kiss her belly, her chest, her legs, and everywhere in between.

"Hey. Let's grab coffee. I got Tad to cover us." She hits me again for fun. "We've the rest of the day off."

I spin my chair fully around and scoot what little I can before jamming into the desk. "Huh, what?" I ask.

"Yeah, sure." She straightens her hair with a few fingers. "Come on. Let's go. He'll be here in a minute," she says.

I'm in full panic mode. *She might sex her way out of missing hours, but I can't.* I'm not cute enough to catch James's eye, no matter how many push-ups or tight shirts I wear. Not his type. "Eh, maybe I'll work a bit. I'm on a roll," I sound disappointed because I am.

Jen rolls her eyes with a hand on her hip. "Take charge of life, man! Come on, let's go," she tugs impatiently on my sleeve.

"Hey, guys," Tad walks over and sits at Jen's terminal. "Were you on sheet seventeen, Jen?" he asks.

"Yeah, thanks," she says, looking at me with a more-than-curious expression, and still taking up my space.

I suddenly can't read what she's thinking. "W h a t?" I mouth silently, cautiously looking past the curve of her hips to our manager drilling on Jen's keyboard. She pets the side of my head tenderly with her fingers as I look. My eyes close in bliss, my shoulders relax. I want to stay like this forever.

"Let's go." She grabs my collar with a yank.

We sit side-by-side in a rusted open-window TempBus for the ride downtown. It's a sweltering day. I offered Jen the window seat so I can occasionally view the top of her breasts jolting with each bump while pretending to appreciate the scenery roll past.

Simply mesmerizing, that scenery.

The depression hit southbound Highway 281 hard. Not riding a bus for years, I now realize the highway is a skeleton of the road I remembered. All the parks leading downtown are burnt dry and full of Collectivist shanty camps. *I'm so grateful I don't live there, paying $100 a month Squatters Fee to the park owners. Ugh!*

As we cross I-35 and merge onto I-10, the world changes. I forgot how San Antonio is the most unequal city in the country. My truck stop apartment in ZIP code 78258 is very far from life in 78207 west of downtown and the Alamo Plaza. Green trees. Clean streets. Posh store fronts and huge houses with armed guards and imposing fences.

We step off the bus on Market and Alamo into a different country. The San Antonio Riverwalk hasn't had a river in the past eight years, I at least remember that. *Too many people kept stealing the water.*

"I love downtown." Jen says, walking through the touristy areas perfectly at ease, looking for our coffee place.

I feel uncomfortable, counting the years since I've been in a coffee shop. *Where's my life gone?* I worry as we enter The Alamo Roast, Jen's venue of choice. I officially feel we're entering a country whose exchange rate I can't afford; one where the idle rich spend their time chatting with friends and finishing private school homework. I stare nervously at the prices on the menu and the miles between the lifestyle of these kids and my own. My throat feels dry. A small coffee is half a day's pay for me. I suck it up and order a small tea once I settle the math, to forgo my weekly bacon.

Jen's tall black coffee is free. No cream. No soy. Just black. She flirts with the cashier and offers to look up his resume in the TempGrace system, to, "See what might be out there…"

Only Tad and the other assistant managers have direct access to the whole résumé database! What the fuck is she doing? I'm greatly annoyed how many blowjobs she'll owe Tad or James for this access. Jen laughs at my visible disapproval and leads us to a small cluster of couches in the corner.

"Tea, Eddie?" she frowns at the economical choice. "We don't make it in the world playing it safe with tea. You could talk your price down and get a better deal. You work at TempGrace too."

"Yeah, but not with the whole database…" I shrug not wanting to talk about this. *I can't wipe off my problems like Tad's spooge on my back.* I've tried sex-charming before when my Mom couldn't afford antibiotics and I desperately needed a raise to buy them. I always wished female bosses stayed around longer, and stopped getting pregnant. But when you have thousands of attractive people vying for favors—or demanding favors; an empty womb doesn't outlast an empty belly in the Temp world.

"Gross," I frown. "You like straight black coffee?"

"What can I say?" She smiles as we sit, "I like my coffee how I like my men: bitter and devoured alive," she toasts. "Ed. There's no one looking out for you *but you,*" she says. "There's no 'free' coffee. No free handouts. Success takes cunning, or we'd all be rich kids."

"Yeah, sure," I shrug.

Jen continues, sounding like a preacher, "Think of the merciless discipline; the courage; the responsibility relying on your own judgment; the days, nights and years of unswerving dedication to a goal; the tension of the unbroken maintenance of a full, clear mental focus, and the intense honesty needed to see new opportunities. *That's* how we make it *big* in this world. Not playing it safe with watered-down tea," she scolds.

I shrug, *She's one intense chick,* and look at the photo books of exotic places lying on the small table between us. *I guess I could use more imagination.* Before my Dad disappeared in the TempTampa office fire, he always tried to coach me to stretch every opportunity to its limit, no matter how small. But I never found much leverage. Nor did my Dad apparently, as he never got out of that TempTampa death trap. I put him and his fiery death out of my mind.

Our chairs are soft with small pebble patterns that ripple in the sunlight once you touch them. They feel like flower petals and sand and smooth warm stones. I've never seen quantum fabric before, but I want to fit in and not gawk. I already sense the odd stares from the private school teens burning through me, wondering, 'What the fuck is this guy doing with a babe like her?' My home-cut hairstyle might as well be on fire. Jen relaxes in her mini-sofa and turns her head to survey the room. *I've no idea what she's thinking bringing us here. I feel humiliated, but my tea is too hot to chug and run.* And I want to stay for Jen.

"Do you think these kids' parents make over $45,000 a year?" she leans forward conspicuously.

I try not to stare at the widening chasm blooming at the top of her fantastic cleavage. "Maybe even $60k," I note. "My cousin once had a job for a whole year that paid $49,000 and her children went to TempEd Houston," I wrinkle my nose. "I don't know if these kids know how lucky they are to watch football games. Have proms. I miss that. We were so spoiled having public school in our day."

"Ya know what," Jen edges closer. "We were *all* spoiled then, and they probably don't appreciate it either. They're taking it for granted too—and one day their letter jackets and boat-owning-parents will fall like stones right into a TempCamp. Humans always take stability for granted, like our good jobs at TempGrace. Every day we walk a razor's edge that determines the rest of our life. Ed, it could be so much worse. *It was worse!* Remember?"

"Gee, yeah, I remember where I was that day. Studying for scholarships. Where were you?"

Jen leans back, thinking seriously about the day the world changed. "I was sixteen in a small town south of Chicago. In the country really," she says, her hand flicking away imaginary dirt. "It was a beautiful blue fall day. We turned on the news in class after a teacher bursts in telling us to turn on the TV."

I lower my head. "October 29th, 2012. Man… Those days were nuts," I say. "Especially the hunger riots. But we all came together and completed President Ron Paul's vision," I notice Jen's face darken. "Today—gee—we can't get *anything* done. We're almost as bad economically, but we don't have that unity now."

My voice cracks a bit, "The fools wasted the biggest era of economic growth in human history. Squandered it. That was terrible. But what disgusted me most was how The Left said it was an 'inside job' and politicized the one-time government, businesses, and society actually came together to work. Whiners!" I blast. "'Oh, the shooter really never had a chance to explain himself before disappearing into an insane asylum and committing suicide.' Jeez, really? He obviously was retarded. What *could* he say? The country deserved closure. To move on. Instead, the North and West Coasts made a huge mess."

Jen nods, "But look, that pain was good for us. We *needed* it to bring us together. To learn. To unify us," her voice explores an odd hunger. "Justice is harmony and agreement among the parts; be that justice in a city, an individual, or a soul. Did you know that?"

I shake my head as she continues.

"We burned away regulations and handouts and made civilization stronger by allowing the *individuals* who make civilization to become stronger too. God, I miss that unity we had then," Jen says, fiddling her cup. "We're so fragmented today."

She seems to deflate. I watch her amazing lips take a shy sip of coffee. She always seemed superglued with the confidence of a thousand guys a day worshiping her; I never thought she'd be less-than-optimal.

Jen perks up. "The Double Think is good for us. Like a beautiful Zen kōan. Ed, this always makes me happy: Focusing on what most benefits the individual, also most benefits society! It's so elegant. Society is made up of individuals. It's our *duty* to civilization to make ourselves as rich and strong as possible—no matter what. No holding back," she pushes away an imaginary restraint.

God she's so beautiful. Her face lights like starlight, her gravity consumes the whole room.

"What?" she smiles, breaking my reprieve.

Fuck. Keep it cool. "I'm just mesmerized, uh, by your, smart talking," I say. *'Smart talking'? Such a turd!*

Jen laughs, "Okay good. I like that," she thinks a moment. "I mean, how stupid would it be for an Olympic swimmer to hold herself back from a gold medal because it would hurt the feelings of the other swimmers? Right? We wouldn't have the Olympics. We'd all be little weaklings 'playing nice' and 'playing fair.' Ugh. Gag me now. Please. I mean, we ought to go for it and be the strongest self we can be, right?" She looks for approval.

"Yeah. Totally," I say with a vigorous nod.

"Okay, good," she relieves into a more reflective tone. "So, Ed, where'd you like to go? In life, work, whatever," she adjusts her hair again.

"Haven't actually pondered that. Gee," I say. "Honestly, it's been awhile. I'm just trying to keep my head down, do a good job. Keep off the streets. I mean, I've 'planned stuff' before. Always wanted to become a Technology Architect. Did 230 credits of TempCollege before I realized those positions were only filled from private schools or the owner's friends. All TempEd seems to do is barely keep me above the cuts. I'd really love a life, of course," I nod. "Who wouldn't? But all my friends relocated to TempOmaha or TempHouston or wherever they could find work. And, well, ha—all the girls move out too fast for anything meaningful," I say, avoiding the various reasons *why* they move on. "You really are a breath of air, Jen. I'll be sad when you move into something, uh, big."

"You really think I'll get big?" she twinkles her nose at me with a coy smile.

"Without a doubt." *Like getting pregnant by Tad or James and subsequently abandoned!* "You're smart and quick and forceful, and have a charm that, er, keeps people's attention." I blush, edging too near the truth. "It's odd," I cough through my dry throat as a nervous electric current surges down my lungs. I take a sip of hot tea. "Sure, some girls are pretty, like masterpieces of nature even, but they seem two dimensional, like, makeup on canvas. With you, there's something else I don't understand. Something intense."

Jennifer bathes in my words. I feel terrified and invigorated. Her eyes are open and pure and soaking me in. I've never felt this comfortable being so honest with anyone, let alone a hottie like Jen.

"Well," she leans forward. "That's because they don't have the hunger I have. *They* hate learning. Hate work. All they want is to sleep all day and be a trophy wife. *Me?* I want the world."

We talk another hour and another tea about how our families made it through the Collapse. My Dad followed 'the rules' and bit it hard not taking control of his 401k, which evaporated with the rest of the world's currencies when the old U.S. Dollars split into Commodity Certificate Dollars. Jen was more vague and dark about her family. She didn't want to talk about her Mom and Dad beyond the fact they died in the hunger riots, and she moved in with her uncle.

At 4p.m., I walk Jen to the Private Bus stop but decline to ride along claiming I have some shopping to do. Another lie, as I have no money left for the fare home.

I arrive at my small-unlockable apartment late in the night after an unplanned and confused sixteen-mile hike from downtown. She's simply intoxicating.

CHAPTER 8—GARDEN PARTY

Jennifer. July 2012

I remove a finger from my belly button when a clunk at the front door startles my sensual focus. My blood pounds. *Who's breaking in?* I worry. Mom jumps from the kitchen table to the front of the house. I set my *King Leopold* book on Dad's cot and tiptoe into the kitchen as Uncle Greg bursts into the house.

"Hey, y'all! Doorbell's broken? Man! I'll tell you," his loud east Georgia baritone declares as two large exhausted bags thunk to the floor, "Chicago has *just fallen apart!"*

Mom embraces Greg and delivers her little brother a kiss on the cheek.

"Hey, Meg! The taxi to the car rental had bullet holes in it. Bullet holes!" he lifts his arms excitedly in the air.

"Welcome to Wilmington. You made it. You're safe here," Mom says.

"Hi, Tom." Greg's tall frame moves deeper into the house with his rugged hand sticking out of a leather jacket like a sack of walnuts to shake Dad's hand. Dad hobbles out of the family room couch to tolerate Greg's confident handshake.

"Other car companies were loading customers in armored buses!" Uncle Greg says. "I knew things were bad the past three years, but not *this* bad. Guards holding machine guns at O'Hare? Did a double take I wasn't stuck in South America."

"Well, we have a nice quiet place for you here." Dad says.

"When have you last been downtown?" Uncle Greg asks the two of them.

"Um, last January I think?" Mom looks at Dad. "We don't get around much. Tom and I saw a show for our anniversary. I guess the city was under a blanket. It was, like, zero degrees that night, right hun?" Mom asks.

"Yeah, January 15th. Suppose not much crime in the dead of winter. We don't watch the news anymore. Too sensational. Too negative," Dad says.

"—Too real?" Greg interjects.

"—Too hopeless, I'd say. And who's to say what's even 'real' these days?" Dad politely hedges with a shrug. "I tire being told to feel terrified all the time. And I hate how the media uses pretty women to get attention and convey messages."

"Holy hell. *Who is this?*" Greg notices me in the kitchen doorway.

"Hi, Uncle Greg," I cheer and step forward, sliding into awkward side hug.

"What did you trade for *this* beautiful woman? Hot damn, it's been awhile," he ogles me up and down. "You're not covered in boogers and mud anymore, huh?" he asks, grinning his appraisal.

"I've learned how to take showers. Yes," I cross my arms.

"—And you should see her chew through books like a termite." Dad beams through a huge grin.

"So, you shit letters like your Pa? Good for you. One day, we'll have to get you that real world education," he slaps Dad and me on the back with a wink. "My, things changed," Greg looks around. "I was nervous on the road down I'd hit a blockade of burning tires and masked gunmen. Then I drive out of Chicago into these beautiful nature preserves and exit the highway at this perfect little town with my head just spinning."

"Yup. Yup. We've worked hard to keep this little town together," Dad says. "We've got Jennifer's room all set up for you to invade," Dad offers. "Hungry? Thirsty?"

"God, yeah. I'm parched," Greg lifts his bags. "Planes are dry as hell. Thanks."

"One *free* tall glass of water coming right up." Dad twinkles his eye at Mom, who stabs him quickest glare of The Look I've ever seen.

I can't help but laugh and cover it before Mom turns her easy glare on me.

"We've the back deck set for dinner if you're not too tired?" Mom chimes, "It's a beautiful night."

"Yes please, that sounds great. Thank you," Greg nods back, following Dad into the kitchen talking about his work in Washington D.C. last week.

I get out of the way to watch Greg lumber past as if he's a character from an adventure movie turned real. He reeks of the world; reeks of shoot first, questions after—if at all. No spinning and tumbling thoughts—and layers of thoughts about those thoughts—like my Dad. The man is action.

Three strands of white lights drape across our deck framing a dark turquoise-blue sky. Citronella candles try mightily to defend marauding mosquitos. The evening's humidity wraps a comfortable blanket against a slight chill creeping into the night.

I intentionally sit with my back against the mansion next door so I don't have to think about how poor we are.

We pray:

"Dear, Lord. You see people grasping, grasping, grasping. Taking, taking, taking. And it must be so hard to see us always that way. That no matter how much we have, we never have enough. Please guide us away from a life filled with worry about what we don't have or 'might have.' Fill our emptiness, Jesus. Let your love, consume us as we consume you. Let us stand in awe of the totality of your love to become one with you. Amen."

We eat. *We never have lamb chops, yet we are tonight! The adults are even drinking wine. I never see Mom and Dad drink wine. They're totally showing off for Greg.* And of course, adults talk about boring adult stuff. I fight not to roll my eyes.

"So, how's Ben been?" Dad asks, sorting through his question with chuckle and a sip of wine.

"Oh, good. Really good," Greg says, finishing a bite. "We're still at that Pangue ranch seventy miles northwest of Santiago, near Valparaíso and the coast. You'd love it. Totally self-sufficient. Solar power. Organic vegetable gardens. Great view of the mountains; and even the ocean on a nice day. Gosh, wish you had Internet. I'd share photos. I didn't bother with a data package for this trip. Prices are insane."

"Eh, tell me about it," Dad frowns. "But I'll admit the web's *way* less of a time suck when you have pay by the minute in the library! And libraries are only open on weekends. Anyway, yeah, data costs a ton," Dad looks sideways at Mom. "I shouldn't complain. We worry technology distracts from being more heartfelt and human."

I smirk. *Even Dad's irritated with our 'give all our money to charity' life. 'Live simply so others may live?' Eh, Dad? Right?* I chide him in my mind.

"Were you and Ben thinking of adopting?" Mom asks, waiting long enough. "Your note a few months back made it seem like something's up," she raises a delighted eyebrow.

"Ah. Hm," Greg shifts in his deck chair. "We're not really thinking kids anymore. It's hard to see how they fit in our lifestyle. Ben *really* wants to adopt. He'd love a little girl to gossip with. But I don't know if we'd have time. So much work these days. I'm traveling a lot with All Corp.; traveling all over the continent each month," he says.

"Well. There's *never* a 'right time'," Mom smiles carefully. "Lord knows Jen was a surprise blessing to our lives. We made it work. Parenting is enriching on it's own levels, even if she's a brat most the week," Mom sticks her tongue at me.

Ugh, so embarrassing, I roll my eyes and slice a roasted tomato.

"Children make life different," Dad says. "They really do. Jennifer softened Megan a lot. Greg, you know better than I, back at Duke, I almost kicked Megan out of class she was so opinionated. Would never let anyone speak unless they agreed with her! Then, the day before Christmas break, she shows up at my office hours demanding I re-grade her final paper, and jumps—ow."

Mom kicks Dad's story under the table as Greg spreads a toothy grin.

"Kids change things," Mom says. "And I don't just mean diapers and stress and stepping on toys. Having a kid changed how I view the world. Jen makes me worry about parents everywhere and how they struggle. Caring about another person more than yourself, is the essence of god's will."

"Absolutely," Dad says. "It's our turn to push this heaping pile of a civilization forward. But the pillars of our caretaker society have been washed away in the name of 'helping the economy'—but only help the rich."

"—Greg." Mom sternly crosses her arms with an eye on Dad. "What fun things did you want to do here this week?" Mom smiles.

"Now wait a sec," Greg holds up a hand. "This is where those books screw with your head, Tom. I work for Mr. Jacobson. He's a billionaire, yes, and also a great guy. Calm, confident, and focused. We developed whole regions with him. New factories. New farms ten times more effective than before! Is he tough? Yes, he'll pound the hell out of an opportunity without holding hands. But if there's room for work, and you have the talent, you can ride your boat on his tide. He can't do it alone."

"Boys. Boys," Mom interrupts, getting bored. "We're talking about children here, *not* politicians and businessmen. Greg, what Tom's *trying to say,* is how worthwhile children are even if they seem like 'an ending'—sure, they end some things—but also add a wonderful richness to life."

"Yeah. But I'm not feeling it," Greg shrugs.

"Greggie," Mom says. "I don't want money to replace a happy life for you. All those rich people? Seriously? That wasn't you growing up."

Greg looks at his plate.

Mom continues, "I worry about you." She moves a hand to his, "Extreme wealth does *extreme* spiritual damage. Serious social science suggests the affluent are less likely to exhibit empathy, respect social norms, and disregard laws. The rich were also more likely to cheat someone than a poor person would."

"Hey, I haven't really changed much." Greg tenses a lip. "And I don't cheat."

"Sure, Greggie. I know." Mom looks at me. "But someone who's merely disagreeable in normal circumstances, with wealth that allows her to get whatever she wants. It'd be easy for her to become pathologically unconcerned with others."

Shut up, Mom. I quietly tense at the barb.

"Everyone's different," Greg shrugs. "Independence is important to me. I like being active. I've things to do and it's for sure a lot of time and money fostering a child with no clear ROI," Greg looks at Mom in an odd way. "I mean our Dad kinda made me wonder if we—I, shouldn't even have kids? I've always wondered what monsters might be lurking in my DNA. Thankfully, Jen's such an angel," he smiles and messes up my hair.

I blow him off with a fake smile and return my beauty to its proper place.

"—But what's really the difference between developing a society and class of children?" Dad asks.

"I don't know." Greg shrugs.

"We make room for children to be successful." Dad crosses his arms. "A family spends *years* of time and money on helpless children without knowing the return. You always think you have to do everything yourself. That's not how societies work. Let's lighten the load, make it *easier* to have successful children? Fund all day pre-school? Free organic lunches and breakfasts for all students? Encourage extra-curricular activities with easy transportation and supervision? It'd only cost a few billion dollars. We can do it. Yet, that was the first thing cut."

"I don't want *my* tax dollars paying for someone's free lunch," Greg says. "Pay for it yourself. I want to spend my money on the life I enjoy: whisky, poetry books, and leather jackets. And if I don't want children, I certainly don't want to pay for your choices."

"The more powerful you are," Mom says, "the more your choices impact other people, and thus the more responsibility you have to act with kindness and humility."

Dad taps his fingers. "And what about *growing* the market? Do we want new customers, new innovations? I'm horrified the next Mozart is stuck serving fast food," Dad shakes his head. "That's probably *already* happened a dozen times. Resources don't naturally flow to who uses them best—power and privilege say who takes what."

"Look," Greg says. "The market always rewards hard work. That 'fast food Mozart' *could* find success if he worked hard enough."

"Well," Mom stands. "I'd love to stay late, but I have to finish my own sermons for service tomorrow. Some in this town actually attend church at 7:30 a.m.," she huffs.

"Oh, sorry, Megan. Um, yeah," Dad fuddles a bit realizing he maybe went too far in Lecture Mode.

"You three behave." Mom kisses her brother. "Say goodnight before you head to bed, Greggie."

"Sure thing." Uncle Greg wraps an arm around his sister.

Mom walks around the table supplying all a mandatory hug goodnight.

"Night, Mom," I hug back.

"You want a blanket, dear?" Mom asks, rubbing my shoulders and arms, warming them up.

"Sure. Thanks," I smile. The night *is* chilly. The stars are out. Jupiter, Venus, and a thin crescent Moon align sharp and bright against a dark purple sky. Mom returns with a fuzzy fleece blanket and a non-subtle yank on Dad's collar instructing he should clear the table and do dishes.

Two fireflies dance with each other in the corner of the yard. Greg and I relax in the sudden peace of the evening. He appraises me for a moment.

"You look so much like Megan, it's freaky," Greg shakes his head clear. "How's school going?" he asks, adjusting his chair.

I look at a fingernail I need to repaint. "I don't go. Mom and Dad teach me."

"Yeah? I heard. More your mom teaches?" he asks.

"Dad too! He's really good."

"I bet. Sure can lecture." He gently lifts a thumb off the table. "But parents can't show you the whole world—only what they know. The world is *the world.* It's never the same as the books, and never what anyone thinks they 'think' it is."

"Yeah?" I ask, fiddling with a sock.

"Yeah," he nods.

"Dad says I'll probably get scholarships at any college I choose," I smile.

"He's probably right." Greg slightly frowns, "But college isn't the world—only a *part* of the world he's most familiar with. Again, the *world* is the world."

"Hm," I shrug, not really caring about the world.

"You might be too smart for college. From what I hear," he reaches into his coat pocket for a cigar, and lights it. A puff of smoke rolls into the air. "College might be an expensive disappointment. I'm not saying don't plan on going," he says. "You're young. School can be a good thing."

I shrug.

We sit quietly. I realize I've never talked to Uncle Greg as an adult before. "What was Savannah like, growing up? I don't remember the South," I ask about my birth place.

"Oh, gorgeous," he shakes his mind awake and leans back into memory. "The old plantation aristocracy built a beautiful city. Today it's a hip town too, great bars, food. Parks. But also like traveling back in time to a classical republic where the people are proper," he chuckles. "Everyone knows where you stand. Some pcoplc, you don't talk with. Some people are better than you, some are less than you, and that's how it is. But we all hate the Feds," he taps his cigar at me. "I worry that seems strange to you kids up north, people hating the government. You should see the total sham governments in South America. *Holy. Crap.*" He leans forward, "Governments are *terrible.* I'm forced to spend $1,000,000 in bribes a year to get basic permits for my businesses. $1,000,000. Direct bribes!"

"Really?" I ask, somewhat interested. "Why? To do what?"

"Everything," he says. "Get a permit. Move a truck. Store grain. Bureaucrats are people who love power. And once they have power, they love to lord it over their subjects and make you bleed whenever they can. Like vampires." Greg turns his two fingers into fangs, "I'm-here-to-suck-your-blood."

I laugh. We both smile.

"Your Dad sees governments academically. Southerners are wary people who know government is perfectly willing to burn it's own city to the ground. One hundred and fifty years ago Savannah was destroyed for the fun of it. We trust our abilities and expect nuthin' from no one." He points at himself, "I have my lot, and my lot's mine." He points at me, "And your lot's yours. Makes sense, right?"

I nod. "But no bad memories down there?" I ask, slyly fishing for background on why Grandpa was sent to jail for life. *No one tells me anything!*

"Sure. Well, the South can feel a bit stifling and unfair," Greg misreads my question. "It *was* a slave society. That lingers. Some families wouldn't bat an eyelash to hold slaves again, but they're a minority," he coughs and shrugs uncomfortably, waving away his smoke. "History's sometimes the same story with different actors and places. The South *was* founded by English slave lords from Barbados. They wanted a West Indies–style slave society: Democracy a luxury only for the rich, with enslavement was the natural place for the poor." He re-folds a napkin. "That's the history of it," he shrugs, taking a few puffs.

"But that's where government was good, right? Freeing the slaves. Slaves could never do that themselves? The North had to rescue them?"

Greg coughs and looks around. "Hard to say. Anti-slavery morality took long to get ahold in the South because it was against powerful economic interests, rightly claiming their businesses would be destroyed if they weren't allowed slave labor. Many argued the squalor of English factory workers were far worse than those of slaves." He puffs, looking hard.

Is he testing me?

"How many slaves were there?" I eventually ask.

"About four million in the United States back then. Seventy percent slaves and only thirty percent masters in some parts. I suspect slaves *could've* organized and rebelled, if life was actually so bad, *could've* rebelled without a Northern excuse for invasion. Some Blacks owned slaves too. You know that?"

I shake my head no.

"Some say Blacks in the South today are poorer than their slave ancestors." He looks around the yard, "I bet a slice workers of any race, when given the honest choice, might prefer the simplicity of working for a good master who takes care of them. No bills. No grocery shopping. Just life in a simple community with plenty of work. I'm all about ultimate freedom, no matter what. Even if that means the freedom to be a slave."

"Sure," I smirk.

Could I choose people like pets in a store? Like Jon Stein? I move my hand down my shirt to finger my belly button through the fabric. *Mmmm.*

"I lean on libertarian rather social control. Being gay isn't the funnest bag of rainbows in the South," he looks at his lap. "Live and let live, I say." His gaze suddenly tilts at mine, *"Your* life needs to be yours, Jen. Who is society to say who and *how* I should love? Be as true to yourself as you can… no matter how strange," he taps his heart.

"Even if everyone thinks it's weird?" my pulse quickens. *Like taking Jon for walks on a leash?* Warmth spreads between my legs. I press a finger harder into my belly.

"Yup," Greg nods. "Even if people think it's weird. You have to be you, Jen."

The sliding glass door opens next to us.

"Um. Are those Cubans?" asks Dad in a giddy whisper.

"Indeed they are. I've more," Uncle Greg says.

"Comrade," Dad grins, opening his arms wide. "That's one regulation even I agree needed to go." He joins the table.

"Tom, I think you're the only Liberal I can respect. These things aren't cheap. Got $15?"

Dad purses his lips tight and slowly nods, "Sure. Yeah." He leans to access his wallet. "Jen, wanna try? Probably scare you straight."

"No. Gross!" I say.

"Don't tell your mom I offered," he winks. "Just wanted to take out the fun in case you felt cigars were cool."

Greg laughs, "Clever, clever."

Dad lights, puffs, coughs, and eventually finds a footing around his smoke. "Human actions are founded on belief, and all beliefs are fueled by emotion. People are always attracted to what gives them comfort, pleasure, and meaning. Yet we're all different about exactly what those things are."

"Tom, that's the first bit of sense you've said all night," Greg chuckles. "That's why I love the free market: *you* get to follow *your* passion. No central committee telling you what to do. No one holding you back taking more than they deserve. The market decides what floats, no one else. Anyone can find a way to float their dreams across a sea of hard work," Greg says.

"Yup, yup. That's fine," Dad says. "I'm not *really* against the free market as much as you think. I don't *really* hate President Paul."

"Wait. What?" Greg says in over-dramatic shock.

"Yeah. Really," Dad says. "I see him as the wacky uncle I shake my head at each Thanksgiving."

"I voted for Ron Paul in 2008," Uncle Greg slowly nods, "and I'll vote for him again this fall. He's a business person; that's why we all voted for him. He's been successful all on his own. We need to run this country like a business."

"Yikes. Okay, but are we *really* voting for Paul's vision this November?" Dad asks, his smoke swirling high into the air. "I worry the libertarianism you and I might agree on is a false-front to *much* deeper de-regulation. That these seductive freedoms of 'anarchy of a total free market' are false freedoms only the super strong win and the rest of us lose."

Greg shakes his head. "In 2009 we burned regulations, handouts, and made civilization stronger by allowing the banks to fail. *'People make their own decisions. This is what liberty means!'* Ron Paul's message blew right by McCain and Obama. A total breath of fresh air. I thank god Choke's industrialist heroes gave Paul's free market message a huge infusion of cash. I've no problem with the fact that they're taking $150 billion a year in profit."

"But where in this administration is the 'hard work and cunning' Libertarians talk about? All I see is dumb, spoiled privilege. Paul was purchased. Vice President Choke walked into Chem Industries with family connections and stepped from a board room onto a presidential ticket! Not a prior day in elected office before that. None of us would ever be able to do that. Never." He takes a puff. "Never."

Greg is silent and relights his cigar with a mysterious smile. "Honestly, Tom, you're just intimidated by the rich," Greg says. "Or jealous. When it comes down to it, they're men like you and me," his hand motions across the table.

"—And women, right, Jen?" Dad winks at me. "Ha. Here men are talking politics, smoking cigars, and ignoring the women. So cliché. Sorry, Jen."

"It's okay. I don't really have anything to say," I lie. *Both of you are wrong.*

"Sure you do," Dad says. "What do you think, Jen?"

I ponder. I never like talking about myself. I swat a mosquito near my neck and casually flick its carcass away. "Hm. From your emotional incentive thing, Dad, is a democracy even stable? It seems like a group of people following their pleasures will always vote nice stuff for themselves and then always vote not to pay for it; because that's their natural incentives? Right? So, um, is a democracy doomed to fail unless it's *told* what to do?" I suggest. "But then it's not a democracy, right?"

Both Greg and Dad sit in surprise and smile at each other.

"Ah. We have a Philosopher Queen," Dad finally says. "Remind me to get you Plato's *Republic*," he grins. "That conflict may be what we're seeing." Dad scratches his chin, "It's hard to say how a democracy will survive this depression. A vibrant democracy should self-correct, and that 'strict guidance' should come from the Constitution. Or, maybe, we do need an enlightened incorruptible guardian to lead the way?" he winks at me.

Yes, please. I bite my lip.

"Let the market decide," Greg says. "Whoever earns the most money, wins. Faster verdicts than any power hungry civic judge."

"But shouldn't our most powerful people be accountable to fellow citizens, not to profits?" Dad continues his conversation with Uncle Greg. "A concentration of wealth leads to a concentration of power, which in turns *protects* the concentration of power... and eventually we're all locked in a black hole of a rich person's pocket."

"Tom, wealthy people are just people, not some smoky conspiracy."

"Eh." Dad frowns, "I don't think a powerful person is 'just' another guy—*or* woman," he smirks at me. "We can't compare power like planets at the science museum: Earth's a little marble, Jupiter's a big beach ball, and the Sun's the size of a house," he moves an arm to outline our home. "Power is sneaky because we can't see the reality of its strength."

"If people have power, good for them. Let 'em be Jupiter." Greg flippantly suggests.

"What if Jupiter finds incentives to gobble the rest of the solar system into an economic black hole? How do we pull back those who aren't respectful with their independent libertarian 'orbits' as you or I might be? A Philosopher Queen, theoretically, has wisdom and truth holding her back," he grins at me. "Megan has faith and religion holding her back. Ron Paul's laissez faire, by definition, has no holds!"

"Relax, man. Laissez faire gets figured out eventually," Greg suggests. "Ninety percent of rich families' wealth evaporates by the third generation. Seriously." He shrugs. "Relax."

"And endure a thousand years in a feudal state? *Some* regulations are critical. Yours and Megan's dad; he's in the slammer for a *long* time. No one would've known if that girl hadn't escaped. No one had a clue. He was brilliant."

My heart jumps as Dad talks about grandpa.

Greg's face darkens. "I half-think Megan joined seminary to wash her spirit clean, worrying the daughter might follow the parent. He never hurt us. Well, never hit us."

"That's what Megan says," Dad soothes, a touch of wine slurring his voice. "But not the case for those women in his dungeon. Anyway. Hey, sorry, didn't mean to bring it up," Dad sighs, looking like a regretful jerk. "Governments can't pick and choose citizens; they *have* to manage the weak, the strong, and the very weird. They have to manage when one man profits on another's pain."

"But a *person* can choose," Greg extinguishes his cigar on the table and stands. "When things are shitty, you go somewhere else, like South America. G'night y'all. I'm a bit tired," he walks into the house.

Dad looks sadly at me with a tipsy sigh.

After a week of hiking, fishing in streams, more dinner parties, even a summer folk music concert at the church potluck, it was time for Greg to return to Chile. He calls me into my soon-to-return room as he folds the last of his laundry into a suitcase.

"Jen. I appreciate you letting me stay here. I know it was probably weird having to bunk with your parents, but, I've secretly always wanted pink sheets," he jokes, laying a hand on my bed. "So, thanks."

"No problem," I lie. "I'm *so* ready for my room back," I smile. *At least he's grateful.*

He zips his toiletry bag and looks at me. "I guessed right. A week was good before I got the itch to move on. I really *am* happy to spend time with your Mom and Dad; impressed with you becoming such sharp tack too," he says, and slowly looks around. "Things… are strange here. Maybe I'm paranoid, or shell-shocked from South America, but I feel trapped in a bubble and worry something *real* is going to pop. Pop hard around here. Maybe in a couple of years, or a couple of days, the *real* world is going to flood this little town. *Flood hard.*"

"Yeah? Okay." I adjust my hair and grab a hair tie off my mirror desk.

I don't really know what he keeps talking about with his 'real world.' Chile and South America can't be that different from Illinois. We have plenty of poor people here too.

"Anyway. Jen." He slaps his thigh and reaches for his bag. "I want to make an investment." He removes an envelope. "An investment in you. Before you go to college, or the summer between semesters, I'd like you to fly down and work for me. Open it."

"Huh?" My fingers work the envelope. A large stack of $50 bills spills into my hand. A rush floods me. "Wow! I've never seen this much money, let alone held it."

"That's $2,000, Jen, and this is a loan. I want you to understand this as a strict and serious business deal. That's my money," he points. "Hold on to it and only spend it to visit me. Return the leftovers when you're on my front door and you can work off whatever you've spent. I've written my address and have my business card on the back. We'll find you a challenging internship, and you'll see more of the world than you ever could in Wilmington or Duke or any other place." He snorts. "I'd like to teach you, if I can, early in life, the idea of a self-respecting, self-supporting, responsible *capitalistic* person."

I love the cash in my hand. *The possibilities of such heft. The security of it. The power of it.* I notice the envelope still has some weight. I peek to see a large glimmering coin, and free it into my grip.

"That's a one ounce American Gold Eagle," Uncle Greg grins at the coin. "One troy ounce of gold today is worth about *twice* that in cash. Tomorrow? Maybe more, maybe less. It's for just in case. Try your best to get *that* back to me as well. Who knows what's going to happen over the next few years."

"Yeah. Sure." I scamper around the bed to give him a great, long hug. "This is so cool!" I feel giddy, like in a dream world, one rich with possibility, and one I never need wake from.

CHAPTER 9—NEW BOSS

Eddie. June 2022

I hobble to work the next morning with blisters on my feet. Each step probably adding more blood in my shoes. My blood instantly cauterizes when I see Tad *still* working at Jennifer's desk.

What the hell is he doing there?! Rage thunders in my head. *This is going to suck huge working with him instead of Jennifer.* I almost start to cry; then, see a note on my monitor.

Eddie,

I got promoted! Tad and I are switching roles for a week. If you're interested, please pack your desk and come to my new office (Tad's old office). I'd like us to work more closely from now on.

Your buddy and new boss,
Jennifer

My knees wobble like I've stepped off a poorly maintained roller coaster into a circus of possibility. *No more data entry? No calls? Will I make enough to afford a door lock? Will a beautiful romance bloom over the long hours we'll need to spend in the office?*

I shuffle files, pens, and protein bars into a box and hurry to Jen's new office. I burst in her open door.

"Jen. What? How? How did this happen?" I grin widely.

She eagerly beckons forward. "Don't worry about it. I've got big plans. The higher-ups seemed interested making them happen."

"Excellent. That's so cool." I plop my box on the edge of her desk and lean an arm on the lid. "Wait. The café yesterday. That 'making it big' talk. You already had the promotion?" I laugh, feeling stupid and shake my head.

"Haha, yep. Was a bit surprised you never asked *how* we got out of work. Ed, I do *really* like how quickly you follow my whims," she laughs. "So, here we are." She covers an excited dry nervous cough with her hand.

"You actually *could* look up that guy's résumé for the latte?" I feel guilty thinking the only way she could escape work for afternoon coffee was sex-ploiting Tad. "I thought you were playing him," I chuckle.

"Was doing both, duh. Obviously." She smirks and moves on to business. "Anyway. Ed. I'd love you to work full-time, with full benefits. How's $80,000 a year sound?"

My jaw numbly opens and closes in pointless shock. "What?" I ask.

This is huge. Only 7% of the population works full-time with benefits, and those roles usually go to the private school crowd or family of the managers!

"Yes. Yes. Double yes," I say. "I'm so tired working two full-time Temp shifts a day. What will I do?"

"You'll be my full-time ass-istant," she cutely stammers. "Organizing and tracking my various projects. It's gonna be long hours. Lots of work. And things will change *way more* than you expect. Way more." She tilts to her head to examine my reactions. "I'm going to fundamentally disrupt the Temp market. Globalization's making the world smaller and smaller, and I hope you'll have fun helping me rip up the place."

My heart's thumping. *This is amazing. I've waited twelve years for a job that was more than slavery in a shit hole.* "Sure. Wonderful. I'll do it," I fumble. Looking around, I ask, "Where will I work?"

"Deep up my ass," she grins. "You'll be with me all the time."

I flush a deep red at her crude language and make a polite laugh, "In your office?"

"Yeah. Sometimes. We'll travel together and hit conventions, but yes, technically. Wherever I'll be, you'll be in the same place." she grins widely with intense amusement and slightly spins her chair back and forth.

Being close to such an amazing woman and going on lonely business trips together? How great is this!? My heart thumps faster and faster as my dreams, fantasies, and reality crash into the moment. "Jen. I'm psyched. Honestly—I'll tell you what I think and give good advice. We'll do great work," I promise to myself and to her.

Jennifer looks at me curiously, "That's why I want you for the job. We had your interview at the coffee shop yesterday. Your contract is here." She points to a thick stack of papers under a small plastic gel cap. "And I'll need your IDs for more paperwork."

"Oh. Sure." I move the paperweight aside and sign it eagerly. "Where should I set my stuff?" I beam, removing my IDs from my wallet and setting them on her desk.

"Your office is right there," she points to the left corner of her desk, collecting my contract and IDs, and filing them with a pleased smile.

"I'm working *at* your desk?" I ask amused.

Jen, with content satisfaction glowing from her beautiful face, places her feet on the desk, "Basically."

"I'm *really* going to enjoy you as my boss," I try not to stare at her legs. "Near this corner?" I place my box on floor and pull over a chair.

"No, right there," she wiggles her bare toes at the corner with the small plastic gel cap.

I scoot forward, "Not much space for my knees… but okay."

Jen laughs with amusement, "No, that *is* your desk. Look closer." She grins darkly at the gel cap.

I look at the small plastic gel cap. "Ha. Funny," I smile. "Where should I put my box?" I point to the floor.

"That's up to you, once you're inside," Jennifer's eyebrow arches knowingly to the plastic gel cap near my hand. After an odd second, she sighs, and grins. "Hey, check out my belly ring, if you accept the job."

Her perfectly pedicured feet wiggle at me. Her hands lift the shirt.

Holy crap. My eyes widen. I nervously swallow.

A beautiful silver and black flower sits as an ornament above her navel; it looks like a moonbeam fallen from the sky locked forever in the tidal forces of her immense feminine gravity. I soon feel the same way, like I'm falling from space through a cold darkness I don't understand.

I awake on a hard surface not knowing why I had been asleep. The place is vast, too vast. As I startle to my feet, god giggles above me.

"Oh, this is always my favorite part," the chuckle thunders.

I spin to see a massive wall of buttons arcing nine hundred feet above.

It's Jennifer! She gazes down. I'm standing on her desk, apparently less than a quarter inch tall.

I scream and bolt. This makes Jen burst into a laughter. I feel vibrations along the wood's surface.

How is this possible?! I pant in terror, running blindly across a desk half a mile wide. *How the hell does she have an Arbrim Device? They can't work on people!*

"You're too funny, Ed," she laughs.

Licking a finger, Jen casually sweeps me up. *How humiliating, picked up by spit on a finger?* I dare not thrash as wind whips at my clothes as I rise. A blue eyeball the size of a house, outlined with dark eyeliner, makes me scream again.

"Shush, shush. We can set up your office later. No reason to panic. We've an 8 A.M. meeting and you need to be my extra little set of ears."

I can only see her smile twinkle the edge of her eye.

"This a big day for the both of us," she says, picking up a white tissue with her free hand. "I appreciate the confidence having you tag along. Don't have much for pockets, so I'll tuck you away."

My adrenaline surges as I'm smeared on a rough white plain. The wad of tissue surrounds my view into an enormously vast bowl.

"Careful in there."

Jen's face is the sky. Her breath washes over me like a warm cinnamon wind. I shout at Jen. I don't know what to shout, probably "Stop. Wait, why are you doing this?" But all that comes out is a pathetic "What-hey?" what little voice I have is lost in the ruffling of tissue as Jen's hand seals off the outside world, crumpling the tissue I'm in.

Jen puts on a black blazer. "Ed. I've always been more woman than you can handle," her chuckle booms.

I scream, tumbling deeper into the tissue, becoming stuck as the tissue is stuffed into her inner blazer pocket. Earthquakes rattle the darkness. Jen's bust lunges twenty feet behind me with her every step. I kick my arms and legs in and out, to see if I can feel anything.

I can't move.

I hear voices. *The meeting? I'm here too,* I realize, already feeling the real world as a strange far away dimension, despite knowing other people are nearby.

"Alright," James's voice booms. "Before we start, I'm sure you're well aware of Jennifer's presence," he says to the other general managers. "She's to replace Tad as Director of Floor Operations for a trial week, but after further conversation, Jennifer promised all the partners and top managers some rather significant *payouts* if we gave her a shot as top manager for a day." Several subtle chuckles rise from the men in the room at the smile in James's voice. "I talked with her late last night, and she has surprisingly solid ideas for efficiencies we could implement immediately. But also wants to share some strategic ideas, that if she were the CEO, she'd want us to pursue. Jennifer, as promised, as our CEO for the day— we're all yours."

"Oh, I'm not too sure of that, gentlemen," Jennifer chides and stands. "I probably won't *have* you all until after the meeting," she coos. "The first item I have is to limit our liability exposure by adjusting the security camera system to a fifteen-minute loop. Then, any indiscretions with Temps, or in this meeting room, won't be recorded. James, may we change that now? Your CEO System dashboard does that, right?" her voice twinkles.

"I don't see why that'd be a bad idea," he says.

I hear clicking on his laptop as the room chuckles.

"Also, let's get all the cellphones on the table and turned off—for security." A reluctant clattering of phones on the table settles before she continues. "Alright, thanks." Jen's voice changes blunt and business-like. "As you see, a larger cost assumption we have in the temp industry is energy for cooling and lighting those large office floors. We have 7,000 workers on eight floors. Ideally, we can reduce our operations to *one office* and rent TempWarehouse to other agencies, *vastly* reducing operating costs by $2.1 million a month while earning an additional $2.4 million in rent revenue." The room bursts into laughter as Jen continues. "This would give us a *huge* competitive advantage over the other agencies, opening the door for many acquisitions," she finishes, slightly annoyed.

"Alright 'CEO', how would we do that?" an amused, nameless voice asks.

"We put all staff in my office drawers," Jen says, to more laughter.

Holy shit. I realize what she's doing.

"Come on. At least have your titties out if you're giving a wild show!" James snickers. "I've always wanted to fuck a CEO!"

The laughter in the room slowly quiets into awkward tension. I imagine Jen's surprisingly smug and calm smile. I wonder if her deep confidence is unnerving anyone in the room.

"The trucking industry shrunk their processes with Arbrim's gizmo and found 30,000% rise in profits, but oh well." Her tone lightens. "I tried, guys, I couldn't do it. You're right, show time!" Jen playfully invites. "Maybe let me first take off my shoes?" The crowd approves.

I feel the world surge forward as tons of boob flesh slam into my back—and I feel I'm about to burst. She bends for six near-death seconds. I'm suddenly much less relaxed about my position in Jennifer's world and intensely aware of how my life might end with her casual slouch.

"Would one of you boys like to lick my feet?"

I hear more laughter and suggestions what she ought to lick first.

"Let's open that shirt too," a guy says.

I feel her blouse unbutton.

"Of course." She stands. "Hey, look at my belly ring or you're all fired," Jen intones with a fake girl boss voice to rambunctious laughter. The room falls silent like the unplugging of an obnoxious TV show.

"Well, that was easy," Jen says. "Ed, I think I've been officially promoted again. Thanks for the help." she chuckles in relief. "I doubt I'd have played it so cool without you. Each time I felt I couldn't do it, I remembered you stranded and pathetic in my pocket, that gave me a rush of security and confidence! *Mmmm...*"

A massive wall attacks beyond the fabric as Jen grabs the tit behind me with a rough squeeze. I try to scream but my lungs are collapsing. I have no air. I descend into thirty feet of darkness before the pressure lifts. *Is she sexually harassing me?* I panic, catching fractional breaths.

"Now where'd those little fuckers go? Hey, guys. I want a foot rub..."

Jen spends the next two minutes slowly walking across the room oh-ing and ah-ing. Her gait suddenly shifts and bends. I have no idea what to make of the world wildly swaying forward other than that it's becoming hard to breathe and I try my best to focus on my immediate survival.

Eventually, the tissue around me lifts and the world brightens into a sudden burst of bright cool air.

"Where ya at?" Jen asks, peering into the tissue like a kid looking for a bug. "Oh, *there* you are," she says. "I wanna show you something."

Two bus-sized fingertips crash against me and place me on a nylon mountain; Jen's foot is curled in the chair, and I'm atop her knee which is the size of a small parking lot. Her massive leg spires beneath me. Her partly open shirt exposes a bra straining to contain a woman far exceeding her natural boundaries.

"Ed, I'd like to introduce our Partners and Leadership Team," she says, proudly displaying one of her shoes and tipping it as if removing beach sand. The company's top nine managers tumble into her other hand. "Don't remember their names; you'll have to remind me," she holds them playfully up to me in her palm, her fingers wiggling. "In our new organization, the top drawer is for top managers." She casually brushes the managers in her desk drawer.

"Who needs office *floors* when we have office *drawers?*" she says. "Boys, it's time for contracts and a choice. You can sign a new employment agreement with me as your new longterm manager or a confidentiality agreement and cash out. Deal?"

I hear a few distant shouts and cuss words but can't understand exactly what's said. I see they are pissed and far too small to climb the drawer's walls.

Jen frowns. "I'll let you think and settle down before we talk more," she shakes her head and closes the drawer. She rights herself and I find myself again at the temporary peak of her leg.

"So, Eddie. What do you think of your new CEO?" she leans back and frames herself for my evaluation.

I'm flabbergasted. *What am I supposed to say?* I remain in shocked speechlessness as her hands buttons her blouse to a more appropriate level. She fixes her hair and tilts her head at me. Her stare becomes fixated. Hypnotized, I suddenly don't think she cares about my answer. She's entirely focused on me yet somewhere else altogether, and I have nowhere to hide from her odd, intense expression. I notice her breath rise and quicken. A hidden smile tightens her lips. With her eyes on me, a finger moves deep into her mouth to scoop a massive amount of spit, which she leisurely menaces my knee-top spire.

Uh-oh.

I run in stupid little circles before a tanker truck of saliva slams into my back and lifts me to the sky. She holds me aloft, her focus intense. She blinks her eyes repeatedly, and once they clear, I'm moved to the side of her head where I briefly see a large ear before tumbling into darkness. Light floods a waxy cave from a distant ten-foot wide opening.

"Okay, maybe I can hear you now, little one?" The world booms.

"Jen?" I squeak.

"Perfect. I didn't think about headsets, shit. I'm not used to interacting with tinies like this. Your new office might have to wait. I'll order some. I *did* say we'd be working closely together. Right? Right?" she laughs.

In shock, I eventually mumble, "Holy fuck, Jen. What the hell happened?"

"I thought you were my extra little set of ears? Didn't you hear? James and the managers gave a verbal contract that I was CEO for a day. I'm taking charge as I see fit," she says.

"Jesus. I don't think this is what they meant, Jen."

"Maybe, but that's what they *said.* Not my fault if what they said, and what they 'may or may not mean,' don't match up. What they *said* is a verbal contract. Anyway, it's their word against mine and yours."

I notice a large clump of earwax stuck to my hand and scoot to avoid it.

"Easy! You're tickling me. I might not remember you're in there."

"Oh," my senses clarify. "Wait. Why the fuck am I in your ear!? Jen? *Shrinking people is illegal!"*

"Eddie. Those rules were struck down as overly restrictive by the Southern U.S. Supreme Court this April. Airlines wanted the same advantages as the shipping industry and paid the courts to repeal the regulations. They can now use smaller planes, fit more people, and charge first class passengers the *privilege* of staying their natural size. A jackpot business model! The freight industry has done this for years, and airlines now too. So why not extend the technology to other industries? It's only a matter of time, Ed. Why not be first? In Chile, this is how prisons have worked since the discovery of Arbrims Theory. It was a *hugely* effective tool for social control and motivation," she sighs. "Now we can finally organize corporate resources fully in line with the corporate power hierarchy."

She oddly makes sense. I certainly see how her strategy could be extremely profitable. "Okay. How long will I be small?"

"As a contractor, the agreement you signed ties your income—and size—to mine. As CEO of TempGrace, I only make three-hundred and fifty times more than you. Not much at all, really. That was industry standard in the old U.S. socialist economies pre-2010. Once we meet a level of profitability I determine appropriate, we can enter the conversation about where employees can go. But we're way under our potential. We'll have to work hard and long. Due to the confidential nature of our trade secret, the company needs you to not talk with any members of the media, friends, or family without strict written permission from me. Which, Eddie," she says, "is why part of your new employment contract is also a lease. I'm your CEO *and* Landlord! How cool is that?" her gleeful laugh rings. "No more wasting time walking to work! You can put that extra time and effort into making more profits for me."

I hesitate, thinking how this sounds close to some of the types of contracts we offer our prospective temps, but Jen interrupts.

"Okay, Ed. I have James's computer. What's the distribution list for company-wide email? I need to update the staff about our meeting this morning. God, why does he have so many baby cow pictures? Is that a thing?"

"Huh? Um, I think it's C-All," I remember back to our corporate-wide announcements.

"Yup. Great, thanks," she says.

I can hardly see the constricted view of the outside world beyond her ear. All I see through the filter of Jen's hair is a few filing cabinets against a wall and a closet door. Around me is the odd and tough mat-like skin of Jen's ear-canal. A few scattered clumps of wax collect in certain places. I'm a bit disappointed she isn't as pretty on the inside as she is on the outside.

"Okay," Jen booms. "I had James explain to the staff they need to expect an update from me. But I can't send an update until the top managers declare their intentions and sign their contracts. So. About that…." I hear the sound of her drawer opening. "Hey. Time-out's over. Out of the corner. All of you—front and center. CEO here," she speaks like a mother scolding her kids. "Thanks for attending this meeting. I'm sure all of you had busy schedules today; thanks for clearing them for a demonstration of our new business model. Obviously, if this pilot project were extrapolated to the whole company, some *significant* profit opportunities present themselves: about $4 million a month, as I mentioned in my presentation. Utilizing this new technology, profits are going to hit the moon. If you envision yourself staying a part of TempGrace under my leadership, please walk to the left of the drawer. If you'd like to resign and cash out today, please walk to the right side and you'll never deal with me again—for better or for worse, I should add. You'll need to sign a non-disclosure agreement with TempGrace before receiving your checks at payroll. So, gentlemen, it's decision time."

Jesus. Jen is busting balls. I notice the second we got small she dropped the cute girl thing to become intensely authoritative. *Who in the drawer was going to help Jennifer lead the company?* I wonder. *Would they be my boss, or would Jen be?*

"What's the word, Jen?" I ask after a long minute.

"Are those your final answers? Really? Ed, it looks like you and I are going solo. All the partners are cashing out. Folks, I'm disappointed but respect your choices. The confidentiality agreement we have here at TempGrace is rather strict. Eddie, may I use your box?"

The question surprises me, "Uh, sure." I tumble as her whole world shifts and moves.

Jen empties the box on the floor. "Your payouts and severance checks will be available at the payroll desk for the next fifteen days. Meanwhile, I'll need to escort you out of this drawer into a holding box until our trade secrets no longer need confidentiality."

I hear the drawer pull out of the desk as she dumps the ex-managers into my old box. The room pivots as Jen walks to the closet door, opens it, and slides the box on a shelf.

"Thank you for your tenure at TempGrace, gentlemen. You're on your own. Feel free to call for future references once our confidentiality policy expires. Best of luck."

I hear the door click shut.

"Alright, Ed. You're the top drawer man now! I'm going to finish some emails, clean out a few offices, and need the day to get organized. Besides, once I order headsets we can talk more tomorrow. We *need* those—I love hearing you, Eddie, but I already almost squished you to a pulp like three times with you itching my ear. Climb on out."

I feel my world slide and lurch towards Jen's earlobe as her head tilts and shakes. I drop through dark long strands of hair into her hand. The world seems huge and cold. The top drawer opens below me as I lower. I turn at her to shout, "Wait, slow down," only to see the side of her face alight from the glow of an email she's reading. Her hand shifts to shake me off the last ten feet to the bottom of the drawer. I receive a quick glance from her to ensure I'm off her hand, before Jen returns to the computer screen. A sharp earthquake rattles my world as I beg her to look down at me—to acknowledge me with a basic fucking smile—but darkness falls without a second glance.

I shuffle around a bit. The drawer is dark and quiet. I sit. *How much money am I making to sit in the dark and catch up on rest?* I estimate that with a yearly after-tax take home salary of $78.5k, divided by the standard seventy-hour work week, I'm earning a hefty $21.50 per hour. Over five times more than I was making just yesterday at $4.13 an hour. I barely contain my excited jitters.

I eventually lay on my back, with my hands on my belly, to rest in a stirring ponder. I don't know how many times I drift in and out of naps as I lay, drunk and dizzy with the potential of my new job.

I hear muffled phone calls, occasional yelling, lots of typing, and the random terrifying *thunk* of Jen's knees hitting the desk.

My throat starts to dry, and my belly rumbles. *I'm not even worried about food or water. I trust Jen. She'll feed me. Right?*

After a long while I hear a key enter a lock above and a metallic latch snaps shut. *Did she just lock me in?*

A long silence descends, even the slight cracks of light around the edges of the drawer eventually fall dark. I start feeling thirsty, but my excitement working as a full-time employee quenches that well enough. I turn off my mind to embrace this exciting darkness, promising to be ready for whatever hard work Jen has tomorrow.

CHAPTER 10—LEAVES OF FALL

Jennifer. October 2012

I hate my parents so much. How are they such professionals at ruining my life? Last month, Mom and Dad begged the school to take me back. Never have I been more embarrassed than on the first day of school in September. *Never.* I had no idea what the stupid TV shows were the girls talked about.

Apparently today I can't walk fifty steps without some boy fumbling his conversation with me. I feel like a battleship cutting a wake of stupid pickup lines and stares through a sea of drool. Headphones should be a clear fuck-off signal, morons, but then some dumb jock puts his hand in my face and asks what I'm listening to.

I irritatedly stop and wait for a path through the cramped hallway to clear. *God, I can barely breathe in this mess.* I glare at the tan hundreds of shuffling feet over the drab linoleum tile like hoofs of cattle. Wilmington High School has *twice* the students it had last year. *I've no idea who these Jackson High kids are.* Their Junior class was cut in half and added to ours like a half-used coloring book pasted in the middle of a mystery novel. *"Here. Read this, kids; should work fine,"* I taunt the deadbeat school admins.

I'm not learning shit in this monkey-ass zoo. I ignore a gauntlet of jocks punching nerds, shouting, "Nerd tax!" as the dweebs pass. *Wish I could just lay in my garden and never go to school—I'd be way smarter reading by myself. Ugh, I hope mom's happy now I'm getting stupider by the minute. She'd love me to be better at swallowing her lies.*

I remember our blow-out fight the last week of summer.

"Jen. Academics aren't all you learn in school." Mom said. "You need socialization. Being demanding and pretty enough to get away with it only lasts so long. Bitch isn't a career!" Her arms crossed as she leaned forward, "So. Jesus and I have been talking; you need high school. We eventually got your Dad on board."

"Mom! No! Who cares if no one came to my 16th birthday party? I *told* you last week I didn't want a party!" I said.

My birthdays always suck. Only Peggy and her Dad, Mr. Davis, came for a awkward stupid chat. And for a whole three minutes a group of teenage boys stood in the street searching for each other's balls and the courage to walk up the driveway to join. They couldn't find either. The rest of the party was only Mom and Dad's friends, but at least I got $200, and Dad loaded my Plato addiction with books!

"You forced me, saying the church ladies kept asking for a party, and we *had* to have a party. Not *my* problem people don't like me because I'm prettier and smarter than they are. So stop picking on me!"

"Jen. I don't care I'm not your best friend," Mom followed as I stormed to my room. "I 'pick on you' because I wish I could go back in time to tell these things to myself as a young *brat.* 'Jesus is right. Love is truth. Nothing else saves us.' Not books, not grades, not cars, not money. We look for love in all the wrong places, but the truth of love is only Jesus. His love is real and total."

"Hey. Mom. I don't want your imaginary friends. They're *your* friends. Not mine! If you love Jesus so much why don't *you* marry him, have *his* babies, and pick on them!"

I want King Leopold's baby.

Mom fought tears of rage while her fist clenched. "I wasn't going to tell you this until college," she angrily sat on my bed. "But yes. I did want to marry Jesus—only I had you instead!" She savagely pointed at me, "I was ready to drop out of school and join Saint Vincent's Convent. Dead serious. That winter before you were born, I wasn't treating myself well. I wasn't treating men well—I certainly wasn't treating your father well. I needed love, comfort, and control, and found it in all the wrong places. Jesus is real, my dear. I feel him every night..." She longingly sighed. "I wanted to surrender my life to Jesus Christ's message of unlimited grace, kindness, and forgiveness. But that week in January that I was to sign the Convent paperwork, I discovered I was pregnant with you." Mom stood, "Now, I'm terrified you're fine settling as a loveless Career Bitch and nothing will soften your heart. We're putting you in school to make friends, discover empathy, learn the social skills of a basic fucking human being. That's final." Mom stormed away.

"How dare you!" I shouted after her, "I don't need the pressure of being responsible for my own actions!" I slammed the door and jumped sobbing onto my bed. "I only want to be me. Why's that so hard for you?"

I cried into my pillow for an hour.

Now I look at all the stupid teens with dead eyes. *I hate this place. I hate this place. I hate this place.*

In American History, we don't have desks, only rows of crowded benches and a waiver from the fire marshal that this ground floor room has windows that open, for the most part. I spot a potential seat between two of the more malleable boys. I enjoy watching their geek faces burn fire-engine-red when the immense power of my body demands they clear room for me. They heat up like flares when I make small talk: "I'm so far ahead I forgot where we are in the syllabus today."

"Oh, cool," one dumbly says.

Boys never question me. Never challenge me. They're so delightful.

"Uh. Chapter four, page 106. Lead-up to the American Civil War: the irreconcilable differences between the North and South."

"Oh? Way back there? Okay."

I'd die with laughter if Ms. Anderson made them write on the whiteboard with the biggest boners in their life.

Ms. Anderson tries her best to lecture this month. Her experiment with democratic education 'self-empowerment exercises' at the start of the year devolved into a nightmare of mass ignorance and juvenile distractions. Plato would be displeased and I imagine him stepping in on my behalf: "Ms. Anderson. Why bother teaching stupid people? Let's not waste a sloppy lecture on a gem like Jen, okay?"

We're all losing here, people.

At 10:11 a.m. Ms. Greene, the math teacher, opens the door and waves for Ms. Anderson's attention over the chatter of the room, and adds with a serious tone, "Jill. Quick, turn on the news," before closing the door to dash off.

Only half of the room notices Ms. Greene's intrusion, or it's effect, until the TV bursts to life and Ms. Anderson's face turns from confused to somber. One-by-one, the side conversations about Jeremy's party, Sara's ugly dress, Nick and Rachel's breakup, morph to a singular focus on the screen.

President Ron Paul: Assassinated.

The news man speaks, "Again, we've received substantiated reports, confirmed from Blessing Hospital staff, that about twenty minutes ago, President Ron Paul died at the scene of a campaign event in Quincy, Illinois from a high caliber rifle wound. He was 77. Our hearts and prayers go to his family, and his wife Carol."

A picture of Paul flashes with the caption: *August 20, 1935 to October 29, 2012.* The jolt of the image pulls a harsh suffocating reality over the room. I feel my chest tense. *Someone killed our President?*

"Due to the nature of the event, and the means of death, we can say with high probability President Paul joins Abraham Lincoln, James Garfield, William McKinley, and John F. Kennedy as the fifth U.S. President to be assassinated. We have a video of his last speech at the event from our affiliates in Chicago. I'm also told that, perhaps fittingly, his last speech was one of his finest. Note to our viewers, its inspiration may be matched by its brutality. We in this newsroom believe, for today at least, the public has the right to know the truth of this historic event."

The news anchor cuts away to a beautiful small town. A large bandstand faces a crowd that fills the banks of the Mississippi River. Islands and trees are painted with beautiful fall colors that make the valley like a painting or a postcard. President Paul steps on stage to enthusiastic applause of a few hundred people.

"Hello, Quincy, Illinois. Thank you," President Paul says. "What a gorgeous day for democracy. Thank you for having me here at All America City Park and for inviting me to your truly fine town." More cheers and a distant 'We love you Paul' whoop.

"Thanks, I love you too," he grins at the interruption. "I'm proud to be here as Quincy prepares to vote in the next act of this great American Pageant we call democracy." Sparse cheers ripple the audience. "Well, I hope you all haven't forgotten there's an *election* going on?" There is sparse laughter as he continues, "Right? That we're here for Quincy's First Annual Puppy Mayor for a Day Election?!" A huge burst of applause erupts as cameras pan wide to reveal a large banner with photos of four adorable puppies. "I am honored to be Quincy's first Puppy Mayoral Election Judge. And with only four puppy candidates, the rest of America envies your simple choice. Are *seven* bickering candidates in our general election giving you a headache too? I mean come on." More laughter.

"As a doctor of medicine and politics, I've long seen freedom to be the truest medicine. Even if it's hard. And like any good medicine, there are those who hate its bitter taste, until they realize later how much *better* the results are. And I also know there are those who prefer the sweet-tooth seduction of easy free healthcare, free lunches, and the mindless yoke of big government. Citizens with that sweet tooth aren't going to be happy with the tummy ache when they wake up to a fascist government, I'll tell you that!

"As President, I've tried my best to be the candidate of liberty—that hard medicine no one wants to swallow. We've sent Wall Street the message they're no longer in control! That bankruptcy means *exactly* the same for them as it does for you and me.

"We've starved the bureaucratic beast and removed the most degrading and totalitarian of all possible taxes—federal income taxes—because you and I know the government does not own a piece of the lives and labor of the citizens it represents!" he firmly nods. "Because small towns, like here in Illinois, are best left alone. They take care of each other *without* state or federal assistance." Applause. "We've even taken Social Security to court. We've slashed the pay of all Federal workers down to $39,000—the same salary as the average Americans in this crowd. The private sector simply works better." A wave of applause erupts.

"We need to starve 'Congress, Inc.' of its profits and hand its power to you." Huge round of applause, "I want 'Terry, Inc.' to grow and innovate on her own. I want 'Mary, Inc.' to breathe without the suffocation of government regulation. I want both to know success is *not* a crime. We need as much freedom as we can stand and then some," another burst of applause.

"But…" his tone becomes serious, "I'll tell you the most important part of freedom, of all this democracy, is the results of today's Puppy Mayoral Election." Large laughter. "I have an envelope," he reaches into his coat pocket, "containing the fully vetted results of 1,954 votes on which a young canine shall ascend to the lofty office and responsibilities of Puppy Mayor of Quincy, Illinois!" As the paper unfolds, he holds a hand to hush the crowd's enthusiasm. "Today," he dramatically pauses, "as President of the United States of America, I'm proud to announce that our Puppy Mayor for a Day is… Ms. Dolly Williams."

A huge cheer blooms through the crowd. The Quincy Senior High School band strikes up a patriotic tune while a dance line twirls flags and batons. The Williams family walks on stage carrying Ms. Dolly, a twelve-week old yellow lab. President Paul shakes the family's hands—and with a medal handed to him by an assistant—places the award adorably around puppy Dolly's neck. The family hands her to Paul who moves to the front of the stage, lifting the mayor over his head to All America Park's raucous approval.

The crowd and Paul is happy and smiling and enjoying this moment when a burst of blood savagely explodes from President Paul's chest.

Dropping the puppy, he tumbles three feet back and slumps unmoving to the floor as the crowd screams and scatters in terror. Black suited Secret Service men pull out their guns and rush the stage.

Our classroom is unified in sharp, sobbing, shock and sorrow.

The boys next to me rest their heads on their palms, pretending not to cry, as the chaos flashes on screen. Our teacher has nothing to say, other than that we are watching American History as it happens.

We watch the news debates. "Are the puppies okay?" "Will there be a second Puppy Mayor Election next year, in light of this tragedy?" "How will President Choke need the support of the people in these trying times?" Video loops focus on weeping families huddled in prayer. Live interviews focus on sobbing children who just wanted a Puppy Mayor for a Day.

We watch his speech and death again and again.

Then we hear more breaking news.

"We've just learned that Vice President Jerry Choke was visiting industrial operations at Goldstrike Mine in Nevada when the news of President Paul's assassination reached him. Amateur digital footage uploaded to social media, by who we believe to be an engineering intern at Barrick Industries, DJerick69er of Reno, Nevada, captured Vice President Choke's response and inauguration. Again, since this event wasn't expected, all we can show is shaky amateur smartphone video…"

A sweeping, vast open pit mine is the backdrop to Choke's podium. He's before a group of thirty individuals wearing a mix of hard hats and expensive suits. A huge mining rig destroys the ground several hundred yards behind him.

"Barrick is a lean and nimble company," VP Jerry Choke says. "With minimal bureaucracy, I see them as a role model for all organizations—even State and Federal ones. Their guiding philosophy is one we all can learn from: 'A small head office manages the company with healthy balance of entrepreneurialism and prudence, focusing on a few core activities: defining and implementing strategy, allocating human and financial capital, and fulfilling the obligations required of a public company. Leaders at the operational level have greater autonomy, responsibility, and accountability, and in a sense, function as business owners—because they *are* owners. And are free from bureaucracy and middle management to focus on maximizing free cash flow...' Ah, hm?"

Two aids interrupt Choke as a cadre of Secret Service agents suddenly surround the podium and stare intently at the crowd. One aid whispers in the Vice President's ear. A second aid asks the small crowd, "Is anyone a notary public?" The question is odd for the group; whose unease becomes apparent.

"I'm one," a chubby guy in an ill-fitting flannel shirt, cowboy hat, and jeans raises his hand.

"Here please," the staffer waves him forward and whispers under his cowboy hat. His eyes blow wide and pulls out his smartphone.

"Anyone have the Wi-Fi password?" he asks, "Can't get no reception," his cheeks and neck flush red.

"Guest1234 with a capital G," an anonymous voice offers.

At this point, the aids leave Vice President Choke, who breathes deep and long at podium, and then speaks. "With great sorrow and regret, I have some deeply sad news for all of you, and, I think, sad news for our fellow citizens. President Ron Paul was shot and killed this morning in Quincy, Illinois..."

An electric gasp runs the crowd and the camera wobbles the frame, before re-centering.

"This is not the ideal time and place, but history calls for an Oath of Office, an oath this Notary Public will provide. Friend, are you ready?"

"Yes, sir," he shakily says, "Please raise your right hand—"

"Wait. Katie," the VP interrupts. "Can you please get the book from my bag? I'd like to swear on that," he asks an off-camera aide.

Katie, the aide, returns and joins the two of them with the VP's bag, holding a book while Choke rests his left hand upon it.

"Alright," he properly raises his right hand and responds to the oath of office of the President of The United States.

"Ladies and Gentlemen," Choke turns to the crowd as his assistants scatter. He looks sorrowful and downcast. "I'm only going to talk for a minute or so. President Ron Paul dedicated his life to freedom and to justice for all human beings. He died in the cause of that effort. In this difficult day, in this difficult time for the United States, it's perhaps well to ask what kind of a nation we are and what direction we want to move in."

A gust of wind kicks dust and dirt through the scene.

"For those of you who are conservative; considering the evidence that there were people on the radical left who were responsible, you can be filled with bitterness, and with hatred, and a desire for revenge. We can move in that direction as a country, in greater polarization filled with hatred toward one another. Or we can make an effort, as Ron Paul did, to understand. To comprehend. And replace that violence, that stain of bloodshed that has spread across our land today, with an effort to understand and expand our love of freedom. We have to make an effort to understand, to get beyond these difficult times.

"My favorite poet is Aeschylus, and he once wrote:
Even in our sleep, pain which cannot forget
falls drop by drop upon the heart,
until, in our own despair,
against our will,
comes wisdom
through the awful grace of God.

"What we need in the United States is not more division. Not more hatred. Not violence and lawlessness, but freedom and wisdom, and a feeling of justice toward those who suffer tyranny within our country. Whether they be liberal or whether they be conservative."

"So, I ask you to return home, to say a prayer for the family of Ron Paul, but more importantly to say a prayer for our country, which all of us love—a prayer for understanding and a longing for that freedom of which I spoke. We can do well in this country. Truly we can. We'll have difficult times. But the vast majority of Liberal people and the vast majority of Conservative people in this country want to live together, want to improve the quality of our life, and want freedom for all human beings. You must forgive me, as I must now return to Washington. God bless and guide us all."

A standing ovation escorts President Jerry Choke and his Secret Service detail past a crowd of weeping eyes.

For the rest of the day, classes are essentially canceled. The whole school sits in silence watching the news loop.

Who? Why? How? No one knows answers.

But the news suspects a Leftist angry about losing their big government treats. All other candidates suspend their campaigns out of respect, despite the election being only two weeks away.

I have a quiet walk home in the autumn chill. The leaves crunch under my feet. Even thinking each little leaf is a little city doesn't make me happy today. I plop my things on the couch and curl up on it. Dad hears me come in.

"Hey, Jen. How was your day?" he asks, kicking off his shoes, toe-by-toe. "Oh," his tone drops in concern. "What's wrong, dear?" He bends next to me and rubs my back.

"Huh?" I look at him in confusion.

"Did you have a bad day at school?" he gently asks. "What happened?"

"Um, yeah! Ron Paul died."

"What," Dad deadpans, taken aback, his face pale. "Really?"

"Dad. You don't know?" I sit up angrily. "Oh my god. He was assassinated! We all saw it on TV."

He opens his mouth to talk, but can't find words. Eventually all he says again is, "What?"

"Dad? Are you clueless?! How can you miss something this big?" I almost shout.

"Um, er. I was tutoring all morning with the Johnson's kid, and helping at the food bank, and then organizing leaves in the yard. My god. Really? *Jesus!*"

"—Hey, watch the language," Mom says poking her head in from the yard, wiping her nose with the back of a gloved hand. "What's all this noise?"

Dad looks at Mom, "President Paul was assassinated today."

Mom's eyes expand wide, *"Jesus fucking Christ."* She drops a rake to the deck in shock.

CHAPTER 11—OFFICE WITH A VIEW
Eddie. June 2022

"GOOD MORNING," a blinding violence of light says.

The force of the opening drawer tumbles me against the back wall with a solid *thunk.*

"Wakey-wake. You're on company time, Ed. Here's your new headset. Came express overnight," Jen says as a massive white piece of paper descends into my drawer like the ceiling of a collapsing stadium.

I shakily stand, checking for lumps and bruises.

"Walk onto the paper so I can see ya', no idea where you are. *Shit.* Hopefully not underneath?"

I stumble onto the vast plane of coarse white paper, not really knowing where to go.

"Oh, good. Gosh, you're slow. Put some pep in those little steps," she says.

Eyes adjusting, I look up to see that Jen is shockingly massive. With a hand on her chin, an odd glee in her eyes, she holds a cup of coffee and is grinning down at me from a thousand feet up. Grimacing from muscles half-asleep on the wood floor, I jog slowly towards the middle of the white plane. *Fuck,* I groggily think, *this is like two football fields end to end.*

"No. Go more left."

I vector left.

"No, *my* left. Whose perspective matters here?" Jen laughs, sipping from her mug.

My jog shifts to the far right. Fifty yards ahead I see a strange mound and aim toward that. I arrive, puffing and out of breath, at what turns to be a large glob of water the size of an old semi. A package floats within it.

Jen's loud laugh startles me.

"Even my spit's bigger than you. *You're nothing,*" she cackles. "I lost the first headset on a blank sheet before I remembered our spit trick from yesterday. Go on and get it."

The glob smells slightly of coffee and morning breath. A few large bubbles pop as the glob slowly settles in all directions. I open my arms wide up at her in disgust, shouting and waiting for a reaction.

"Go on..." Jen smiles reassuringly, not noticing my protest.

I can't argue with her. She can't even hear me. I remove my shoes and tentatively inch my feet into the large pool; it's warm and almost thick enough that I trudge the first bit until the glob becomes so deep that I have to swim. Jen burst into hysterics at my struggles. I am soon floating about five feet above the headset. I can't reach it. My eyes clench shut and I surface dive into the pool, my hands frantically searching the thick goo for the headset. My pinky hits something hard as I locate the package, then struggle to the surface.

Jen is unabashedly enjoying herself as I paddle awkwardly to the nearest edge.

"Feel free to pick any chunks of egg you find for breakfast." She says.

I ignore her taunt and crawl out of her spit, dripping in disgust. *This is a terrible start,* I quietly fume, fumbling with the wet plastic box.

"Such a brave strong man! You made it! Like the headset?" She asks, putting one on herself.

I fumble opening the packaging--the fucker is slippery--but I finally get it in my ear. "Can you hear me?" I say looking at her. A chill settles as her spit cools.

"Perfect." Jen claps her hands and leans pick something off her desk—my drawer briefly darkens as her boobs create an expansive new ceiling. She returns to lower an object and a sudden whoosh of air hits me from behind as Jen's giant fingers place what look like a large tan gel cap pill next to me.

"Alright, here's that new office. Climb on in," she says.

I slowly realize *this* fifty foot thing is the odd thing Jen placed on my contract yesterday. But it looks huge!

"Get in, Ed."

"Okay, um. Sorry. Hold on, this is all a bit strange, Jen. What the hell *is* this?" I complain.

"Your office. Get in," Jen says. "We're transforming into the most innovative company in the world. Get used to doing new things."

"I know. Okay. But a door?"

"Figure it out. You're a manager now."

I silently grit my teeth and walk along the smooth edge towards the tip, noticing a hatch with a circular handle that opens to a small set of stairs. I lean forward and peer inside.

"Get in," Jen says.

I look up nervously to see her staring darkly at me and step up the stairs, closing the hatch behind me.

"God, I love telling you what to do," she sighs through the headset.

My world unexpectedly blasts upward and I tumble onto a couch, up against a wall, and into a few plants. The capsule walls are transparent from the inside and to my horror I see the whole open world whirl around me.

A giant eye settles on me.

"Keep your screaming down when I do that. Jesus. I'm gonna move you around. Holy shit. Get used to it." Jen says, "I can't have anyone see you until they *also* sign onto my new Temp reorganization. But rather than playing in my earwax, I want you to see what's going on. Figured you could be a proud part of my necklace."

My floor drops and the room churns and churns as Jen's huge fingers fasten gold chains—probably wires—around the capsule. My world flips upside-down and automatically re-orientates as the capsule's double hull resettles.

A 270-degree vista beholds the underside of Jen's chin, half the room is against a wall of tan flesh, and the other half reminds me of the hotel at Grand Canyon Pepsi Park in Arizona—the hotel which directly opens to the vast ancient canyon rock but instead of the painted sedimentary lines of the North Rim, I see Jennifer's desk in the mid-ground and her door several miles away.

I timidly scoot forward to touch the plastic wall. It's solid and smooth. If I wanted to lean forward, I could peer down Jen's blouse, but my nerves are overwhelmed enough, so I only take a quick peek.

I'm so insignificant in Jen's office someone could talk directly at her and would never know I was here. Am I just an ornament around her neck?

Inside, my new space is part mini-workstation and part studio apartment. A set of plants, an exercise bike, a sofa bed; fit within less than an inch on Jennifer's scale. The walls and floor not transparent to the outside are oddly sturdy, like redecorated bulkheads of a navy ship. I move aside a thin wall curtain to read a small placard of instructional Spanish that confuses me further. A small sink next to a microwave produces a clean trickle of cold water. *And I have a small shower all to myself!* I smirk in satisfaction at it's healthy flow.

I sit on the thinly padded couch to comfort my nerves.

"How is it?" Jen's voice pops through the wall speakers.

I see a poorly folded blanket next to me on the couch and dry off the rest of Jen's spit, "I haven't vomited yet—so that's good…" I say, half in shock. "Jen. This is nuts… I'm black and blue and drenched in spit. What's going on?" I ask.

"Don't be so sensitive, Ed, just having fun with you. Jeeze." Her hand raises as a massive thumb gently rubs the outside of capsule. "Just wait and see all the cool stuff I have planned. We're going to work together on a level so tightly coordinated we'll leave the other agencies in a dust so thick they won't have a clue what happened." Her hand moves to completely darken the view into pure blackness. "*This* is our new world. And it's nice having you close to my heart," she says.

I sit numbly on the couch, staring at the floor as a few dim lights automatically blink on. Twenty seconds pass. I reflect on the realities of my position. The absurdity and frustration drain slowly away. I realize this is three times the size of my old apartment. And outside of Jen, it's highly secure. No brats stealing my food and shampoo. I see how my salary is five times more than I dreamed I *ever* could earn.

And where do I really need to go? What other opportunities did I have better than this? All jobs suck and are demeaning. Jobs are hard work—that's why it's called 'work' and not 'fun relaxation time.'

I root my resolve and dedication into Jen's needs. *I will focus all my heart and energy into what the job requires—and not my selfish needs as a worker. I'm better than a moocher. Better than a taker.*

Jen removes her hand and the world brightens.

I walk to my workstation, power it on, and unmute my headset, "Alright, Jen. Let's do it."

CHAPTER 12—ELECTION NIGHT

Jennifer. November 2012

A sharp crack of orange and pink twilight glows sharply around the edge of a grey overcast sky. *Like a goddess peeking under the lid of the world to check inside.* I muse, pretending I was that Goddess. *A whole little city hidden in a butter case in my room? That would be fun.*

I tug at Mom's wool scarf keeping my neck warm against the crisp wind of my walk home from school. The trees are bare. My backpack pinches my shoulders as home appears around the next street corner.

"Hello, dear," Mom says, leaning around the kitchen door with a big smile as I walk in. The warm humid air feels soothing on my chapped cheeks. I smell tomato, basil, and homemade spaghetti sauce cooking. *Yum.*

Dad grunts barely a "Hello" from the couch. He's glued to PBS's all-day election coverage on the small fuzzy seventeen-inch tube TV he hauled from the basement. He hasn't shaved in over two days. I see an empty box of crackers beside him and a jar of peanut butter. A truck driving through our house wouldn't get much notice from Dad since Paul's assassination. I think he's gotten thinner?

"Want hot cider, hun?" Mom asks from the kitchen.

"Yeah, sure," I say, thunking my bag against the wall.

Mom's stepped up her cooking duties since Dad's fallen into his mopey funk. I enter the warm kitchen for an even warmer hug.

"How's school?" Mom asks, pouring a pot of cider into a mug, adding a cinnamon stick to stir.

"Eh," I shrug like I always do. "Did you two vote yet?" I ask.

"Of course. Dad and I were at Christ Lutheran by 9 a.m.," she waves off the question. "Did you know Mary Kelly's children both got into the University of Chicago? Received early acceptance letters yesterday."

"Yeah?" I blow across the mug to cool the streaming cider, "That's neat." *Kate and Tim are total dumbasses.*

"Think you'd want to apply there one day? I said you probably would," Mom says.

Already forecasting my future to her friends? "Eh. Yeah, maybe. I don't know…" I say, a tad annoyed. "More winters in Illinois sounds sucky."

I've thought a lot about Uncle Greg's idea, maybe visiting South America before college for a summer. I've never told Mom and Dad about Greg's offer, or his money, or his gold. I hid his envelope in the back of my shelf and cradle it at night when I feel lonely.

"We should sit down one night and map what colleges you have interest in," Mom continues, stirring her sauce. "Never hurts to be prepared. We can ask other people what they think too," she says, planning subtle ways to show off her daughter.

"I'm sixteen, Mom," I say, before braving another sip of cider. *Still too hot.* "Maybe… I dunno," I shrug.

Dad walks in with a sigh and shoves the peanut butter in the fridge. "What we really need to talk about are scholarships. Financial aid," he mumbles, not looking at us.

"Yes. Well, I assumed that too," Mom says, returning to the stove. "Honey, will you please set the table," she tightly informs him. "I've been cooking."

"Of course," he says without eye contact.

I sense they've been fighting a lot today. *Their problems aren't my problems.* I bring my cider and book bag into my room and flop on the bed.

Eventually, it's time to eat, and Mom prays.

"Dear, Lord. Please forgive us our sins and guide us to your eternal love. Teach us to share our hearts and resources with all your creations. Guide our community and our nation along the path of love and justice tonight. Amen."

No one talks. Dad starts his salad with a sigh, picking at small parts of his plate for two minutes of silence before speaking his worry. "Jen," he looks at me, "it's not a proud day that—that I as a father who wants everything for his little girl—has to tell you that your Mom and I won't be able to provide much financial support for college," he says, looking intermittently at me. "With private student loans at 17% to 24% interest, you'll need to rely a *lot* on scholarships to avoid crushing debt. It's been hard, with the food-bank and all," he angrily glances a Mom, "to save up a nest egg, let alone a college fund. And I don't see much changing for the better the next few years." He sighs. "You're definitely not going to get any support from the government, that's for sure," he says, stabbing his fork into a cherry tomato.

"Oh pooh-pooh, Mr. Grumpy Pants," Mom teases. "There's *no* way President Choke's getting re-elected. We'll get someone sensible. Someone who cares about justice and fairness. This greed nonsense is a temporary slump. The election's been too close to call all year, you know that."

"Not the past few days!" Dad says. "Too many candidates distracted the electorate. Choke's been climbing the past ten days and leads many critical exit-polls. Ugh. I'm sorry, Jen, it's not looking good," he shakes his head. "The country is becoming a corporation, not a nation of citizens."

Whatever. I twirl a fork of pasta. *I don't care.*

"Honey. Choke in the White House again? It's *not* going to happen," Mom says. "Everyone I know has been praying. Even the more conservative church members don't like him. How can he win? Anyone *that* money-driven can't lead this country. He swore on *Atlas Shrugged* for heaven's-sake," she says with a disgusted curl of her lip.

I don't understand why it was such a big scandal when that news came out. Who cares what books he likes? I'm not even sure who this Ayn Rand is. Dad dismisses her books when I ask, saying I wasn't missing much.

Mom continues, "It was a dumb spontaneous choice. A huge slap in the face to every faith-based person in the world, and thousands of years of divine guidance. Stupid. Sure. But just a dumb choice. No one is bigger than God. No one."

I eat gods for breakfast and sprinkle them on my dessert. I correct her in my mind. *Yum.* A familiar warmth tingles me. I envision Zeus and Athena drowning in my spaghetti as I tighten it around them, and then bring my divine fork into my mouth.

"Are you sure it was so 'spontaneous'," Dad asks, making slow work of his salad, having not touched his dinner.

"Tom. I'm not interested in your conspiracies anymore," Mom says under heavy breath.

"—And I'm having a harder and harder time with your blind faith. Blind faith on *this*," Dad awkwardly corrects. "Look. How many 'Puppy Mayor' elections has Quincy, Illinois had? *Zero.* Why was the event located next to so many trees and totally exposed to the river? Why did so many Federal pay cuts practically chase out experienced secret service agents? Why did Choke's speech so closely resemble RFK's? A systematic analysis *strongly* suggests a corporate coup of this country. Our country," he bangs his fist on the table and the plates dance. "I swear. Power hypnotizes people into turning off their minds." He plops a napkin on the table.

I'm so annoyed with Dad's blowhard mood. I *envy* the unity I've seen on TV. It's been an incredible week. "We are Paul" banners stand proud on the neighbors' lawns. *The whole world is together, in line, obedient, and harmonious in mourning. "Our Civic Soul stands united," and Plato is pleased.*

"Whatever happens," Mom says. "We'll get through this. Good things will come, either in this world or the next," she says through a thin smile. "Harvard has some fantastic scholarships too. Just you wait, Jen," she warmly smiles and grabs my hand. "But, this means making sure your grades are top notch the next two years. Even if you think classes are dumb. Even if it means getting involved in sports. Maybe the school newspaper? Volunteering in the community? Oh, Tom." She tilts her head sideways with a ingenuous smile, "Maybe she could start a *second* foodbank in—"

"Mom, no! I don't want to do those things," I say, throwing my hands in the air. "I'm sick of living my life for causes I don't care about. God!"

"Hey, language, missy," Mom snaps.

"Look, honey," Dad's face is heavy. "The world's changing *way* more than I thought it could. Cheap easy-access education like your mother and I had is gone. College prices are skyrocketing while financial support is plummeting. I swear, we're practically *trying* to create a class of serfs. Really, starting *this* semester," he reaches his hand to mine, "you'll have to decide if you want to go to college at all. And I mean, at all. That means building a solid academic and extracurricular resume so you're not trapped inside a crushing lifelong debt that devours your life. This new oligarchy seems *intentionally* eager to burn the ladders of social mobility and build a moat around themselves. Anyway," he throws up his hands. "Or not. We'll see tonight. Sorry. I'm too agitated to eat. I'll wrap this up for later," he pushes his chair back and stands. "The sauce is great, hun," Dad kisses Mom on the cheek. He shuffles to the refrigerator and places his food next to several other saran-wrapped dishes of his, and returns to his hole in the couch in front of the TV.

Mom's scowl follows Dad and lightens as she turns to me, "It's okay. I have faith. We'll be fine tonight. Some can say billionaires paying no taxes is fine and legal, but there's no way a *whole country* can shut down their heart and moral sentiments like that. No way. Just you watch and see," she smiles. "That the strongest of us owe the *least* is entirely against the idea of common citizenship."

I'm done with reading in bed, and turn off my table light to sleep.

At 1:14 a.m., I hear an anguished scream. Curious, I lean in the hallway to see Dad standing in the middle of the living room, his hands clenching his hair tight. Mom sits tense on the couch, her hand covering her mouth in disbelief. I squint at the TV and see loud election-night graphics announce President Jerry Choke is re-elected in an election landslide.

"No. What? No. That monster! It's not possible," she says to Dad, who remains frozen. "I, I, didn't see this coming." Mom eventually mouths, "I'm sorry, dear."

Dad lowers his hands, "It doesn't matter. If people lust for their own repression, there's nothing we can do. I'm out for a pack of smokes," he walks to the coat rack.

"Really?" Mom asks.

"Yup," he says, not looking at her.

"…You're not going cliché on me?" she asks with a hint of worry.

"Nope. Just need air," he zips his jacket, opens the door, and walks into the night. Flashes of amateur fireworks crackle and silhouette him against the street as the neighborhood celebrates.

I enter the living room and sit next to Mom after the door shuts. "He's pretty upset?" I ask.

"Yeah. Oh, hey honey. Sorry we woke you," she hugs me and looks at the time.

"It's okay. I was just reading," I lie, playing with the ultra-soft cotton of my pajamas.

"Of course, you were." Mom grunts half a smile and leans to kiss my head. Her arms slide around me. "We're so proud of you," she sighs.

The TV pans to various landscapes of stunned crowds across the political spectrum. Black people in Chicago have their heads low. Women cry in shocked huddles at Hillary Clinton's camp. At Jeb Bush's independent headquarters, an angry squabble breaks out. Choke's concert hall is exuberant. Champagne foam rises into showers of confetti. The news analysts discuss the This and That of each campaign and highlight the disaster of President Ron Paul's death and how America found President Choke's genuine leadership so attractive.

Eventually the pundits take a break. The victor of the night is about to speak. President Choke bursts on stage looking sharp, handsome, and ravenously confident as balloons and streamers explode majestically around him.

He speaks.

"Thank you, America. Thank you. Tonight, the world's greatest democracy has chosen true political and economic leadership. Yet, before we celebrate. I'd like our Nation, and the world, to respect a moment of silence…"

The roar of the crowd slowly settles. The camera pans over a sea of bowed heads. Some eyes are closed. Others wave at the camera like morons.

After an almost too long and quiet moment, the President continues. "The *peaceful* transfer of power is the hallmark of Democracy. Unfortunately, deep elements of fear and hate within small, petty, and jealous sections of our country sizzle with disgust at the freedoms President Ron Paul stood for. These jealous people valued their egos at the expense of our democracy. They valued their *arrogance* over the life of a great man." His eyes mist as his voice breaks. "And yet, America is strong. Our national week of mourning has healed the soul of America, and tonight I'm honored to announce to the world: *America is back."*

Wild cheers.

"Yes, we're back."

More cheers.

"I respect this election is unique in American history, and that not everyone listening enjoys tonight's results. I respect some see only the 'successful man' and not the flawed human I am," his hands touch his heart. "I respect this friction. Real change involves politics, and all politics creates friction. It takes leadership, and the willingness to create friction, to guide true social change. I'm okay that we all don't agree. I only ask a chance to prove myself. Our sole focus the next four years is teaching America the techniques and discipline to *finally* end this depression and catapult our workers towards decades of prosperity!"

Lots of cheers and hoots as cameras pan wide.

"The unfortunate nature of justice is that we don't always see it in our own time. The Founders who wrote and ratified the Bill of Rights did not presume to know the extent of freedom in all dimensions, and thus offered future generations a charter protecting the right of all persons to enjoy, and evolve liberty as we discover its meaning."

"We need government to better acknowledge the liberty of *you*. The freedom of your choice, your work, your opportunity." He pounds a fist on the podium. "Government needs to acknowledge the real world; a world that is fast-paced, digital, and market-based. Acknowledge that extreme income inequality reflects *merit,* not a threat!" he smiles. "Our problem sits not with those who take risks and work hard, but with our political system, which fails to keep markets competitive and the opportunities to raise your lot plenty. Our system distorts markets in ways where the poor and the unions can—and unfortunately do—exploit us.

"From our strength, today we find our greatest dangers lurk *not* from empires across the sea, *not* from monsters hidden within our land, but from entitlements that rot our minds and repress the dreamers by seducing them along a False Path. We need to acknowledge that helping other people *actually does them harm.* For decades, our civilization has been misguided that caring for each other is virtue and not the vice it is!"

Wild cheers.

"American industry and might was *not* built by those who sat on the couch cashing government checks each week. No. America was forged on wit and strength suffering the frontier. America is a country of pioneers. Pioneers, who '*debouch upon a newer mightier world, a varied world, Fresh and strong was the world they seized, world of labor and the march, Pioneers. O pioneers. Down the edges, through the passes, up the mountains steep, Conquering, holding, daring, venturing as we go unknown ways, Pioneers. O pioneers.'* Our moment of history calls, delivering a radical opportunity: *meaningful* change to the processes and systems that have chained the potential of our country."

"America. Here is my radical position: Only *you* should hold the creative power to rule yourself."

Wild cheers.

"This is my moral obligation. My vision for this country. I believe in an America that doesn't ask you to justify your good fortune. An America where creative, entrepreneurial, and unique types understand that the power of individual brains ought to replace the power of government bureaucracy."

Crazy wild cheers.

"Over the next few weeks, even before this month is done, I'll challenge Congress to enact an Economic Reforms Package to build a world in which the creative power of the people, via the frontier of a wild and truly free market, decides who earns what merits. Let our frail America of today, become a vibrant New America of pioneers! Let us once again enter a frontier where cunning and hard work rule us all. Thank you. Thank you, America. Good night and God Bless," President Choke waves at the cheering crowd.

Massive applause.

"'God Bless'? Seriously?" Mom asks, bitterly muting the TV. "So…" her head coolly turns. "What'd you think?" she asks.

Mom and I look at each other. "Wow," is all I flatly say, unsure if my giddy inspiration is acceptable. *A whole new frontier to conquer and claim? What an adventure!*

"Yeah," Mom rolls her eyes. "Seems like someone sounding bigger than they are. Zero humility before God. Where's the love? Where's the fellowship?" She scoffs. "Wealth should serve the people. People should *not* serve money and wealth."

"What's wrong with trying hard on the frontier and being successful?" I ask, feeling off-put.

"We don't need *more* risk, Jen." Mom shakes her head. "No. We need more love of God. Frontiers are for the power hungry and the anti-social. Do you take children to the frontier? No. Do you take old people to the frontier? No. Where's the compassion leaving those people behind so only the strong and greedy can surge ahead?"

"A little bit of competition could be fun. Like an adventure race?" I ask.

"Maybe? But ultra-competitive environments only encourage the ruthless—not those who are more creative, ethical, efficient. Ultra-competitive frontiers are where narcissists flourish, because they're willing to do more to get ahead than an average person would. I can't believe he pulled it off." She leans against the back of the couch staring at the ceiling, almost in prayer. "The super-rich want society surrendering to *them* while they serve themselves. The narcissists!"

"What do you mean?" I ask. The muted TV turns to annoying commercials and I power it off.

"Hm. Oh, dear," Mom looks at me with a sudden nervous flush, a hand rubbing the back of her neck. "Well, it takes a narcissist to know one," she sighs with an awkward smile. "When I was younger, I did whatever I could to rise above others and be in control," she frowns. "Like Choke, I entered relationships charming and seductive, but warped them to be all about *me*. There's no space for anyone else. Just me," she laughs. "And Jen." She looks at me. "This is why I worry about you. I want you to have a happy life *with* others, not apart from them."

I shrug, "Eh." *No way! I need to be above everyone. I can honestly never imagine my life any other way.*

"So yeah. Anyone providing me admiration, support, or sustenance," she lists, "I treated as if they were a part of me, because I saw no boundary between me and 'other.' I wanted everyone to be part of *Me*. Look at Choke. He's bending the whole economic world to the whims of his friends with total disrespect to other people's needs—yet people love him for it! He's removing as much government as he can so we have *only* corporations and his rich friends to bow to. No community. No Jesus. No love. *Only them.* He's manipulating us; removing our restraints; coaching us to be as financially empathetic 'givers' as we can to support his narcissism."

"Wait. What's 'empathetic giver'?" I ask, unsure what Mom means.

"Oh, Jen," Mom's face bursts with joy. *"Jesus is an an empath."* She slaps my knee, "He's an unlimited and selfless giver. His agenda is love, healing, and care. He gave his life for the sins of the world. For *our* sins. Yours and mine." She holds my hand warmly in hers. "Though, here on earth," she frowns, "there's no balance between empaths and narcissists." She rubs the side of her neck. "The more love and resources an empath offers, the more powerful and in control a narcissist becomes... and that *can* be really fun," Mom blushes. "But with Jesus. His divine love is unlimited. We can take and take, consume and consume, and he can forgive and forgive! That's why Jesus is so important. 'Whoever oppresses the poor shows contempt for their Maker, but whoever is kind to the needy, honors God.'"

I tire waiting for Dad to say goodnight and tuck me in bed like he often does, so I stop bothering and flop under the sloppy covers.

Stop taking from others and sharpen your own wits? Why is it bad that Choke tells us that? I want to be my own pioneer! My own ruler! *'We need more love of God?' Mom, no!* I toss left then right. *Who even is 'God'?* I ask, looking at the ceiling with my mind afire. *Where's the evidence? I mean come on. Does that make-believe matter if god's not real?* Thinking back to dinner: I'm tired of Mom's fantasies too. *Who cares if narcissists care about only themselves? Ignore them and worry about your own things.*

No one in this house is happy! I don't have a college future. Mom is drunk on Jesus Kool-Aid. Dad is miserable, sacrificing his potential to work at a food bank and tutoring nine-year-olds. What are we getting helping other people? We are *in a tyranny of 'others first' at the expense of our own lives!*

I see Plato walk out of my closet mirror and sit on the edge of my bed.

"Jen, you're right," he says, helping tuck me in. "Tyranny of the mob is real. And tyranny is the regime with the least freedom and happiness. Only the wisdom-loving soul is equipped to judge what is best through mindful reason. The mob, by definition, has no mind. Just desire."

I frown at him, "I don't want to live other people's desires! I want my own life."

"I know," he pats my knee. "You're wise to know we all have roles. *Justice is fulfilling one's appropriate role, and giving to the city what is owed.* An organization is like a body with mindless cells, critical organs, and the executive brain who controls them all. For a healthy city, country, business; we should do what we can or get out of the way."

Plato has helped me understand this a lot.

"I guess. Probably not *all* men can sharpen their minds, right?" I ask. "And be aware of their place? They need to be told."

He ponders, "That's why those who are sharp are so important. Some minds are brittle and crack. Some minds are too malleable and bend any way they're told. Jen, with your wits and charisma, *you* can be the wise golden soul who binds everyone together in eloquent reason. *You* can add a piece of your golden soul to the center of everyone's souls. They crave your wisdom and guidance." He touches his heart. "And since the regime, soul, and body correspond, you'll need to be their regime too. You'll need to be their everything."

I look sincerely into Plato's deep wise eyes. "I'll need to do that?" I ask, feeling awe, intimidation, and pride at how special I am.

"Without a doubt. Yes. You must," he stands, "because democracies are easy to manipulate. Authoritarianism is the default position of men's souls and bodies. Democracy needs informed citizens to pay attention, and have the courage to hold politicians accountable. Do citizens ever do this? No. Pinning hopes on a great leader with a golden soul *frees* citizens to surrender their own judgment at the altar of the leader's wisdom, *your* wisdom. Once they trust their basic instincts of submission, your golden soul will radiate harmony over all. It'll be hard work, Jen. But that's why you have the wisdom to be so noble. The wisdom to rule the world." He walks towards the mirror.

"They can trust me. I'll always do what's best," I promise.

"I know, Jen. That's why I'm here with you. Good night." Plato disappears beyond the mirror.

CHAPTER 13—WALK-BY™

Eddie. October 2022

It feels strange to be important, I realize as I Walk-By™ dozens of busy rows of call center temps with the chafing gate of a new pair of shoes. My shoulders are wide. Workers hush as I near and look busier than they supposedly were. I've never felt this tall. Tad, now an assistant manager, is a half-head shorter than I, and provides a summary report I didn't even ask for. He's the second tallest employee around. Most temps only rise to my chest, and few only to my waist. Jen's TempWork Contracts™ communicate a clear picture of who is in charge of who: *Anyone taller than you is your boss.*

I'm pleased we pay so well; almost all employees' sizes are within a factor of two. The shortest person earns $40,000 a year, only half as much as me. Jen certainly wants to ensure our enthusiasm is focused on the new opportunities with her, so our employment contracts reflect her ambitious goals with ambitious rewards.

I don't *need* to walk the floors now—most managers come to my office via a series of ladders in Jen's desk if there's anything serious to discuss. The System provides a clear picture of company operations. I walk the floor because I want to connect with workers and show that management has a human face. Call centers are my roots. I remember how it was. I remember how the System never accurately reflected what *really* happens on the floor. Besides, I've honestly felt lonely the past months and want to interact with other people.

I know work comes first; bad habit, I guess.

I eye empty desks as I walk, worrying about runaways. Jen's non-disclosure rules are strict. No communication with the outside world. Period. This is hard on some employees who didn't really understand what a contract with her meant. We try weeding out employees with young families and sick relatives. Jen's employment contracts hold a Job Sponsorship™ clause legally binding her workers to her. We, like workers at all agencies, are not permitted to leave our jobs without employer's permission. If an employee runs off, they become 'absconding workers' who are fined, thrown in jail, and Blacklisted™. There's little workers can do if managers choose not to pay them. Thankfully, Jen's checks sail into our bank accounts like warships.

Ultimately, I walk the floors because I want workers to know management cares for them. I smile and nod at my subordinates, "Hey. Good afternoon."

Jen's voice bursts into my ear, "Why aren't you in your office?"

Shit. I unmute my earpiece, "Hello, Jen. Just checking operations on floor three. I'll be back in a few minutes. What can I do?"

"Why? What's wrong?" she asks.

"Nothing. Wanted to be visible and ensure we're running smoothly."

"Leave that to the assistant managers. I've been waiting for you to answer an email," a violent earthquake rattles the lights above. Coffee, water bottles, and anyone not at their seats— including myself—spill to the floor. Three acres of warehouse ceiling lift to the sky, causing me waves of vertigo.

Jen's scowl looms five-hundred feet above. "Where the fuck you at, Eddie?"

I stand, purse my lips, trying to remain calm as I'm humiliated in front of hundreds of temps. "Main aisle, center," I politely say.

An enormous, expensively manicured finger descends, stirring screams of terror from my neighbors.

"Is this you?" she asks, veering towards a cowering temp whom I realize was walking thirty-feet behind.

"No, I'm to your left," I say.

The giant finger shifts over me to be joined by a thumb. I hear a workstation or two crunch and clatter as a violent pinch rockets me to the sky. The pressure releases and I catch my breath sprawling on the room-sized spire of Jen's fingertip. Fearing the thousand-foot drop on all sides, I dare not stand, and tightly clutch the large grains of her fingerprint for support.

"How's *this* for management visibility?" Jen sasses the cowering temps below. She lowers the ceiling and latches the drawer lock. "Eddie, *I'll* handle the 'management visibility.' You do what I tell you. Clear?"

I behold her cold, massive presence a hundred feet away and say the only thing I can. "Yes, Jen."

Her face brightens. "Okay good. Thanks."

She brings me close to her face and lifts me in amused appraisal. "Jeez, how bad-ass was that for those workers? We need more cameras so I can record the *god* cracking open the sky to smite their manager's *manager* from their midst," she laughs. "That'd look incredible. I bet drawer three's productivity will skyrocket this week. Maybe I should do that once a day?" she asks herself.

"Employees are very aware you're CEO. I don't think they need all that much reminding."

"Good to hear." She nods her massive head. "Let's see how this week goes. Nothing wrong with a few demonstrations of who's in charge," Jen laughs, bringing me much closer to her cold blue eyes. White porcelain skin expanding like the side of a cliff. "Like, I wonder how my top manager, who's not always at his desk, would enjoy working inside my nose?" Jen slowly lowers her fingertip down the length of her face below her nostril.

A thirty-foot dark hole flares above me with large spikes of hair ten feet long. "Um. Jen?" my voice cracks as a warm wind washes past me. The nostril flares wider on an intake breath and I clutch tight as the breeze becomes a strong roar.

"Jen, stop!" The roar shifts to a soft warm exhale.

"I wonder if he'll be more focused, working and living as my booger?" She laughs as another finger shuts the other nostril. A hurricane blast of air lifts my legs off her skin. My hands cling impossibly tight. My grip slowly slips.

"Jen, STOP!" I scream.

She laughs so hard her finger moves away. My heart is a dry coal burning in my throat as my lungs heave in terror.

"Eddie, I was barely breathing. You're such a coward," she says.

"I had to hold tight to not get sucked in! *What were you thinking?*" I ask.

"Phsh. *You were fine.* Don't be so insecure. You're always so insecure, Ed. Don't be a loser. Worse come worse I'd eventually get you out with a tissue or a sneeze," she says. "You could probably crawl out later tonight. Yikes, relax. Don't forget how good you have it. Be thankful you have a private capsule. Your co-workers sleep in dorms. Remember?"

I note the stern motivational suggestion. Jen leans and opens the top drawer containing my capsule resting next to her purse, a few hair pins, and a notebook. She lowers me in.

"Call me inside," she says, placing me near the office.

Her thousand-foot arm twists away. Eyes fixed on her computer screen she closes the drawer without a glance.

The world shifts and darkness falls. *Why doesn't she look at me?* I fume. *That's always the worst part, when she can't bother to look. Am I just another pen or paperclip she uses to get work done?* I click on the flashlight I long ago learned to carry, and navigate across a large notepad towards my office.

I arc the light across the vast space of the drawer. A sudden wave of gratitude rushing over me makes me stumble. *Fuck.* I imagine what it would be like to solely depend on this small light to navigate out of Jennifer's sinus. I sit to steady myself, and breath deep through the panic.

Jen was once my co-worker. The hot new temp. Gorgeous smile. Tight skirts. An ambitious spirit. But working with her, in unvarnished practice, has become increasingly more terrifying and humiliating than I ever expected. Minor infractions or disagreements are met with the absurdly sharp whip of her will. I always knew CEOs were a huge force in an office, but I didn't realize how many resources Jen would soak up or what damage the traumatic the razor bolts of her spite could cause. The office is dominated by her. We live and work in her fucking desk like staplers. I grip my fist tight.

Pull your shit together, I shake to reality. *The company is depending on you. The technology of the market is moving faster and faster than anyone can understand, and this means change happens fast.* I stand to my feet with purpose and quickly enter my office.

A wall monitor glows a live-stream of Jen working on her computer. Sometimes she doesn't display herself, but right now she is typing away, looking gorgeous and wonderful and human—almost as if I was video chatting with a normal co-worker. *Only we aren't remote,* I keep reminding myself. *We're inches away.* A second monitor next to her live-stream occasionally shows her desktop feed—this is currently dark. I never know what she's exactly working on until she shares it.

I have two monitors of my own. One monitor has a camera facing me so Jen can watch me work at all times. I always assume she can see what I'm doing on my desktop, because *my* monitor allows *me* to view the work of all my assistant managers and their direct reports. This is the beauty of the System. Only Jen, as the CEO, can turn hers off. The modern workplace has scaled up several factors of productivity from even a few years ago, simply because managers directly monitor what their employees work on 100% of the time. TempGrace enabled this technology well before the arrival of Jen.

"You're so slow, Eddie," Jen says as I sit.

"Sorry, Jen. My flashlight was dim." I try to lie before Jen cuts me off.

"—Ed, you're on mute," she says, watching me.

I sheepishly adjust the volume, feeling like my day isn't going too well, "How's this?"

"Good. We're going to need all employees to work harder and faster the next few weeks to make up for the disruptions of last month's re-organization."

"Alright. I'll tell the managers the System is evaluating them on an extra 3% more work hours?"

"No, 15%," she smiles, leaning forward, her blouse straining for my attention. "This is an emergency. Our revenue only grew 27% last quarter!" She groans. "I don't want us leveling off. We're focused on my profits, Ed."

"Okay, sure," I say.

"Hang on, let me display some files." Her eyes dart at her screen as her free hand fondles her gold necklace. "I miss you being closer to me. That was nice." She briefly smiles into the camera.

Funny, she misses me. I allow my heart to flutter.

I treasure the moments her monitor is on. The view is less visceral than those first days when my office was mounted on her necklace. Then I seriously worried that I was just an ornament to make Jen feel good. Once TempGrace's warehouse floors were transferred into Jen's office drawers, she placed me closer to operations. Now, I only have HD monitors to interact with Jen—for the most part.

"Okay. Here we go." Jen's second monitor brightens, displaying her CEO dashboard. "We need to request a quote on a new Enterprise Performance System. TempGrace's System is old-school. Yes, I have an accurate picture of basic operations and cash flow and can map performance of whole divisions down to an individual, *but* I don't have access to other roles like Chief Operations Officer, Chief Financial Officer, Comptroller, Director of Human Resources, Chief Technology Officer, and Security. I bet an updated Systems today is simple enough to allow one person to run a large company with the ease of a Mom and Pop shop. A company ought to be managed by only a few people; ideally one."

"Okay," I soak in her demands, biting my thumbnail. *A new System? Ugh.* I worry. *How many people are we going to lay off this time?*

I see technology displacing more and more workers as globalization minimizes those who remain. I notice the economy is getting crueler and crueler; not nicer. *I don't remember the last time I had dinner with friends. My social life is gone. All my time and energy is totally consumed by Jen's work.*

"Jen. If this project is what the business needs, I'm happy to help. But, this System upgrade could be really expensive. Wouldn't it be cheaper and faster to hire more managers, like a CFO?" I ask.

"Cheaper?" she snorts. "Technically, yeah, from a short-term perspective." She frowns. "But the strategic long-term *cost* of giving my authority and confidential methods to other managers is way too high. The more I can do with less employees, the better I'll feel today *and tomorrow.* A new System will be expensive but so worth it," she grins. "If I'm to get bigger and bigger and acquire other companies, I need to spend less on pointless administration and double-checking numbers, and more on thinking *bigger.* I need more technology to automate and expand my will—my vision. I sent requirements in that email you were too busy to read."

I open her important email and try not to roll my eyes seeing it was sent seven minutes ago. *She really wants me at her beck and call, eh?*

I read.

"Jen, are you sure you want the data center on premise? Companies haven't hosted their own servers in a decade. Data centers are *way* extra overhead. And why this much extra battery power?"

"Eddie, I'm not expecting you to understand. Just do. You don't see the *big* picture. I do. These are security and confidentially points that'll make sense later."

"Okay, and fifty-thousand System Seats? We've only five-thousand employees." I pinch my chin.

Yikes! I cringe. *The hell is she planning?*

"Again. Ed. Do this my way. *I have plans.* I don't want to always renegotiate with you," she says. "This is exactly why I don't want a ton of other executives, jeez! Request a few proposals and let me know who responds. Also. You'll be happy to know we have new tenants taking over the six unused TempGrace warehouses floors. MatchTemp signed their lease today. We'll see how they perform—might be an acquisition in the works sooner than expected." She claps her hands with giddiness. "God, I *love* being a landlord. I'll give them a good discount on rent the first few months, and then charge them whatever I want until they leave." She brightens the screen with a care free maniacal grin. "They didn't read their contract closely. Alright, bye."

I nod. Her monitors darken. I carefully research a few vendors and submit Jen's requirements to worthy vendors by the end of the day. I do so quickly and directly. *Don't want the System thinking I'm goofing off on the Internet. We'll find Jen exactly the server and System she wants.*

I feel good being helpful. I'm pleased to see she wants so many seats. I was worried she wanted to cut jobs. Whenever I explore System design, I try preserving as many human roles as possible. Humans can work hard, but machines can always work harder and cheaper—without sleep. I once designed a System automation to cut by 60% the time we spent paying invoices, but rather than retraining the four accounts payable people my new process cut, the company simply laid them off and gave the CEO a record bonus that year.

Working in the Temp Industry, I worry Homo Sapiens will split into a few deities and their servants. Forecasts suggest huge swaths of jobs getting washed to sea: "The low-skilled factory workers, replaced by robots, do not have the same skills as programmers and analysts. The pace of technological progress explodes inequality." The longer I study the numbers, and the fact Jen doesn't want a CFO or several other roles, makes me worry technology will displace white collar jobs too.

Maybe one day, only a few people will own all the robots, technologies, and everything else; and the rest of us will struggle to survive on their crumbs. That's why I work hard for Jennifer. Once we're profitable enough, Jen's employees will be so rich we'll easily survive the terrible day the world is a few human titans surrounded by thousands of human-ants.

CHAPTER 14—THAT NOVEMBER

Jennifer. 2012

The paper in my pocket sends flutters through my heart, and this beautiful sunset is a fine finish to a spectacular day. I skip home. *How great a Christmas present is no more school, forever?! Who needs it?* Didn't Mark Twain say, "Never let school interfere with your education."? Ms. Anderson sobbed handing out the official fliers. The students in our Civil War class jumped and cheered.

No more stupid boys leering at me. No more bullshit homework. Mm, the idea of so much freedom is so invigorating I've been clenching my fists with excitement all afternoon.

"Mom! Dad! Guess what?" I burst into the house, then toss my hands in irritation at their silence. "I'm home! Hello, it's me… Where are you?" I wonder, plopping my stuff in my usual spot for the last time.

I find Dad in the backyard, watching the sunset smoking a mini-cigar. *At least he's shaved today.* I slide the door open and walk outside.

"Hi, Pops! How *gorgeous* is that sunset?" I cheer the rich red and orange glow arching it's divine lattice above the bare trees. Dad slowly acknowledges me with barely a nod. He stares at the glow. We stand in silence.

"The sun set forty minutes ago," he eventually says. "Chicago is burning."

"Really? It's beautiful." My amazement not wearing off.

Dad shares a sharp look and taps away a bit of ash. "Kinda. Hundreds are dying in those riots," he takes a shallow puff. "Thousands?"

"Wow," I say. "Guess the glow *is* coming from the north rather than the west."

So gorgeous!

"'Wow' indeed. How's school?" He asks with distant interest.

"School's closing at the end of the year!" I cheer, waving the paper flier and jumping up and down, "Yay!"

"Yup," he nods, not taking his eye off the glowing horizon and not looking at the flier. "How do you feel about that?" he asks.

I feel like I'm hoping for a bigger reaction. I silently complain. *Why can't I be more significant than the economy, eh, Dad? I hate not having influence on him anymore.* "Um. I dunno," I lie. "I learn faster at home with you anyway. I think it'll be good," I say.

"Yeah," he half-smiles. "You *are* my little bookworm," he wraps a heavy arm around me. A thin sigh passes through him, "I suppose your Mom and I can pick up full-time teaching. There'll be plenty of students. I *have* wanted my own classroom again," he says. "But, we won't be charging much, and this means no more one-on-one teaching, Jen. We might have *twenty* students crammed in the house all day. Mom might have *forty* kids at her church. It'll be hard to let you intellectually wander when we need to respect the greater community of students."

"What?" The pit of my stomach drops with my open mouth. "That sucks," my foot stomps the ground. *Piss, didn't think about that!* My eyes sting. *Why can't they just focus on me?*

"Ah, um," I sputter. "How am I supposed to get as smart as possible—for Harvard?" I add, feeling highly dejected.

No one's gonna let a dummy rule the world. At least not for long.

"I know. Sorry, dear." Dad sighs, "That's how it is." He takes a long puff.

His flat response doesn't make me feel any better. *Adore me! Feed me.*

"This is the direction chosen for our country," Dad says. "Privatization of the whole education sector starts January 1st, 2013 with the rest of Choke's fucking 'economic slavery' package," he spits some cigar bits on the ground. "The Department of Education—gone. A fine New Year's gift for families struggling with this Depression. That's why Chicago's burning, Jen," he points to the horizon with his smoke. "That's the dreams of millions of poor families going up in smoke. We'll get by in Wilmington—band together like we've done. But Jen, this'll be the hardest winter of our lives."

"Why's everyone so upset?" I ask, blowing my nose.

"Ha," Dad snorts, "Their opportunities for an even marginally better life—no matter how hard they work—will never happen."

"Why? I thought the Economic Freedom Package was supposed to *improve* things?" I ask.

"It will improve things!" He laughs. "But for *who*? Not folks who have disabilities, get pregnant, have children, or want to defend themselves against abusive managers," he lists. "Collective bargaining? Outlawed. Minimum wages? Outlawed. Corporations can now *sue* the government for lost revenue due to regulations. How ludicrous is that?" he shakes his hands in rage.

"I don't know," I frown.

"Capitalism *already* generates arbitrary inequalities that hugely undermine democratic societies. I feel sick," he looks at me and taps his heart with his thumb. "The wealthiest sixty people *already* have more money than the poorest three and a half billion people combined. Combined, Jen!" he spits again. "*Already!*"

"Wow. Really?" I ask. *To be worth a billion people? That'd feel incredible.* I bite my lip as a friendly warmth tingles. *I know what I'm doing after Dad's done blubbering...* I move a finger under my coat, and press into my belly button with pleasure.

"Yeah. Now, Choke's economic enslavement package empowers the government to move all the public's assets to our oligarchy. The parks, lands, healthcare and educational systems—that in a 'democracy' benefit the common good—will only benefit billionaires. Basic consumer protections? Gone. The FDA? Gone. The EPA? Gone. The National Parks? Gone. All in the hands of the private market through a political 'justification' falsely claiming all the poor and the government ever do is destroy our economy," he looks at me with tears.

"Okay." I shrug.

"Jen. Hey, this matters because real economic growth may never return in my lifetime. 'Market growth' *needs* a market. Not just dirt-poor serfs serving mansions with moats. Zero growth gave us Genghis Khan. The Middle Ages. Eras when the only way to advance was conquest and subjugation."

"Though wouldn't that be obvious to people who care so much about money?" I ask, ready to go inside.

"Totally, you'd think. Right? But I suspect something darker, Jen. I suspect *some* people don't actually care about economic growth. Some just want the economy to be small enough to be *theirs*. So they can feel their sick power thrills."

Well, maybe then I'd matter more than the economy, huh? I grumble, feeling ignored.

Dad shrugs, "Honestly, Jen. The only way out is revolution," he pounds his smoke on the deck railing and looks me coolly in the eye. "Your generation is gonna suffer that." He lights a second mini-cigar. "Might be *your* revolution. I already have a PhD, a career, a house. A family," he smiles at me. "I'm lucky… but my story might not be your story unless you seriously take charge, Jen. And I mean *seriously*."

Finally, validation. I cross my arms against the cold wind. "Yeah. Taking charge is important to me," I finally say the truth. "I've thought a lot about living a powerful life," I gently kick the deck post. "It's something that really excites me. I want to matter to lots and lots of people."

"Huh. Really? Good for you," he grunts. "Keep it up. I'm already talking with people," he confides. "Jack McHardy and I agree: anything's better than this. *Anything*." He acknowledges the struggles beyond the horizon. "Maybe, Uncle Greg is right. Maybe you won't need college. The real world will be your education. Come December, Jen, the streets will flip their shit."

"Why December?" I ask, shivering.

Dad wraps an arm around me as we walk to the house.

"Choke forgot winter will kill all illusions of his false paradise. Ice offers no shelter, no forgiveness, unless we melt it with a sharing compassion."

We spend Thanksgiving Day at the foodbank spending our life savings on the dirty poor people who will never pay us back.

"The truest Christian thing to do," Mom said.

I've totally seen Billy Chloe driving a car all summer, and yet here he is, tenderly receiving the business end of my fake smile and his free slice of my sacrificed college education.

"Hey, Billy. Happy Thanksgiving." I grin at him like I've done with every dirtball before him. He spends a half a second looking at my tits before meeting my fake smile with one of his own.

Faker recognizing faker.

Fucking free-rider.

Thanksgiving is so fucking socialist. How can this even be an American holiday? Thank god Normington's has some sweet deals tonight to make this lame day tolerable: *45% off all jeans at 7pm!* Black Friday deals at least give balance. I'm sick of this sharing-caring bullshit. Really, where did 'sharing' get the Native Americans four hundred years ago? They should've slit those sick and starving Puritans throats or watched them freeze to death while laughing and enjoying cornbread. Or at least kidnap the stupid colonists as slaves…

Mmmmm, I imagine Pocahontas tying John Smith to a tree, shoving a gag in his mouth and beating him with a branch. She's forcing him to learn *her* language. Forcing him to do *her* basket weaving and grind her maize. *"You work for me, bastard. My way of life is going to consume your fucking soul,"* she bends over him with a vicious grin and runs a menacing finger along his chin before flicking him in the nose. She spits on him. She binds him to the tree for days until he is so cold, weak, and desperate that he eagerly submits to her without question. He's *thankful* to work for her without pay or respect.

Now that's the kind of Thanksgiving I want to see.

"Hey, Jen."

I hear my name and am shocked to see Peggy Davis and her Dad. She's clearly embarrassed, her face turns bright red.

"Oh. Hey, how are you guys?" I skittishly ask.

"We're okay. Dad lost his job again," she whispers.

"—Jen. How are you?" Mr. Davis loudly grins behind Peggy, laying a fatherly hand on her chubby shoulders.

"I'm good. Good," I say to both, not knowing what else do.

"Sorry we can't help here as much," he trails off, looking around. "Loved serving here last year."

"Well, um, no problem. Good to see you," I smile and immediately ready the next tray. *Ugh, Peggy!* I mutter to myself. *How embarrassing! I'd rather* starve *than have someone I know serve me at a food kitchen.*

—Oh, my god! My heart jumps when I look from the mashed potatoes and see a tough tall black guy leering down at me.

"Hey gorgeous. How you doin'?" he grins.

I turn beat red, "Uh, hi," and hand him a tray.

"Now we know God exists because here is an angel—a pretty lovely angel. Thanks, honey," he moves along the line, lingering a few stares back at me.

Creeper, I shudder and look at next person. *Holy crap, the whole line is black people,* I notice. *We have like only four or five blacks in Wilmington. What the hell's going on?*

I serve five more trays. The sixth tray I imagine is a calculus textbook that I'll never get to open. The seventh is a lab notebook I'll never write in. The eighth is a track shoe I'll never wear.

"Bye bye future," I whisper into each lost dream.

Dad arrives with another load of sliced turkey and hefts it into the serving rack for me to assemble more trays.

"Oh-my-gosh, Dad," I say. "The line's out the door."

"Whoa. Um, wow," he says.

"Do we have enough for these people?" I quietly ask, before I smile and quickly serve another tray to an old black guy who grunts and walks on. "Who even are they?"

"Don't know. Might be from Chicago?" He shrugs, and raises his voice, "Friends, where are you all from?"

"Englewood," says the next lady.

"Wow. How'd you get here?" Dad asks. "That's fifty miles!"

"Me and Sam," she nods at her little boy about seven years old, "We took the train as far as it would go and then started walking. Been slow going. Military locked up the highways."

"You *walked* here?" Dad asks.

"Yes… been walking all week too. Just walking south to one day find some warmth and some grace somehow, somewhere. Folks in Joliet were all full up. Said, 'try Wilmington.' And so we kept walkin' to Wilmington. Anything, anywhere, is better than last week."

I hand her and the boy a tray.

"Thanks, child. First warm meal all week," she says with a thankful smile, and then to Dad, "Happy Thanksgiving to you both," she moves with a slight limp to grab a few rolls.

"Happy Thanksgiving," Dad cheers as the lady smiles back. "Jen, keep up the good work. We'll serve as long as we last, I guess."

We last another forty minutes before the food runs out. Normally we wait and wait serving dinner until 6:00 p.m. and it's *so* boring. But it's great to be done by 11:30 a.m. today! I have the whole afternoon to plan shopping.

Mom's livid. She tells over a hundred waiting people, "Sorry, we're out of food! We'll have more Sunday night."

I glare at the cold, sad people with anger. *Oh, god. Just go away. I'm so done with you. And now I'm dragged into this Sunday?*

Mom notes my expression as she walks in, "This is how we truly worship Jesus, Jen, following his service for the poor."

"No, Mom. This sucks…" *I'm so sick of helping your imaginary friends: God and Jesus, and these poor people who don't give a shit about us beyond a free meal!*

At 6:00 p.m., I grab a $50 bill from Uncle Greg's cash pretending I'm reconnecting with Peggy. What I really want is to head over to Normington's. *I'd love black high heels with spikes, but don't think I can get away with those in this small-ass town. If only this town needed an executioner, I'd wear black leather all day!* I laugh. *Until then, those jeans that make my ass look great will be fine. Guys drool after Wendy and Sarah half the day; I want to wear the same brand. Screw radioactive spiders and gamma ray bursts. A great set of T&A are the only superpowers I need to make boys do anything I want. Mind control, bitches.* I cheer, stepping into the hard November wind.

Brrr, it's fucking cold. God, I can't wait until I get a car. I tighten my jacket against the dark swirling wind. *I'm flooring the gas outta here and heading south. I always forget how much winter sucks.* Although, I do admit the smell of bonfires make the walk feel cozy and romantic—like I'm hiking through a campground on a crisp fall night.

Tonight, I count ten bonfires. *Wow. That's weird?* I observe. *So many campfires on a windy night? Football parties?* I notice the middle school athletic field has a few dozen tents and three huge bonfires. *I must be right. I wonder if the junior high teams are having a party? Future perverts I won't have to avoid, now there's no more school!*

I turn the corner onto Ryan Street and see a lady wrapped in a blanket, sitting on the curb of the sidewalk with a "Please Help" cardboard sign. She's chattering her teeth and asks, "Can I please have a dollar? Fire burned up my home."

Of course not. "I barely have anything. Sorry!" I quickly duck my chin and walk past. *Wilmington never has beggars! Why the hell now? Don't fucking try and make me feel guilty, lady.*

On Water Street, there's more normal people. *Hopefully, now it's a straight shot to Normington's without being asked for another fucking quarter. Beggars should pay me a quarter for wasting my time.*

"You sure know how to make a wiener stand, girl!" a dirty white guy says from inside his ghetto car on the far side of the street. "You're a walking Hot Dog factory, toasting wieners left and right!" He howls.

I slam a glare his way. He laughs and speeds to the next intersection. *Thank god,* I turn in disgust to watch him drive away. Instead, his car makes an illegal U-turn and races along my side of the street.

Fuck. I steam forward and clench my shoulders tight.

"You've got fiiiine written all over you, girl... Why you walking so fast? Cold? You'd get warmed up a lot faster riding with me," he says. "A lot faster!"

I'm hella scared. "No thanks." I grit a smile between my teeth.

"You suuuure?" he asks. A car honks behind him; it receives a middle finger.

"Yep. Go away," I don't look at him and keep walking.

"Bitch. Fuck you." He peels off.

That was humiliating, I fume. *Who the hell hits on someone walking down the street? Like, was I a prostitute to him? These Chicago people are terrible!*

I finally arrive at Normington's. *That walk took forever,* I complain, rounding the corner. My steps freeze. There's seventy Chicago people in the parking lot shouting at a terrified assistant manager blocking the doors.

"I'm sorry," his teenage voice says. "I can't let anyone in until the police get here. A lot of people have been shoplifting today. I have to close the store."

"We're freezing. Let us buy some clothes you dumb shit. Let us in!" a lady yells.

"I'm sorry. No. I can't, not until—" his voice cuts off.

Five big guys shove him aside and rip the door open. A dozen figures jump in the store and run down the aisles. The crowd erupts in pandemonium as it shoves in. A few people fall and start screaming as they're stepped on.

What a fucking mess. Why can't these people let me do anything fun? I wanna live my life too! I return heartbroken to the night as three cop cars scream down the road. *Why's the world against me?*

I hear gunshots that scare the shit out of me and run.

"Those people from Chicago are invading our town!" I burst the door open into our house. "Couldn't even get to Peggy's. Ghetto camps on every corner. Gunshots! People yelling rude things at me the whole way. It was terrible." I cry.

"Oh, dear. I'm sorry," Mom stands from the kitchen table to wrap me in a hug. "You okay?" she places hands on my shoulder for comfort.

"Yeah. I guess," I say, settling my nerves and catching my breath.

Dad sits darkly on the couch. "How many people did you see?" he quietly asks.

"I dunno. A couple hundred? They have campfires all over."

On hearing me, Mom and Dad share an odd look with each other.

"Public good. Private cost…" Dad frowns.

"—Don't care about your 'Collaborators Dilemma,'" Mom says. "Jesus would do it. No matter how much it costs," she sits firmly next to him on the couch.

Dad glares at the floor.

Mom looks at me, "Jen," she reaches to hold my hand, "it's not okay you felt threatened. I'm sorry. Let me know next time you want to go somewhere and I'll drive if I can. But don't hate. Hate gets us nowhere. Forgive desperate people. This Depression is changing us. Out there, tonight" Mom points to the door, "millions of people are losing their identity, their self-respect, and their hope. Research says, 'it's harder to recover from joblessness than losing a loved one or suffering a life-altering injury'. A Depression isn't just economic, but psychological," she taps her head. "Unemployment sucks social spirit dead. Imagine having no idea when you're going to eat next *and* having to tell your kids that? Why be polite and respectful to a system allowing that?" she questions.

I fume and sit next to her on the couch, "I didn't take their jobs. I didn't make them poor. *I* don't deserve to deal with those problems."

"But, Jen. Look," Mom turns fully to me. "You're not 'just you' in other people's minds. Jen, you're something more, a beautiful white girl the system will be infinitely kind to—a seductive ideal so many people want, or at least *think* they want," she laughs. "Whether they actually get along with you is a different story." Mom sticks her tongue out at me.

"Mom." I complain.

She moves to the kitchen, and holds up her papers. "We need to send their anger to those narcissists sucking every possible dollar for themselves. Your dad and I are going to network with those camps tomorrow. We think if people feel more welcome and understand they have a place here, we'll *all* get through this without feeling 'us versus them.' You wanna help? Would be eye opening. Good college essay material," she says.

I stew as my parents' expectations bore into me. *What's an excuse not to waste my time helping rotten people?* "I saw Peggy's family at the food bank today. I wanna try again and see how they're doing."

I'll get my jeans somewhere else.

Two weeks from Sunday, I walk arm and arm with Dad. A thin layer of soft, wet snow crunches like Styrofoam beneath our feet. My cheeks feel cold. My nose too. A crisp fog announces each breath. *I'd rather be shopping. But what I want never matters to this family.*

Dad and I walk along side-streets toward the food bank. We know neither of us want to be here or go the food bank. Mom's voice compels us forward: "Jen, this is our test from God whether we can live radically simple lives close to the poor. Can we replace ambition with humility and devotion? Can we support love above all else?"

Mom, no.

We walk beneath rows of trees stripped of their branches, standing as tall lonely towers encouraging travelers past a ghostly town I hardly recognize. We can't attend the last days of school because the place is full of refugees. Those who couldn't get in for warmth illegally cut trees at night for their camp fires. The last of the smaller trees were cut for firewood days ago. And now our largest trees die at night, murdered by a horde of scum. We pass a few houses burned to blackened skeletons. *Spring's going to be so ugly! All my cottonwoods will be gone. How will I dance through a star field of cotton in the wind?* I fume, *these shits.*

I feel Dad's slight warmth seep through his coat. *More,* I crave squeezing him closer against the winter wind. *More heat. More heat.* I silently demand with a shiver. He subconsciously obeys and places an arm around my shoulders with a squeeze.

Yes.

We eventually turn left at the Historic Route 66 sign and stop.

"Holy Hell," escapes Dad's lips. He releases me and walks forward a few steps alone.

Thousands of people surround our Food Bank, extending past the gas station, past the closed Lombardi Chevrolet and Buick dealership, and past the Gemini Giant and the abandoned Launching Pad Drive-In. The entire road is blocked with refugees.

"We can't handle this," he shakes his head. "We can't."

"Where's Mom?" I nervously ask.

"Where she feels needed most," he shares heavy eyes with me. "Where she can give everyone else the most hope and love; in the middle of all that." His chin points to the dark throng before us, "The physicalization of inequality itself. Ha. Jen, did you know inequality spreads? 'Demographic instabilities drives migration and conflict, leading to the cultural or physical extinction of egalitarian societies,'" he cites.

"What're we going to do?" I ask, more than ready for home.

"Don't know." He laughs loudly, shaking his head. "No idea. We can't save in a day what's been devoured by years of greed. The wealthy globalized markets and manufacturing. They greedily introduced new technologies faster than they empowered social safety nets and education systems. Systems that'd 'give people ripped in globalization's teeth, opportunity to adjust,'" he frowns.

We look silently at the thousands of cold people huddled together.

Dad turns and smiles at me, "Well. Come on, love. Let's support your mother—because we love her. And see what happens," his smile and gloved hand beckon gently forward.

I hesitantly accept his direction and walk into the throng. Into the hungry masses we march. As we part the crowd, random people start shouting, "Hey, Mr. Tom. How you doing?" with big smiles.

"Who are these people?" I whisper, feeling the sudden burn of their stares. "Do they know you?"

"Apparently," he laughs with a whisper and kisses my forehead. "Great. Hey, thanks guys. Thanks for coming out." He says to the crowd as people make room.

Why do I feel like a celebrity? People look at us with deference, with awe. *It's so nice.* I smile, wishing I felt like this all the time. *Dad and I are heroes to these people! We're saviors. Whoa.*

I finally understand why Mom loves this stuff. *She's saving these people. She's feeding them and giving them hope—giving them life—by fueling their spirits. They owe her their spirits and their hope. She's their 'god' on Earth.*

Is this what actual, real power feels like? I relax my tense shoulders, imagining the crowd as my worshipers, like Mom must. *I feel so comfortable.*

We spend fifteen minutes pushing through hundreds of tough, sad, and smelly people who brighten at the sight of us. The crowd becomes dense and think. We eventually arrive at the Food Bank.

My heart stops when I see who's at the door. *Shit,* five huge black gangsters block our way. *We're about to be beaten!* I clutch my coat with wide eyes. Yet, Dad walks forward and does a fist-pump-hug-pat thing with them. They smile and let us into Mom's Food Bank.

We enter and see Mom sobbing on the floor. The storeroom shelves are empty. There is no food.

"Huh? Megan?" Dad rushes to her. "What happened? What's wrong? *Where's the food?* I thought Trinity Lutheran and City Hall were giving 300% today?"

"They *did,*" she sobs at us. "Gone in ten minutes!"

"What?" Dad asks.

"The food. It's gone. All gone…"

"But Megan. There're *thousands* of people out there. *Thousands* of hungry, cold people," Dad says.

"I *know!*" Mom shouts at him, her voice cracking. A drop of spit lands on his forehead, he casually wipes it away without noticing. "Jen. Honey," Mom tensely smiles as she sits and wipes tears from her face. "I want you to go. Please, baby, go. We'll be right behind you. Come give me a hug."

My throat suddenly tightens, "Um, yeah?" I swallow hard, rapidly moving forward to feel the damp heat of her face against mine. "Are you sure, Mom?"

"Yes, Jen, of course. We'll be fine. Dad and I'll be fine. God is with us, love," she releases.

"What about the police? Where are the police?" Dad asks with dead seriousness.

Mom almost laughs, "Ha. They're protecting the *real* bank," she sniffles and slowly stands. "Couldn't get them to come," she adjusts her ponytail. "Tom, all we have are these protein bars," she angrily thrusts a small box. "Please, take a few and make sure the children get some. Only the children; no one else matters. If they can't grow up with hope who knows what they become. I'll take some too," she says, opening the box to hand half of them over before putting the rest in her pockets.

I slowly move to the door, my heart quivering like dry sand thrown in the wind. I look at the door and hesitate. *Where will I go without them, in that crowd?*

"Jen. Wait," Dad's arms wrap behind me in a strong hug. "Have Money Joe and D-Bill walk you out. Guys!" He opens the door and leans into the cold, "Can you please walk Jen out?"

"Yeah. No problem, Professor Díaz," the biggest guy says with an eager nod. "Hey. Y'all get back. Back." He shouts, pushing a narrow hole in the wall of faces. "We're coming through."

I move forward, leaving my parents behind.

"Bye, Jen. We'll see you at the house. Love you," Dad manages a strong smile. Mom stands next to him and sends a frightened wave. I lose sight of them as the massive crowd reforms behind Money Joe's immense frame. We plunge forward.

After a minute I hear Mom on a bull horn: "Hello, Wilmington. Hello, friends."

I try to turn my head as guttural cheers rises from the crowd and surround me like a warm hug. Mom's sitting on the shoulders of the two other gangster-guards. I smile, proud what a massive effect my Mom has over these people. *That power.* I feel the crowd surge as an electric jolt through my veins. I close my eyes and smile as time slows down.

"God's love is here." the bull horn praises. "Right now. God loves *all* of us—all of you," Mom inspires. "He feeds in heaven those whose hunger is not fed on earth. We are not defined solely by this life... but how we choose to enter the next... Compassion, Love, Faith, and the Grace of God—*forgiveness!* These are true meats and breads, the true sustenance we share with our fellow man, woman, and children. Friends—" Mom's voice cracks, "in Wilmington, there is no more food today. We're sorry."

A heavy disappointed collective shout erupts. People shove hands into the air with disgust.

"We're hungry!" one shouts.

"I ain't eaten in three days."

"Fuck you, lady!"

Mom continues, "We know. We know. Jesus, once took five loaves and two fishes, and looked up to heaven with a blessing—"

"—They lyin'! They've taken all the food themselves." An angry scream interrupts Mom. Her face drains pale as she struggles with someone in the crowd.

"Look. Fuckers have food in they pockets!" a few power bars arc into the air. The crowd's anger erupts and surges for a chance at the bars. Somewhere, a lady trips and screams in agony, begging people to step off.

A red brick arcs slowly across the sky and hits Mom hard in the face, crushing her skull. She shouts pain and blood and drops from sight.

"Megan!" I hear Dad scream.

A large rock smashes his shoulder. A lead pipe hits someone near Dad. The crowd is in a frenzy and panic; half try to run while half fight with anything their anger can throw. Money Joe and D-Bill become intensely tight in front of and behind me. I see nothing but a raging human mass of arms and elbows and screaming faces. We shove hard to escape.

I can't breathe. I can't breathe.

I struggle as the ground softens and becomes lumpy, and would trip if not for the gangsters strong hands. I think I'm standing on someone but can't look down to check.

Eventually, I see a giant smiling over at us. He's holding a silver rocket ship high above the rage. We walk closer and closer. Eventually he's looming high above, calm and unmoving. He's above life and death, above hunger and defeat. He's the Gemini

Giant, the thirty-foot spaceman of the old Route 66 drive-in diner. His space suit technology and size make him impervious to our mortal pushing and screaming. He perpetually smiles, uncaring. God-like.

Suddenly, the crowd thins.

"Run home, little girl. We gonna get your parents," Money Joe huffs as he pushes me away and reluctantly turns around.

I run.

Hot tears carve layer upon layer down my freezing face. I feel so empty. I never knew feeling empty could hurt so much. So much. *I never want to be the 'little' girl again. I never want to be poor again. I don't want my parents to live in a hospital. I don't want to feed Mom with a straw. I don't want to lose our house. I don't want us to starve.*

I want to be the giant—the strongest of the strong. I never want to be hungry. I always want someone to eat.

I burst in the house and throw myself on the couch to sob into the dusty fibers. Trembling and numb.

I hope they're okay, I hope they're okay, I clench the fabric. *I wish we had cell phones. Why can't we have cell phones? Please, someone call me,* I beg. *Please…*

An hour later the doorbell rings. I burst it open to see a policewoman. Her squad car lights strobe harsh red and blue shadows in the falling snow.

"Are you, Jennifer?" she asks.

CHAPTER 15—CORPORATE HUNGER

Eddie. December 2022

Jen's angry face explodes large on the monitor. "Our growth is stalling. You people even working?"

I'm eating an apple for breakfast. It's 6:17 a.m. Fresh fruit is now a once a month treat that I refuse to let Jennifer ruin. I half-wish I *hadn't* told her about my protein bars. The largest staff complaint, after the lack of natural light, is the monotonous protein bar meals Jen sells at 350% markup. I've seen the invoices. I know she buys them at a rate far better than I ever got with a fifty pack. Since the atoms in our food must be our size to be digested, Jen buys and shrinks seven large crates of bars every week. I know her time is expensive and the markup makes sense when the CEO serves us food, but that's hard to communicate down in The Drawers. The delivery guys have confused looks on their faces as they cram Jen's office full of seven large crates of bars every week. The MatchTemp™ folks give Jen lots of strange looks too.

And I never did figure out where she stores that Gizmo to shrink everything. I take another bite. But I never know how or why she does most of the strange things she does. *I dunno. Whatever. I choose not to think about it.*

I'm better at handling Jen's insecure outbursts, at least when she's on the monitor. I'm not the best at handling her face to face, for the obvious reason that her face is two-hundred feet wide—it's hard to talk with someone who's three-hundred and fifty times bigger than you and holds your life in her hands. I need to work on that. *New Year's resolution?*

I finish chewing my apple. "Jen, we've extended work hours twice. We're a cash cow! Profits are sky-high since re-organization. Maybe productivity is a fixed quality here? For some reason," I swallow some apple, "adding more hours actually lowered median worker System Scores last month. Even though they're working longer and harder."

"That's not okay with me. I need more," she half-listens, reading something else on her computer screen.

"Um. Okay," I say. "Well. Remember, Jen, you've done it. We're a huge success," I remind her, not knowing what else to say. "You're making great profits."

What's the point of all this efficiency if profits don't satisfy her?

Jen types on her keyboard. I look at her quizzically. *Please look at me? Please?* I beg, subtly trying to engage her eyes through my monitor. I'm unsure if we're having a conversation or if I should return to work.

I read in an old TempSchool book that "Low levels of emotional intelligence create climates rife with fear and anxiety. As the tense or terrified employees have short term productivity boost, their organizations may post good results, but neither the employees nor the productivity last." But I can't find the quote in the newer TempBooks these days.

I decide Jen's done with me and read another report, finishing the apple.

"We need an acquisition," Jen blurts. "Shake things up," she looks intense. "I want workers to compete for their jobs and assignments—bring free market efficiency directly into TempWork Life™ as much as possible. With duplicate roles, I can keep the best performers who work hardest for the least money."

Huh? What kind of mess will that be? "Uh. Acquisitions are risky. Sometimes groups don't mix," I say.

"Our numbers aren't getting the returns I need, Ed!" she says. "I'm not making decisions because workers can't be friends. Workers need to be happy they *have* jobs and grateful I'm *saving* those jobs by keeping our business above water. No success is forever. Look," she waves a tablet reader, "I've read how BIUSA, our number three competitor, made sudden killer returns the past two quarters. I want to know why. I want to know if they've replicated my competitive advantage. This isn't rocket science. Anyone can consensually shrink workers with technology as much as they'd like. I need scale and to reach market sustainability *before* other companies catch on. I need to see what BIUSA is up to."

This is new. She seems nervous? I don't think I've ever seen her nervous. Which I realize is oddly frightening. "Alright, Jen. Um, I can set up a few calls with—"

"—No," she says. "I can't be 'the little girl on video.' I know how businessmen think. I need to build the relationship in person," she scratches the back of her neck, reading another email.

"Sure, okay." I keep what I suspect that means behind a neutral face. "Where is BIUSA? I think in Georgia?"

"Yeah. Bought a ticket for Atlanta this morning. I'm leaving in thirty minutes for the airport to make an offer."

"Whoa! Jen. Are you sure?" I say. "We just started talking about this."

"Key word 'WE', Eddie. Yes. I'm sure," she says, finally glaring at me. "I've been worrying about this for a long time. If I told you my secrets, you'd be shocked, Ed." A savage smirk cracks her concrete face, "*Shocked.*"

No shit, you psycho, I think guiltily. *Are all super hot girls so crazy?* "Okay," I sigh. "Anything you want me to do while you're away?"

"Yes. I'll wear video glasses. They're so fashionable, nobody will notice. Take meeting notes and research questions I ask over instant messenger. Only, Ed," she smiles darkly into the camera. "I doubt they'll let me stream video through their firewall. I'm smuggling you in! It's more cost effective that way. I only need to buy one plane ticket." She displays her airplane phone pass.

Oh gee, I grimace.

"I can't allow anyone discovering my strategy. Not yet," she stands. "Got to see what BIUSA is doing and I'm worried about airport security picking at my jewelry. So, Ed, I have an office relocation for you while we travel," she maniacally grins.

An earthquake opens my drawer as the hash artificial light of her office fills the translucent walls of my capsule.

"Ed," she licks her lips as my capsule lifts into the sky. "I hope you're not afraid of the dark. Enjoy your new home!" Her hand arcs to her upturned face. "See you in sixteen to thirty hours, tasty guy." She laughs, craning her

neck and opening her lips wide to lower my capsule past her teeth and into predatory darkness.

"Mmmm," the inky blackness harshly rattles my wall monitors and the mug on my desk. Then the ceiling slams into my head as the world violently pivots ninety degrees. Gravity disappears, my lamps unplug, papers scatter as I'm flung through two seconds of swirling chaos. A sudden stop slams my head against an invisible table.

I awake to my phone ringing. *I don't have a phone in my apartment. How could it ring?* A ghostly light casts a blinking glow in my strange dark place. Then I remember where I am. *Wrong apartment,* I mutter.

I frantically turn on my flashlight to see a gooey darkness beyond, as I search for leaks in the capsule. I turn on lights as the phone rings. I feel like it's been two hours since Jen swallowed me, but it might have been two minutes or two days.

I answer the phone and start shouting. "Jesus fuck, Jen. What the hell is this!?!"

"Hi. Ed? Oh. Um, I thought I was very honest with you about what this job meant? You're employed and boarded on *my* terms. The details of the contract were right there. You signed them. You didn't ask questions. You didn't do the work to cover your ass—so now you're gonna end up in mine!" Jen laughs, her monitor blinking on to display a pleased expression on her face. She's now wearing a sharp looking business suit and loading a few printouts in a travel bag. "Anyway, this is *great* for me. We can get more work done. Nothing to distract you but what I need you to do. You're right in here," she smacks her belly and the whole world booms around me. "Treat *my* word like law—because for you, it is."

"But this is sick and absurd!" I shout at the phone and pound my desk with an angry fist.

"I dunno," she shrugs. "It's your choice if this doesn't work, I can flush you out," she smirks, leaning into the camera. "But then I can no longer be your responsible landlord unless you're an employee. Serving me."

Her words land as dangerously.

She notes my anger.

"There's no reason to fight it, I am your one true desire and I know you want to give your all to me. Because all that's 'yours,' including you. Now belongs to me. You should've read that contract, Ed. I own you." She casually returns to her packing. "It's the burden of the approver to understand their contract. A responsible person doesn't make a promise or a decision without thinking of all the consequences and being prepared to meet them. What you've signed away to me, Eddie, is intense, and you've no one to blame but yourself. You signed an employment contract," she begins to list. "A confidentiality agreement. A landlord agreement. A full arbitration agreement. A lifetime 360-degree copyright agreement; meaning everything you say, produce, or write—for as long as you live— belong to me. A power of attorney agreement. Eddie, it's only fitting I've actually consumed you. I did last summer!" She laughs, "Yummy."

I give up.

Damnit, I cringe. *I guess I should've been more responsible. I've always known actions have consequences—only I've never had the money to become a Contract Attorney nor the time to stay with all the changing rules! Fuck,* I cradle my head, *she has my IDs too. Maybe I* was *lazy? Too over eager?* I cringe at my stupidity. "Okay, I probably deserve this." I fail to contain a sniffle. "*Technically.* But why would you do this to someone you like?"

"Um, because it's cheaper than buying you a plane ticket? Duh. That's obvious?" she says. "Look. I understand this is a shock. New things always have pushback. You're fine. It's going to be fine. You'll adjust," Jen says. "Your capsule used to be part of the Chilean Navy. And on the plus side, you can't distract yourself walking around anymore," she laughs. "More productivity for me."

"Jen…did you *ever* like me?" I ask. The question falls out of my mouth before I can catch it.

The words make Jen awkwardly shift. "Uh, sure, I 'like' you. What do you mean? I gave you a promotion. I don't understand why you'd ask that," she says.

"I mean, I thought, like, maybe you'd *really* like me? Like, maybe we'd date?" I say.

"Huh? Ed. No!" She stops what she's doing. "Don't be frustrated with me because *you* let your expectations inflate. *Sure, I like you.* I mean, I'm just not in a position for a normal relationship," she looks away. "I prefer trophies over love. The corporation comes first."

What the hell was I thinking? If a girl like Jen wanted a real relationship she would've found one years ago. She's single because she wants to be single. And why change that for me, a CareerTemp™? She'd enjoy her pick of any private school boy in a café or college guy in a bar. Hell, pro-athletes would outbid my attempts at her phone number. I'm so stupid.

"Ed. I've been your whole world since the minute I showed up—that's why I like you. Now, I've made that official! Ha. Now you're a part of me. We both get what we want. Nobody cares about you but me, promise," she shrugs. "Get your office organized and adjust. I'll call you once I'm through airport security. Rest well my little gut-bug. Welcome home," she laughs her gorgeous face into my video feed before the screen darkens.

I feel sick, sit, and focus on breathing, rocking my head in my trembling arms. *I didn't expect the vast personal freedoms Jen would ask me to sacrifice to keep a job. She's entirely consumed my life!*

But after a few cathartic sobs, I think it through.

If I did good work, put her and the company's needs first— I'd get rewarded. Right? She's ultra-capitalistic and hard work is the foundation of success. I only need an attitude adjustment, and to look at the big picture. TempGrace *is* making tons of dough. I've seen the numbers. We have great customers. Jen is one hell of an ass-kicker. That dough will soon trickle down into higher wages and bonuses for us.

There's a silver lining here, I admit with a smile. *One day, once things settle, what other guys will she be familiar and comfortable with? Only me!* I nod as I re-pot a plant and scoop in the loose dirt. *People marry co-workers all the time these days because those are the only people they know!*

I reassemble my office with a fresh smile.

"Made it to the gate B3," the speaker phone awakens with Jen's voice. "Airlines are gonna piss themselves when companies skip buying tickets for team travel, using the same strategy the airlines legalized—carrying miniature people inside them!" Jen says. "Eating you saved me $1,750 bucks! We're on the frontier, Ed. It's you and me against the world."

"I suppose," I say, uncomfortable with my situation.

"Oh. Mr. Mopey Pants. What's really different for you? Were you going to the mall today? Driving to the beach?" she sasses. "No. Ed, you were working in the office all day. Are you in your office? Yes. So who cares *where* that office is?" She jostles her bags. "We need to fundamentally rethink how workplaces operate. Technology is changing the world and we need to adapt. The free movement of people is the next great wave of globalization. No one is ready for that wave but me."

"The next wave?" I ask. "A wave *after* information tech?"

"Yup. Globalization making the world smaller and smaller has only just begun." An airport announcement blares through her phone. "Oh. My. God," Jen snorts. "I just got to the gate. The coach passengers are lining up for their shrinking gate, and look humiliated. Oh, this is so fun. Hah! Oh, god, it looks their Coach Travel Tray is missing—they have to walk into a paper cup! How funny would that be if an attendant forgot and poured my coffee into it? You'd have lots of company!" She guffaws.

Jesus. I frown at her tone.

"Anyway, Ed, I'm getting on the plane. Find BIUSA's past annual reports, map their earnings, highlighting anything odd. My secure local data link is our normal password with JEN added to it. Now that we're not on corporate Wi-Fi, *I'll* be your only conduit to the world. How fun?" Her voice radiates a grin.

I tense my lips at her amusement, unable to fathom Jen's need for absurd and absolute control. *How's someone even like that? Why can't I have my own mobile data plan? They're $80 a month. But no, my whole life needs to flow through her.*

At TempGrace, I'm the only employee with external web access, and the System logs my every click. I get a nasty email from her if I read the news, and my System Score™ drops 10% with an automatic distraction penalty. I'm terrified to even touch the web unless she specifically tells me. When I research what she asks, I have to remind her to manually override my System Demerits™.

I get that confidentiality is critical to Jen's innovation strategy. I respect the needs of the corporation. I can't shake the selfish thoughts of wanting to live my own life now and not in a few months when Jen finally feels secure enough that she's making enough money to let us grow to the size of normal workers.

GERRrrrr-SHQUEEeeeeeeeee! A high-pitched rumble pierces my thoughts like a chorus of dancing whales. My world gently sways side-to-side in the currents of Jennifer's consumption. I think I recognize a piece of lettuce in the murk.

My monitor beeps to life with an instant message from Jen: *Did you d/l those reports? plane doors lock in 15mins.*

almost, I reply.

Really?? haven't seen any data traffic from you. get your shit together before you become a pile of mine… LOL, Jen responds with a wink.

Not funny. I ignore her and busy myself with clicks, typing, and searches, finding three-year's worth of BIUSA's annual reports with five minutes to spare. I begin the slow task of highlighting and tabulating information for Jennifer as the smashed remains of airplane pretzels fall like a gentle rain.

By wheels down at Atlanta International Airport, I send Jen a solid summary of BIUSA's past three years of reported revenue, market size, cash flow, and special projects. I watch on Jen's video monitor as she walks through the airport to meet a smiling white-gloved limo driver who opens her door to a black sedan. Two porters lift her leather Chanel luggage into the trunk. Jen jumps on the phone with me once she settles in her seat.

"It's forty-five minutes to their headquarters. How was *your* trip? Where are you now?" she asks.

"It was fine," I say. "Still in your stomach. Almost forgot where I was, except for the non-stop gurgling."

"Oh good. See, Ed. I'm *not* a crazy monster. You had more room than I did! You could stretch your legs and go to the bathroom anytime you wanted. I had to sit like a cow tied to a first class reclining chair. And thanks for the summaries, they're great."

"No problem," I thank, grateful for the rare praise. *She's in a chipper mood.* This acquisition talk gives her a huge boost—it gives me the jitters. I have no interest being so reckless and headstrong. *But that's why I'm not the CEO.* "Their revenue spiked September 2022. Reports mentions a 'Project Peach' spinning up, but no information on what that meant. Should I keep looking?" I'm not searching the open web without her direct permission.

"Yes, wherever you can. I'm reviewing background on the Execs. Oh, um, wait a minute. *She's* cute. Ed, check out the CFO. Too bad you couldn't charm some information out of her. Check your email," Jen laughs.

I open her attachment to see the dour face of a seventy-year-old woman.

"Ha. Ha. Jen," I fake laugh. "You don't pay me enough for that…" I say.

"Oh yeah? Maybe I should pay you less and less unless until you agree to a new Pimp Clause? That sounds fun."

"Gross, Jen. That sounds distracting. I'm trying to work here. We've only got thirty minutes and I'd like to leave your guts alive when we're done."

"Hmm? Who says we're gonna be 'done'?" she teases.

"Um, you'll have to puke me out sometime?" I ask, not looking forward to that ride.

"Oh. No, Eddie. I hate puking. You're with me the *long haul*. I'm done with you—when I'm done with you."

"Well, shit," I say, as my heart sinks.

"Exactly." Jen guffaws.

"Jen," I angrily realize for the first time how long my fucked-up ride with Jen might last. "You know, it's hard to work when you treat me like a piece of crap. Like, an actual piece of crap." I throw some pens on the floor.

"Oh, whatever. Life is hard, Ed," she says. "Work is hard. You're a big guy—er, a *tough* guy. Haha. We all eat shit in our lives. Your career track is now my GI tract." Her voice is firm yet oddly supportive. "This is what the company needs from you. So, focus."

I have zero interest in this merger or research, yet Jen controlling my every fucking move offers me no options beyond supporting her demands. I'm not feeling inspired at all.

"I'll keep looking," I say, "and see what I can find on Peach."

"Mm-hm," Jen says, already thinking about something else.

I drop deeper into Jennifer's guts. Millions of little fingers wave at me like seagrass, their hypnotic seduction coaxing me deeper and deeper into Jen's psychotic world.

Jen's arguing with a BIUSA receptionist.

"Why isn't my meeting on his calendar?!" Jen shoves her smartphone calendar in the poor girl's face. "Jesus. If this *wasn't* confirmed, why in hell would I fly from San Antonio, and why the hell would that limo be there?" she points to the black car idling beyond BIUSA's main doors.

"I'm sorry, ma'am," the miserable receptionist frets. "I don't see anything in his email or calendar."

I squint at Jen's video feed to see if I can read the receptionist's name tag; either Katie or Kathy.

"Do you know how many millions of dollars are on the line today?" Jen demeans. *"Millions.* The future direction of this company."

"Um, I see Mr. Thompson's schedule is free for a half-hour at 12:30 p.m. I'm sorry it's not your promised half-day," the receptionist trembles.

"Maybe that'll work," Jen says. "I'll wait in the lobby like a jackass for the next forty minutes," she huffs.

"Sorry, don't know how Mr. Thompson's calendar got messed up. I'll tell him you're waiting."

"Of course." Jen elegantly storms towards the drab lobby furniture that looks as if it was stolen from a hotel.

I give her performance a dramatic slow clap. "Probably didn't need to make her cry, but nice work getting a meeting by showing up." I applaud. "Bravo."

"I know, right?" Jen says into her phone. "Eh. Needed to be one badass bitch with her. Couldn't flirt with her like the guards. How stupid were those guys?" she laughs.

"You've got more balls than me."

"Duh, Ed. I own *your* balls. You and three-thousand other men in the TempGrace drawers. Oh, hello, Jim." Jen's video feed pivots as a tall silver fox strides in a panic towards her. "You're even sharper than I remember. I'm, Jennifer Diaz, CEO of TempGrace." She rises to shake his hand. "Thrilling to see you again," she says.

"Yes. Hello, Jennifer? Sorry to have missed our appointment. What was our agenda again?" he asks.

"We talked about a large transfusion of cash for BIUSA and maybe a partnership at a party a few weeks ago. You had so many clever ideas. We were both, um, more than drunk, but thought it was wise for us to keep in touch," she adds, placing a hand on his arm.

"Sure. Of course. Sorry I forgot. I'm on a call with the board." He points to his muted smartphone. "We'll try and end early. Kathy has lunch for us. I'd love to hear more then."

"Eager to refresh your memory, Jim. Thanks," Jen allures with a second hand on his arm. "See you soon."

Jim Thompson shares a lingering nod, clearly impressed with Jennifer, and briskly returns to his call.

"You know, Ed," she returns to her phone. "If men are this easy to manipulate, no idea why it's taken so long for a woman to take over the world. I mean, seriously. No way a *guy* could walk over an important dude's day like I did. *No way.* Quick, what's Project Peach? Gimme gimme."

Her question jolts me to work. The video feed makes her masterful manipulation seem abstract and far away, like a movie.

"Er, still looking," I say. "It's been a whirlwind. Nothing obvious."

"Piss. Keep looking. Cut the chit-chat. Receptionist's back. IM me."

Okay, I instant message her.

Jennifer leans on the executive conference room table as the caterers shuffle the last parts of lunch. Her tight business skirt rises above her knee. The room is filled with plush leather chairs and the smiles of BIUSA's leadership team, who, except for the old CFO Jen wanted to pimp me to, are all white men in their mid-fifties.

"Alright, Brian, Kyle, Jim, Samantha," Jen wipes her mouth with a napkin. "TempGrace is San Antonio's largest temp staffing agency with over 5,000 employees, and the third largest temp organization in the Southern United States of America. Our revenue growth is 38% quarter-over-quarter, with a profit margin rising *over 600%* the past six months since I've been CEO.*"*

The room gasps.

"We're on course to raise revenue growth by an astounding 350% by the end of my fiscal year. I'm one hell of an ass-kicking CEO, loaded with cash because I personally strive to ensure TempGrace is as close to a total free market paradise as possible. Today, I'd like to explore a world where BIUSA joins the fun."

"Jen, those results are amazing. Fantastic," Jim, praises. "May we see your latest financial reports in detail? I'm sure we'd all like to study them."

The room nods in agreement.

"Unfortunately," Jen sighs, "I'm a private corporation with very little public information to share. I do, however, have contracts for you to sign… if you'd like to know the private parts of my organization, more in depth," she says seductively. "You'd be welcome."

Fat contracts plop in front of each executive, raising their eyebrows. "Sign these," Jen says, "and I'll show you exactly how TempGrace works, with every naked detail." Her hands adjusting the thin hem of her skirt.

The men raise their pens.

Samantha, the CFO, glares at Jen. "I'm sorry. No." She cuts with a sharp interjection of her hands. "We don't sign anything unless Andrea, our SVP of Legal, reads and approves the contracts. We'd certainly *love* to see if your financial results are true," she says. "Not by signing a stack of papers an inch thick, an hour after you show up."

The men sheepishly lower their pens.

"Oh. Er," Jen says, "it's hard to *show* how successful I am, without the agreement." She leans into her computer. The room waits awkwardly as she types.

that cunt. they didn't bite! pops onto my screen as an IM.
ask about Peach? I type.

"Um, meanwhile, maybe we can talk best practices? In abstract?" Jen recovers, and sits in a plush chair that makes each adjustment sound like a fart. "As an industry, we all share an interest in fighting government regulations. I read buried in your annual report some great success around a 'Project Peach'. But I couldn't tell what it was. I'm an investor in BIUSA. I personally bought 8% of the company's shares last Tuesday. So, I'd like to know the scoop." Jen's smile makes the room uncomfortable.

"That was you?" Jim clears his throat after receiving a nod from the CEO. "Of course. Jen, we have a great relationship with the State of Georgia. Last August, the Governor's re-election campaign approached us with, an incentive, to hire one thousand temps in the parts of the city his poll numbers were close. To prop up a campaign pledge around improving unemployment—"

"—Are you kidding me?!" Jen shouts.

Her outburst surprises the room, including me.

"Hey now," Jim defends. "Alright. You should know BIUSA hired the temps for only three months and laid them off immediately after the election and sat on the rest of the state-allocated money. Gave record dividends that quarter, I believe?" He finds agreement around the table. "Incentivizing more capital. Including, yourself?" His eyebrows ask.

Jen stands abruptly. "Well, I've got turds smarter than you people." She slaps her belly. *"Handouts?* Seriously? You're puppets," she points an angry finger at each person in the room. "Pathetic. Government. Puppets. Government isn't after the wellbeing of anybody. They only want power and *you* wiggled your little tails over, giving it like crack whores on a salty dick."

Jen shoves the contracts into her Chanel bag and storms out of the stunned room to her limo, blindly sending Kathy the finger on the way out. "Fuck off."

The limo delivers Jen to the Mandarin Oriental, Atlanta's most expensive hotel. Jen removed her earpiece and turned off her phone a while ago. I'm stranded without communication beyond her video feed. On the drive from BIUSA to the hotel she mostly looks out the window.

Funny how Atlanta looks so much like San Antonio, pockets of opulence surrounded by a sea of squalor, I observe.

The hotel bell boy tries to flirt with Jen in the elevator, but his smile freezes from what I assume is one hell of a withering look by Jen. He leaves her executive suite without bothering for a tip.

Her room is spacious and gorgeous; white walls with ornate gold trim, large crystal chandeliers—all enclosed by a wall of windows. Jen flops on the couch. My whole world tips and slides as her movement overloads the double-hull bearings that orient the floor of my capsule with gravity. *Any trivial new direction from my CEO sends my little world scattering,* I bitterly note as all the contents of my shelves fall to the floor. Her video feed spins violently towards a small coffee table. The glasses settle upside down, framing her shoulder and the side of a head of hair. I tilt my head at the view.

I want to reach out to her. Talk with her. I caress the screen softly with my hand. *I'm so ironically close, yet a thousand miles away.*

I drop into her large intestine as Jen takes a long nap. I look outside my apartment to again reaffirm: yes, everything I do gets me covered in shit. I read a book on my sideways couch trying to ignore the metaphorical and physical realities of Jen's crap piling up.

A sudden motion tosses me off my couch. *Did I fall asleep?* I see it's 3:34 a.m. Jen's video feed remains upside-down but is missing Jen. I check my computer for any updates but lack data connection. Her phone is off. I shake my head to clear rising feelings of claustrophobia and the worries of a prisoner. Suddenly I'm falling. My well-placed cushions scatter as all my belongings rise in a split second of weightlessness before crashing into a mess all over the floor.

Goddamnit!

I'm surrounded with an eerily solid darkness. A darkness that holds no life, no rhythmic sway of Jen's breath or gurgle of her digestion. A tomb like stillness. *What the hell?* My pulse quickens.

My speakers crackle to life. "Good thing I was working late and awake enough to remember you!" Jen laughs. "If I was half-asleep, you'd be a swirling goner!"

I realize what happened and bury my face in embarrassment.

"I paid $5,000 a night to shit in a bathtub! Gross, I think I see you."

A massive tissue scrapes at my capsule and lifts it into a gushing waterfall. Jen dries my capsule walking through a massive hotel suite to a grand dining table hosting her own midnight party. A computer, a few dozen books, and a large stack of files lay jumbled across the table's surface next to a few messy plates from room service.

Jen's indeed working through the night.

She slumps into a chair with a long sigh and sets my office a few feet from her work area.

"May I walk outside?" I ask.

She looks sternly at me, before softening her face, "Of course."

With eager relief, I grab a headset and dash through the door onto the table's vast surface. I feel giddy to simply walk and breathe fresh, non-recycled air with a grin immense of pleasure.

"Eddie," Jen says, wearing a simple tee shirt and a ponytail, several hundred feet from me,. "I'm *so* glad I didn't hesitate to devour you. We saved a plane ticket *and* a hotel room. Another $400 in my pocket." She slaps her hip.

"Yeah, sure," I say without bitterness. "I support personal sacrifices for the company."

"And I love you for that," she says, her chin lowering to the table.

I blush. The warm wind of Jen's breath rolls through me smelling of lavender and French fries. I kick my feet at the rough table grain, avoiding her intense eye contact.

Her eyes tighten. "The BIUSA guys were total fuckers. Those spit wads haven't stolen my advantage at all. Thank god.

Once I knew that, didn't give two squats. I can't believe they sucked government money down like whores. I was so repulsed I had to leave the room immediately. Money's never free, Ed! Never, never, never," she raises to shake her head. "I guess I just realized how much work I still have to do." She lowers her shoulders and looks at me. "I've been slacking." She pounds a stack of books.

"What are you working on?"

"A plan for free enterprise to win and government to lose."

"Alright. Cool, I'll leave you to it," I say, focusing on some basic warm up stretches. The table's massive enough I don't wanna get lost or accidentally crushed. *About half a mile in each direction? I guess.* With Jen around, I need to stay where I feel comfortable.

I jog in circles a bit around stacks of books I assume to be safe. After a few minutes, negative thoughts interrupt my relaxation.

Damn. Would it hurt to give me a private room and my own plane ticket? Jen spent $10,000 today on limos, an executive suite, and a first class ticket purchased the fucking day of travel? She already makes three-hundred-fifty times more than me. What's another $400 to her?

I once calculated Jen earns in a day what I earn in a year.

I struggle and finally subdue the unproductive thought, only to be interrupted by the burp of another. *It's been months since I've seen the sun.*

I snap to reality.

Deal with it. Yes, she's looking out for the corporation first, to bring jobs back! As things trickle down—and they're going to because this is America—little folks like me will get richer too. My negative thoughts don't respect the efforts of job creators like Jennifer.

"So Ed." Jen interrupts, leaning casually sideways in her chair. "Had an idea after my nap. When States wrote laws banning collective bargaining, they also broke government unions. What if *all* government offices were run by temps?" She grins excitedly over a stack of books. "I *love* that idea of whole governments working for me," she sighs. "We could have contracts with all thirty-six states in the Southern U.S." She holds a print out, "Each technically allows their governments to be administered by Temps. I could provide a patriotic service *and* save taxpayers loads of money!"

Jen looks at me strangely hot and bothered.

"The whole state of Texas working at TempGrace?" I ask.

Her smile moves to the distance. "How neat that'd be." Her hand moves gently along the top of a breast.

"Um, yup," I say not knowing how to respond to her all-consuming ambition. "Temps as bureaucrats? Would probably save a lot," I nod.

"Ed, having you inside me today has made this one of the best days of my life." She rubs her belly. "I already ache that we're apart. You're my little productivity secret. I felt so effective." She sighs. "Like, I was omnipotent enough to actually get things done. I felt like I was *more* of a person than before." She moves closer. "Walking with you hidden away gave me thousands of jolts of electricity."

"Um, yeah?" I nervously edge closer to my capsule.

"Yeah. Ed, we've shared something special. *The first symbiotic corporation.*" She throws arms at the significance. "Historians will mark today like the first personal computer, the first powered airplane. The first time a corporation *in-sourced* her workers! Imagine a world with *total* in-sourcing," she dreamily stares. "I could work in the park *all* the time. Or the beach, reading reports in my bikini all day in the sun, and all of my employees would be with me." She tenderly rubs her arms.

Jen lowers her chin to the table. Her adoring stare fires intense heat.

"Sometimes, I worry my visions are deeper than rationality," she says.

Her hot breath again rolls across the cherry tabletop. A massive airplane-sized finger arcs to gently pet the top of my head.

"You and me. At the forefront where technology needs the modern office to become. More agile and more productive, with as small of a workforce as possible. Pushing teams doing more for less money. All of us coming together in a total free market paradise." She looks heavenly. "So beautiful it hurts. Eddie, that you're doing whatever the corporation wants without much complaint is such a thrill. Honestly. Really." Her eyes gleam. "I felt so connected, so significant, so capable. I wish we could have this every day," she sighs. "Oh. Fuck it. Why not?" she grins.

Jennifer stands, towering massively above the table, and throws off her loose t-shirt to expose a magnificent set of breasts.

"Holy hell," I mutter. Terrified how Jen's mood is unraveling, I immediately dash in my office and latch it shut.

Jennifer's hand reaches, and the world blurs as my capsule aggressively re-adjusts to the table's edge. I arch my neck to look through the transparent ceiling at Jen's face, glowing like a titaness a thousand-feet above.

"This has been an intense week." She brings the full height of her torso a few inches from the table. "I hope you don't mind if take a bit of time to, decompress, before we get back to work?" She leans her hands coyly on the table. A colossal pair of thumbs hook the elastic waistband of her pajama pants and drop them below the table. Her voluptuous hips shift as she steps out of them.

Three-hundred-foot-wide bikini panties radiate before me like the sunset.

"Look how small you are, Ed," Jen whispers as her thumbs hook the front of her panties. "I could make you disappear forever." Her thumb slowly drifts to the right to reveal massive and naked vagina lips.

I'm petrified. Mesmerized. I feel a man about to die.

"All I'm going to do, Ed, is lean slightly forward and you'll totally disappear," she says.

Her legs shift open slightly as the massive shadow of her belly descends to rest fully on the table. My last glimpse of the outside world becomes the smiling maw of Jen's glistening lips as I enter a new form of darkness. The world distantly *ohhhs.* I feel it shutter and twist. A sudden lurch tumbles me forward and an earthquake jolts me twenty feet up and down—up and down. I hear slurping in the dark. I feel the hard *thump thump* of Jen's heart pound through the walls. A light breaks overhead like dawn at the bottom of a well a hundred feet deep, and I glimpse a massive finger circling above. A rib bruises as I slam into the side of a bookcase. Her heartbeat is the stampede of a thousand horses. The world tilts another ninety degrees at a rush of pressure. The capsule massively shudders, settles, shudders again, and falls into silence.

Her heartbeat relaxes, and I feel entombed in stone.

I'm alive. It's so quiet. What's going on? How can she fuck her workers like this?! I fume in tension, feeling utterly insignificant within the thousands of tons of woman surrounding me.

I wait. An hour? I can't tell. I unclench my spine, relax my sore muscles, and check for cuts and scrapes—wary any second my whole sense of truth might violently lurch. After what feels like an eternity of tense waiting, a light shines like a distant star. A crude finger clumsily eclipses it searching for me. I'm out of reach and the darkness returns. *Am I lost?*

I wait.

Eventually, my world pivots.

After a lazy twenty minutes, the world rocks up and down, the light returns much closer than before, and a finger scoops me out.

Jen's hotel bedroom is intensely bright. I clench my eyes tight but force them open to see something normal. Something real. Jen lays naked on her bed, extending me arm's length above an angelic smile. Her hair casually splays across the bed sheets. She glows.

"Oh my god. I feel so much better! Thank you, Eddie," she dreamily stretches, exploring her peace.

After a few glowing breaths, a mischievous smile lights her face. She flips to her belly and brings me close to her face. "Tonight, was your rebirth, Ed. A baptism in a new era of capitalism I've been dreaming about for *years*. Now that I'm relaxed, and you're properly orientated, I think we'll get a lot more work done the next several months. Thanks, love." She kisses the capsule and rises to her knees with a dark glint in her eye.

'Love?' I blink, taken aback at her term.

My heart softens to match her glow.

"Ed," she leans closer. "As your landlord, and for the sake of our mutual productivity, I'd like to permanently relocate your office..." She lowers my capsule past her stomach and around her lower back. "I can already tell you're the best ass-istent ever." She laughs, bending forward a few inches. "Let's get you back to your brown nosing," she says. "I need *all* of you, Eddie."

Oh god. My heart sinks. *No, no, no.* I pointlessly pound the clear plastic walls as the ass which has distracted me from months of work, now officially opens to devour me alive. For the third time today, I disappear into the all-consuming ego of Jennifer's world.

CHAPTER 16—NEW YEAR

Jennifer. February 2013

"Morning, Peggy," I mumble as cold milk and cereal dribble down my chin. I obviously find it hard to care about my breakfast manners.

"We need to wait for Dad," Peggy meekly scolds, reaching into the fridge in annoyance. "He wants to spend breakfast with us before we go to work."

I shrug.

Peggy angrily thuds the bland cheap design of a TempOJ™ container on the table. "And you *didn't* set the table for us?" she says, a hand on her hip before pouring herself and her father a glass of orange juice. "That's not kind."

You're so annoying, Peggy. I shrug.

She opens the cabinet for two bowls and a box of TempCereal™ and pours some flakes into her bowl.

"All we have is each other, Jen. We don't even have this house anymore. It'd be nice to appreciate our last week's here together and be happy. Your part of our family too!" her big eyes plead.

I stare at my milk. Two corn loops swirl and bump together. I ignore the sting in my eyes until I forget to breathe and force my lungs open. I refuse to let my lip tremble, but it does anyway.

Why won't Uncle Greg answer my calls?

I shrug again. "Oh well," and rapidly scoop the last of the cereal and then turn the bowl to my mouth with a loud long chug. I drop my dirty dish on the table with a hard clunk and walk out of Peggy's small-ass kitchen. "I need more time to get ready anyway," I say without looking at her.

I love combing my hair in my underwear. Every time I look in the mirror I'm astounded by how perfect I am. Each and every time. I slink side-to-side, modeling for myself. *Fabulous.*

My makeup kits and brushes devour the whole bathroom counter. I smirk, *Peggy and Mr. Davis have only a quarter the space*

I have. Mom and Dad never let me have that much stuff in our little bathroom.

The police car lights flash a sharp red and blue in the falling snow. Mom's face is so crushed that I puke all over the coroner's green linoleum tile floor.

I adore the significance I lord over Peggy's home. The Wounded Princess. The Child of the Fallen Heros. Over the past month Peggy and Mr. Davis have bent-over-backwards to offer me all they have. I've been their superior, their Alpha. Now Peggy wants me to drop to her level? *Nope.* I'm *done* pretending I'm not beautiful. *Done* pretending that I'm not better than this stupid city! *Why has it been so long since I've worn makeup? I don't need to follow my parent's rules anymore.* I eagerly sort through dark green and blue eyeshadow. *It's time to be honest here people. Hello! I'm a Goddess.* I tug on my bra straps and ogle at my amazing jiggle, before applying a purple shadow under my eyes.

Worship me.

I continue my beauty therapy. Eyeliner. Dark red lipstick. Curl the ends of my black hair. I smile when Mr. Davis gently prods from the hallway: "Jen you're making us all late…"

"Just a minute!" I open the door without bothering to cover and flash him a billion-dollar smile.

"Oh, alright," he says with wide eyes.

Mind control, bitches! It feels so good. Control might really be the best drug ever invented. I love it so much.

I fix my hair again. This is my first week in the senior TempEd™ classes, and a girl needs to make her impressions! I'm already *two* TempGrades™ above Peggy. She's almost as smart as me, but not smart enough.

TempEd™ encourages and rewards our best. *What a novel idea, eh?* I grin at my opportunities. *Hell, I'm only three classes behind Peggy's Dad, Mr. Davis.* My new TempTeacher Rick™ is so fucking hot. He personally lobbied to have me skip into his class after brushing past me in the hallway. I look forward to his TempTheory™ discussions every day.

"Jen. We're gonna get LateDemerits," Peggy pleads through the door. "We can't afford $6.00 each. Come on, let's go!"

Keep begging, bitch, I smile. "We don't have to always do things together, Peggy." I adore myself in the mirror.

I like how TempSchool incentivizes good work and being on time with cash and uses fees to punish. *Totally makes sense. I earn what I deserve.* Certain subjects offer bonuses to study "depending on the market needs." *Rick's TempTheory™ class even pays to attend!* I'm simply amazed how all these schools miraculously popped up on New Year's when we needed them most. The TempSchools seriously saved this town from those mobs.

I hear Dad screaming, "Megan!" as the violent crowd surges around us. Money Joe pushes me forward. I'm suffocating. I'm suffocating. I'm suffocating.

Hunger destroyed our minds. I'd never been without food my entire life; it was always easy to open the fridge and eat. Until last December, I never felt myself go crazy with hunger. None of Mom and Dad's credit cards worked. I couldn't find Uncle Greg's cash either, some stupid-fucking-ass packed it away! Come New Year's, the town craved the TempCamp relief. The cold, crazy, poor, and starving people could attend TempWork™ and TempEd™ for warmth and food. Our houses stopped getting broken into. We stopped getting mugged.

The Temp System works!

We have cheap food, warm dorms, clean clothes—and the options of various TempLife Packages™ we can either purchase or work off when short the cash. Weekly micro-loans can pay for morning classes at TempSchool if we want to spend the afternoon working to help actual businesses! *I earned $35 dollars last week. A fat stack of Lincolns, baby. Fuck yeah.* The can-do attitude of the TempStaff is incredible. A thousand times more focused and effective than my feeble parents.

Dad's casket locks shut, never to open again. The fine maple grain is solid against my hot cheeks. Through the sideways blur of my tears I angrily watch a church full of remorse. A congregation choking on the pain and guilt of My Pain. You cowards caused this. *I grit my teeth at them. I turn my eyes in rage at the cross and the wooden Jesus strung up in well-deserved-pain.* Your stupid lies made this happen! Your stupid fucking lies. I HATE you, *I silently scream.*

I open the bathroom door to the irritated faces of Peggy and Mr. Davis. "I'm ready. Coats on. Come on, let's go!" I prod. We hustle into our winter gear and trudge through the wind and snow to the old high school.

"Welcome. Hi! Good morning." The TempCheerSquad™ applauds and hoots as we enter. I can't help but bashfully smile and shuffle forward, stomping snow off my boots. *These guys are so fucking positive. TempLife's going to take over the world, I can see it. God, can't remember when a government school made me feel this welcome.*

Such a simple thing.

A "Hard Work is our Safety Net™" poster extends along the hall as we walk to our pay-lockers. Peggy, Mr. Davis, and I each deposit a dime, hang our coats, remove our workbooks, and hurry to our respective classes as blaring rock music counts the final thirty seconds before morning sessions start.

TempTheory™ time with Rick, I squeal in delight, hustling to his room. He's already talking.

"It's sad how elements of society hate freedom. Hate work," TempTeacher Rick raises his arms, enthusiastically welcoming my arrival. "I don't understand," he says, "but it's oddly true. Thanks for coming in, guys," he welcomes the last students rushing into the room. "Funny how there's a deliberate campaign to cripple and close these schools by people who think making money *working* is wrong! How silly's that?"

The class chuckles.

"We're here to teach you how to make money, how to work, how to be rich. How to be the best *you*."

He points at me.

"At least until some bureaucratic *tyrant* tells us what we *can* and *can't* think." Rick leans his fabulous baseball player butt against his desk, rolling the sleeves of his dress shirt over his muscular elbows.

What a hunk. I need to be careful not to drool. He winked at me twice last week when my attention was a tad too fixed. *I'd destroy that man and there'd be nothing left,* I chew on my pen as my eyes dart to check him out. It's no accident most of the women are in the front row paying solid attention to our lessons. *Because, yum.*

"Governments are fundamentally about control," he continues. "They want to take god's place—have all your thoughts, actions, and dreams accountable to them! We'll break that," he pounds the desk. "TempLife is about ensuring *our* choices rule *our* lives and nothing else. Because only *we* are truly responsible for our destiny."

"I'm flabbergasted at the news this weekend. 'TempSchools Under Attack All Over The Country?' We need to be alert against government takeover. I mean seriously." He looks intently at each of us. "State Legislatures on the coasts, and here on the Great Lakes, are in outright revolt and anarchy? For the first time in U.S. history, states are rebelling *against the lack of rules and regulations* from the Federal Government! What? How crazy is that?" he asks. "Why do these states want to take away *your* freedom to be rich? See how oppressive governments can be when they lose their dose of control over you? Control is a drug, people. An addiction bureaucrats crave and can't let go." Rick shakes his head slowly and thinks, "It's startling what cruelty rises when one person controls another…" he sighs.

"Be careful what you hear in the news. Tyrants love poisoning public information. They spin the news to *deceive* the public into giving them more money or power. That's what governments do." He shakes his head.

When someone as hot as Rick speaks, I'm focused on his every word. This makes me think of all the attention men lavish on me.

Beautiful people hold so much power.

"Ask yourselves," he continues, catching our attention, "what kind of world do you want to see?" He holds up a hand. "One that incentivizes hard work and wealth?" He holds up his other hand. "Or one that incentivizes laziness and poverty? It's that simple. That's why we choose cutting the state over taxing the rich, why we reward the comfortable rather protect the needy. Incentives matter. Poverty happens *because* governments incentivize poor people to be lazy. TempSchools want you to work towards your dreams. Encourage you to own the horizon in every direction if you can. Because we need more consumption, more growth, *more you.* In focusing on what most benefits yourself, you benefit the rest of us; *that's* how we make this economy thrive."

I realize my purpose. *I want to make people free. I want to use my smarts and beauty for the freedom of all—by empowering myself!*

Outside the classroom we hear hooting and a stampede of footsteps down the hallway. *Oh, god. Fucking activists again,* I moan.

In busts two masked clowns dressed as jailbirds in black and white stripes. They jump, shouting, "Hey. Come on. Let's go! Together we can escape greed. Come on, come on!" They eagerly wave us to the door.

No one moves.

No one cares about your fucking beliefs, dude! Shut up. I roll my eyes.

"This school is private property. You need to leave," Rick angrily jumps towards them.

One jailbird jumps out of Rick's charge "—You've no right to occupy this stolen public space," she sasses back.

"Security!" Rick interrupts, shouting down the hallway. "Get out of here, losers," he shoves one as another moves to the opposite side of the room behind a desk. Three security guards rush in, and after an awkward chase, finally escort the jailbirds out.

Lame…we need a safer space for these lessons. Away from public influence and interference.

"Sorry," Rick apologizes, shaking his head. "Today, I'm compensating you double." The mood in class lifts. "I'm shocked how many people fight *against* their own freedom. Folks *willingly* lock parts of their mind away because they like to ignore things that —if they really looked—might cause them pain. I guess the best traps really are when the guy *keeps himself in jail,*" he taps his temple with a chuckle.

"The complacency I see in people is sad. Fascism is never on their minds, not at first—not until it's too late. There's lots of blame to go around for this Depression. But the biggest failure I want us to admit, until recently, was the old giants of industry *failing* to defend and protect free markets. We call this 'nationalism without a whimper.' With our new economic package, that song has changed. Next week we'll introduce the Business Awakening that shocked the world and propelled Ron Paul into office. This same movement is saving communities all over the country this winter." He nods approvingly. "TempSchools are founded by the wealthiest people on the planet so *everyone* can learn the same ingenuity and zeal that made them rich."

Fuck yeah! I eagerly lean forward. *I'm sick of being poor—time to be rich.*

"As we end. Please, please, help us de-nationalize, help us privatize as much of the public space as possible and expand corporate personhood to be as huge as possible. It's up to *you* to fight public tyranny."

In book VIII of *The Republic,* Plato's clear on the worry of tyranny to democracy. His fret was that a "towering despot" would inevitably rise in any democracy to exploit its freedoms and seize power by representing himself as the protector of the people against that fear.

Thank god people like Rick inspire us to be as strong as possible. I think for a moment. *Could I be a second towering defender, ready to fight against whatever government monster arises in this stupid democracy?*

Rick hands us each a crisp $20 bill as we exit. *Best money I've ever earned.* I like when teachers actually teach. Some courses are self-taught bullshit; the instructor only provides guidance on a per-minute fee.

I can hardly pay attention in my Accounting class because the teacher is so damn boring. Old prune. *Fuck accounting. I only earn $2.00 a class here. I don't care how the fucking banks work, lady.*

I'm slouching in the bank chair, arms angrily crossed. Mr. Davis tries his best to argue with the over-muscled bald guy behind a large desk, a guy who keeps raising an eyebrow and frowning at his computer screen.

"Sorry, Jen," Mr. Muscle Man says. "Your parents were great people, but when they, uh, passed, your house was already double-mortgaged and late a few payments. I'm really sorry. The bank needs to seize your home by the end of the year. Please move out by December 31st or the sheriff will be involved. So sorry," he says with sincere bland eyes.

Fuck this guy who keeps saying 'Sorry' about helping me despite how strong and rich he is.

My parents were so fucking stupid. No one gave a shit about their 'giving.' It's take or be taken. Eat or be eaten.

I cry the car ride home.

I wish Rick was my teacher growing up. Would've saved so much pain and trouble. He'd stop the false fantasies, pointless guilt of my parents and gotten me set right: *Improve the world by improving yourself.*

A large banner hangs in the dining area: *Have an opportunity? Provide a Service, Receive a Compensation.*

Hell. Lunch is expensive here. I glare at my $25.00 bill. *Obviously, there's no free lunch, but $25.00 for a plate of spaghetti and meatballs!? At least allow us to bring our own food then...* I look for a place to sit. *Someone should totally start another Sandwich Stand like when Jake Anderson sold PB&Js a few weeks ago for a dollar each. Not sure why he closed down or why they threatened to kick him out of TempSchool.* He said he can't talk about it because he had to sign something.

By far my most expensive class is TempManagment™. *Balls!* I can only afford the first fifteen minutes of lecture before a ticket agent escorts me out. *It's like you need to be already rich to be a manager? Fuck that. How are we going to grow into titanic managers if they make it so hard to attend advanced classes?* Here, I only see the business people in town who already have big jobs. I'm sick of being poor, and listen as hard as I can. *Thank god the teacher is another boring lady, and I can focus.*

"When it comes to managing employees," the lady introduces, "squeeze workers as hard as you can. Workers naturally want to take. To mooch and slack. They'll overestimate the time it takes to accomplish a task so they don't have to work as hard. To get the productivity you really can—squeeze them tight. Set 'impossible goals' with your vision, and even as workers fall short, you'll be amazed at how far they go. It's important to be careful 'being nice.' Altruism is an expensive hobby. A corporation has *no* moral obligation to anything beyond the interest of maximizing its profits, and altruism logically permits no view beyond viewing people as parasites on the resources of the provider."

Whoa. I never thought of altruism like that before. Mom totally loved having the whole town, all those lost hungry people, as parasites on her. *We prayed at every meal and made us love the idea of Meekness with all our heart—but, it was all about her control.*

Shit. I fume, realizing her congregation was always the most popular on the days she provided meal bags. Duh! We took in rioters and unionist alike. We offered all we had like some starving shepherds selling their last rags to buy oats for a flock who could freely graze wherever they liked!

Providing food and comfort kept them close to her, gave her control.

"Capitalism and altruism are incompatible," the old lady continues. "The choice is clear: either a new morality of rational self-interest, with its consequences of freedom, justice, progress and man's happiness on earth—or the primordial morality of altruism, with its consequences of slavery, brute force, stagnant terror and sacrificial furnaces."

Altruism *is* a moral corruption. A naive, sinister, karmic fantasy of 'repayment' masquerading as a passive power play.

So many lies, I fume.

On Christmas day, half the congregation is at my house packing pans into boxes and swinging them into trucks. They bring little tributes and gifts for me. The ladies bring casseroles for lunch. The men follow my every order.

"You all gotta listen to what I have to say." I beam, the first time I can truly act how I feel. I determine when they arrive. I tell them when they leave. I tell them what goes in what box. Fun!

I sort through my parents' room alone. Fold Dad's cot next to Mom's queen size bed and drag it into the hallway. Under Mom's bed, I notice a few wrapped Christmas presents. My eyes sting as I quietly open them. A pair of jeans and a gold necklace for me. I clasp the pendant around my neck and cry.

I don't want any of Mom's frumpy clothes. I dump each of her dresser drawers into a donation box—as I do, a large black dildo with a crucifix over the balls tumbles to the floor at my feet. What the fuck? *I stare at it.* Oh. My. God. *I realize what it is and see Dad sleeping on the cot as Mom fucks Jesus all night. So messed up! So messed up,* I panic. *She really was in love with a fantasy? Gross. Gross. So gross.* I kick it into a trash can.

I struggle to regain my focus on my last few minutes of TempManagement™.

The instructor continues, "Be rude if you need to. Break the previous assumptions on the role between companies and employees. Seize the global trend towards the commodification of employees' basic needs and allow market efficiencies to thrive within your organization. Because in our optimal economy, each person is a free actor who makes decisions purely in his or her own sclf-intcrcst."

Suddenly, a ticket agent taps me on the shoulder suggesting I either pay for another fifteen minutes or leave.

Goddamnit, I rage, gathering my notes.

Afternoon is TempWork™. *I'm better than this,* I mutter, stuffing envelopes and stamping postage. About three hours in the Direct Marketing Room™ is all I can handle, even if it is where I make the most money. *I can stuff fifteen envelopes a minute! That's nine-hundred pennies an hour, bitches.*

Jason Ericson seated next to me can stuff twelve a minute when he's not trying to start awkward conversations on me. *Shut up dude. I don't care about your Mom or your cat or your stupid paper cuts. I need to focus here.* Each day this job gets more competitive and the compensation lowers; only the most profitable workers are allowed back the next day.

Every day's an audition to keep your job, dude. Jason might be motivated to work harder if he noticed this yacking slipped him to #13 on the productivity screen. A point I don't tell him because I want my spot at the top preserved. Seeing "#1 Profitability" next to my name makes me smile.

Yet, if Jason does get wise and catches up, I have a few flirty questions ready for him: *Have you had your first kiss yet? What do you look for in a girlfriend?*

I hear screaming in the hallway.

Activists again, I barely flinch. *I'm making $0.01 an envelope here folks. Get lost.*

The door bursts open, "All managers out!" a gruff voice shouts, "All workers, go home."

I turn mid-stuff, expecting to see a bunch of hippies—but my throat clenches at the sight of three masked men with rifles, dressed in black.

"The 99% is re-occupying this public school! Everyone, out. Now!" they shout, moving through the room lifting workers by their elbows.

"What?" My mouth drops, *"Holy shit."*

"TempClasses are permanently canceled. You'll be notified when public classes resume in a few weeks. Come on, out. Out." They say again.

"Don't fucking touch me!" I say, jabbing a sharp finger as a guy approaches me.

He jumps, startled. "Miss. *Jen—*" he whispers. "Come on, it's time to go," he kindly waves me out.

"Fuck you! Take off that mask." I lunge toward him, but he's too tall and strong, and easily pushes me to the door.

How humiliating.

The hallway is chaos. Papers strewn all over the floor. Some people are running. A line of ten children holding hands are crying as a masked woman leads them out. A few administrators and teachers are shouting at masked men using axes to chop open locked doors.

TempSchool is overrun! My hands tremble opening my locker for my coat.

I arrive home to see Peggy and Mr. Davis crying together on the couch.

"What a goddamn disaster," I rage walking in. "Hey. You two okay?" I ask.

"Yeah. Mostly," Mr. Davis says a bit shakily. "I've known for a long time, a long time, that something was going to crack in this town. But I hoped it'd at least be better organized. None of this 'few weeks' crap he said, 'until we'd get something up and running'."

"How are we going to eat without TempMeals?" Peggy asks in halting sobs.

"Whoa." I join, sitting on the edge of a chair. "I didn't think about that. Shit. Food shelf?" I hesitantly ask.

"They've never reopened, after, after, um," Peggy timidly tests.

"—Oh, yeah," I plop heavily back, waving off the conversation none of us wanted.

"All we had were TempMeals," Mr. Davis' eyes go wide. "Jack went too far closing the school with everyone there. Reckless. Totally unsafe."

"Jack McHardy?" I ask.

"Yeah," he nods.

"Oh," I quietly say. "He's a friend of my Dad."

"We should've at least been told to buy more TempMeals," Mr. Davis continues.

"We've only four left," Peggy says. "I don't want to have to worry about things anymore… I just want to work and not be sad," she cries.

"A total screw-up," Mr. Davis says. "In the older class sections, we were already worried the TempInstitute might blacklist TempSchools in Illinois due to political instability. The Administrator was direct: 'Only states with the most favorable Temp Policies will receive TempSchools' continued investments.' He was warning us against supporting Senator Obama's Public Spaces Amendment. Look, I don't believe in temp politics, but what are we supposed to do until some 99% School opens and collects enough donations? Huh? Eat our shoes?" Mr. Davis blasts, "Who has money to even donate these days besides the rich? We've nothing. Nothing. Sorry, girls, we're really going to have to scrape through this one," he says, reaching for a tissue to blow his nose.

We? I lean back darkly in the chair thinking of Uncle Greg's hoard of cash and gold hidden in my room. *Or you?*

There's no way you're going to push me into my parents' fucking Altruism Trap. I'm not going to spend My time, My money, My life supporting someone else. No. I am me. You are you. I glare at the room. *You are nothing and I want to be something.*

There's no future here, I realize.

CHAPTER 17—HIDDEN LIABILITIES

Eddie. December 2022

We arrive late the next afternoon in San Antonio to broken locks on Jen's office door.

"Fuck, fuck. Fuck." Jen's video glasses stare down at the splintered chunks of wood of a kicked in door. She frantically runs to her desk to confirm all drawer latches are secure—she'd locked her desk before leaving. All staff is accounted for.

Jennifer collapses into her chair in highly agitated relief, cradling her head.

"Sorry, Jen," I say. "What a fucking irony that'd be—worry about your business model getting stolen, fly a thousand miles to investigate, only to have your neighbors discover five-thousand workers living in your desk because they broke a $10 lock?! How much would that suck?" I ask, clearing my throat. "People want to know how we're making all this money with only one office."

"Can it, Ed," she removes her glasses and rubs her temples. "I think they just stole my computer monitor," she sighs. "Probably wanted my laptop. Maybe I've been naive? God. What if something *really* happened when I was gone? Who?" She slams a fist on her desk. "A disgruntled, laid-off worker? Or the families of my so-called 'missing' workers? *Fuck.*" Panic enters her voice.

"—Uh? Wait. What? Jen, what 'family members'?" I ask.

"Ugh," she angrily says. The question hits a nerve. "Police call me for information."

"For what information?"

"Where my subordinates are," she says. "A fucking violation!"

"Wait. Jen." I ask. "How long's this been happening?" I probe what she clearly doesn't want to explore.

"Every month. They're on a special assignment and taken care of—which is totally true! God. Next round of contracts, I'm going to make employees sign a Do Not Contact Claus to clear this issue altogether. So annoying." She looks at the ceiling.

I feel increasingly upset. "Jen. You're not telling me things."

"*Eddie*, you didn't need to know," she says. "The *company* is family. I video-link the employee with the detectives or ex-family members or whoever, and provide bonuses if they perform *exactly* as I want. No one's asked about you," she harshly finishes. "I'm the only one who cares about you."

In one stab, I realize despite everything I do for Jen, she isn't including me in all her initiatives. The twist of the knife comes after all this time, no one's bothered to wonder where I am.

Is Jen really all I have?

"It's beyond clear I need better security," Jen says with a dark edge. "I'm never coming back here again." She opens her laptop and searches for moving companies. "The liability that someone could physically carry off a whole division, or torch my Operations Desk, already gave me nightmares. I feel *vulnerable* leaving so much human capital in my desk when I go home at night. You specks obviously need to move into my home office."

"Sure. Moving us into your home makes sense, for security." I warily nod, keeping my doubts quiet.

She's blurring the line between the company and herself even further?

"Yeah. Why should I waste *my* time commuting?" Jen paces the room. "Pisses me off that no matter how many weights I lift or miles I run, I'll never be strong enough. If someone could kick in that door, they could abduct me in the middle of the day."

"New project, Eddie." She suddenly shifts. "Research as much as you can on nanotech. I read that artificial blood cells can allow someone to hold their breath underwater for, like, *three hours* and be strong enough to outrun Olympians! *I want that.* Gather a report by morning. It's not okay to be weak. Too much is at stake." She unpacks her closet. "And look for nano tech on immunity. No cuts, disease, and germs for me either."

Yikes. Always 'more more,' I mutter. *This project makes me uncomfortable. Jen's already intensely strong.* My head spins. *And how expensive is this shit going to be?* Out of the corner of my eye, I notice Jen reach in the closet to grab my box. "Oh, shit. The old management team!" I say to myself, as I peer through Jen's video feed into the box to see what happened to them. I see nothing as Jen casually plops it on her desk and throws in her files and books.

Did they escape? Did they eat each other? Did they die of thirst? I spend a whole fifteen minutes, with my thumb over the unmute button, wondering what I should ask Jen. I examine the implications of each question and the implications of each of her possible answers.

No. I don't want to know. I bury the issue. *I just want to do good and work hard.* Jen packs her office as I research.

Simply incredible. I had no idea Abriams Theory revolutionized nano-production so much. *Of course, it would. Components can be built large, then shrunk down.* Several companies stand as leaders: MicroMenace, NanoLogistics, and EverLast.

MicroMenace had the artificial blood cells Jen mentioned, in addition to a product they call *Guardian*, an improved and programmable auto-immune system.

NanoLogistics had a different approach, creating a parallel logistics system that transfers resources, cells, and repairs from one part of the body to the next.

EverLast didn't have any products ready, but had early development for a protein called p16 that manually purges old, dying, and inefficient 'senescent' cells twice a week. A simple process that extends average lifespan by at least a quarter. For only $100 a week! *Damn, wish I could afford that.*

The only thing holding back these amazing techs is the Southern U.S. Food and Drug Administration.

How come we free the economy from this red tape and it keeps crawling back? I wonder. *You'd think the free market would eliminate toxic and shitty food on its own? No one wants to eat crap!*

I stand and walk through my small capsule suppository to stretch my legs. *Yet the regulatory agency keeps springing to life after rampant abuse of pharmaceutical and food suppliers who willingly lied to those too dumb to do their own food quality testing. The pending round of appeals in a Federal court in Atlanta ought to eliminate the Southern U.S. FDA for good. That's great.* I smile, already hearing Jen's pissed off rant about 'government regulations' as I sit and continue typing the report for her. She'll want to know that regulations won't be a problem. She can do whatever she likes with nanotech without oversight.

At 11:14 p.m. my monitor suddenly blinks on to display a spectacular living room from Jen's laptop and video glasses cameras.

"Edd-dyyy?" her voice explodes through my speakers. She's laying on a couch.

"Wow, is that your place?" I ask.

Next to her are several piles of books and reports.

"Yes. How arrre youuu?" she asks. The two wine bottles on the coffee table suggest she's rather drunk. "How's it goin', man? You're, like, the onnnly guy I can talk to."

"Ha, yeah?"

Hurray! I pump my fist in victory.

"How ya doin', man?" she grins.

"I'm rocking this report. Half done, I think."

"Super. Cheers to Eddieee!" An exuberant wine glass half blocks the room and zooms towards Jen's face. The video view tilts to reveal extravagant moldings carved near the ceiling. "I really, *really* want to say how realllly grrreeat you are. Ed. I'm sorry you think, like, I might be, like, a huge bitch or something—*I'm not.* Really, I'm not," she says.

"Oh?" *Shit. She must be drunk.* I extinguish the thrill in my heart. "No. Jen, you're the smartest and coolest women I've ever met," I say, trying to be supportive. "The biggest ass-kicker ever."

I'm terrified enough of her when she's sober. I've zero intention of pissing her off in who knows what-volatile-drunken state.

"Aww, *really?* Hey… we're buds. Right?" she slurs.

"Yeah. Of course, we're buds, Jen. Great buds," I confirm with concerned amusement.

"Even, after, yesterday? You were really mad at me," she stifles a sniff and dabbers her eyes.

She been crying? Holy crap, this could be severe.

"Ah, Jen. I was *really* surprised," I struggle. "Really surprised. I've never been, uh, consumed by a girl before. *Like, three ways* in one day," I admit. "Um, I'm still shoved up your ass, actually."

"Ha, yeah. New Things Eddie!" she cheers with another sip, nearly falling off the couch as she does. "Whoa. Crap. Hey, did I scare you?" she asks.

I risk the truth, "At first. I get nervous when I don't know what you're doing with me," I say, my worry deepening. "You have a *huge* impact on my life."

"Eddie, I want you safe. I want you in me forrrever."

My heart plummets. *What? Will I never escape Jen's company?*

"I want everyone together and happsy," she says. "I never *want* to scare you—it's just, like, my fun and stuff. You know that? I felt soooo incredible sitting on the couch, working, 'membering you inside me. I thought about yesterday, how mad you were, and I got scared you hated me and didn't like me. And I was like 'but we're so close!' Like right here." She pats her belly, "I should talk with him. So I did!"

"That's great, Jen. I'm glad you did," I slowly nod, a tension tingling through my chest. "Jen, could you put me someplace safe tonight? I worry you might forget me—and I'll disappear down the drain in the night. How sad would that be?"

Tonight I'll break for it and run.

"Oooh no, that would be sooo sad. Nooo, I don't want you gone. Ed, you'rrre mine. Mine. Mine," she says. "Oh. The room is moving. Stop it room! Damnnn winnne… Ugh. Water break!" Jen lurches and wobbles through the massive living room into a spectacular kitchen. Copper pots hang around *two* incredibly fancy stoves. Her fingers tickle an extraordinary and vast Italian marble countertop.

I count three sinks. *Three fucking sinks.*

Jen grabs a cup and slowly leans across the counter to the nearest faucet in deliberate focus. She slams two tall glasses of water like a champ. As her system expands and readjust to the sudden load, her guts groan like a herd of hippopotamus suddenly discovering a new lake, screaming in pleasure.

"Ugh," she slowly grunts, standing still with her hands on the counter. Then she rapidly turns back into the sink to puke an extraordinary amount of pink and red fluid. The roar is angry and massive as the video glasses capture each heave in splashing high definition glory.

I look away as best I can, grossed out as Jen's deep insides rise and churn angrily around me. Yet, slowly begin to see that I can't turn off the reality directly outside the capsule.

Jen coughs and sputters. "Oy," she moans. "God, why do $1,000 bottles of wine taste so good? That's a month of your salary I puked up! Bye, bye! Too funny." She burps. "Oh. You'rre right, Eddie. Time to empty the other half too. Bathroom break!"

She stumbles, her hands guiding through the kitchen hallway to the bathroom.

"Ah. Jen, if you can. Feel free store me somewhere else tonight while you get better."

I can hide in the house. Outsmart the cleaners. Find freedom. I'd rather live alone as an ant than permanently locked in Jennifer's psycho chaos. The sight of that empty box and it's horrific mystery. Jen casually throwing her stuff on the corpses of the old management team haunts the edges of my mind.

"Eddie-Freddie." Jens stumbles into the bathroom looking at her gorgeous self in the mirror. "You're such a pain in my ass. Ha." She slaps her hips. "*But I like that.*" She sits on her throne, removes my capsule. "No peeking," she whispers, laying me in the sink.

I sit at the bottom of a porcelain bowl as terrible noises escape Jen. *There's no way I can climb these walls,* I frown with a hand to my chin.

"Ahh. But now I feel too empty!" Jen rises, frowning above the sink, adjusting her pants. "I don't like it."

Water gushes around the sink as she washes her hands and my capsule. "How about we go for a late-night snack?" She enters the kitchen and pours herself a glass of milk. "Hello, cookie," she laughs as she holds me up to her face. "Meet Jen's belly."

She lifts her t-shirt to shove my capsule repeatedly into the deep soft flesh of her tummy next to her silver and black belly ring. "Cookie—Jen's Belly is empty. Can you please make her happy again? *Please, please?* 'Okay, Belly.'" Jen pretends the capsule is talking with a mock cartoon voice. "'That's the whole point of being a Cookie. My reason to exist is to be inside a Belly. Thank you so much for giving my life meaning.' 'Of course, Cookie... *and thank you.*"

Jen flashes a grin as she lifts the capsule into her mouth.

I witness the brief line of light between her lips vanish as the rim of a glass fills my view. A torrent of whiten washes me away with an immense gulp.

With no escape plan to execute, I finish my research at 2:09 a.m., consumed within the belly of my passed-out psycho CEO.

CHAPTER 18—ARRIVAL

Jennifer. April 2013

I slap $643.67 in exact change on the O'Hare International Copa Airlines counter, fuming that the taxi from Wilmington took *three* hellish hours. Should've been only an hour!

Oh my god. Get the fuck out of my way you whining protesters! No way I was paying full price for that taxi. Fucker totally wasted my time not taking charge of the road and now I'm late. *Seriously. All of you: if I miss this flight because of your whining, I'm gonna eat your living hearts.*

This Copa Airlines lady looks slow. She better not be slow. I tap my fingers eagerly on the desk.

"I need a one-way flight out this mess to Santiago, Chile. Now. —Please?" I ask, remembering to be polite.

Passport? Check. Life in a suitcase? Check. Balls of steel? *Yes, ma'am, I got them all.*

Sixteen hours later I reek of grime, B.O., and the unrestrained thrill of freedom. *I don't need sleep. I have freedom—and it's dirty and stinky and mine.* The battered truck I negotiated from Santiago lurches through the foothills of the Andes. After an hour, we randomly halt at the gates of a long, dark driveway in the non-existing town of Pangue Curacaví, in the hills far west of the Santiago Metropolitan Region.

All I see is a gate? I check the paper in my pocket to ensure I have the right address. *This better be the place or I'm kicking Pedro in the nuts,* I chuckle, stepping out of the truck door to look for a bell or some way in. *At least I think his name's Pedro?* As I search, Pedro unloads my suitcase and bags and peels away, leaving me in a small cloud of dust.

"Wait!" I shout. "What the hell? Pedro." I pointlessly wave my arms. *Why doesn't Pedro want to see my uncle?*

I'm in the middle of nowhere. No lights, no other houses.

"This better be the right fucking place," I say to inky black stars.

My god, the stars!

I've never seen so many. Millions and millions of bright diamonds cut against the jagged hills and sprinkle across the biggest sky I've ever seen. *Beautiful.*

The chirp of crickets and bugs dawn in the darkness. A warm breeze wraps me like a hug. The air's so clean. *OMG. Is this how peace feels?* I laugh in dumb amazement. I laugh again, realizing this is first laugh I've enjoyed in months. My jaw and cheeks stretch like a cautious armadillo. I realize how wary I've become. How tired.

And now, so free.

A mosquito pricking my arm refocuses my appreciation. *Fucker,* I eagerly slap him to death. I awkwardly drag my baggage through the gate and along a winding dirt road.

Goddamn useless Pedro, I mutter, feeling residual anger at my abandoned ride. It's increasingly clear I'm not in for a short walk.

At least there's no snow, I cheer, smiling again at how warm the darkness feels.

I haul my dirty luggage for ten minutes through trees, past a hill, and into a wide savanna of grass. I stop in amazed wonder. *Jesus H. Christ, there's my uncle's house... my uncle's mansion!* A sprawling estate imposes glowing grace over a well-manicured garden hillside. Long warm shadows from many windows ignite a sparkle of dew on the grass. I collect my shock to move hurriedly forward, tears already stinging the edge of my eyes. *This is real, this is real*, I chant at the pounding of my heart. I yank Greg's envelope out of my pocket, recklessly bang my suitcase up the steps and pound my fist on his door as hard I can. The door opens.

"Hello?" An annoyed silhouette of a large man eventually answers.

Fully sobbing, all I can do is hold up my tattered envelope.

"Jen? Oh my god! Jen, I'm so sorry!" The shadow steps into the porchlight as Uncle Greg wraps me in a hug. "I was in a corner of Bolivia. I didn't know until after Christmas. I didn't know. Oh my god, I wish I'd been there. Terrible. Just terrible," he cradles me. "I tried calling the house," his eyes water up. "No one at the bank could give any information," he says. "I'm so sorry. Oh my god, I'm glad you made it. Amalia! Juan! Ven aqui. Lleva la maleta de mi sobrina al cuarto y. Prepararle un baño caliente!" he shouts in Spanish.

Two sleepy servants hurry to grab my things and pull them up stairs.

"Are you okay?" he asks with honest eyes. "Let's grab a snack?" He leads me into the massive house.

"Yeah," I sniff with a meek nod.

Uncle Greg brings me into his kitchen.

"How come you never answered my calls?" I ask.

His brow furrows tight, "Calls? Jen, what calls?"

I point to the envelope, "I tried calling you for months."

He looks at his writing from last summer, an eon ago, and his hand rockets to his mouth. "Oh, God. Crap, I changed numbers last fall. I'm so sorry!" He gives me another hug. "Jeez. Jen, once a few projects wrapped up, I was totally going to fly and look for you. I've been crazy busy," he moves to pour me a tall cup of juice. "A *lot's* happening these days. It's insane what's going on. Total insanity," he shakes his head with a huge grin. "Is grape juice okay?" he hands the glass.

"Sure, thanks," I nod. "This is a beautiful house," I marvel, looking at several copper pans hanging from the wall.

"Yeah," Greg smiles. "Ben and I worked hard. He's with family this week. The opportunities out there are insane, Jen. Just insane. The market is crazy; whole sectors of the economy are up for grabs. Mr. Jacobson, sorry, my boss," he laughs. "Just a couple weeks ago, placed a $5 million low-ball bid for Dry Tortugas National Park—as a joke. He won!" Greg spreads his arms wide. "Jen. *He won.* Didn't even give a shit. Seven islands, one hundred square miles of reefs, and the most massive coastal fortress in the Western Hemisphere, Fort Jefferson. Everyone I know has barely slept the past few months."

My nerves settle after a few sips of juice. I reach for a nearby paper towel and blow my nose.

"The U.S. Federal Government *used* to own mineral rights for 2.5 billion acres of land and sea. More than the surface area of Canada! The oil and gas resources alone *were* worth $128 trillion. They've been idling for decades. Until last month, when they sold for a fire sale discount. Now the private market can *finally* put them to good use and spread that wealth around, to you, to me; to everyone…"

We sit quietly for a second as Greg's giddy adrenaline sobers up. I remain still, looking at the floor. He rubs his knees nervously.

"Hey. Yeah. So, um, it's been super busy. ...How's Illinois?" he asks. "What's, um, what's it been up there? How've you been?" He picks sheepishly at his hands.

"Bad," I frown at my empty cup. "Poor people ruined *everything*. Chopped up all our trees. We couldn't go to the store without being groped by the police because of shoplifting," I raise my eyes to his. "The churches gave too much, we all cared too much. We were Mom's beacon of hope and we attracted every hopeless insect in the region to us." A darkness surges within me. "They ate us alive. Like locusts. Took *everything*," I sneer. "Mom and Dad kept giving and giving but *they* took and took—and took. There was no miracle. No god. No happy light. Just, stupid death."

We stare at each other. Uncle Greg doesn't know what to say. His lip quivers. "Holy hell. Oh, Jen..." he releases a long sigh. "I'm so sorry. I'm happy you're here. Look—well—we made life too easy for slackers. Their 'social safety net' was a hammock, lulling people into dependency. When people lose incentives to make the most of their lives, they get *mad* when they're told to work. Sadly, for most, violence is the easiest answer." He makes a sour face. "That's why I have these gates and walls. Dependence on others is basically evil. *Only your independence is good, Jen.* Independence proves you're willing to do your own work. Oh," he slaps his knee, "I think Amalia has a warm bath ready for you. Juan has your things in your new room." He excitedly grabs my hand. "We can talk in the morning. Settle in. You must be exhausted."

"Yeah. Sure." *I love this man. He's strong. He cares. He smells like leather. He smells like freedom.*

I awake in a huge soft bed. *A queen size bed,* I smirk, realizing where I am. Who I am. A peaceful morning breeze floats in my room through billowing window drapes. Outside, birds chirp freely amongst conversational Spanish and the laughter of children. I see my room has a beautiful white timbered ceiling and wide soft green walls. A large wooden desk sprawls next to an elegant double-door closet.

"Am I in heaven?" I wonder. "Yeah, probably." Is my own divine answer. Smelling breakfast, I pleasantly stumble downstairs a touch sleepy.

"Hola. Señorita." A warm voice eagerly welcomes me to an extravagant breakfast spread of pineapple, eggs, pancakes, and a sizable tower of toast and jam.

This smiley guy is Juan? The house servant who carried my luggage up last night? I sit down and shove breakfast directly into my face. "Thanks." I cheer through a mouthful of deliciousness.

Juan eagerly offers me another caramel roll.

This guy's so pleased to serve me! Good. I munch his work down and eagerly devour half an elegantly carved pineapple, marveling at the effort these people did to serve me.

A shame Peggy didn't understand that. I wonder if she's still dragging out her pointless life? When we still talked, briefly, sometime last week I think Peggy had lost another tooth from her lack of food. *At least she finally lost weight,* I smirk. *No way in hell I was sharing a protein bar from my stash. If Mr. Davis had found my hoard of Uncle Greg's money, he'd have taken it all and I'd never have flown to Chile to wake up like a Queen today!* I eat more pineapple.

I need to be the predator; not the shepherd. A wolf stuffed full of the lives of others. Yum, yum, yum, I eat.

After breakfast, I change out of pajamas so Uncle Greg can tour me through our beautiful estate. He meets me at the bottom of the large wide staircase.

"Much of our design," he points as we walk down the hall, "follows the old Galloway House in Savannah down the road where your mother and I grew up." He chuckles, "Ben and I loved the idea of a 'modern old south.' Bringing that old comfortable lifestyle 4,500 miles away. But, I also love rural Europe and that old-world charm. We'll see that later." He escorts me through another room.

So many rooms! I'll get lost without Greg. Nine bedrooms. Five bathrooms. A massive library with old maps, books, and a large set of reading chairs next to a huge fireplace. *Amazing. Amazing. Amazing.*

Greg and I walk through the mists of a greenhouse with tropical fruits, plants, and birds. Outside, he shows his solar panels and geothermal cooling pond that's *also* a natural swimming hole with a tire swing.

"When the boys finish working the ranch," he says, "they often take a swim at 3:00 p.m." He winks, "Just sayin."

Mmm, I bite my lip, wondering how many boys I could wrap around my finger. *That'll be fun.*

We walk a forested path of grass under the canopy of huge trees.

"And here's the garden that rules our little world," Uncle Greg admires as we approach a vast vegetable garden. "85% of what we eat comes from this ranch. The chickens, beef, corn are over there," he points behind the house. "And here," he highlights our new surroundings, "the lettuce, tomatoes, carrots, and most produce we need. Butter, sugar, cheese we buy in the store—it's too expensive to do that ourselves," he shrugs. "But we could." He adds, "I like to be independent, but only to the point it makes sense. When the government decides to control the food chain, I want to be ready to fight back or at least hold my own."

I enjoy the hot sun searing the skin of my neck. "It's beautiful. Mom loved gardening too," I add sadly.

Greg's face pains for a second. "And great lessons here." Greg continues, stepping around his dead sister. "A gardener shouldn't tell a tomato to be a cucumber, or a pineapple to be a carrot. Right? Nature wants to grow on its own; just like our democracy and free enterprise." He kneels into the dirt next to a tomato. "If you *tie* a plant to a stake, *because* of that outside support, it won't grow as tall or strong than letting it grow freely in the wind!" He brushes some dirt into the breeze. "My goal in life, and business, is a lot like this garden: pull the weeds of government at the root. No regulation choking natural growth. No minimum-wage laws over-supporting what conditions will nurture on its own. Let the strong be strong, and let the weak wither and learn on their own."

"Totally. How'd you get so into politics?" I ask. "You bring it up all the time. I remember last summer on the patio with my Dad," I say and feel sad again.

"Well. You know Mr. Jacobson, my boss, is the uncle-in-law of President Choke?"

"No," I frown.

"Yup," Greg smirks. "Politics is shop talk I've *had* to pick up. Always been an interest. Work practically makes it a requirement. You're young; I want you to learn how the *real* world works. If I had these lessons at your age? Man…" He dreams into the hot sun. "I would *be* Mr. Jacobson, rather than work for him.

But, hey, life's great. Come on." He waves me forward. "I wanna show you something."

We round a corner of his vast vegetable garden to see an incredible old stone building next to a romantic stream cluttered with wildflowers. We appreciate what is obviously Uncle Greg's favorite part of his estate that looks ripped from a romantic painting.

"Best for last. My tavern," Greg approves as we walk into a cool, dark drinking hall. "It's modeled, stone-by-stone, from a medieval tavern in Albergo Diffuso, Italy. The arches in the basement. The planks in the guestrooms upstairs." He stands in awe with his hands proudly on his hips. "All match their historic counterpart. The timber frames, the thousands of candles, the thatch roof too. Even the old barrels of beer and wine. All accurate. True luxury, Jen," he suddenly turns to me, "is the total control of reality. Those villas in Europe—my god, they're so unbelievably charming. I wanted to mix that charm with a bit of home." He places a hand longingly along the door frame with marvelous nostalgia. "I wanted a place I could relax and have things exactly as I envision. Even if other people think it's just a dumb fantasy. To hell with them," he smiles, wrapping an arm around me for a side hug. "Who doesn't want an opportunity to be a King or a Princess for a day?"

"Totally," I genuinely return.

"My place is real enough for me. Had some grand parties tucked away from the media. Once," he laughs, "we had a full-on medieval festival." He points to the cobblestone area outside, "Tents and streamers. All of Mr. Jacobson's direct staff and their families came. Tried to make the feudal era as real as we could and dressed up like Camelot. Even asked the catering and cleaners to dress as serfs—paid them an extra $20 each, and they agreed!" he laughs. "Amazing, what you can get people to do by throwing money at them." He grins, "They'll ignore their dignity and their rights for a chance to crawl into your wallet." He taps his pocket, "Mr. Jacobson was obviously the king. I was just a lower duke. Ha. Oh, that's right," he remembers with a hand to his chin. "Even Jerry Choke was here. How did I forget him?"

"Wait, the president?" I stammer.

"Yeah. He was a musician at the time. Before he got into politics. A fine performer. Still is, in some ways…" Uncle Greg snickers, waving away any questions. "Anyway" He leads me down the dirt path to look at the stream as he explains a native plant restoration project.

I half-listen, in awe that such a powerful person was here, serving such a lowly position. *'Just a musician'? From a performer to President of the United States? Wow!* The range of what's possible blows my mind.

We continue, walking to the servants' village. Most of the staff actually live full-time on the estate in cute, simple houses. Greg says many of the children were born here. The old ones die here. We see a communal kitchen area where some women wash pots and pans next to a large cooking hearth of boiling stew. The village is so happy to see us! They stand, smile, and shout 'Buenos días!' as we pass.

I feel like royalty.

Two women laugh together as they draw water from a well. An old grizzled man repairs a wooden cart using a manual lathe and sends us a toothless grin. *These people are happy.* I feel like I've walked back in time. The rest of the world could disappear and everything here would be unchanged in its perfection. *Imagine if the entire world could be this beautiful? This happy.* I dream as we return to the house.

Uncle Greg shows me his office, but then excuses himself after quickly checking his calendar and becoming worried about a few phone calls.

His office door shuts behind me and I stand in a suddenly empty hallway. I feel as if my entire life has stopped with the lock of Greg's door. I feel like a used candy wrapper. Thin. Disposable.

I'm alone.

I peek through the glass at his clock: it's only 9:23 a.m.! The whole day, the whole week, the rest of my new life lay before me, empty. *And he's leaving me?* Anxiety acid drips down my veins as the panic of being alone hits me heavier than a truck. I never want to be alone. *No, no, no. Why is he rejecting me?*

I move away from Greg's office, hating the idea of him seeing me break down. *How is his work more important than me? No way whatever he's doing is worth more than me.* I feel needy and stupid. My chest hurts. *Ugh. Am I really this weak? Can I really not light my own way in life without the reflected attention of someone else?*

"Why do you think you're alone?" Leopold II simply asks from a large stuffed chair in the library down the hall. He closes his book with a healthy snap and gently looks at me.

I meekly walk the long hall to sit in the chair opposite him.

"Jennifer," he leans forward. "This house will turn into a *museum* simply because *you've* lived here," he advises. "Tourists will queue up from all over the world. The children of Greg's servants will boast to their friends and relatives how their parents served a historical figure. You, Jennifer. You." He points a long wise finger at me. "And here you are moping that you're 'so alone'?" He shakes his head in disappointment, "You need to look to the future, Jen. See the artifacts, the placards, and the tour guides walking down these halls—and you'll never be alone."

"Yes, I'll try." I turn my head to peer honestly at the future ghosts of a world yet to come. They look at my large oil paint portraits. They hush at the sight of my comb with strands of my hair behind a velvet rope. *Such inspiration.* "How easy I forget," I wipe a tear from my eye. "Thank you for reminding me." I settle my breath, before asking him as simply as any teenage crush can, "Will you dance with me?"

We dance.

After lunch and a tough morning of thought, I agree it's time to relax. I open the balcony door outside my room with a five-month old *National Geographic*. My bare feet burn as I step on the sunlit parts of the tile floor and drag a white wicker chair to the balcony shade. After browsing a few pages, I shift and shift, unable to settle. *Too antsy to read,* I sigh disappointedly, throwing the magazine on the balcony table, and stand at the railing to overlook our estate.

I feel a heady dose of power looking over the world from the spire of my fantasy book castle. Below, I see a fountain and the mosaics on the driveway as servant kids play kick ball. I watch the kinetic joy of the boys' little bodies. A quilt pattern of fields stretches past the yard towards large green mountains. To the right, pastures with black dots of meandering cattle roam, impervious to the dry summer heat, as men on horseback slowly weave through them.

Mmmm, I wonder what those rough cowboy hands can do. I close my eyes and imagine mixing them with my body.

I glance left to see an old woman on her knees in the vegetable garden, pulling out weaklings. *Yes. Let me do that! I forgot we can do that anytime down here. How great is Chile?* I change out of my dress into basic clothes and walk downstairs into the hot afternoon sun.

The old lady speaks smiling Spanish at me, her hands waving me away, suggesting I should shoo. I shrug, pointing to my ear that I can't understand a damn word she says. She nods, hobbles up, and hurries away. I'm left in peace to get my hands filthy in the destruction of lesser beings.

I wish Dad had taught me Spanish. Another of his failings, I sigh. *I wonder if the name 'Díaz' embarrassed him in a small white town? So many questions I'll never ask.*

The sun's heat reddens my shoulders. *I'm going to get sunburnt. Oh, I can tan! I wonder if my swimsuit even fits? Probably not,* I smirk, looking down my shirt at my awesome tits. *I'm fucking armed.* The more my body develops, the stronger I feel.

The old garden lady awkwardly returns with Amalia, the other house servant.

"Miss?" Amalia meekly asks in her broken English. "No need to do this. We do this," she smiles, pointing to my little shovel.

"That's okay. I like gardening, even if it's dirty," I proudly hold up my messy fingers. *I control what lives and dies, woman.* I playfully demean her ignorance.

"Okay," she slightly frets. "Do you need lemonade?"

"Oh my god, yes." I beam up at her, wiping a small trickle of sweat from my forehead with the clean back of my wrist.

After an hour, my back starts to hurt and I tire of this old lady's frosty glares. "I'm not taking your job, lady. I'm way better than this," I pointlessly assure her. *Prune.* I lean back to arch and stretch my spine. *Emperor Leopold II should massage my neck,* I dream, rubbing it alone. *Maybe that will be a line to get the cowboys' hands on me.*

"Hola, chica bonita," a charming tenor floats across a row of green beans.

I look to see the brilliant beaming smile of a middle-aged man in clean, bright yellow shorts and a tight orange shirt striding towards me.

"Uncle Ben?" I squint, sensing a vague resemblance to a few family photos.

"Yes, bring it in, girl," he approaches, demanding a hug. "Honey, my god. You're a woman now! Amazing. Gorgeous. Welcome. Sorry, I didn't know you were coming," he sincerely squints at me. "I was in Santiago and came once I heard. I wish I'd known, I'd have picked you up at the airport myself. Has Greggie given you the tour?"

"Yeah. I found my way here," I shrug. "It's okay."

"I'm so happy you're part of the family now! I have no one to gossip with," he whispers. "And baby, the sunlight is going to do wonders for that pale skin of yours." He laughs, touching my arm. "I thought your father was Mexican?"

I grin and roll my eyes at him. "Yeah…though everyone says I'm a lot like my Mom. —Was like," I correct, not knowing what else to say. I tense my lips demanding they not embarrass me.

I miss my dad. I miss my mom.

"Oh, baby. I'm sorry," Uncle Ben cringes slightly. "That was crass of me. Here's another hug." He excitedly wraps me again. "Welcome home, baby. Welcome home," he soothes. "Hey," he looks at me seriously. "Have you ever had a calimocho? Vino cola? Do you like wine cocktails?"

"Um, no. Never had one," I smirk shyly, feeling like a dumb kid.

"Oh. Really? Little Sister, let's break your cherry. Come on, come on," he eagerly grabs my arm. "Let's clean you up and talk life. And please. You *must* tell me what people are wearing in Chicago."

We walk inside and do just that.

On the morning of my fourth day, I yawn and stretch out of bed, feeling happy. Refreshed.

I actually feel like me, I grin. Under the door I see an envelope.

Who's obsessed with me today? I smile, skipping over and thinking about the ranch boys. *Maybe Raul? Maybe Jose?* I excitedly open my love note; yet, instead read an itemized bill for the week.

Breakfast, laundry, bath water, and three nights come to a bold total at the bottom of the page: $1,103.65!

CHAPTER 19—GARDEN INSTALL

Eddie. May 2023

I awake at 5:30 a.m., like most days, to peddle my exercise bike. I obviously don't get out much. I ignore the gurgling around me and the reasons why. Peddling recharges me and the batteries that power my capsule. *I'm so grateful Jen enjoys energy efficient lights and computers or I'd be here all day rather my typical hour and a half!* I towel my forehead as I appreciate Jen's self-sufficient mindset. *She doesn't want to depend on outside sources of power when she can Jen-o-rate it herself,* I chuckle, remembering back to our first days.

 God, I even miss CoffeeFlave™, I sadly realize.

 I feel comfortable with my place in Jen's organization, with the cycle of her patterns, with my responsibilities. *I was covered in shit at work before. Who cares if I'm covered in it now? Jen's crap isn't all that bad, considering.*

 I *could* sit in jail with nothing to do and no a job at all, watching my prison debts add and add each day. I *could* fall into the false promise of progressive economics like the assholes up North. Sure, GDP growth in the Northern U.S.A. is out-pacing the South economically 5:1, *but that's true for all ponzi schemes!* I *could* spend years hunting crumbs on Jen's dining room floor, running in terror from getting absently stepped on or vacuumed away, but I've never gotten the chance. *Oh well.*

 Live the best life I can, all considering. Focusing on the positive parts of my week helps. I'm a productive member of society, serving a greater purpose. And there's certainly meaning in the selflessness of teamwork! I enjoy mentoring staff with the latest management gems I read in the TempScience books. *I gave Sarah Peterson a 0.5% raise for her truly great work last quarter; she gave 40% more effort than her peers, and deserved a 40% raise to match, but Jen has salaries on lockdown and that 0.5% scrap alone was a herculean effort—so worth it,* I smile.

 Another positive to boost: *We're the only Temp service to actively encourage equal salaries between men and women! I bet with our female CEO, we might be the most forward-thinking Temp service in the nation?* I'd suggest a press release if Jen didn't regularly refuse all media involvement. *Oh well, whatever.*

I've tried my best to let go. Accept Jen's directions. Half the day I don't even know where my capsule is. *Why does it matter? It doesn't really change anything.* I respond to her emails. I make my phone calls. I do my work. *Funny that most of the time I don't even notice now when the CEO fucks me, without warning or a conversation.* I take a drink from my water bottle as the energy meter nears 93%.

Considering the uncertain world, especially these days, Jen's concern for control really does make sense. Even if odd to me, I respect that Jen values control, privacy, and self-sufficiency. Our laissez faire free market is the most powerful force in human history, providing great rewards and riches to the wise and cunning, and dealing severe punishments to the lazy and weak. *Jen needs to be smart, strong, and prepared for whatever comes next.*

Near the end of my workout, Jen's monitor brightens to life.

"Wake up, Eddie. It's here!" she beams. "Oh my… *You're* a hot mess. Ooh la la," she teases, noticing I'm already awake. "You always exercise at this time?"

I blush. "Morning, Jen. Yeah. Have to recharge for the day."

"Hm… Yum. I'll have to spy on you more often," she winks. "Hey, my servers are here." She tilts her camera to three large crates in her home office.

"Servers? Oh, wow, the new System? Didn't we order that months ago?"

"Yep. Yep. I added some customizations. I've had, ah, special contractors add a power source. Anyway," she looks cutely at the screen. "I need you to migrate my old data to the new System. Then, grab a team to check and make sure all the processes transfer. Then, I'll need your help *physically* installing it," she grins. "I emailed new sets of access credentials."

"Alright, sure," I nod. "I'll get the managers to test it with me over the next few weeks. It'll be a *lot* of data." I say in confident-man-tone, wiping myself down with a small towel. Feeling buff.

"Thanks, Tiger. Grr," Jen grins. "I might need you to charge your bod—I mean your pod—again this afternoon. Oops, did I say that out loud?" she winks.

"Ha. Anytime, Jen," I boast.

Damn, she's really digging me! What an energizing start to the day. When she's in a positive mood I feel infected with motivation.

I hit my mini-shower; focusing how nice it is to have easy access to warm recycled water rather getting nickel-and-dimed at the old truck stop pay showers. *That place was the true shithole,* I muse. *This capsule isn't too bad,* I admit with a smile.

I put on a dress shirt and tie and call an early video meeting with the fifty middle-managers spread through the drawers to provide updates.

"Please explore the local differences between the two Systems in your respective areas by next Friday. Any questions?" I finish with a slight cringe.

All meetings are recorded. Jen expects employees to criticize each other continually, pressing for errors, all under Jen's gaze through the System.

"I'm impressed a cutting-edge System install is actually happening," Sarah Peterson offers. "I'll admit I was feeling cynical about TempGrace's ability to *actually* keep up with technological trends. 'All show and no go' has been my worry."

I nod at her complaint. "I promise Jen's committed to forging *beyond* the technological cutting edges," I reassure. "Some of my research for her would blow your mind. If I could tell," I smile.

The most interesting research project she's charged me with is on Superorganisms.

Jen asked one night, "Eddie. Our bodies are full of microorganisms: they make up 90% of our cells! Did you know that?"

"No."

"'Humans aren't unitary individuals but superorganisms, huge numbers of different human and non-human individuals struggle inside us for control,'" she reads, and then looks at me. "I'm not 'just me'. I'm a walking, talking community. An entire ecosystem lives within my body."

"Well. I guess I'm there too?" I nodded to the surrounding contents of her stomach.

"Mmmm, totally," she darkly smiles, and reads again. "'You could look like one person, but have the cells of *another person* inside you. Effectively, you have always been more than one person. A superorganism.' Eddie!" she leans with giddiness to the camera. "I want to not *just* be a superorganism. I want to be a SuperCivilization."

"Okay, sure, whatever you want," I say. *This at least sounds like an interesting project to read about.*

The readings hit home for me. I've felt like Jen's lost little twin, swimming through her, ignored and alone. That *'consumed twins and microbes can influence their superorganism,'* was inspiring. *Sure, my role is subordinated for now. In time, Jen will grow bigger and bigger, and I'll grow with her. Maybe I can improve her mood? Nudge decisions for the better?*

As I close the System Install meeting, an IM from Jen pops on my screen: "Actually. I know you said 'weeks' testing the data, I want it done this Monday. Thx."

Are you shitting me!? My eyes pop wide at Jen's unreasonable demand. I pretend to listen to Tad's testing action plan as my nerves and rage swirl.

Suddenly, I feel the world shift as I fall out of my chair and natural light shines bright through my capsule windows. *Oh, she shit me out again. Goddamnit, why now?* I focus as best I can to maintain the composure of the meeting.

"Is that natural light?" Tad interrupts himself to ask with envy, seeing my video from his screen. "Where are you? When can *we* get some?"

The rest of the team eagerly agrees as the meeting tips sideways.

Fuck, I readjust and climb into my seat. "Honestly, I don't know where I am now." Which is partly true. I could be in the sink. The bathtub. Or swirling down the drain for all I know. I certainly don't want them to know how deep up Jen's ass I've been the past few months. That's too awkward for any of us to acknowledge.

"I'll ask about more natural lighting. Seems like a reasonable request," I nod. "I know productivity and mental health is always better—" suddenly my capsule windows fall dark, "—when workers have natural light," I point disappointedly to the ceiling as my artificial lights flicker automatically on, "but not even I control these things."

My capsule starts rocking back, and forth. Back, and forth. Back, and forth, and forth with increasing aggression.

I can barely stay in my chair as I grip my desk tight. The violence of the motions increases. *She's actually fucking me while*

I'm on this call? Jesus Christ. "So. I just got an update." I acknowledge my computer. "I know I said we have weeks. Jen now wants our tests done by Monday."

Groans rise all around. Tad throws up his hands and suggests impossibility.

I tumble to the ceiling as gravity inverts and shudders.

"Ed… Where *is* your office?" Sarah Peterson probes again.

"That's all for today. Make those revisions. Bye." I verbally cut the meeting short from the ceiling, as my office violently twists and contorts. One by one, the video feeds darken in wary disappointment.

I structure our summary report after Jen finishes fucking me.

Test results float in through the next two days. Most of them positive. Jen added customizations that I nor anybody else understand, but over all, our compressed agenda went well.

I tell Jen the good news Monday afternoon, and she playfully demands I exercise for her.

"That was so perfect," she beams at my finished effort.

She was excited—telling me to peddle faster, longer, harder—that I wonder if making me work hard turns her on? *She's so odd.*

I'm happy she's in a good mood, considering how little attention she's given me the past few weeks. I've had no idea what she's been working on. Her total non-response to my reports has hurt my feelings. *Why the hell am I doing all this work if you don't even read it? Nanobots? Haven't heard a word about all that work. Whatever.*

Jen interrupts my thoughts, "Let's officially install the servers tomorrow. Have the managers fix those last problems overnight, and we should be good to launch. Rest up, Eddie. Save your strength because I'm planning an exciting day. Been looking forward to this for *years*," Jen chirps happily.

Her monitors blink off. "Huh? How could anyone be excited for a server installation?" I mutter.

I enjoy my favorite protein bar for dinner. Since none of us were allowed on the open Internet, I sit on my pull-out couch to read an old-fashioned book, waiting on the last-minute data problems. *I'm so happy we're almost done. Getting this monkey off my back and focusing on something else will be great.*

I eye a chart near my desk that marks my saving progress towards buying a clarinet. I've redrawn it three times, especially after Jen said all employee salaries would phase from cash into purchasing company Business Units preparing for our IPO. *Oh-well, whatever. I just wish it wasn't so hard to keep track of the BU/cash exchange rate.*

Tad looks a haggard on the video screen after his call wakes me in the middle of the night. We address his issues by morning, and by dawn the new System tests well.

I dream I'm on a tire swing. I'm two feet tall, a child free to play in summer. My mother is Jen and she loves me. She pushes me back and forth. Then I'm falling out of bed.

What the hell kinda of a nightmare was that? I worry.

I notice my capsule is dramatically swaying. I see Jen's monitor is on, but she's not at her desk. *Where are we going?* I turn on lights and see only tightly pressed palm flesh through the walls. *Thank god I'm finally out of her ass.*

I find my headset. Groggily, I ask, "Jen, where are we going? What time is it?"

"Morning sunshine! You totally slept through my wakeup call. I saw how much work you all did last night and gave the staff a personal day. It's 10 a.m. You and I are going someplace special."

Jen's fingers open, blasting my dim view into a wall of light.

"Last fall I bought a private park near my house to relax. I thought we could visit and do some fun work," she continues.

My eyes slowly adjust to the green grass and a beautifully manicured garden. Trees and flowers are smartly arranged around a patio.

"Jen. This is beautiful!" I stammer at lush glimpses between the shift of Jen's gait. "Nature is such a privilege these days!"

"Yup. Hard work pays off, Eddie. Don't you forget. The first time I came to TempGrace, three years ago, I walked by this park and knew I wanted these acres all to myself, so I bought out the prior owners."

"Wait. You *bought* this three years ago?" *Holy crap! How much money does Jen have? How could she spend millions of dollars on a park before we even met?*

"Yeah," she acknowledges. "The grounds crew waters. Keeps the riffraff out. The whole world deserves to be a paradise exactly like mine."

"Wow," I stammer in a trance. "So much green." *This must cost thousands of dollars a day to water. I haven't seen this much nature in Texas since I was kid! Before the old public parks were outlawed and auctioned in President Choke's Privatization Act.*

Intensely cool.

"How big?" I wonder.

"Only six hundred acres. But with a nice swimming pool, three patios, and two miles of walking trails through the trees. A perfect place to plan and think business. And a nice write-off!" her voice grins.

I'm become overwhelmed with the fantasy of Jen normalizing me. We'd splash each other in the pool. Sunbathe on the patio, cheers our cocktails to the beauty of life. She would need a back rub. *I was good at those once; my hands would remember.* My heart beats fast.

"So, what shall we do?" I jokingly suggest. "I forgot my swimsuit."

"Ha, Eddie. You won't need one of those. I want us to install the new server!"

"Oh," I deflate and my shoulders hunch. "Yeah, sure."

Jen walks towards a set of reclining patio chairs overlooking a large garden pond.

"But, I want to do it while I sunbathe!" she teases.

I'm confused as the capsule whips to settle on a small table next to a reclining chair, now filled with a goddess sitting in a sundress.

"Come join, Ed! The weather's fine." She inches up the thin fabric of her sundress.

Never have I run out of a room as fast. I felt like those old cartoons where the bird is covered in dust and he runs off so quick only a cloud of his likeness remains. Only my cloud wasn't made of dust, but common sense and dignity. I hadn't seen the sun in five months, and here my only interest was seeing what was under Jen's dress with my own eyes.

Her dress passes over dark hair and sunglasses to reveal a bright smile and an amazing body restrained by two thin pieces of a bikini. Relaxing fully in the chair, she becomes a half-mile landscape, one that I need to turn my head 180 degrees to fully appreciate.

The sun, the fresh air, her massive basking presence; I feel overwhelmed, as if a breeze might lift me away. *This's Jen's private garden, a vast wilderness totally owned by a creature already inescapable to me.*

"What do you think?" she grins, tying her hair back.

"Gorgeous place, here. This patio," I fumble as the blood returns to my language centers.

"I know, right?" She beams, shifting towards me to dig into her bag below the table. With a twinkle in her enormous eye, she returns with a bottle of suntan lotion. "Hey, Ed. Who would you kill to have the chance to rub this lotion all... over... me?" she teases, nudging a fingertip of lotion at me.

"All of humanity," I gasp.

Jen slowly applies lotion to her neck, arms, breasts, belly, and each individual leg with seductive grace. I stand like an idiot unable to do anything to quench the thirst in my mouth or the bulge in my pants. She finishes and relaxes into the lounge chair with a sigh.

After a quiet few seconds, she turns to me.

"Eddie. Our new servers. I'd like them implanted in my belly button."

That breaks my reprieve. I need a full three seconds to fully catch what she said. "Wait. Your belly button? I don't understand."

"Yes. My navel needs to be the center of the corporate world. Your world. Our data goes where *I* go. I want it safe and inaccessible to anyone but *me*. And I want *you* to place it there. If I'm to sustain my vision, I need total independence and control of our System. Is this something you can do?" her big eyes ask.

How do you say no to a mountain, glistening in oil, wearing small patches of fabric?

"Um. Okay, sure, Jen. Whatever you need."

She's so fucking weird.

"Wonderful. Thanks for agreeing. This is beyond your contract, and I need your consent."

"Wait. Hmm?" I murmur in confusion.

Jen's facial expression cools to a stern crust. She delves into her bag removing a small plastic bag and gently pours its contents at my feet. Out tumbles a backpack my size. I pick it up.

"Did you grab the backpack?"

"Yeah."

"Open it," she curtly orders. "It has video glasses, some water and snacks, a rope, and a black rectangular box. Do you see it?"

"Yup, it's all here," I say. "Where is the server?"

"In the black box."

"Oh, really? Wow!" I examine it. "How is it powered?"

"Batteries, kinda. No more questions," she snaps. "Put on the video glasses. *Now.* I need to see how significant I look to you." She bites her lip.

I wear the black frames as Jen pulls a tablet out of her bag. I shoulder the backpack and drink a bottle of water, noting the sun's heat beginning to build. A huge smile explodes on Jen's face.

"Look at me," she orders. "Oh. My. God. *I look fantastic!"* Jen poses and flaunts herself, for herself. "Is this how you *always* see me? No wonder you do everything I say. Wait. Stay still. Look more to the right." She looks at me and back at her tablet comparing the two views, waving at herself and guffawing several times.

"Okay, get ready, my little Goddess Cam," she teases.

Two fingers eclipse the sun and pinch me high into the air to dangle over a vast expanding landscape of tits and stomach, as a field of skin rushes at me. I'm placed below her sternum in the shadow of a pair of hundred-foot tall boobs and can't help but look dumbfounded at them before awkwardly remembering who's watching.

All I smell is coconut oil. My feet slip along Jen's greasy skin. I turn to survey the vast plane of her stomach which ends at a cute bikini bottom, splitting a pair of legs, each a thousand-feet long.

"Damn. I. Look. So. Hot. I'm grabbing so many screenshots here. Alright, young man, march south." Jen demands with awed pride.

I turn, expecting to see her massive face, but view the back of a tablet bridging the span of her chest.

"Wrong way, mister," she scolds.

"Couldn't you drop me there?" I ask. "It'd be easy for you."

"Nope! Can't help you without reason, just because you 'need help.' Besides, you need the sun. You're getting a pale," she taunts.

With a frown, I compare my white skin to the rich bronze of Jennifer's terrain and admit she's right. I start down the gentle slope of Jen's belly towards her navel a hundred yards away. I note her belly button piercing is gone. *Wonder where that went?* I adjust the backpack. *Need to watch out so I don't trip in the piercing hole.*

The floor of Jen's stomach rises and falls like a slow-motion fun house with each relaxed breath. Drops of sweat condense near stalks of hairs as tall as I am. For a liberating moment, my thoughts roam beyond work and Jen. I admire the green trees around the patio swaying in the wind. *I miss that sound,* I close my eyes and listen. *Jen was right to have me take it slow.* Beyond Jen's fantastic legs lay an elegant mix of wild flowers encircling a pond of lily pads and cattails. The pond's surface simmers in a soft forever dance with the wind.

It'd be amazing to grab a music stand and practice clarinet on a nice sunny day. I imagine playing out the cobwebs in the forest on a warm rock without disturbing anyone. *Gotta get back in my groove.* I absently finger my forearm as a melody tumbles through my thoughts.

I feel the world abnormally shift and turn to see Jen reading a magazine. She looks a quarter-mile away.

Wait.

How long have I been walking? Shouldn't this be a two-minute walk? I notice Jen's hairs are now as tall as normal trees. My skin prickles in tinge of realization.

I unmute my headset. "Jen…have I gotten smaller?" I coldly ask.

The ground heaves and knocks me to my ass as Jen's laughter shakes my bones. Around me, large pools of sweat collect and slosh into each other.

"Holy crap, I can barely see you! Yes, you've gotten smaller—part of the new contract terms you've accepted to install the server. Keep at it tiger, you're doing great," she giggles, returning to her magazine.

I barely see the rim of her navel and aim towards my best guess where it is by what I can measure of her legs. A half hour passes before I'm drenched in sweat—my own, plus the random puddles of Jen's I need to wade through to save time. I see her reading at what seems like ten miles away. *This is fucking ridiculous,* I fume. *I thought this was going to be a relaxing day on a patio, not a death march through an alien jungle of hair, dead skin, and giant stinging globs of salt water.*

An hour passes. The air is humid and oppressive. I now have no idea where I am. I have no desire to talk to Jen. Her stupid little belly hairs are the size of city skyscrapers, and I'm doing a ton of work for something she could have saved with a split second of her fucking time.

I sit to take a fucking break.

After a minute or two, a voice whispers, "Eddie…you're not in my belly button yet…"

"Damn it, Jen! It's a humid death trap here and I have no idea where I am."

"Hmmm. Oh, Eddie," Jen says. "Then I think we have a problem; I have no idea where you are either."

"You don't know where I am?" A minute of panic chokes my thoughts. I swallow anger. I want to live through this day. *And, yet, I agreed to do it,* I remind myself. "Could you please point to your belly button? I don't know which way to go," I stammer, hiding fear as best I can. *I can't even see her chest or face,* I panic at the rolling tan plane of broken pores and hairs.

"Maybe. Get on your hands and knees and *beg,*" Jen demands.

"What? Jesus." *The smaller I am, the more she wants to bully me into deeper submission?*

I have no choice.

"Okay." My knees sink into the mushy ground. "Please, Jen, can you tell me where to go?"

"No. Say how insignificant you are. Say how lost you are without me. How you pathetic you are walking across my stomach. *Say that I am your world.*"

Tears sting my eyes. *Why is she doing this?*

I say those things.

"Good. Say it again," she muses.

I say them again.

"Okay, look up. My finger is pointing where you need to go."

The sky darkens as a massive structure blots out the sky above me.

"You're pointing right at me, Jen?" I ask.

"I'm pointing *at* my belly button," Jen corrects. "Ha! Are you *that* tiny you can't see what's right next to you? Oh, yum." Immense glee drips in her voice.

"Oh." Feeling stupid, I hike to what I perceive her finger's center. Two hundred feet away I see the rim. The sky brightens as Jen removes her guidance. I gasp at the site of the vast canyon a mile wide and a mile deep.

Watching the video feed from my headset, Jen asks, "Ooo… I wonder what's bigger? The Grand Canyon to me or my bellybutton to you?" The ground heaves hundreds of feet in multiple directions as Jen laughs in delight.

I feel myself floating mid-air as her belly-quake knocks me into the vast space before me. In seeming slow motion, a wall of flesh rushes past me until a ball of sweat catches my fall a few hundred feet into her crater. I'm stuck to the side of the wall with thousands of feet above me and below me. Jen laughs harder. My globe of sweat dislodges, avalanching with other globs as I slide thousands of feet to the belly button floor.

I swim, dislodge myself, and stand on uneven legs to catch my unsteady nerves.

"You made it! Look around, Ed. I want you to *really* appreciate how insignificant you are."

The wrinkly valley floor waves with layers of large hills and crevices. I peer to see only sky and the far away skin of the crater rim. The world sags and shifts as the valley floor tilts. Jen's face rises on the horizon like a distant moon.

"Oh. Wow. Eddie," her voice drips with awe, "I really am your *god*. Look at me. I must be two hundred miles tall compared to you. Unreal," she coos. "Wow. Okay, walk into this needle," a huge silver shaft rapidly appears in the valley. "I think this is deepest wrinkle here," she says as the needle probes a large fold on the valley floor, "Come on over."

Seriously? What the hell is this? I walk fifteen minutes towards an upside-down needle nearly four miles tall. Her arm practically enters the stratosphere.

"Get your rope out and enter the eye. Your adventure isn't over yet, my little belly lint." She laughs, "Tie yourself in and clutch the backpack tight."

I glare at her grin. *What is she doing?* I'm so tired, my nerves simply aren't processing this. I just obey; I obey so all of this can be over. I unpack my rope, tying myself into a little ledge of steel.

Jen shifts her position to see. "See Ed, if I did this alone I couldn't know if such a small thing was properly set. I'd be devastated to lose the server in the shower or during my morning jog. I've done self-piercing before, so consider me an expert. But never with a live person, until now! Hold tight... Ouch."

The floor drops as I plunge into hot suffocating darkness. The walls of Jen's flesh rip at my sides and tug violently at my ropes like an elevator ride straight to hell.

"Ow. Ow. Oh. Can you hear me? That stings... Mmhmm," she moans.

Beyond my headset, a ferocious gurgle raises from the depths below. I can hardly breathe.

"Fuck! Yes. Jen, I still have the backpack. What now?"

"Ensure the black box is placed *below* the needle. Mmm...this feels wonderful, Ed," her voice radiates bliss.

Is Jen getting off on this? I angrily force shallow breaths. *How bat-shit is she?* I worry, already knowing the answer.

"No rush, take your time," the world rumbles. "You're *only* a half-inch down. Mmm."

I lean along the side of the needle to drop the server package below. "Okay, done. I'm done with this," I strain, securing myself into the needle.

"Good," her response lingers.

Nothing happens.

"Jen?" I ask. "Can you hear me? I'm ready. It's hard to breath."

"Yes. *Good.*"

Nothing happens. I wait a minute. Her darkness is oppressive and violently close. "Jen, please?" I beg.

No response, then a long sigh. "Oh... fine."

A force bites my gut as I lurch and spin. I feel my tether loosen until I suddenly stop—feeling dizzy and sick.

"Thanks, big guy. Wait, your monitor's dark? Did the glasses fall off?"

I check my face and ears for my camera. It's hot and dark. I can't move. "Jen, they're on—*I fell off!*" I scream, terror gripping my chest.

She laughs. Huge contractions jostle my world and I feel myself slip deeper down the tunnel the needle left behind.

"Jesus, Jen, stop laughing! I'm trapped. Oh my god, Jen, please get me out. Please, please, please." I panic.

"Easy there, Eddie. You've been trying to get inside me all this time and here you are, all a mess?" she laughs. "What's a girl to think?" Jen teases. Huge thunk-thunk pounds above as she pats her belly. "I'm fine with this if you are."

"No! I can't breathe," I hyperventilate. "Please!"

"Bummer. Hm, what to do? What to do?" a grin in her voice darkly taunts. "Tell me that you *want* to be an insignificant speck, and *maybe* I'll turn over and you'll fall out."

This bullshit again? "I want to be an insignificant speck," I gasp.

"Louder. If my laughter can end your life, you better mean it."

"I want to be an insignificant speck!" I shout, panic and tears sobbing down my face.

"Eddie. You're so demanding. Okay, if you really insist on being that pathetic," her smile slithers.

"Yes!" I shout, fighting for life.

"You should've been smart enough to understand the risks when I asked you to do this, Eddie. You tied your *own* knots with that rope. The choices we make have consequences. You're lucky my back needs some sun and I'm ready to turn over. Otherwise, you'd need to find your own way out," she sternly instructs.

Up suddenly becomes down as Jen flips. I slide the opposite direction as Jen's world shifts and adjusts.

"Good luck on your escape. If my opinion matters, I think you feel great just where you are."

I'm getting out. I'm getting out, I chant. *I'm not dying like this.* I'm make progress but have no idea how far I need to go. I start feeling light headed.

"Mmm, Ed. Here's a sexy thought." A sultry voice enters the headset. *"What if you die in there?* If you couldn't get out. The path heals shut? You'd be entombed." Her stomach clenches tight as she sensually sways side to side.

My descent slows. "But, Jen, we have work to do. I want to help you. I do!" I beg.

"Shh. Let me enjoy your struggle for life," her voice is detached and dangerously aroused. "Oh, Ed…"

"What the fuck, Jen?!" I shout, unable to believe what's happening. *I'm going to die?*

Massive belly muscles undulate around me like a trapped pod of serpents. My descent is erratic. Pressure builds, and I stop moving. All I can hear are her sharp inhales of breath and low moans of passion. *She's masturbating to this?* A massive primal groan surrounds me as the world hops and spasms. The lack of air makes me dizzier.

"Crawl," she gasps.

The churning becomes so great and violent I feel sick. I can't move. Can't crawl. Jen moans and clenches in withering passion. I feel a new darkness, a buzzing like a tunnel collapsing around my ears. Through this buzzing I hear—more feel—Jen scream in passion. My lips are numb. The world around relaxes into a deep peace. I feel myself falling in darkness.

A flood of cold water chokes me. I cough and thrash in shock, treading water in a pool about twenty feet wide.

"Wakey wakey, little belly lint," Jen whispers.

The air smells fresh and wonderful, like coconut lotion. Birds chirp. The sun is low, yet bright.

I realize my 'pool' is water in Jen's navel; I'm the size I was this morning. *Why am I alive?*

"Jen," I sputter, swimming to the edge. "I thought you killed me."

"Um?" She dreamily acknowledges. "Yeah. I wondered that too," she smiles.

The pool sloshes and spills as Jen sits higher to look at me. I slosh on the skin of her belly, my knees weak. My rubber feet force me to collapse.

I no longer care.

"Jen, you're a royal sick fuck!" I shout, angry pointer finger jabbing at her face, a thousand feet away.

"Eddie, Eddie, Eddie," Jen shakes her head. "That's not how to address a woman who's practically, and technically, your deity. I'm beyond your Boss. Beyond your Queen. Since when do *I* have a responsibility to coddle and protect you? IIm?"

"Fuck you!"

"You sure did," she cheers. "I was so blissed in pleasure I fell asleep. Got a solid sunburn on my ass you can be happy about." She laughs.

I'm unamused. "How long was I out?" I rub my arms against the chill.

"About two hours? When I woke, I can't say enough how hot it was to lay here not knowing where you were. You could've been sealed in my flesh or a smear on the recliner." She sighs heavily, "Squish. Eventually, I checked my tablet and saw you wedged in a belly button wrinkle, returned to your originally contracted height."

The wind feels cold as I drip dry. "Jen. You're a monster."

"Maybe," her middle finger swoops down to trace tender circles around me, "but we *do* have a special relationship, more than just work. I agree my interests are odd. The more helpless a man is, the more powerful I feel, the hotter I get! Feel satisfied your pathetic situation flooded my swimsuit. Like three times! No guy's done that before," she winks. "I knew today was going to be hot, *but once you fell,* I didn't realize how soaked I'd get watching you suffer," she coos, her massive finger tenderly encircles tighter. "I'm good for more of this if you are. I love owning your life."

No, I'm done. I spit to myself, recoiling at my situation. I think about bolting. *Right here and now.* I glance at the patio. *Disappear into the grass. Fight bugs for crumbs and dew. Fuck Jen and her contract. Just go. Be a man. Do it. There's no chance for a normal life in today's workforce. Start over.*

"This was a wonderful day," Jen continues in bliss. "Ed, I think I love you."

What?

This breaks all my thoughts. I don't know what to say.

"Hm, did you hear me?" she asks with a smile.

After an increasingly awkward minute of quiet, all I can say is, "Jen, I'm tired. Let's go home."

This brings her back. I feel her skin tense, her eyes don't know where to settle. I think she expected some joyous confirmation; a full return and embrace of her sadistic love.

"…Oh. Um sure," she stammers. "Do you want to go back to my room?"

"Doesn't matter," I mumble with my head down, not looking at her.

The sun drops behind a tree. A wind spikes fields of goosebumps along the long arms and legs that Jen's small bikini can no longer warm. She rubs her chill, looking distracted. Eventually, she brings my capsule next to me. I quietly walk in and shut the door.

"I'm going to put you in my bag. Okay?" she gently asks.

"Yeah. Sure," I mutter.

"Do you want to talk?" she asks.

"I'm tired, Jen. Sorry," I generically mention.

"Rest up. I'll let you know when we're home," she awkwardly smiles.

I jolt awake from my nap as the walls of the top drawer zoom past. The capsule lurches at touchdown.

"Okay, we're here Eddie. See you Thursday," Jen says.

"Goodbye, Jen."

She doesn't respond and my drawer shuts in darkness. The next morning I'm grateful to enjoy my first day off in seven months.

CHAPTER 20—MS. WARDEN

Jennifer. August 2013

My favorite part of the day is reading in a patch of afternoon sun near Uncle Greg's romantic stream.

Eek! I never knew towels could be so soft. I aggressively nuzzle my new softness with the side of my face. Grasses and flowers gently sway in the wind. Uncle Ben has taken me shopping so many times I don't have enough closet space for dresses and shoes! The whole winter we sampled every shoe store and spa in the region. Days with Ben are such beautiful days. His questions always hilarious. How this women stuff works blows his mind. *He's addicted to having me around.*

I lay watching the wind dance in the treetops and sigh into relaxation.

After an unexpected nap, I stretch and return to my book, "Serial Killers."

This big world is so crazy; people are nutso fascinating. I always thought kidnappers were 'mean people' who wanted to be bad because they 'were just bad.' I never understood the *sexual* aspects, that people actually get *turned on* torturing victims. Crazy. That's never mentioned in the news!

For some, the thrill of control was so intense that people's fantasies overtook polite restraints and practically forced antisocial fits of passion. Some views on the matter were more complex: "He is sadistic because he feels impotent, unalive, and powerless. He tries to compensate by having power over others, by transforming the worm he feels himself to be into a god: 'Who's alpha now, bitches?'"

Fascinating.

I mean, I love control. I totally sympathize with that buzz. I never felt godly enough for Mom, yet I've always wanted to feel 'godly' myself. No wonder I never liked jocks: *Alpha males? No way. I'm the Alpha Bitch!* I see this more now, especially after what

I've done with my cowboys, Raul and Jose. Devouring their friendship was so hot I couldn't help myself. *Holy shit, it's so fun to see power as a sexual dynamic. Why've I never thought openly about it before?*

I read more.

"The female psychopath may look different on the surface because the behaviors are different. Underneath her exterior, though, the female psychopath operates from the same conscience-free, bent-on-manipulation and winning mindset. If a woman is a psychopath, she can be just as dangerous as a male psychopath—perhaps more so because, based on social conventions, we're less likely to see her coming. Females tend to fly under society's radar as they are less likely to commit criminal offences, just moral ones. She will use her social tools to dismantle one's life and soul and greatly enjoy herself in the process."

Fun! I laugh.

A bee drifts through the flowers around me, content and working hard for his queen. *How perfect,* I smirk at the timing, appreciating his effort on his Queen's behalf. *The power to control someone's life—to be that Queen Bee. To even take that life because you want to...so intense.* I bite my lip.

Am I already a serial killer? I suddenly wonder.

If Peggy and her Dad starved to death last spring, am I a murderer for not sharing my food? Or were Dad's crazy activist friends the murders for shutting down TempSchool? Or was Choke's Economic Progress Package guilty by ending food programs for the lazy? Or was it no one's fault but Peggy and Mr. Davis?

I look at the stream and watch water race over the pebbles. *Is any person with real power a 'serial killer'? If people love power enough and are willing to set aside lives for their psychological thrills, then is George Washington a hidden serial killer—only his thrill was American Liberation from the British Crown and a place in history, rather the cliché gagged and bound sorority girl?* I scratch my chin. *Why is one 'thrill' more noble than another? Could the smartest most skeptical people believe any nonsense or contradictions if they breathed it every day?*

I hear footsteps in the grass as Greg's solid frame stomp towards me.

"Hey. Glad I found you," he approaches. "We've got to talk finances, Jen. It's time to work hard and pay off the expenses of your first few months."

"Oh, god. This again?" My irritation stirs as I sit.

"A $27,000 debt is out of control for a teenager," he angrily shakes the layers of invoices he's dutifully placed under my door the past few months. "I'm sensing basic chores aren't working here," his chin tilts to the fact I'm lying on a towel in my bikini.

"Ben needs to stop taking me shopping! That's totally unfair," I counter. "I'm reading now," I say, holding my book. "This needs to be later." I turn to ignore him.

"No. Now," he stomps into my line of sight. "And, um, it's not Ben's money to give—it's *my* money. He *has* stopped," he complains, avoiding details of what must have been a larger argument with Ben. "Also, books aren't the real world, Jen," he frowns. "Hard work is the real world. Fiction or nonfiction—books are just words some loser wrote because he never made it in *the real world.* You need hard work."

"Don't you care what I've been through?" I stand and cross my arms in rage. "I've *moved* into a cheaper room. I eat *toast* for breakfast. I spend *half* the day making $4 an hour sweeping floors," I bite. "And the servants hate me. What more can I do?" I nearly yell.

He has so much wealth. "I have nothing. We're family. And you ignore my needs!" I pick up my towel to storm off.

"Hey. I didn't build *my* estate running a charity," he tensely waves his invoices and grabs my arm. "I want you to drop the idea you're entitled to take money or support from me because we happen to be relatives. I want you to understand clearly—when you're young—that no honest person believes he should support his relatives. Pull your own weight. So. I found you an internship," he offers. "There's an Assistant Parole Administrator role at Valparaíso Prison. A pal of mine needs help, and it's one of Mr. Jacobson's investments, part of All Corp. There's lots of room to grow big once you're in the family," he nods. "Your first day is tomorrow, if you don't screw up the interview. Pay Juan $10 each way." He firmly nods and walks to the house, and then turns. "If you find any downtime from all your hard work, I'll give you worthwhile books to read."

I fume. *This sucks. I don't have time for a shitty ass job like this!* I throw my book in the grass and clench my elbows tight to my side. *What a horrible day!*

Why does 8:50 a.m. feel so goddamn early? Juan woke me up at 7 a.m. I rest my chin in my hand and yawn as I sullenly observe Ms. Ruth. She has a bossy, stately grace. Based how she snapped at me to stay quiet when the guards escorted me in, she has the confidence to demand what she wants and not waste time. *But she sure doesn't mind wasting my time,* I mutter. *Why did I get here so early if she's spending twenty minutes on the damn phone?* Stupid.

I watch her expensive high heels tap her desk while she leans into an executive chair, dropping torrents of irritated Spanish into the phone. The shoes look *really* expensive. I can't tell the brand, but I love them. I want them! She's not wearing a wedding ring. I wonder if she's been divorced. *Early forties?* I guess. Her hair is a silky raven-black. *She must really work out and have great genetics. I hope I look that good when I'm old.*

Her desk is layered in binders. Two phones: a black one and the red one she's holding now. A gold "La Directora de la Cárcel" nameplate sternly appraises me. Her office is big, luxurious, and on the third floor of the prison overlooking a long city street.

She suddenly slams the phone without a word to me and writes in her notebook. Five minutes pass. After exhaling a long slow breath, she warily peers at me.

"Hi. So, how's Chile for you?" she suddenly asks in clear, perfect English.

"Wow," I say in genuine surprise. "Your English is amazing. Um, it's nice here," I nod, playing nervously with my hair.

"I grew up in L.A.," she shrugs. "Came back after the election."

"Oh. What election?" I frown, not knowing what to ask.

"Ha. Wow…how old are you?" she smirks darkly, slouching deeply in her chair, balancing a pen between her fingers.

"Twenty," I lie.

Ms. Ruth slowly nods. "Uh, well," she clears her throat. "There were several years when Chile wasn't working well. A total unsafe mess. Companies weren't investing. Roads, schools, banks: a total disaster," her head shakes. "Businesses fled to the States because nothing got done with all the corruption and communists."

"Communists?" I ask, confused. "I thought they were gone?"

"That's what most think," she frowns. "Not here. They're underground…hiding. During the 2009 depression, Chile got so bad, General Ormo couldn't stand it anymore. He took action. Got things working and saved us from much worse. Now's a wonderful time to live in Chile," she points past the window to the city rolling on the hills. "You can walk the streets with safety. Your family is respected. And the stupid are in their right place," she says pushing her thumb on the desk. "The people, they have honored the general to be our president."

"Wow," I nod.

"That was *him* on the phone," she looks at me, waiting.

"Him?" I eventually respond, confused, not sure what she wants me to say.

"Yes. The General." She rolls her eyes.

"Oh," I say, feeling insecure and annoyed.

"I don't know how we're going to handle all these new inmates," she pinches the bridge of her nose and rubs her eyebrow. "Thanks for coming in. We need the help. I trust you've never had any corrections experience before? Never worked in prison? Never been to jail?"

"No. Never," I frown.

"That's okay. It's not hard. What's *hard* is knowing who to trust. And because you're Greg's daughter—"

"—Niece," I correct.

"Whatever," she waves her hand. "And because you're related to Greg, that gives you a lot of trust here. Don't fuck that up," she emphasizes. "Don't talk to anyone you don't know. Here or anywhere."

"I don't know anyone," I shrug.

"Good. Keep it that way. Trust me. You need to be strong. Not a wimpy American girl hoping men will do all the work so she can boredly read fashion and makeup magazines," she sneers. "Can you follow and enforce rules?"

"Um, yeah." I agree. "What do you mean by 'not wimpy'?"

"As strong as possible, and then some." She sternly waves a finger. "If it means one day of freedom, most convicts would slit your throat," she glares. "Not all of them, but most of them." Her eyes drift vacant for a slight second before refocusing on me. "We have a strict no fraternization policy here. Do not befriend. Do not *flirt.* Do not trust these people. They are beneath you." She points another sharp finger at me, "You are right. They are wrong. You are god. They are dirt. Got that?"

I nod and perk up. *Yum.*

"Other rules," she continues. "Never answer the red phone. Only I answer the red phone. Let it ring. Never touch it. Always ensure the guards have prisoners properly restrained before you enter an area with them. *Don't* trust the guards to keep you safe…be smart. We executed a guard last month because he allowed insurrectionists access to wire and a knife. If there's a prison riot, they will storm this office to rape and kill us. Understand?"

I hesitantly nod.

"Uh, what else…" she taps her manicured fingers on her chin. "I'll think of other things later," she waves. "We'll figure this out as we go. Basically, we're overcrowded and inmates are sleeping on mats on the cell floors. Budgets are tight for the new building…is $6,000 a month a good place to start?" she asks me quizzically.

"Hm? Start what?" I ask, perplexed.

"Jeez, I thought Greg said you were smart. For *you,* honey— for your salary," she rolls her eyes. "We'll try and find some incentive pay. Let me work on that before you say no," she consoles.

"What? Oh. Oh." I nod. *Holy shit.* "Wow. Yeah, sure, that's great!" *That's so much money!* I squeal.

"Really? Okay, good," Ms. Ruth looks relieved. "Since you're the only girl around, I'll probably promote you just to have conversations *without* someone staring at my tata's all day. Consider that too before you look elsewhere," she adds defensively.

"Would other employees be okay with that?" I ask, recalling how the servants glared at me when I took their jobs at Uncle Greg's estate. "Could we get in trouble?"

"No trouble," she smiles. "I'll tell you a secret: I'm Ormo's big sister."

"Who?"

"Uh, the President of Chile…aye-ya-aye! Mr. Red Phone," she taps the item on her desk. "I'm his sister," she whispers.

"Oh," I say, feeling really dumb this morning. *Maybe Uncle Greg was right about how little I know?*

"'Oh' is right, girly-girl." Ms. Ruth laughs, "God, at least you're cute." She shakes her head. "You're going to be useful. Wanna know my favorite LBJ quote?"

I nod, not knowing who LBJ is.

"'I never trust a man unless I've got his pecker in my pocket.'" She laughs, "Guys always care more about what my body looks like than my mind and ambition, and that fucks them more than I ever will." She smirks, "Nothing's more dangerous than an attractive woman who knows what she wants." She adjusts her blouse. "Think on that. Men *think* they know what they want until a pretty face tells him otherwise."

We tour the building and meet a few of her favorite guards. I get an ID badge. Fill out paperwork.

There's not nearly as much staff as I expected. Ms. Ruth says the previous administration had a huge bureaucracy, and now with Ormo, it's basically her, the guards, the prisoners, and the occasional investigators who come and go. "Beautiful efficiency," she says, outlining those facts.

Ms. Ruth introduces my first task of the day.

"I don't really have much for you this month," she says as we walk over to a lone file cabinet in a large room down the hall. "Make sure this form," she opens a drawer, takes out a folder, and opens it to the second page, "is in all the files and signed within the past year." She points to a date on the page. "Note which files are old or missing the form and drop those outside my office. I'll see you tomorrow at 9 a.m. I have to, uh, interrogate a prisoner," she finishes.

"Okay. But Ms. Ruth, is there anything *else* I can do?" I quickly ask, noting it's only 11 a.m.

I worry I won't be free of Uncle Greg's debts and annoying financial sit downs for months!

"No. No more work yet," she shrugs. "And *you* can call me Valentina. Or Val. 'Ms. Ruth' is for inmates and normal staff."

"Okay, sure. I'd just like to get more hours," I request. "I don't wanna get paid for only this morning."

"Oh," Valentina laughs and slaps the grey file cabinet with her hand. *"Hours* don't matter, honey. You're salaried. That means you get paid no matter when you work. Some weeks you might need overtime, some weeks are quiet. I'll say this: people in cages don't need much supervision," she winks. "We work on other stuff: Are the cooks passing drugs? Is the cleaning crew planning an escape? Are the investigators getting the interrogations they need? Is the public pacified and sedate? The prisoners watch TV all day," she smiles.

"All day?" I wonder.

"Pretty much. They love *The Young and the Restless.* Sometime there's chores to be done. But yeah. Have at it." Valentina slaps the file cabinet, eager to get going.

The folders contain the backgrounds of each inmate. I make a game of looking at their photos and trying to decipher their occupations before they arrived in prison: médico, científico, abogado, profesor, panadero, estudiante. I do a poor job guessing! Each cover sheet has "Insurrección" stamped in bold red ink.

Sorting through five-hundred personal folders takes twenty-five minutes. Five files have outdated forms.

That's it? I'm all done with work? I calculate personal finances walking to Ms. Ruth's office. I made $32 a day doing chores for Uncle Greg, and $38 *an hour* sitting on my ass? And that's if I do 40 actual hours this week. *How is an hour here worth more than a full day of hard chores at Uncle Greg's?* I wonder. *But what are the taxes? That will take half; $19 an hour isn't bad either!*

"All done," I chirp, walking into Ms. Ruth's office. She's not there so I put the files on her desk. *She must be hard at work too.*

I call Juan on Valentina's black phone but he can't pick me up until 4:30 p.m. *Goddamnit. I wish I could just read in the sun,* I complain and grab my lunch bag to walk around the administration floor.

I find an empty break room. Many empty offices. *No wonder Valentina wants someone to talk with.* I find a comfy chair at the end of a hallway with a nice overlook of the city. After gazing at the sunny sky over Valparaíso, I reluctantly open one of Uncle Greg's books. A few hours melt away and I hardly notice.

I've discovered heroic individualism.

"Selfishness is not immoral, but the highest of morality. The moral purpose of a woman's life is the achievement of her own happiness. She does not subordinate her life to the welfare of others. She does not sacrifice herself to their needs, the relief of their suffering is not her primary concern. Any help she gives is an exception, not a rule. In a free society, we are not forced to deal with one another. We do so only by voluntary agreement and by contract."

Ayn Rand, wow! Thank you for guilt-free capitalism!

"Givers are never blessed; the more they give, the more is demanded from them until they are subhuman. Until they are nothing."

Selfishness is our best protection, I grin. I've found permission to be me. Me first and always.

Valentina walks dreamily past my sunlit alcove, looking disheveled. I rapidly hide my book to obscure I've been reading at work.

"Hey, Valentina! I put those files on your desk," I cheer to distract in case she notices. "There were only five…"

"Oh, hey." she sheepishly blinks at me, apparently not noticing I was there. "Thanks work. I mean great work, thanks." She chuckles, fixing her hair.

She looks tired and drunk at the same time.

"Are you okay?" I ask, wanting to be helpful.

"Hm? Yes… More than…" she glimmers a sigh.

We stand in awkward silence.

"So. What have all these people done to get in here?" I ask, trying to learn more.

"Huh? Um, doesn't matter," she quietly shakes her head. "Not our job. We supervise. We ensure they are contained. Where they belong. And things are smooth," she waves her hand slowly along an imaginary line in the air.

"What if someone's innocent?" I ask. "What do we do then?"

"Ha. Unlikely," Valentina's fiery aggression lights up and she turns to walk away. "And if they weren't an enemy before, then they sure are one now!"

"Oh, okay," I nod. "So, once they're here, they're here forever?"

"Practically. Hence our overcrowding." She waves her hands in casual distress. "Your job, as a Parole Administrator, is to give them hope. You keep them passive. Distracted. Find clever ways to motivate them towards a bright future while keeping them trapped and going nowhere." She walks away, calling, "Good night, Jen. See you tomorrow." Val slinks down the hallway.

That's strange. I cautiously open my book as she drifts from sight. *Was she off doing drugs?* I wonder with a smile.

I spool my spaghetti around a fork, wary of splashing sauce on my new work blouse. I glance across the table to measure my jealousy on what Uncle Greg and Ben are cutting for dinner: An elegant five courses of sear-roasted duck breasts with grapefruit-balsamic sauce, all next to some exotic grains I can't pronounce. *Keenwah?*

They've already enjoyed a fancy soup and salad as I waited for my noodles. Spaghetti is cheapest on the house menu: $13.80! The incredibly rude shock of Greg charging me meals and treating his home like a hotel and restaurant has never worn off.

I was furious. We didn't speak for days. I always assumed, as a family, because that's what families do. I paid for my own birthday cake last week. *Outrageous!*

"Families share because they care about developing each other," I remember Dad saying.

But now Greg is mixing new rules from his corporate life with family life. It's disorienting what a different world he lives in.

Didn't give a shit I was angry. "Many companies discovered offering customers a taste of luxury enhances their bottom line, even if it stirs envy and resentment," he smirked. "Class segregation creates a dream for people to aspire to."

Wait, I realize as my plate arrives. *I have a job. After I get paid next week, I can eat with Greg and Ben. Hard work does pay off!* I marvel, *maybe Greg's right?*

If he's right about that, what about the words that have haunted me for months: *"If I had these lessons when I was younger, I could be Mr. Jacobson, not just work for him."*

Nobody knows how much Jacobson is worth or how much power he has. *And one day that could be me?* I suddenly grin.

"How's your first day?" Uncle Ben warmly asks me.

"Great. Valentina wants me back tomorrow," I smile at Uncle Greg, who nods with suspicious relief.

"That's awesome," Ben encourages. "Val's really fun. Great taste. Take notes on her style for me. You'll get along smashingly."

"Did she offer a salary?" Greg simply asks.

"Yup! $72,000 a year!" I grin.

"That's a little cheap," he tenses his lip. "I'll give her a call." He thinks for a second.

"She said she's working on it," I offer, rolling a bite of spaghetti.

"Okay, good," he nods.

"How much do I have to pay taxes on that?" I wonder, drinking a $1.50 cup of water.

"Ha! Practically nothing," Greg chuckles. "Not in Chile. You'd need $100k in the States for as much take-home pay," he gloats. "Here the cost of living is so minimal, the buying power practically sets you up like a queen." He smiles. "Besides, she'll probably pay you in cash. A lot of stuff is under the table with her group."

"Awesome…" I grin. "Greg, when I finished work and was waiting for Juan, I cracked open your book," I hint.

"And?" His skepticism towards me visibly evaporates.

"I'm half done," I smile.

"Wow. Already?" he eagerly nods. "You *are* a bookworm," he muses, swirling wine. "She's teaching you how to live, Ayn Rand. Best advice I've ever had. Cuts through the 'sharing caring' bullshit. *Selfishness* offers irresistible clarity for business: focus on the owner's interests," he shrugs. "That's it. Which is hard for people to understand; we're brainwashed to help each other." He eats his piece of duck. "I'll tell you," he speaks through bites. "The biggest shock of the past year was the volume of hatred the radical left had being freed from their own economic enslavement!" He shakes his head.

"Yeah. There was a lot of anger." I remember my Dad bitterly smoking in the backyard.

"How can anyone resist the rising dominance of the market?" he shrugs. "Nobody can. The market dominates us all, and she always will," he vigorously nods. "That's the truth they wanna ignore."

"So, if I embrace the free market," I open my hands, "I'm guaranteed to kick ass?"

"Easy. More than that," he says through a mouthful of salad. "You'd own everyone's ass, *if* you can keep the government out of the way. Look," he emphasizes with a hand, "we need to smash the one remaining thing in the world that holds us back—governments. By definition Collective Thievery to stop any single person from rising too high or making too many of their own choices. Government intentionally kills greatness. Why do we allow that?" He shakes his head at Ben and me. "You'll never be as great or big as you can be with a government blocking your way."

"But governments can do good things, right? Like roads?" I wonder.

"Barely. All Corp built that nice highway from Santiago to Valparaíso. And we did it at half the cost and in half the time. Before Ormo, I had to pay $150,000 in bribes *a month* to forty different people just to keep operations going. It was exhausting. Now, we work with one person and things get done. Simple," he nods. "Chile is great for business. America? Not yet, but Choke's getting us there. Give it a few more years," he encourages. "Up there, we need more help privileging the market over citizens."

"How can anyone do that if people always want free stuff without paying for it?" I wonder.

"Indeed," Greg nods. "I'll tell you, turning corporate self-interest into a movement of and for people on the streets was genius. The pain will be worth it, for the economy," he cringes. "The depression will end. I didn't think it'd be this bad. Don't think anyone did."

"It's just terrible. The fighting up there," Uncle Ben frowns, looking worriedly at his plate.

"Real freedom's never free," Uncle Greg sadly shakes his head, considering the Second U.S. Civil War tearing North America apart.

"But freedom's so important," I lunge. "I hate being told what to do."

"Totally," Greg furrows his brow. "The more efficient the market, the more freedoms a population has to buy and sell, create and consume, whatever they please."

"I'd *love* to buy and sell anything I want." *Like people,* I think. "How does All Corp work? What do you guys do?" I demand.

"A lot of people wonder that," Greg chuckles.

"I don't even think Mom and Dad really knew what you did," I add.

"Probably not. We keep quiet. Look. Here's the basics," he adds, his elbows to the table. "We're an under-the-radar private equity firm, excelling at political maneuvering: winning government contracts, shaping public policy, and recruiting former and current public officials to our needs. We never *directly* contact policy makers and governors," he clarifies. "The companies we control do."

"But what do you *do?*" Ben asks. "I never really know."

"Lots. Everything. We replace poorly performing banks and fund projects governments can't or don't want to afford. Private railroads and other infrastructure projects like stadiums in exchange for access to resources. Coal. Gold. We built Valparaíso prison a decade ago and we're trying to build the new one too," he points.

"Oh, really?" I raise an eyebrow.

"Yup. The project's going so-so."

"Why?" I ask.

"Can't tell you," he smirks and continues. "Private equity was once 'corporate pirates' who took over failing companies. Now, we manage projects previously in the domain of banks and regional governments. And even tech startups and research labs."

"Where's your headquarters?" I ask, curious where I should move if things go well.

"Actually. We're the world's first *metanational.* All Corp exists everywhere and nowhere."

"A *metanational?*" I rub my forehead.

"Metanationals rip apart old definitions of a 'global superpower.' Because today, the most powerful laws are not government sovereignty but those of supply and demand. We have no government accountability, as governments lack basic understanding what we do!"

"So, Metanationals have total freedom?"

"More and more, yeah, I'd say so. We lift market freedoms and efficiencies to whole new levels."

"Fascinating." I grab some sweet candies Amelia offers the table.

"Easy now," Greg warns with a chuckle. "Those candies are $15 each!"

"What? That's crazy?" My mouth drops as I return one. "They were only $1 last week!"

"Yup, a bastard in the UK cornered the sugar market. Buy low; sell high, Jen. That's the number one rule. He bought a ton of things no one ever thought would be rare. Purchased whole factories, only to shut them down. Bought all the good sugar beet land and let it go fallow or switched it to soy. He owns all the corn syrup plants in Asia and North America too! Brilliant bastard's making billions."

"That's nuts!" I tilt my head. "Wow. What's 'low' now?" I cross my arms with intense curiosity.

"Labor probably has the best value. Everyone's so hungry for work, but it's not a commodity. Policy makers fail to see globalization requires the mass migration of workers. No one knows how to get the right labor to the right needs, across national boundaries."

Greg's speech continues as my mind drifts.

If someone can unexpectedly corner the sugar market; can I secretly corner the labor market? I glance at the kitchen. Juan cleaning the dishes. Ben's eating his second candy, texting friends. *How? Can I buy and store labor low, and sell high to others when the time is right? Can I store labor in a vault, like De Beers who controls 40% of the world's diamonds?* I absently touch my collar bones and the gold necklace Mom gave me for Christmas. *Workers like diamonds around my neck; that would be a dream come true.*

At work, at lunch, in the car; all week I page through Uncle Greg's awesome business books.

At night, I read in the warm candlelight of my newly affordable second floor balcony room. The chirp of crickets on the fresh evening breeze is instantly relaxing. I do my nails and girly things, but with radical individualism as my best girlfriend.

"An individual owes no obligations to others beyond those explicitly, contractually agreed upon; obligation to the common good makes no sense."

"There is one and only one social responsibility of business: to use its resources and engage in activities designed to increase its profits so long as it stays within the rules of the game, which is to say, engages in open and free competition without deception."

No deception? I pause to look out the window. *Should a company* never *hide its intentions? That makes zero sense. I love the advantages of my Feminine Mystique: Who do I like? What am I thinking? Boys, you'll never know…*

The business "rules" I read sound like recipes to play nice and get boiled alive by someone who doesn't care about the rules. I toss the ethics book aside. Innovation is about ignoring cues about danger or punishment. *If the market is totally self-regulated, it'll find equilibrium on its own.* "If you make money, you succeed. If you lose money, you fail." *Money is the ultimate points system. The ultimate reward.*

It's that simple, people.

Use money to buy power, and use power to make money. That's the real world: get as many points as you can.

I walk to the balcony, my mind afire with potential. Overlooking the sweetness of the sleeping estate, I feel a thrill flood my veins, a sense that I can be powerful, that I can be a hero. *I really can care only about myself. That it's moral to care about myself above all others—and damn that's so intoxicating!* Grin, and shimmy my elbows on railing.

"The man who builds a factory builds a temple," and *"the man who works there worships there."* I smile though a giddy shimmer, when I remember a reading about Calvin Coolidge. *If I managed a factory, people would worship me. I'm glad I don't have friends. If I feel lonely, I'll always find men to wrap like a diamond around my finger.*

I want to be limitless.

I want to be an infinite growing loop of more power and more money.

A Goddess made real above all else.

CHAPTER 21—TOTAL PRIVATIZATION

Eddie. June 2023

I find comfort lying on the floor. Facedown is most soothing. Grinning stupidly, with my forehead pressed into the cold metal grain, I realize it's my therapy: *Floors are solid. They support you. Everywhere normal has floors: schools, offices, parking lots. Even jails have solid floors and a standard orientation.* I've never been more grateful for a standard horizon than this past week since the garden—a whole week free from Jen's warped reality. *With Jen, there is no orientation. Only her.*

We're more distant now, and I don't care. I wake up early some days to walk and marvel at the flat, solid, real floor of my top drawer.

Our new metal desk doesn't have the tunnels we burrowed in Jen's old wood desk at TempGrace. Our new desk is all secure for our protection. I dare not call the police. False imprisonment is still a crime, but our ambition agreed to this, our contract allows no crime. The police have no regulations enabling them to seize corporate property. Besides, the anger of Jen's spite would not only be career ending but life ending as well. *And who would know?* A chill tingles along my skin as my face feels solid and cool against the solid ground.

A familiar quake of the drawer opening rattles into my forehead.

I, however, remain unmoved.

"…Eddie," a cool distant voice drizzles. "I'm worried about your performance this week."

My face remains on the floor, bound to something real.

"Eddie. Look at me. This floor thing is weird."

Weird? I clench my fists. *What right does she have to call anything weird?* I roll over, annoyed she can make me do whatever she wants, and then realize today is one of those days I forget the massive scale of our CEO. Jen opened the drawer standing at her full height. I feel a jolt of shock at her distant frown looming two-thousand feet above me like a cloud.

I refuse to let nerves attack my cool and place my headset into my ear. "Good afternoon, Jen."

She tilts her head, crosses her arms, and asks, "What is this?"

"This? My life?" I raise an eyebrow. "Good question, Jen. Been wondering that too. Not really sure."

"Eddie, easy: Sacrifice your life so I can run a business."

"Oh yeah?" I ask.

"Yes."

"Why?"

"Because I love you. That's how this works." Jen points at the two of us.

"Humph," I grunt. "No idea what your 'love' means, Jen."

She frowns, thinking with a hand on her chin. "I love that your entire life is focused on me. That you want me to be happy with no thought of your own needs." Her hand moves to her heart. "I love being your entire source of truth, information, and direction. I love how your service makes me feel, Eddie." She leans forward, eclipsing all sight of the world beyond. "I love this thrill of being huge. Massive. Watching you dwindle away. Becoming a piece of my property. Something I own. A human speck entirely obedient to me."

I have nothing to say.

"And I love that your life is for the corporation," a fresh smile lightens her face and warms the drawer, "having your soul consumed into something much greater than yourself." She leans over me.

"Your 'love' is burning me out. You're a really harsh boss, Jen."

She grins. "Yeah. Ed, that heat's only going to get more intense. The corporation may seem harsh only because she needs more energy than you're currently giving. I'm *not* devolving 'from ruthless predator to a sluggish bureaucracy.' My hunger saves us from a market that *will* devour everyone you know and love, Ed. You, the thousands of temps in the drawers, everyone." She brightens, "Gone." Her head tenderly rests on the edge of the drawer. "A paradise is coming. Submission to hard work keeps the corporation safe, submission feeds her."

Jen shifts, and for the first time, her face looms inside the drawer above me. Her lush lips pucker into a fifty-foot kiss that rapidly consumes my world. I make no effort to move as I melt into her enormous sudden warmth.

A long, "Mmmmmm," rattles my bones and crushes my chest as a massive wet tongue parts her lips to suffocate me in a soggy, sensual Titan French kiss. Between laps of her tongue, I briefly glimpse the dark terrifying roof of her mouth and the endless abyss beyond.

She lifts, her eyes closed, and tenderly wipes a glob of spit from her smile, briefly checking to see if it was me.

"Because, Eddie," Jen stands to her full two-thousand feet, "I'm a business. I want to maximize the amount of work I can take. You're my nutrients," she pats her belly. "You feed me. Today's special," her mood lightens again and she re-ties her ponytail. "I've made a few acquisitions. Tell all staff to pack their things. Today everyone gets their own capsule based on your prototype. Have them ready to move by 4 p.m."

I'm lying on the floor, soggy and wet. My hand moves to my earpiece to unmute.

"Sure, Jen. I bet they'll love that."

She bursts a grin. "Yeah, it's gonna be a huge boost!" Jen calls as she walks away.

I slouch to my capsule and towel off, wondering why I feel so terrified by her excited grin.

"Almost forgot. You get a new capsule, too," Jen randomly alerts an hour after I updated the staff. "Quick. Get your shit out." She lifts me onto her desk beside a nearly identical capsule.

"Wait. Why?" I ask annoyed. "What's wrong with this one?"

"Made upgrades. You'll see," Jen hums. "Out, out."

I sigh, pack three boxes, and walk each next door. Meanwhile, Jen easily moves several absurdly large boxes into the office by herself. *She must be really working out.* I note the absurdity of her lifting strength.

I notice it's 4:20 p.m. when she finishes, and Jen swings to my area to check on me.

"Are you in this one?" she asks, picking up my old home.

"No, the new one. On your desk."

"Good. This *was* once part of a shrunken submarine." She displays my old capsule between two fingers. "It's reinforced titanium and carbon fiber. And strong. Check it out," Jen's hand trembles for a half a second and suddenly the whole structure crumbles and cracks like the cookie she once pretended it was. A wry smile darkens her face, "I've gotten a *lot* stronger today."

She lifts my new capsule and walks to a tall cylinder in her office I've never seen before. It is about four feet tall, a foot wide, and half filled with clear fluid.

"In you go, number one," she declares.

My capsule lurches into the tank and casually feathers to the bottom. *Seriously, now what the fuck is this?* I wonder, hitting the bottom of the tank with a thunk.

She crouches low, peering at me. "Ed, I need to be free. Cast aside old corrupt laws and inefficient rules. I have the moral obligation to give *everyone* access to the opportunities of a truly free world. I've created the freest market in the world." She pats her belly. "This is the right thing to do."

"Huh? Okay," I say, organizing my office. *I at least want to be comfortable.*

"This is going to be amazing!" Jen claps excitedly as she jumps to her feet.

Watching Jen's video feed, I see her lay a large six-feet by three-feet flat box on her desk with ease. She rips the perforated top off to reveal one thousand small capsules like mine, aligned in formation. She looks at me in the cylinder with a grin like a kid on Christmas, practically skipping around her desk to open Drawer Five, lifting the dorm section of one thousand employees into the middle of the small field of capsules.

"Alright, Five, out!" she announces. "Office relocation time. Pick any capsule, they're all the same. Once you enter they will automatically re-adjust to your contracted height, so don't worry if it's too big for you at first. I promise that will change," she smirks, looking at me. Jen then leans with her hands on the table, intently watching her dominion below like a kid would her new ant farm.

I notice her face relax into a peaceful bliss as thousands of workers scurry below.

After what appears to be a few oddly delightful minutes, she says, "Stragglers will get sucked in the vacuum. Make sure you find a home." She laughs and tosses the empty dorm in the trash. She picks at a thin plastic film at each the corner of the box, which forces all the capsules to tumble into a center pile, and raises each corner.

Through the walls at the bottom of the tank, I see her enormous stilettos clack on the wood floor, and then dumps Drawer Five into the open top of the cylinder. She crouches, watching the slow rain of her staff join me at the bottom of this strange bath.

Is she doing this so no one can walk outside? I wonder. *What a bitchy thing to do.*

From Jen's video glasses, about 10% of the cylinder fills with our little pebbles. She repeats this four more times until the fluid rises to the brim and the cylinder is half full with capsules of the entire staff. She leans over her computer.

A System Invite™ alerts us to an All Hands Call. Jen pulls her chair before us, sits and crosses her legs, folding her hands on her lap.

"Hello, team," she cheers into her headset, her dark red lipstick curling a smile. "Thanks for your hard work today. As we know, the only certainty in our industry is change. At TempGrace, we've done well using technology to stay ahead of these changes to become an immensely profitable enterprise. Due to your hard work and sacrifice, I've made a few acquisitions. I'd like you to be the first to hear that I've purchased MicroMenace, NanoLogistics, and EverLast Technologies. All leaders in the nanotech world."

"Holy shit." I stop my unpacking and stand at the computer. "Where did she get money for that?" I wonder in dull surprise. *The market cap for each was around five to ten billion!*

Jen continues, "I want to not merely be a stunningly successful outlier, but the pioneer of all future workplaces to come. Globally, we're well into a total transformation of the labor force. I'm certain the path to market sustainability and success is the path we're on now. In this economic climate, if you're not first—you're last." She leans forward. "Technology is changing our operations so much that the proud history of TempGrace no longer makes sense as a brand. Due to the portfolio of our recent acquisitions, and the many more acquisitions to come..." She happily smiles, "Today, we are rebranding to, *Jennifer Incorporated.* So, please use *Jennifer, Inc.* in all your email signatures and official letterheads. After all, corporations *are* people." A bright grin spreads across her face.

She stands, walking closer. "Team. Nanotech is immensely expensive. I leveraged TempGrace 40:1 to ensure enough cash was on hand to privatize these nanotech firms." Her hand lovingly caressing our cylinder. "To maintain our market leading synergy, a substantial round of pay cuts and rent increases will be necessary."

My stomach drops. *Oh no...*

"To keep the maximum employment and productivity, all my subordinates pay will *decrease* twenty-four times. The workforce needs downsize *some* way, and this is my choice. Effective, now."

The room immediately explodes in size. Jen's video glasses confirm our cylinder shrinking from four feet, to two inches tall.

Jen slinks toward us like a cat to a bug.

"I also tire of the manual logistics keeping you fed and alive," she continues, towering ten miles above. "A dull waste of time. Ideally, I don't want to think of you. I only want to think *bigger,* and the manual annoyances of supporting your lives needs to automate. It's not *my* job as an employer to take care of your individual needs. I'm willing to compromise. As part of Jennifer, we're going to automate that dreary life support with nano technology I've onboarded from NanoLogistics, which is now integrated into the System."

"So that's what those strange System customizations were!" I mutter to myself.

"This provides Jennifer additional benefits. Certainly, secrecy, clearly key to our effectiveness. I now have the guarantee that no one will see or know about my business operations, except me." Jen bends and gently lifts the vial of staff before her admiring face, without spilling a drop. "We can no longer risk haphazard security practices. With Abrims technology legal for broader use, the nature of the workplace has permanently changed," she says, walking us to a table where parts of a syringe lay. "Great thinkers have said that 'Civilization is progress toward a society of privacy.'"

"Welcome to the pinnacle of civilization," Jen picks up a needle and an injector, and screws in the cylinder. "Total privatization." She holds us to the light and watches her subordinates twirl like fine sediment.

"Witness the natural evolution of the outsourcing of labor, to the *in-sourcing* of labor: The ultimate privatization!" Jennifer eases into her chair and places our syringe on the desk. Her hand slightly trembling, she rolls back her sleeve. "To be successful, market economies *need* inequality to function. The more unequal Jennifer is, the more Jennifer will thrive in the market."

She grins in pure delight, savoring every second. "And think of it this way: 'Happiness is to be dissolved into something complete and great.' I agree!" She raises the syringe before her eyes. "Jennifer, Inc. has an amazing vision," she continues. "You are the first residents of a truly free market frontier. A new paradise. Welcome home."

Jen lowers the syringe to the vein of her left arm. Her breath quickens. Her thumb quivers above the injector.

A sensual gasp escapes Jen's lips as our world becomes a vortex into a permanent abyss.

CHAPTER 22—HARD WORK

Jennifer. July 2015

Does work always need to be this boring? I toss my book on the patio floor of the prison's rooftop garden to stare pointlessly at the wide blue sky. I'm waiting for my afternoon parole hearing with Simón—the *one* thing I should do all month!

I've visited all the best beaches in South America. Old news. Greg took Ben and I to Vienna last Christmas. Beautiful! Yet after the fifth magical night of snow covered Christmas markets—boring. *How did my life become so lame?* I muse, stretching beside a large potted plant. *Where's the thrill?* I eye the skyline of Valparaíso, wondering what it'd be like to stomp through the streets like Godzilla.

Fun.

"People need to achieve things to feel a lasting sense of purpose." One of Greg's business books haunts my mind.

What have I achieved? I need my purpose. Reading whatever I want all week is the easiest job in the world; although, two years of parole hearings in a prison no one leaves sure is one hell of a slog.

I grimace, kicking my bare foot against a side table as I stretch my calves. *The little work I do for Val is practically pointless.*

I love playing games at the parole hearings with the English-speaking prisoners; the inmates are so educated that most of them speak English. The problem is no one is eligible for parole, so I endlessly pretend to handle appeals. The prisoners and I, we each play our dance of seduction with well-rehearsed sob stories and lies. Our connection becomes so intimate it feels almost romantic.

"I shouldn't be in prison! I didn't do anything," this kid, Simón, moans. "Please help me. I wrote a stupid blog!"

"But sweetie, blogs are illegal. You know that." I pat his hand with a loving touch.

He tearfully nods.

Students are the most annoying. *Ugh,* he's five years older than me. *I keep forgetting I'm only 19 next month. Yet, I'm already a thousand times his superior.* I caress his arm as he becomes a puddle on the integration room table. I tenderly play with his hair. I soothe his sorrow, saying, "There there, love…I'll try my best for you. Let me see what I can do." *I don't care about your B.S., dude.*

The prisoners love me and think I'm their angel.

I'm not. Not even close.

We talk about Simón's performance, what he's done for the prison. How well he's behaved. Blah blah blah. He's a big guy, one of the star college athletes, but here with me, he's a small thing. Weaker than a hamster.

I nod as he talks, filling in a form for him with scribbles and doodles—I've drawn a cartoon bee in a flower and several rows of curly cues. Valentina will throw it away unless someone spits up some intel, but that's more the Investigators' jobs, guys in dark sunglasses who occasionally come and go.

A few weeks later, after Simón asks three times for an update, I schedule a meeting to break the bad news.

I love watching him enter the interview room with so much hope. I warm the room with a smile as Simón is seated and restrained. I've sustained his fantasy for months. He's been dreaming about me all day. I want to take as much as possible from Simón while giving as little as I can. He's warm, timid, quivering in my hand with both joy and fear, unsure where his life is going. Now I crush him.

Pretending I'm his best friend, I gently say, "Simón. You've been an excellent prisoner. Exceeding expectations. But there's no parole this year, sorry." I frown. "There aren't the resources. Budgets are tight. We don't have enough parole officer slots to accommodate you! Sorry." I raise my hands in defeat. "We agree parole is a great idea for you, truly we do. Keep up the good work and we can try again next budget cycle."

It turns me on, denying this kid's future. If I could torture people all day, I'd do this forever.

Some conversations don't end well. I've been spit on twice, and the guards knocked their faces in. We take away privileges, like having teeth, from those who misbehave. No hot showers. No media room.

Simón agrees an extra ten minutes of media room per day is a fair compensation for another guaranteed year of imprisonment. It's amazing how easy the small stuff controls these guys while I try my best to lock them forever under my thumb.

Executions are a thrilling jolt of activity. I like those. From nowhere the red phone will ring as Val and I are paging through fashion magazines, comparing makeup colors and styles. Valentina answers. Her eyebrows rise. She'll say "Sí, General," and unlock a special drawer in her desk to remove a special form. She calls five of her best guards on the black phone and they walk into the prison to deliver the news and the deed.

The rest of the time though, I'm mostly reading.

I'm hungry, I realize a week later. *Not just for food,* as my stomach growls, demanding lunch. *I'm meant for more than sitting around.* I put down my last book. *Probably know everything I need to know anyway. Time to be one serious Bitch of Action.*

I grab my lunch. *Time to ask Val for more responsibilities. I need things to do and be in charge of.* I poke my head in her office. *God damn it, she's not here! She always disappears half the day. Fucking druggie,* I huff. We haven't been as good of friends as Uncle Ben hoped. I half suspect it's because she's never actually around. She's always out somewhere.

When the weather is stormy, like today, I enjoy lunch in the Video Control Room, rather the rooftop patio. Watching lives scurry below me is soothing. The omniscience is amazing. Walking in I notice the video room is a mess. *Don't want to eat in filth,* I frown. No one ever cleans the room because only Valentina and I are allowed inside, and we clearly have better things to do. Wanting to make myself more comfortable, I grab cleaning supplies and fix the place up.

One-by-one, I tenderly wipe each monitor clean like a mother would the messy face of a loved child. The video feeds stream to Central Security so Ormo's investigators may monitor all prisons in the region. Beneath Valparaíso's peaceful veneer, a handful of people with centralized power use their wealth for clever surveillance to aggressively neutralize critics. Uncle Greg says countries, small, rich, or even poor, buy commercial spyware or hire and train programmers from All Corp to develop hacking and surveillance tools. Allowing Ormo to easily punish families and individuals who speak out, and track those who might. In June, Ormo cancelled the passports of four brothers whose mother was charged with "undermining the state." But with the prisons so full, weekly beatings were the only justice he could deliver.

There. Much better, I coo, pleased at taking ownership of my clean environment. I watch dozens of silent black and white video screens display the private moments of my prisoners as I eat.

I remember Dad blasting before the election: *"Megan, we have to be careful if Choke wins. Technology today makes it far easier for oppressive regimes to weed out dissidents and perform surveillance. We could have a permanently stable corporate tyranny, rather than the ones throughout history that get sloppy and are eventually overthrown as secrets build against them. Technology brings omniscience, which brings omnipotence."*

But I like prying into private moments, I counter Dad's ghost. *It's fun. Watching my kept souls is meditative. I feel peaceful. Content. In charge.* I eat my sandwich and watch the screens.

No one is too violent. The militant rebels stick to themselves. *I'm glad they never bother for parole.* The professionals clump together. The students and professors entertain themselves with lectures. I watch a calculus lesson today feeling a touch nostalgic and out of phase.

What would my life be if I'd gone to Duke or Yale? A slight twinge pulls my heart. *What would I learn? Who would I meet?* I watch the silent lecture. *Could these have been my professors and classmates if I'd studied abroad? Now,* a warm glow floods my center, *they're my prisoners.* I'll order new books for the nerds, as long as they're not politically charged, when their request comes through.

Valentina rolls her eyes, saying 'whatever' as I hand in the request.

"But it's so cheap to keep academics controlled. Why not?" I say. "All they do is talk."

I wonder if Val's intimidated by smart people? I realize as I finish my salad.

I notice three of the monitors aren't working: "The Isolation Block." *That's odd,* I frown. *That's where the opposition leaders are. Investigators will want those feeds.* I now worry that my cleaning damaged something. Already hearing the angry phone calls from Central in my mind, I pick at the control panel to expose the guts and circuits of the video room, using my smartphone flashlight to peer beneath.

Yup. Three of the cables fell out: I456, I455, and I454. I plug them in one-by-one. *Good,* the first cable lights video of the isolation hallway. The second video is a the door to a cell, and the third monitor illuminates the inside of a cell where two naked people are entangled on a bed.

"Holy fuck!" I panic, jumping up. "Two people in Isolation? How? Valentina!" I sputter, running to her office. "There's a security bre—Damn it!" *She's gone!* My throat dries tight with adrenaline. I rage, eyeing the red phone. *Not doing that. Where the hell is she?* I fret in panic.

Wait.

Oh god.

A cold chill floods my spine. I run to the video room for a closer look. A man's hands are bound behind him, his face is ears-deep into the ass of a woman with raven black hair tossing in pleasure. She turns her head to shout soundlessly at the man, grabs his hair, and pulls him harder into her with intense passion.

Oh my god. Oh my god. That's Valentina!

Intense curiosity replaces my shock. *Holy shit.* I smile. *That's hot.* I sit stunned, with growing arousal. *Whoa.* I try looking away but can't. I then slap my eyes to the computer server labeled, "Central Feed," in a bolt of terror, its glowing blinking lights recording all. *Shit. This is streaming live to Central!* I duck under the console and unplug the three cables.

I tensely contemplate the three black screens.

Did anyone in Central see her? My heart pounds. *Holy crap. If they know, will she know that I know? Maybe. Can she take me down with her? Fuck, fuck, fuck.* I panic. *Who's in Isolation?* I suddenly wonder.

I walk to the personal files and open the top drawer for the prison cell assignment sheet. The "Aislamiento" box has only one name this month: Antonio Andrés.

Who the hell is that? I whip out my smartphone and search the internet for an English explanation. *He's Ormos main opposition leader? The fuck she doing? Humiliating him?* I relieve with laughter. *Funny. Why not? She can do what she wants. She has the power and authority. Have some fun!* I smile. *Good for her.*

A week later is my two-year anniversary working at the prison. Valentina and I enjoy a gourmet six course lunch brought in on the beautiful prison rooftop patio garden. Lunch is paid by the prison, of course. We cheer to my hard work with glasses of expensive wine.

"This is fantastic," I praise the sautéed green beans and the general beauty of the day, looking at the city.

"I love Valparaíso. Best place in Chile. The colors. The seafood. The air. The mysterious people. You can't beat it," she thinks an extra second. "You know. I'm glad I took this role and not the cabinet position in Santiago. Way too much drama and backstabbing there."

"Oh. A cabinet position?" I ask.

"Was going to be Justice Minister," she shrugs. "This is lower key. The more intimate justice I prefer."

"Oh yeah?" I smirk, thinking of her humiliating Antonio. "What are the guys like these days?" I slyly ask.

Valentina looks a touch uncomfortable and scrunches her nose. "Needy. Pathetic," she spits. "I can't date online. The security problems and embarrassment would be absurd. Can you imagine someone like *me* on a blind date?" she laughs. "No, I have to date within The Party. And those guys have bigger hard-ons for my brother than me." She twirls her hair in frustration.

Interesting, interesting, interesting, I muse.

A ruckus erupts below on the street. Surprised, we carry our glasses to the rooftop edge to watch a stream of three hundred people round the corner.

"Is this protest authorized?" I nervously ask, "What do their signs say?" I note the large banners and colorful posters in Spanish.

"No. Not authorized. 'More jobs. More work.'" she reads.

"Annoying as hell," I flinch at the absurdly loud whistles and cover my ears. "I'm surprised Ormo let them get this far."

Val shrugs, "He prides himself as a social scientist, not just another 'thug'. Look, officers are walking the edges." She points here and there at them. "They're taking notes for now, making sure no immediate chaos breaks out."

So many people, I watch hundreds of ants stream past, casually waving my hands over them to force a perspective that pretends they're insects crawling under my hand. *This is fun.*

"I've been thinking about more projects for you this month. Honestly, I haven't found anything," Val consoles.

"That's okay," I shrug, swallowing my irritation.

I have my own project for the next few weeks: How to spy on Val and Antonio without Central watching. I'm plowing into the guts of system management. Powerful tools hide in technology that no one knows about. My goal: get Antonio's video feed to stream encrypted to my smartphone with no one knowing. I'll buy the service myself from All Corp's Intelligence Division for only a few hundred bucks.

"How's the new prison coming?" I change the subject.

"Ugh. Thanks for ruining my mood," Valentina sours, setting her wine glass on the rooftop ledge and closing her eyes. "The new building's stalled in design. Again." She shakes her head. "We only have a $100 million budget and Ormo wants to hold 10,000 *more* prisoners." She points to the crowd below. "How? There's no way. We either need to stick with 500 prisoners or add a billion dollars!" She shoves her hand in the air with a go-fuck-yourself shrug. "Seriously. I tell him we should shoot the fuckers if we *really* need room. Why are we paying for these shits?" She sloshes her wine at the prison below her feet. "But he wants things as quiet as he can," she huffs.

"Hm." I think about my business books. "Could they work? The prisoners?"

"No, they couldn't build the new prison. Could build their own escape tunnels!" she scoffs. "Besides, they wouldn't know how," she dismisses.

"No, I mean real work," I clarify, laughing. "Like, jobs that earn money for us." *Maybe Val is kinda dumb?* I wonder.

She thinks a bit. "Probably won't earn enough revenue for a new prison," she shifts.

"Maybe…but if we put our 500 to work now and see how much we earn, we can extrapolate what ten thousand prisoners might earn? The more people we lock up, the more money we make! I'll ask my uncle what simple projects prisoners might do by hand and how much that work could be worth."

"You know, yeah. That's great, Jen. Wow." Val steps back a tad taken. "I never thought of that. Wait. Shit, laws," she frowns.

"Who cares about rules? Screw those," I encourage with another sip of wine.

"I can't…no. There're implications if *we're* breaking the law. There'd be riots. We're the law and order group. Ormo doesn't want to 'just be another dictator with Labor Camps like the asshats in Venezuela and Argentina.' Direct quote," she points. "He wants to be a noble Custodian of the People. He saved us from a civil war and has lots of admiration for that."

"What could be better than lowering their taxes as thanks?" I offer.

"73% the country is a bunch of moochers who despise work and would vote Communist if it were not for my brother. Rock the boat and they'll storm this place." She taps her fingers irritably on the stone ledge. "If we were perfectly hidden away, I'd be fine with whatever," she waves her hand. "Sure. Labor camps would be amazing. But we're in the middle of the city." She looks at the thinning crowd below. "There's a shifty squalor here," she says, her words darkening.

"I thought we're under Martial Law? Use the red phone. Spitball some ideas, see what the president thinks," I suggest. "He's the one who wants the new prison and can't afford it. Maybe we *all* can make money?" I emphasize.

Valentina's eyes bubble, but her words drip with worry, "I don't know."

The commotion on the street evaporates and we return to our table.

"Valentina. We can build a wonderful industry here," I encourage, pointing to the prison underneath. "We *own* these people. I know we're surrounded by the envious and less gifted," I nod to the city. "I know their hate burns and wrongly victimizes us. We've earned these privileges." I caress the gourmet table. "They don't understand. Maybe they've never had the chance to work hard and earn money? Val, we need to see ourselves as heroes, job creators delivering the gift of hard work."

Valentina sighs, smiles at me, and pours us another glass of wine. "To arrest his political opponents, my brother shut down congress, rigged the media and courts, and reformed most civil rights," she lists thoughtfully.

"Wow, right?" I encourage. "So put 'em to work. The hard part's done!"

Valentina nods and slowly continues, "Martial Law allows him to set his own law into statutes." Valentina twirls her hair.

"What's the problem then?" I grin, waving my hands excitedly in the air. "We should *charge* for prison time. Like

$15,000 a year? That'd be $7,500,000 a year for our five hundred. Prisoners families could be on the hook for the bills. We can sell loans and pay ourselves extra with interest!"

"Careful," Valentina cautions. "We don't want to be *seen* as running a slave labor camp. That's my worry. Jen, yes, we have power, but we aren't free."

"But why have power if you can't have freedom?" I complain.

Fucking cowards. How disappointing. "Why should the powerful be the *least* free when they should be the freest?" I prod.

"Actions have counter-actions," she balances a fork on her finger. "Even if people are predictable, one of the keys to power is to allow people to *think* they are free and unconstrained...even when they're not. That's always my advice for your parole hearings, right?"

I nod. *How does that work in a truly free market?* I briefly wonder.

"Once that illusion is broken, shit hits the fan." She pinches her blouse at the heat. "Hits the fan hard."

"Look. How many people need jobs?" I ask. "Tens of thousands? Maybe he could select the most politically convenient people and their families for our work-prison, and we can keep an eye on them?"

I'd love a whole city working for me.

Valentina frowns. "Well, focus. Our real enemies are all the dark places the fungus of socialism grows. College campuses, the media, intellectual and literary journals, the arts and sciences," she lists. "The pulpit—the religious fundamentally believe in a higher power above the state, and we can't have that. This fungus would never volunteer for your TempCamps up north. I wonder if that's why they're having so many problems and that stupid war?! In Chile, we locked up our troublemakers right away," she gloats.

Reports are that southern Illinois, and much of the rust belt, is a wasteland of militias.

Would Mom and Dad have ended up in prison if we'd lived in Chile, rather than Illinois? Would I have been punished too? Or would Uncle Greg have saved us—for a fee? It's crazy how my world could've totally turned another direction on a random fluke. More reasons to always be in charge, I confirm.

I shrug, ceding Val's point. "I guess I don't really care who, as long as I get lots of workers." I want as many people under me as possible. *I'd never be bored then.*

I watch on my smartphone as Antonio kisses Valentina's neck and moves his lips slowly down her arm. He tenderly sucks her fingers one by one. I see her eyes glaze in bliss as her whole-body sighs happily against the isolation room wall.

I watch as they talk, laugh, and snuggle. I watch as they play card games. I watch as they have *really* rough sex.

She isn't interrogating him. She's dating him. Valentina and Antonio are in love.

What the hell? How stupid is she?

I take screenshots of their kinkiest things. *He willingly sucks her toes? That's a thing?!* I laugh in amazement. *Some people* are *actually attracted to their own submission and repression, like Dad said!*

I take screenshots of their beautiful tender moments; she rubs his shoulders and runs a hand through his hair. I record as they hug long goodbyes.

I watch Val and wish I had what she has. *One person consuming the dignity of another person?* The supremacy. The various forms of humiliation she puts her guy through. *What a treat.* I laugh one night, watching them on my phone.

My greatest pleasure is taking. Growing more powerful, more dominant. Holding power over Val. Torturing prisoners.

No wonder a normal social life fails me. *I doubt I'll ever have a basic romantic relationship. Nothing lasted with the cowboys, they wanted a little woman to protect, while I would have preferred to eat them alive if I could.*

Is a master/slave relationship the only intimacy I can have? Power dynamics are so impossibly sexy for me, and this is not the kind of control that can be given, like, 'Okay, you pick the movie tonight.' No. This is the kind of power where, like it or not, I'm calling the shots.

I have single-minded determination to do whatever it takes to fulfill the hunger of my dreams.

A few days later, the Red Phone rings. We have approval to put our prisoners to work; if administrative costs never outpace revenue, we're all go.

And I'm in charge.

CHAPTER 23—JEN FEST™

Eddie. June 2026

My shuttle docks with a shudder. *Shit*, I lean towards the mirror and quick comb my hair, darken my bathroom light and run into the bedroom for a sport coat. The majestic view beyond my windows forces a grin. *I love these green mountains so much.* I grab my coat from the bedroom chair almost feeling the altitude. *Gotta thank Laura and her team for the view. The morning glow is delightful,* I note as the 7 a.m. sunrise highlights a layer of clouds.

"Sir, your transportation has arrived," an electronic voice insists.

"Be right there," I hurry to the door, shoving arms into my coat, sleeve by sleeve. *Thank god shuttle tickets are 15% off for JenFest today.*

My door opens with a hiss. I see a steep funnel condensing into a thin straw. *Damn it,* I frown. *An extra small ride today,* and walk forward. The funnel becomes a short hallway as my size dynamically adjusts smaller and smaller with each step. I look at my massive apartment behind me as I tap my payment card against the bus door. *First of many of today's humiliations…*

The door slides open to a festive atmosphere. Balloons are on the shuttle ceiling. I smell gin, and smirk at five twenty-somethings slyly holding red cups in the far back row.

Only three people recognize me at first.

An old lady in front offers me her seat.

I warmly smile, "No thanks. I'm alright."

Immediately, a guy across the walkway insists I take his seat as he stands.

I politely refuse again with an increasingly thin smile. *Come on guys, let's not make a scene.* He firmly demands again. The shuttle gets quiet as one hundred and fifty people whisper about who the newcomer is. *Goddamn it,* I blush, slouching into the guy's empty chair. "Thanks," I admit with a thin wave of my hand.

"We BioMechs are helpful types," the man nervously stutters with a curt nod.

"Yup. Totally," I awkwardly agree. The Senior Biomechanical Engineer moves to the third walkway and several rows back.

I quickly glance around. My co-workers avert their eyes, pretending not to stare. We're on edge this week, worrying about the direction our jobs inside Jennifer and what the new directions might mean for our lives.

Why is it impossible to have a normal life? I scowl, despising the mix of awe and fear employees have for me. They think the System Admin has so much power. I have only slightly more influence on Jen than they do, or any other fly, ant, or insect working in her cockroach motel.

I want to be on the employees' side. I *am* on their side. Jen is so impossible. *Why don't they understand that? She decided to mix Company Updates with JenFest,* I curse.

JenFest used to be a true congregation of the human spirit. A Welcome Party where employees came together for meaning in the company of each other, and to welcome our new Jen-Members™, like normal human beings.

I watch three people on the far side of the bus laugh their asses off. *Having fun. Being nice to each other. How great is that?* I marvel. *Humanity is almost too resilient, they're all accepting Jen's world like champs.*

I turn from the life around me with a lonely sigh to watch the flat grassland passing beyond the shuttle. *Must be Kenya? Or Tanzania?* I lean closer to the window and see only slight pixilation.

Two years ago, my biggest masterstroke was demanding Jen simulate natural countryside images outside every shuttle, building, and personnel capsule. Sure, some of the themes were repetitive, like the farmland ones. Ten looping miles of corn! Simple as hell. Nonetheless, I demanded Jen spare no expense on the high-quality holograms. They look real enough and suicides have fallen to an all-time low.

I calculate my Scenery Initiative prevents 13.45% of our co-workers from taking their lives each year.

We took forever to convince Jen the extra money was worth it, as she only faintly cared about the mounting loss of life. *'Economic growth is never even,'* Jennifer muttered, lazily reading a tablet by her massive pool, her response disturbingly casual to the chaos of human life drowning within her. *'Don't impose your values on my profits with your 'social tax'! If employees can't handle the truth of their choices and would rather die—that's not my issue. I've no problem naturally culling opportunities from the weak and giving them to stronger workers who are more effective with my market-driven labor ideals.'*

Goddamn homicidal sadist. I clench my fist around the cloth of my pant leg until it becomes too tight. *How has she sucked us all in so easy?*

I darkly remember with vivid terror that she *enjoys* the thought of people losing their lives inside of her.

Eventually, I painstakingly proved to Jen that hiring new staff takes several months to reach peak productivity. *'Hey, money talks.'* She provided reluctant approval a few weeks later after seven hundred more lives were lost, while munching some chips. Her sadistic Free Market Paradise would indeed become less efficient from the huge turnover, as new staff struggles to lift projects from the deceased.

Or the liberated?

I bite my lip, moving my mind along familiar ethical ruts like a tongue would a lost tooth. *Suicides slow her business and cost Jenifer time and money. No one is really living their own life here anyway. Right?*

I understand the courageous want for a freedom none of us can afford beyond the ultimate price. But then again, the amount of *coordinated* human loss would need to be huge, and simultaneous, for our sacrifice to make a dent in her numbers. She wouldn't care about the loss of humanity alone, as she never cared about humanity in the first place. *And what would stop her from simply injecting more and more naive and brainwashed workers?* There are billions of unemployed ready and eager for a chance.

A young couple flirting across the aisle makes me smile. Seems like they've just met. *The new employees are so young. They look like teenagers.* My thoughts cloud. *Will the next generation of workers even understand the world beyond a life 100% consumed by a corporate monster? Whole cultures have collapsed and disappeared before. Why couldn't they do so now?*

Jen is always chanting her mantra: "This is an era of radical privatization. Climb aboard or drown!" I think she really means it.

A guy moves across an aisle to coach a crying newbie seven seats over. I can tell she's a newbie from the dazed terror. *Good for that guy,* I approve of the mentoring.

Why is compassion a rare thing? I wonder. *Our Welcome Parties were once only every few months. Productivity never meaningfully dropped,* I bitterly defend. *We didn't spend much money. Tons of us volunteered, buying FreeTime™ passes.* We wanted to embrace new staff injected into Jennifer on their first traumatic day. We 'Pioneers' didn't enjoy the luxury of a warm welcome. Our first night in the frontier of Jen's Free Market State was as isolating as it was terrifying. We were in shock. How could she *totally privatize* us?! And nothing worked. Whole teams were accidentally Flushed when the SupplyBots couldn't locate their pods' defective tracking.

Tad didn't deserve to die like that.

I shudder, remembering calls from co-workers who realized they were lost in Jen's bladder or bile duct and were moments away from being Flushed.

Horrific.

Naturally, Jen's response was more horrific: '*What? So, I'm not supposed to piss, shit, or sweat for a whole month while you get the System YOU said was tested and ready to go? Fuck that, Ed. I'm running a business. A for-profit business. And I'm not hiding from that. Fix it. This problem is your responsibility. Not mine.*'

How could we understand, or even imagine, such scenarios when we tested the System so long ago? *Fucking hell. I even installed the System.* My stomach churns, remembering the experience in Jen's navel. *How can I alone fix a System that fucked up?*

The first Welcome Parties were to ensure all new employees, upon injection into Jennifer, had the proper tracking in the System. And to hold secret memorials to those Flushed by Jennifer's selfishness. Marketing eventually recommended "Welcome Parties" be re-named "JenFest," to properly celebrate the success of our CEO. Soon, the events became weekly. Then daily. Now, Jennifer injects herself with new staff *several* times a day and no one can keep track. Not even me.

Ha, I laugh at the dark irony. The staff looks at my System Admin position with reverence, jealous of my 'Sight Outside' because I have Jen's video feeds and summary analytics.

Funny, I look at the staff in reverence for their privileged ignorance. Jen doesn't speak to *them* when she's without the digital touch ups that hide her dead soulless eyes. *They* don't watch the bliss spread across her face as savage throes of pleasure thrash her body after she injects whole companies of people. The staff doesn't need to know how much of a 'party' a Welcome Party *really* is for Jen. They don't need to know injecting humans is Jen's top drug of choice.

"More, more, more." That's all I hear her monstrous voice say.

Why let the staff see the infinite darkness of Jen's totalitarian consumption as they jet from one nameless vein into another? Why let them know they've been stuck in a pimple for two days? Why let them know they've been working under her toenail for seven months? As long as the staff is in the System, and accurately tracked, let them focus on achieving their near impossible objectives and goals with as little pain as possible.

I don't want to poison coworkers high on the promise of Jen's Free Market Paradise like I once was. *Those days,* I smile remembering TempGrace, *when I believed in her, were the most intoxicating of my life!* Sure, now my coworkers are so drunk on Jen's Free Market propaganda they don't have a clue what's really going on. *But hey, they're happy.* I nod.

I look past my ignorant co-workers. *I hate my life. I hate knowing what I know. But at least I have a life.* I eventually admit with stinging eyes, thinking how much serious pain this Depression is hammering across the ruined economy.

I blink back tears and turn to appreciate the warm grassy countryside. *A pleasant savannah,* I watch distant hills stroll past, wishing I could sit for hours listening to humans being human.

I need to stop the insanity of my own thoughts, I mutter, wishing I could afford anti-anxiety medication. I rub my temples to massage tension along my jaw and refocus on the slightly cheaper professional advice. "The best defense for employees who choose to stay in a narcissistic corporation is to protect narcissists boss's egos and avoid challenging them," said an article. The author's advice to employees living with extreme narcissists is that we, "remain sane and reasonable," instead of meeting them in, "battles they'll always win. Narcissists feel superior to others, but they are not necessarily satisfied with themselves as a person."

We arrive.

The bus settles with a soft thunk at Central Terminal. The core of our civilization, a small knot of structures implanted in the lining of Jen's stomach wall. I force myself to smile as passengers eagerly gather their things and push into the aisles.

"I'll see you in the Free Street bars. Have a good time," I pleasantly wave my co-workers ahead. "I'm in no rush. Have a good day! Bye now. Bye now. Have a good day."

I pretend my hesitation is a courtesy. A few people send me stupid grins while others refuse to look at me. The truth of my hesitation is actually a cowardly avoidance for the start of JenFest 2026. I know this JenFest is different. We'll all want those hella expensive Free Street bars and nightclubs to distract our reality with whatever shameful doses of humanity we can grab. Whores. Booze. Gambling. *Sure, enjoy them all while you can,* I spit.

Free Street is owned by Jen. The distilleries. The hotels. Brothels. The amusement parks. All their rip-off prices go to Jen. *We're owned by Jen too, all our profits go to Jen,* I pointlessly remind myself like a jilted lover in the vortex of circular thought.

If she doesn't respect us now, will she ever in the future?

I watch the last passenger stream past as I linger near my seat on the empty shuttle. My chest deflates with a sigh as I stare at the emptiness and move sluggishly to the exit.

The green and purple walls of the Transfer Center teem with thousands of bustling workers. The staff walks and laughs in a hurry as if today is a busy normal day in Times Square. *Actually, this is our normal.*

I drag my fingers along the fake plastic windows that display colorful structures of a stunning yet false metropolis full of proud towers soaring into a false blue sky. I touch the steel support beams arcing thinly along the hallway. I run my fingers over anything real.

"Fat cell storage." I shudder, remembering Jen's voice excitedly outline her vision.

Steel drums rhythmically clang louder and louder around the next corner. *Street Bands!* I hurry into the expansive air of Free Street. One hundred yards wide, eight miles long, Free Street is the main pedestrian artery of The Core. Several off-shoot avenues allow pedestrians to explore bars of New Bourbon Street or the brothels and headshops of New Amsterdam. For a toll. Loud colors and

Worship Money advertisements attack the hundreds of thousands of workers surging forward.

I shove towards the music to see Jamaican musicians drumming in front of a Loan Office—always the first shop outside any Terminal.

These guys are good, I grin at their rhythm. *Fantastic!* I wish I was with them, my clarinet playing a groovy tune. My fingers dance. A damp chill sweeps me as I increasingly sense my musical life as more ghost-like: a parallel soul locked forever in a parallel life that I'll never see.

I note the large crowd listening in front of the harsh lights of the loan office. *I wonder if this performance is paying a debt? I've seen it thousands of times.* Payday advances. Micro-loans. Jen eagerly sells them to us. When you're hungry, you do whatever it takes to eat—even a loan to pay for a loan.

Jen's Debt Prisons will become a forced choice for many. "Free sustenance. Free shelter." *Debt Bondage,* I laugh. *No other life beyond Jen's confinement? Sure! Jen will enjoy us all tied up like that.* I cringe, irritated that I'm allowing Jen's pending announcements to soil my walk, the one thing I was most excited for this week. *Appreciate the music, dumbass. Be happy with what you have.* I force a smile and eventually slip the drummers a Business Unit coin and move on, Jen's needs again ruling my day.

"Celebrate the Rich," billboards flank the mile walk towards Central Arena. All billboards display Jen's $643 billion dollar smile or some other overpriced gimmick of hers.

"The Market is God. It destroys as it blesses," with Jen's smile.

That fucking inescapable face. I try to grip reality as my brain's reward system fires. "Our bodies drug us when we simply look at a person we desire." I feel my heart stupidly melt and soften for Jen.

Blue and purple shadows illuminate the massive Jennifer Free Market State Arena. Four hundred thousand employees enter through multiple sides. MechGuards, with "F.M.S." stamped on their chests, line the hallways ready to enforce the peace. Or whatever Jen's will happens to be.

Ha, I confidently run my fingers casually along the chest of a mech without fear. *All this time I've worried about the machines coming after us. It's not the robot army, no, it's the psycho who owns the robots I should've been worried about!* Robots are predictable. Hard-coded. *Jen? No fucking clue what she's gonna do next.*

I wander the crowded curves of the hallways soaking the humanity flooding the massive space. "Beer for the 9 a.m. rock concert? $45!" "Pancakes and a juice? $29.99 special!"

Ten minutes before Jen's show starts, I sit in my reserved front row seat, glancing a nod at Jim Thompson, and the old BIUSA executive team twenty seats away. At 10 a.m. the arena darkens and starts an energizing light show. A movie inspires us with summaries from Jennifer's 'Amazing Year.' The acquisitions. Jennifer with world leaders. Jennifer with business tycoons. Jennifer on the front page of magazines and newspapers across the globe. *Jennifer is everywhere.*

Suddenly, the lights fade black. The cheers and hoots intensify.

Jennifer is here.

A door on the stage illuminates. Jen steps out to rapturous cheers, her thirty-foot figure fills the stage. She grins, sending me a wink as she waves at her adoring crowd.

I faintly wave back. *She doesn't care. I know she doesn't care. Right?* I wonder. *She looks magnificent.* I breathe heavily.

The staff clearly loves her.

I'm falling in love with her again. *"Love alters not with his brief hours and weeks but bears it out even to the edge of doom."* Funny how love deactivates the advanced areas of the brain. Areas involved in rational decisions.

I shake my head. *She's so here.* Jennifer's real-time digital blemish removal edits her image flawlessly. She radiates grace, sophistication. Radiates intelligence. Her hologram is so real.

"She's so tall," a lady nearby gasps to her friend. "I didn't expect her to be this big in real life." Both ladies clearly forget the whole arena is a speck in Jennifer's belly.

Morons, I chide, as their comment shakes me awake. I see this all the time. Jen's actual nature is entirely ignored because her scale escapes conception. *Of course, she's here. We're buried hundreds of miles in her guts.* But that seems so abstract, and she seems so perfect.

Reality hurts so much that I doubt hardly anyone in this arena ponders it. Jennifer is a world to herself, "an assortment of

~37,000,000,000,000 cells plus a similar complement of allied microbes." Add us employees and our Logistics Bots to Jennifer's system (a measly nine million), and all that humanity amounts to a small bacterial nuisance captured to Jen's SuperOrganism bidding.

Her SuperCivilization.

"Thank you, Jennifer employees. Thank you, Pioneers!" She blows loving kisses. "Thank you for changing the world. Our network brings together thousands of members to advance a vision of a free and open society. Our Free Market State has grown 1,500% the past quarter alone. Friends, it's official." Her eyes glimmer, "You are part of the largest, most profitable enterprise in history!"

Feet stomp the floor like thunder. Chants of "Jen. Jen. Jen." drench the air.

"You. Make. Jennifer. Strong. You are Jennifer. This greatness," she points to herself, "is you. By making Jennifer as strong and profitable as possible, Jennifer strengthens the economy, while delivering the Free Market dream executives and philosophers have searched decades to attain."

More cheers.

Jen walks forward to stand near the edge of the stage. Her thirty-foot illusion stands nearly on top of the front row. The thinness of her hologram is occasionally cut by the stage lights above.

"Thankfully, our pending IPO is only a few quarters away."

Ha, I snort to myself, looking directly up at her, fighting flashbacks to my first few months in her drawer. *She's been saying 'just a few more quarters' for years!* It's hard to not be too sarcastic with the new folks drunk on their initial paychecks, wholly ignorant of the *true* costs of living inside Jennifer's F.M.S.

"Keep working hard. Keep buying Business Unit Manna. And when Jennifer is respected and feared all over the world, we all can retire on tropical islands!"

Wild cheers.

If the IPO does eventually *happen, I'm looking forward to making enough bread to leave Jennifer for good,* I aspire.

"Jennifer consists of the most prestigious and unique work force in the world," she beams. "The Free Market State Trade Zone has become a unique attraction to governments, businesses, and immigrants across the earth looking for more efficiency. More freedom. More profits. And more work. Jennifer is willing to be that hero and deliver the innovative leadership the markets sorely need."

She shifts tone, "Pioneers. The market absolutely *loves* Jennifer. Loves that we've expanded the private frontier to the governments of Mississippi. Oklahoma. Arizona." Localized cheers erupt with the names of each State. "We have privatized their operations into Jennifer, saving taxpayers 3.6% their annual costs. Jennifer has privatized over *half* of all Southern U.S. public employees into this room!"

Wild cheers.

That boggles my mind: *How could any legislature surrender their operations to Jennifer's contracts?* I thought it would never happen so I never bothered fighting her idea. My jaw fell through the floor when it only took a month for Jen to consume the entire bureaucracy of Texas.

"The market loves Jennifer so much they're practically drooling for a taste of Jennifer's private Free Market State. I'm getting so much attention I have to fend investments and partnerships off with sticks," she grins.

I jealously imagine dozens of Wall Street douchebags trying to fuck Jennifer, without a single clue of the kind of predator they're getting in bed with.

"And I'll tell you, personally, it feels amazing to make this dream real. Leading Jennifer feels intense." She touches her heart. "Working with you brings out a power and sense of responsibility I never knew I had, and I've never been happier in my whole life."

"We love you!" someone in the crowd shouts.

Her tone becomes more sensitive. "And I you. I love the Free Market State because I know Jennifer offers the best opportunities to the best employees worth escaping this depression. Jennifer is a Financial Heaven to weary hardworking souls looking for a chance. Because friends, times are dark," the room sobers. "Reports are unanimous that markets are tanking. Down another 23% last month alone, while unemployment rose an additional 17%. To my surprise, even supposedly safe banks collapsed," she frets. "Behemoths that have lasted over a hundred years have fallen to the crashing waves of the Market. Yet, Jennifer BUs remain solid. Keep buying them. Jennifer's success is a resounding endorsement of my Free Market State principles: total hard work, total free market, total privatization."

The audience claps.

"Jennifer is a beacon of stability in a chaotic world. Thus, this deeper depression presents an interesting opportunity," she grins. "Full customer base integration! Can you imagine not only visiting Free Street, *but city after city after city?* To shop? To party? To make new friends?"

Wild cheers as the crowd jumps to their feet.

Oh god...

"So many people and organizations are desperate to join Jennifer that, to support this new Free Market economy, our very idea of Labor needs to become the ultimate resource it's always been."

I cringe. *Oh shit, here comes the pain.* I eye if there are enough MechGuards to settle a riot. *Probably not,* I note after a quick count, seeing only one guard per exit.

"In our shrinking globalized world, people are less sure about themselves. They want peace in a world with no free handouts—but lots of private opportunities, as nothing should be free," she articulates. "No free air. No free water. Not even our time is free. You are part of Jennifer's system, part of something great and secure. Outside? Only increasing dissolution, struggle, and savagery. In Jennifer, you have a home. Stability."

"Labor needs to become the ultimate commodity, as the Free Market never knows what skills are needed when and for how long. Thus, when the debts of a Jen-Member raise too high, and when all their resources have depleted, there is need for a safe place, an afterlife, to accept the total surrender of the weary and a refuge for those unable to repay their debts of manna to Jennifer."

Fuck fuck fuck, I brace, looking panicky at people's naive curiosity. I eye the exit again. *That's far. Fucking far. Why did I agree to sit here?* The first sign of 'boos' and I'm bolting.

"I'd like you to be the first in the world to hear about Jennifer's Strategic Labor Reserve. When debts can no longer be repaid, Debtors will no longer be Flushed to fend for themselves, but enter Jennifer's Strategic Labor Reserve—for free."

The crowd gasps.

I sit in tense silence, trying to decipher the open mouths around me.

Hoots and wild yells erupt as people jump, applauding, to their feet. "No Flushing? How lucky are we?" "Whoa. We never have to leave? Even if we totally screw up?" "That's a free deal even I'll accept."

What? I gasp. People are happy for this? What the serious fuck?

"Yes." Jen continues. "No more Flushing. Ever. Jennifer knows times are hard. From today until the end of time, when staff hit the bottom of their Profitability Scores, rather than be Flushed outside to fend for themselves, staff with zero profitability will enjoy a basic and safe life in Jennifer's Strategic Labor Reserve."

Hoots and cheers.

How do people applaud their permanent imprisonment? I scream to myself, pulling my hair.

"The smartest and strongest of you earn the reward of employment, with all the Free Market freedoms and joys you can handle—and then some. While those whose profitability falters, even temporarily, will enjoy the basic comforts of Jennifer's Strategic Labor Reserve. Free oxygen. Free sustenance. Free shelter," she lists. "And nothing to do for a period of weeks to possibly years, depending on conditions of the Labor Market," she mumbles. "This industry pioneering method enables Jennifer to throttle up and down labor operations on the slightest whim of Market needs."

I scan the auditorium in shock.

How does no one understand the costs of this? Jennifer wants to corner the Labor Market. Permanently! If Jennifer owns most of the possible employees—all the temps, all the experts, all the freelancers—she controls the economy and can charge for services whatever she wants. If Jennifer controls the economy, she controls society; all while making herself look good. Yes, she's sheltering and nurturing millions of the poor and destitute in her sick fat cell storage system, but no one realizes how *strategically* she wants to store the debt soaked saps in her fat cells.

"I'll be 30 this summer." I remember Jen's private conversation with me. *"I want to preserve my physical beauty as I age. Beauty, my one superpower I least control. I worry about losing it,"* she darkly leans towards the camera with her dead baggy eyes. *"A side bonus: I can massage my firm tits and slap my perfect ass in lust, knowing millions of you poor are locked inside,"* she eagerly looks to the ceiling, running her hands across her chest. *"Amazing!"*

This is all about Jennifer's carnal wants. Not our development. Not our economy. All her twisted truths are for her own sense of power and gratification. *And the whole auditorium applauds!?*

The joy eventually quiets down.

"Thank you. Yes, thank you," Jennifer beams. "You have no idea how much this means to me. We're on the frontier. Comfort is not permanent," she shrugs.

"Throughout history, primitive societies have foolishly held back upstarts and strong leaders with ridicule, Collectivist Norms, and regulations. Forgetting that the strong can do the most to protect and uplift the whole tribe. Philosophers say 'Civilization is the cultural shift from cooperation to extreme individualism and competition.' Greed is our salvation," she expands her arms like a preacher. "Greed for life, for money, for love, for knowledge, marks the upward struggle of humanity. Worship billionaires and make more money; any compromise is a betrayal of the fullest potential of yourselves."

She's quiet a moment. The space is tense.

"You might already know…people desperate for handouts murdered my family." Her eyes are big and intently scan the arena. "Jennifer is a fundamentally moral corporation, and it's our moral duty to save others stuck in the savage public world," she shakes her head. "It's time for civilization to advance. We must privatize whole regions and industries so that Jennifer grows bigger and bigger, as for thousands of years, larger groups consistently outcompete smaller ones.

"I can't promise work. Not all will have jobs in Jennifer. But I can promise belonging," she hugs her chest with a tender smile. "Let's take back the North. Let's outcompete their socialist system with rock bottom prices on our services. Let's make our next goal expanding Jennifer to all corners of the earth!"

What? Whoa. My blood drains as I feel faint and need to sit.

Hoots and cheers.

Jennifer moves to the center stage. "The stronger Jennifer becomes, the stronger *you* become. Let's make you part of the strongest entity in human history. Thank you!" She waves goodbye.

CHAPTER 24—SETUP

Jennifer. November 2017

How blissful is this? I slap Giorgio across the face with my leather paddle. He's a tough rebel sergeant, but this week he's my little bitch.

It's fun to be strong, sexy to be strong, I grin to myself.

In my interrogation room, I don't have to pretend like I do in the real world. I'm free to be me. Free to be whatever I want. *Ironic that getting prisoners to see the truth, allows me to reveal my own truth?* I muse at the endorphins surging through my veins, wrapping me in a glowing, meditative bliss.

We need pain to survive, to stay honest. Suffering is a sharp reminder that we're alive and there's a struggle to endure. Love, comfort, and altruism? That shit drowns our potential. Sogs our mind in laziness and ties on a pair of cement shoes that are *hard* to take off when Free Market tides surge around our neck.

I see that workers are naturally lazy and need punishment—or its threat—to stay productive. My new role as Line Boss at our prison factory isn't to make my workers happy, it's to prepare their character and moral courage for a ruthless world where the snap of the free market is as cruel as a dominatrix's whip.

I'm that whip. I'm that dominatrix.

I very much enjoy this power play aspect, having complete control over Giorgio's situation. He's prey, at my mercy, subject to my every whim. I can toy with him as I please. His fear excites me. Knowing I can drag the torment out as long as I want is simply the best.

I'm beating the shit out of Giorgio all morning because he's not working hard enough. Actually, he's not even trying. He's distracting the workers who obey me, so today my performance reviews are violent. *Why can't I just make him work? Goddamnit.*

Three-fourths of the prisoners work fine. I control them physically *and* mentally; they happily assemble shoes and boots according to my client's specifications. The other quarter? They rebel. Operations won't scale if one-hundred guys refuse to work. Thankfully, we're spinning up and I don't *necessarily* need them, yet. But I didn't foresee this disobedience, and it irritates me.

I control Giorgio physically with my guards. He's my prisoner strapped on the cold cement floor. I define his day, his week, his life. *But I cannot control his mind,* I think, looming imposingly above him. *Today we're working on this.*

I want to bring as many people into my workforce as I can and shape them in a style of workaholism that benefits me, and then cast them aside once they're no longer useful. *How do I best ready workers for my needs?* I slap Giorgio again. I find satisfaction inflicting extreme pain and greatly enjoy the process of transforming a man into a mindless slave.

I remember the TempCamp back home rewarding the hardest workers most eager to enslave themselves for the least pay. *Clever.* I only now appreciate the benefits of the sly method. Desperate workers are so important to management success. *I'm such an amateur!*

Hire half the working class to destroy the other half.

However, the greatest lesson of my life is learning some people *enjoy* their own oppression, are even attracted to it. Watching Antonio and Valentina has been fun. Really fun. *Some men get turned-on having a woman bark orders and spit on them? Perfect.* I watch them steam up my phone most evenings and intimately relax. *Mhmmm...* gimme, gimme, I coo as their little bodies writhe in the small screen in my hands.

Some people love feeling oppressed and I'm more than happy to love them back.

I think of my Mom and Dad and their messed-up relationship, wondering what weird shit they were into. I remember how frustrated Dad would be watching so many poor people eagerly vote for corporate tax breaks and the minimization of public services that would directly benefit working and middle-class families. *'The insanity!'* he'd say, watching a blue-collar guy on the news glorify the needs of the market and executives.

Although, I see some people hate feeling oppressed. They're like me and Giorgio; they rebel. They fight my love and affection. I'm getting faster at identifying each type—the controlling and the submissive types—because each need a totally different approach. I want to walk into a room and identify, based on posture and how someone stands, who are the vulnerable targets I can have my fun with and who I need to fight.

I prescribe Giorgio a series of random electric shocks. He'll learn there's nothing to stop the pain and give up trying. Scientists call this "learned helplessness." An interrogation technique that limits a prisoner's "sense of control and predictability" and brings "a desired level of helplessness."

I give all my prisoners these shocks electrically, socially, emotionally, and financially—whatever delivers the most chaos for the day. The CIA's *Human Resource Exploitation Training Manual* suggests, "The purpose of coercive techniques is to induce psychological regression in the subject by bringing a superior outside force to bear on his will to resist."

"I'm your superior force, Fucker," I lean to slap him again.

But how can I control his mind? I need to conquer his mind before I can take his spirit.

"Giorgio," I taunt, slowly stepping onto his chest and looking at him far below me. "I hold the key to your freedom," I jump twice on his ribs, "and with me, you'll never be free *unless I rule you."* I run a toe tenderly along his swollen jaw. *"When I rule your wants, your life, Giorgio, the world is so much better. I do these things so that I can love you, so I can bring you peace! Don't you want that?"*

All he does is groan and look at me through swollen eyes. I love looking down on him. It's so gratifying, to have this power over him. I step off and reach for a towel to soak my sweat. *Interrogations are a great workout.* I drop the rag on his face and tell the guards to leave him in the dark for two days with only a bucket of water to either drink or kill himself with. *If I can get him to do the most extreme or outlandish thing ever, I can get anyone to do anything!* I hope.

We're an artisan prison. My prisoners handcraft glamorous high-end women's shoes. I love that months of their collective lives will be wrapped around my feet and the feet of sophisticated women all over the world. I charge $300-$600 for each pair of women's shoes and over $900 for a pair of women's boots. The retailers charge twice that in stores, but whatever, I'm only starting. Even in this depression the high-end luxury market is bonkers! Uncle Greg connected me with the best young experimental designers in Milan, Paris, and New York—all looking for economical yet highly controlled work environments to protect their designs and guarantee zero knock offs. Unlike the manufactures in Asia, I have my workers *entirely* controlled, which is perfect for business.

Becoming craftsmen has significantly raised prisoners' morale. They're happy to remove their minds from their situation—even for pennies a day. I have no problem stealing wages from inmates. Firstly, they're criminals. Secondly, it's not stealing if they never earn it. I keep the profits. That's what companies do. I get to decide where the resources and profits go, and I decide they go to me!

Success isn't earned; it's taken.

Hard work won't make you rich. The nerdy prisoners are great workers. Eager to please. Yet I will always pay practically nothing beyond a smile and an extra satellite TV package for the break room. Hard Work is the suckers game, an important 'truth' for Giorgio and the rest of my serfs to understand—and for me to ignore.

Owning things makes you rich. Owning resources. Owning processes. Owning people. Ownership, control, domination—these are the true paths of wealth.

After my morning workout with Giorgio, I have two or three hours of administrative work. I type some reports and track invoices on my fancy thin laptop like Uncle Greg taught me.

Yet, today is special. I'm working at Valentina's desk while she's off with Antonio. I check my phone and see them snuggling and laughing.

"Boring," I mutter, tossing my phone aside.

I'm the one doing all the work here, which is fine, as I'm taking all the reward. 75% of prison profits are mine. Valentina gets 10%. Ormo 20%. The guards 4%. The prisoners collectively get 1%.

All my stakeholders are happiest not knowing the truth.

Valentina walks in the office late in the afternoon. "Making yourself right at home, eh?" she jokes and awkwardly brushes the sex from her hair.

I don't laugh and barely move my eyes from an email outlining terms to a curious designer in Los Angeles.

"Val. I think we need to switch roles," I dryly state.

"Too funny. No, Jen," she laughs and sets her purse on my desk with a hand on her hip.

I keep writing my email.

"Wait. Are you serious?" she eventually stammers like a skittish teenager. "You *are* serious," she rages. "What in hell gives you the right to demand that?" She slaps a hand to the wood surface.

"Because you're in love with a prisoner." I half look up, finish typing, and lean back in the chair.

"What? That's ridiculous. *How dare you!* Get out," she violently points to the door. "You're fired!"

I cross my arms. "No. It's true. I've fixed Antonio's video feed to my phone," I say, holding my smartphone. "I have *months* of videos and photos." I stab a sly smile.

Valentina stammers something wordlessly and then shakily sits in the chair across the desk. "Oh, god. Who knows?"

She looks pale and sick.

"Only me. I think." I emotionlessly peer at her like a cat would a grasshopper.

"Hey, look. He's *wrong!* I'm rehabilitating him," she thinly says.

"You're loving him." I plainly nod, adjusting my ponytail.

"He's a socialist!" she bursts with mixed emotions. "It wasn't my intention. Not at first." She frets. "He's principled. He's cares about everyone. Not just himself. He cares about me."

"Hey, he's cute," I suddenly spread a warm smile to lighten the room. "I understand. He's a hunk." I stand and lean on my desk. "I'm not judging what I've seen," I plainly assure.

I get my kicks from imprisoned men too! I laugh to myself, *it's not like I can hit dating sites either. If Uncle Greg's cowboys weren't so fucking macho and insecure, I'd get more attention. I need a man who'll let me eat him alive, not one who 'will show me who's boss.'*

"Oh, god. You've seen everything?" Her eyes pool open.

"Yeah." I turn my smartphone around and play a quick video. Ant sitting on the floor, sucking her toes. Ant giving Val a shoulder rub. Both of them playing board games, sharing a bottle of wine.

Tears well in her eyes. "He's the only *man* I've met. He has an unbreakable edge. A conviction. None of the other suck-up shits in my life hold a speck of his character!" she begs.

Is this why Mom liked Dad so much? They never got along, but they never got divorced. Codependent dysfunction forever addicted 'that edge' of being just out of reach?

"I promise," Valentina affirms. "I control him. He's secure. I've *never* compromised my brother's work," she jabs a thumb to her heart. "I'd never do that."

"You're in love with a prisoner." I point with a raised eyebrow, "And this is a problem."

She nods. "Hey, you still need me," she bitterly defends. "I handle the red phone. Ormo will *never* trust you! You need my signature for Death Warrants," she glares. "This is a dark new side of you, Jen." She chokes a sob.

"Sure, fair enough," I scratch behind my ear. "I don't hate you, Val. I actually look up to you." I smile. "I really do. But I want more, and you're in the way," I taunt.

"Hey. Have more!" she bursts, her hand angrily dismissing the office. "If that's what you want, have more. Just give me Antonio," she pleads, wiping her eyes.

"Okay," I nod. "Deal."

She pulls her purse off my desk and storms out of the building. I don't see her for a week.

Now that I control the prison's budget and guards, I ask Uncle Greg to tour and evaluate our operations. He happily does, charging $700 an hour, of course. I paid $1,000 for *each* email address of his designer connections—and *they* were totally worth it. So, why not?

After a quick overview, he's impressed with how much we've accomplished. Fifty of the smart prisoners are trained to build templates and monitor operations. I've successfully delivered prototypes for designer approval and made adjustments at their request.

"We've completed small test batches. I'm wearing a pair now." I model for him.

"Wow," he whistles, impressed. Yet, Greg notes a lot of prisoners aren't working. "Jen. I can't stress enough: Efficiency, efficiency, efficiency. That's the best way to lower costs and raise profits."

"Totally. But I don't have the room!" I complain. I'd never allow lazy disobedience. "My small parking lot is overflowing with steel shipping containers full of raw supplies and finished products. Guards are running ragged moving around materials."

"Well, talk about being a victim of success," he smiles, as we overlook plant operations from a guard observation point. "Usually companies have a *labor* problem. There aren't enough affordable high-quality workers around, and they pay workers way too much," he advises. "That's not your problem. Your problem is logistics. How do you move *and* assemble your supplies in such a confined space? Hmm…." he ponders. "Let me ask around. We're working on something *special* you might find useful." His eyes glimmer. "It's under tight wraps, but, because your operations are so secure, you could be the perfect test environment," he says, looking excited.

"Alright, sounds interesting," I nod.

"Jen, imagine if your crammed closets could hold anything. *Anything,*" he iterates. "A whole warehouse. Tons of spare parts. Imagine a small vehicle delivering a *literal* mountain of bulk material. One day 'shipping' will mean much more than the little packages on our front steps," he grins.

"Huh? What the hell are you talking about?" I ask, highly confused.

Greg smiles, waving his hands in defense. "I'll need permission from Mr. Jacobson himself," he winks. "But a secret team of ours is looking for a secure place to test real world applications of the Gizmo." He holds a 'shush' finger to his lips. "Let me ask and catch up soon. Will you be home for dinner?"

"Absolutely," I vigorously nod.

"I should know more by then." He gives me a big hug. "I'm so proud of you." He pats my back as we walk to meet Uncle Ben for lunch at his favorite spot in the city.

A few weeks later, Dr. Arbrim's team arrives and installs the Gizmo in a cleared-out storeroom. I watch, with my own eyes, as a bulk package of toilet paper shrinks from one cubic meter, to one cubic centimeter.

"Amazing. How does it work?" I lift the package and gently squish it between my fingers like a small marshmallow. Technicians around Uncle Greg and I fumble with cables.

"I'm not totally sure on the science," Uncle Greg laughs gently, peering at the small toilet paper. "The lab works on it," he nods at the team. "It's so hush-hush I'm unsure they even want to explain. Secrecy is absolutely key being an early market mover here," he sternly advises. "Absolutely key. You'll need to be the only one who accesses and enables the Gizmo. Sure. It might cost $60K a month to rent, but you'll now be able to store and ship as much product as you'd like. We'd *love* it if you could accelerate your business processes. This will be a brilliant case study."

One of the technicians asks for the toilet paper back for more tests.

"Hey. How does this work?" I ask her incredulously and hand the toilet paper over.

She looks warily at Uncle Greg, who shrugs and nods. "How much do you know about particle physics?" she muses.

"Nothing," I frown.

"Good," she laughs. "Less you know, the better. Because the standard model is totally wrong. No one knows *how* wrong yet. Researchers have taken so many wrong turns, for so many decades, in calculating the masses of particles," she chides. "The amateurs. Fundamentally, the universe does not include the concepts of 'mass' and 'length.' Nature actually lacks scale. Sure, galaxies appear bigger than atoms and people *seem* to outweigh ants, but size differences are illusory. Scale Symmetry blows away old assumptions about how elementary particles manifest properties. We can invent scale."

"What? Scale?" I ask, squinting my eyes.

"Yes. We invent scale. With the Gizmo, we slightly re-adjust the universal defaults. Agravity blends the laws of physics from all scales into a coherent picture, allowing the Gizmo to manually scale the weight and length properties of the core matter to whatever scale we'd like." She tosses the miniature toilet paper package in the air a few times.

"To *any* size?" I ask, amazed.

"To any size *and* weight. Although, it's *highly* recommended that length and weight remain tied, to avoid damage," her voice gets harsh. "Imagine a shrunken car weighing as much as a full-size car—it'd crash right through the floor. Wouldn't it now, Jake?" she sneers at another technical guy nearby.

"Ha. Yup," the guy tech sheepishly nods.

"Does it work on people?" I ask.

The whole room pauses awkwardly. "Whoa. Hey now," Greg nervously laughs. "Um, no, we're just thinking business processes here. Not social processes. No. That's too much."

I look coolly at him. "Well, aren't they the same? Business processes *are* social processes."

"Um. Maybe? But that's out of scope," she easily dismisses. "I don't even think the question of 'people' even came up?" She looks at Jake, the guy technician, who frowns and shakes his head. "It *does* work on organics. We transported a herd of cattle in a test box. Organics aren't on our development roadmap due to the obvious ethical concerns. We *have* some limits. In theory, someone could shrink a thing small enough to create a black hole!" Dr. Arbrim laughs, "And that would be a problem."

"I'd certainly never want to be a black hole," I grin.

Greg takes a phone call and excuses himself as the doctor and I continue.

"Well," I say to the doctor, eyeing Greg to ensure he's involved with his call. "We *need* to enable the Gizmo for organics. We store lots of food," I offer, hoping to have as few limits on my Gizmo as possible.

"Sure. Makes sense," the doctor agrees, making a note.

"Alright, Jen," Uncle Greg returns, having finished his call. "This is a powerful technology. We're installing a retinal scanner key at the door and the trigger. Only *you* and visiting technicians can use it. Got that?"

"Makes perfect sense," I grin. *So much potential here!*

"And nobody can know what you're doing. Not even the guards. Only you and Val."

"I'll do my best."

I spend the rest of the month organizing my cute little shipping containers into clean rows on the closet shelf. With all the closets consolidated into a single room, the whole prison seems twice as big! The guards are happy. Piles of stuff no longer force us to walk sideways down the halls.

But my blessing is not without disruption. I demand all operations—the kitchen, shipping dock, and factory floor—all plan their activities so that I have to distribute or restock from the closet only once a week. As much as I love the Gizmo and making things change size, I don't want to interrupt my day every damn second someone needs a bar of soap or can of soup!

"Valentina. Red Phone's been ringing," I bark when she *finally* returns from another long lunch. *How annoying.*

She tightens her lips in passive annoyance. "Oh. Thanks," she lifts the red phone and dials a set of numbers.

"Hola," she listens to Ormo. "Bueno, bueno," she nods and laughs, as they talk about whatever. Then, after a few minutes, her eyes blast wide as she visibly stiffens. "Si, General." She shakily sets the phone down.

Val unlocks the Death Warrants and lifts one with her trembling hands.

Oh, shit. An execution!

She holds the warrant in a daze before collapsing on the floor in tears.

"Oh, no," I cover my mouth. *It must be Antonio! Fuck.* The tension and pain in the room is tight and dark. *If she loses him,* I realize, *I lose her. Shit, shit, shit.*

Then, I have an idea.

I hurry over, bend, and give her a hug. "Oh, god. Hey, I'm so sorry. So sorry." I sit next to her on the floor. She leans over and hugs me back. After a moment I patiently ask, "Do you want me to call the guards?"

"No!" she screams, pushing me away like a crazed, wide-eyed animal.

I slowly stand and look down. "Then we have a problem. This is our job," I sternly cross my arms.

She looks up at me, paralyzed. "No, please. I can't. We can't," she whimpers, her hand tugging tightly on my pant leg.

I remember Valentina boasting about how a single piece of her jewelry could pay for two hundred young Chileans to attend college. I remember thinking how *hot* that much wealth made me feel. *A whole classroom of students dangling like a bracelet?* I tenderly run fingers over my wrist. *Yes, please!* Ormo and his supporters own so much of the economy, anyone seizing their money would crash banks.

"Hm." I squint down at her, walk away, turn up the radio, and return. "I have an idea," I tap my fingers playfully against my arm. "We *can* let him live, but I want all of your jewelry. Can you go home and bring it to me? All of it."

"Oh, thank god!" she bursts as if breathing for the first time. "Yes, sure. Whatever." She jumps to her feet and hugs me tight. "Thank you! Thank you, Jen," she cries, her face hot and wet.

"You're welcome. Okay, okay, enough already. Go. Get the jewelry," I smile, leading her towards the door.

She runs out of the office.

Thirty minutes later I open three heavy jewelry boxes.

"That's almost $80 million dollars, Jen," Valentina scowls, sternly crosses her arms.

"Yeah? Yeah," I try not to drool as I run my hands through more wealth than I can imagine. "Yes, this will work."

"If this *doesn't* work…I don't care what happens to me, Jen. So make sure it works," Valentina stares intently.

"It will," I whisper. "Okay. Grab a gun. Make triple-sure it's *unloaded*. Fill out that warrant."

Her hands shakily work the warrant.

I continue, "We'll walk down and *pretend* to shoot him in his cell so Central has video proof. Tell him through the door what's going to happen, so he'll know how to react when you walk in and shout 'Bang.' Then we'll drag him to the Gizmo."

"What?" She freezes to stare at me.

"Yes. Valentina. We can't have him walking around. And we can't free him to the opposition. They'll kill us all! *He needs to disappear.* Let's shrink him," I assure her with a giddy smile. "You've seen me minimize cans of food and supplies. Why not him?"

"The Gizmo? It'll work?" She bites her lip with worry.

"For sure. Totally," I lie. *I have no fucking idea, but I wanna find out!* "We don't have a choice. This is perfect. He'll be in isolation, only with *you* and not the prison," I laugh. "You two love birds can be together. And if the conflict quiets down, you can unshrink him, and live quietly together sipping mai tai's on the beach. Sounds like a dream to me," I boast.

An easy $80 million! Glee nearly floods out my ears.

"Okay, yes. Let's do it," she slowly nods.

We walk purposefully to Antonio's cell. Valentina bangs on his door three times hard. "Baby. It's me," she mourns with an edge of dry panic.

"I already miss you. How did you know? Come in, Peach. Come in," Antonio gushes with a warm baritone.

I roll my eyes.

"Baby. Wait. Stay put. We have the cameras on. Do you trust me?"

"Huh? Really?" His tone sobers up, "Um, yes. What's up?"

"We have a plan to save you. Will you do *exactly* as I say? ...I've signed your Death Warrant."

Dead silence.

"We have to make it look like you die, for the cameras," Valentina pleads.

Dead silence.

"Antonio. Do you love me?" Valentina begs.

"Sí. Sí," a heavy answer affirms.

"Will you do exactly as I say?" she asks.

"Sí."

"You'll always be with me, Love," she affirms. "Always touch me. Breathe me. Taste me. You'll never leave me. We can always be together. It won't be the life you want, but it will be *a* life. And a life I'm willing to give you. What we're going to do is walk in, point an *unloaded* gun at your head, yell bang, and you'll drop to the floor, limp and unmoving. Can you do that? Can you make this look real?"

I hear a sob.

"Sí," he sniffles.

We drag his 'lifeless corpse' wrapped in a bed sheet down the hallways. *Ugh.* I wipe the sweat from my brow and unlock the room to the Gizmo. *Who'd think this hunk of man could weigh so much? Won't be a problem for long!* I gleefully laugh. *It'll be so easy to pick up and move people when they're small.*

We move him into position. I activate the Gizmo.

CHAPTER 25—DISCOVERY

Eddie. October 2027

"If it's not done right, do it yourself," Jen mutters, reading the fucked invoice on her computer. "Supply chain is gonna kill us this month," she complains, massaging her temples. "You didn't plan this well at all, Ed."

Actually, I had. I silently tense, watching Jen sip wine. *But you didn't want to pay for emergency reserves.*

In two days, Jennifer's Nano SupplyBots™ will be unable to deliver food to the staff. We can last a week without eating, I calculate, slightly lowering the urgency of that priority. Staff pods are self-sustaining for water and air; thankfully the basics aren't a problem.

The timing of our logistics collapse is problematic in more serious ways beyond food and air: the nuclear batteries powering Jennifer's System, our network connections, and the various Core Cities™ like Free Street™—have been running low for some time. We were scheduled to change them five days from now. *Fuck.*

"Shit," Jen blasts. "Finding a new vendor to manage the red tape for Uranium-233 and Thorium-232 ore is impossible."

Logistics is an all-consuming job that pushes workers to rigidly conform or burn out. Workers at Jennifer's huge logistics yard near an old Walmart hub on the edge of San Antonio are dropping like flies and failing to get our daily shipments into Jen's breakfast schedule. Walmart's shocking bankruptcy next door destroyed our synergy and took down many of our mutual logistics contractors with them.

This Depression cascades and cascades, getting worse and worse. I clench my jaw.

Walmart seemed so stable! Bargain prices for buyers desperately needing bargains. Makes total sense. A rock-solid business. This week, the company is dust in the free market winds.

No one can afford to buy anything these days except the super-rich, and they don't shop at Walmart.

Now it's 2 a.m. and we're trying to troubleshoot how to feed and fuel the 9.3 million employees and residents coursing through Jennifer's system beyond the next seventy-two hours—or all of Jen's operations will come to a total halt.

"These prices are absurd," I say, reviewing Jen's notes. "But I feel uneasy going around a regulator's back when we're talking nuclear power," I say, covering my ass. "However, your efficiencies doing so could be huge," I add, soothing Jen's greedy ego.

"Bypassing regulations is obviously rational," she notes. "With the savings, I can privatize an actual mountain of thorium ore, and we won't have this problem until long after you're gone, Ed," she stabs. Jen's fingers pinch the bridge of her nose. Her massive beach home-office sprawls behind her.

I hear faint ocean waves crashing in the wind as a thin glow of a lingering sunset layers the horizon, which suggests Jen is at her Hawaiian estate this week.

We're in Hawaii too, I remind myself, pointlessly wishing I could see the island.

Jen thinks, biting her lip. "We're just going to do it," she bursts. "Refined ore is already enroute from Asia to Texas for processing. I could have the new batteries for lunch by Tuesday, maybe Wednesday. Take a squad of thirty bots and meet the shipment then." She types up the orders and approvals. "Feel free to grab any food floating around if you're too hungry," she laughs. "Hey!" Jen takes her glasses off, sighing some stress away. "Ed. I can't believe it's been almost five years since you installed the Server Core! Time sure flies, eh?" She tilts her head and sips a large glass of red wine. "We sure came a long way."

Ugh. Really? My heart plummets. *Five years?* Jen laughs at the obvious pain crossing my face.

"You're funny, Ed. I'm sure you'll have *tons* of fun bringing the ore to the System Core, just like last time," she winks.

I hate today so much. The 'Bot armada and I rock and sway in the unfathomably vast ocean of Jen's stomach. *She's an hour late for lunch.* I fume at the time, watching my day waste away. Usually the 'Bots automatically capture Logistic Supplement Capsules, but Jen insisted I attend today considering the sensitive cargo she was devouring: one ton of Uranium-233, a whole thorium-232 *refinery*, ten-thousand industrial office batteries, and three hundred new quantum encryption components for our System network.

All crammed in a special gel cap tens of thousands of times larger than I am, I muse, thinking about the daily Industrial Supplements she consumes holding our logistic shipments.

"How big *is* one of those fuckers?" I research data on supplement standards and instantly regret my question. "Just over eighty miles," I deflate, remembering these gel caps are of the smaller variety too. The first time I dropped into Jen's stomach was in an original capsule, over two hundred miles long compared to my size today.

How have I allowed myself to get this small? I angrily reflect. Already knowing the answer, I request that Jen enlarge my size for this operation via Instant Message. *All of our pods and SupplyBots can adjust size whenever Jen needs them to. Why can't I?*

"No," is her near instant reply. "The bots will handle that. You stay microscopic, my silly little gut bug." She adds a smiley face.

I pick up the phone, "Then why am I here?" I ask. Her video feed opens. "I can meet the bots at the server."

She's sitting at a table. "I wanted an opportunity for you to eat. A reward for your hard work!" she cheers, grinning into her laptop camera.

My stomach growls. "No! There's nothing even here." I refuse, "Let's get going. When are you eating the supplement?" I impatiently tap my fingers.

"Soon," she raises a fork into her mouth and an incredible noise floods her stomach. Jen chews and swallows again. "Watching my simple things totally rock your world never gets old." She takes another bite of salad. "I regret I haven't had time to torture you. And I'm sorry about that," she says, shimmying side to side.

My world rocks violently.

She laughs. "Ed, this *is* a delicious salad. And you look famished and cranky. You should enjoy a bite." She devilishly smiles, typing on her laptop.

I hear my outer airlock door open as a flood of green goopy material blasts into the small space, violently hitting the inner door.

"Jesus Jen, no!" I jump. "Don't open the door!"

"Come on man." She leans. "Do it," she demands. "Open the hatch. Join me for lunch."

"No!"

"Don't you deserve a dividend for all your hard work? Hey. None of the other employees have eaten all week. Let me help ya out." Her hand lingers near a key.

"No! Jen. I'm serious! Don't!" I shout.

"Huh?" A false confusion crosses face as she takes another bite. "I thought you wanted more dividends?" she pouts, chewing. "I'm trying to be nice here."

"No!"

"Bummer." She frowns, swallowing. "Sorry to hear that. Just trying to share the wealth." The outer door closes. Jen's face brightens. "Well. At least enjoy a complimentary snack."

My inner door opens, flooding the living room with saliva and massive chunks of spinach.

"Fuck!" I jump on the chair as goo sloshes around the floor.

"Yum, yum," Jen laughs with glee. "Eat up! I'll down the pill after dessert," she laughs, reaching to close her laptop.

"And when the fuck will dessert be?!" I shout at Jen's dark monitor.

I wait another half-hour, cleaning Jen's unnecessary mess.

The armada approaches the server.

How huge it looks. "How small was I when I implanted this?" I ask, refusing the math this time. I was naive to think the enormous mile long black cube was only a set of System computers; *it's a nuclear-powered data factory.*

Sections of the Bot armada divert to their respective areas. The ones I can see being docking and opening hatches outside the enormous cube. *Going smooth.* I nod, reviewing the complex status feeds. Smaller supply robots detach and enter the opened doors and latches on several areas of the cube that hosts the System. Nuclear power. Hardware for quantum encryption. Faster and lower power processors. Batteries. *All looking good.*

I'm most worried about the remodeling section and getting the new ore refinery directly integrated with the uranium processor and the nuclear power stations.

My stomach growls. I eye a large chunk of Jen's spinach in the trash can. *I hope she gets food shipments soon.* After this server headache is over, staff hunger is my next huge problem. I eye my unopened email folder: 5,000 unread messages.

I don't dare read any email unless it's from Jen. My safest view of the world has been mainlining the truth directly from our CEO—a pure form of truth with less distraction.

"Sir. Untracked anomaly located," the System chimes at me.

"Huh? Where?" I groggily shift my attention.

I've slyly dedicated code in all of Jen's nanobots to directly report anomalies to me anytime parameters might match a lost employee pod with broken tracking.

"In the System Core," the computer voice dryly reports.

"The System? Here?" I peer into the gloom, "Where?"

"Main Server, Corridor J."

"Oh. *In* the System? The server rooms?"

"Approximately. Area undefined."

Sabotage? A lost pod? Possibilities rattle my mind. "Can you access the pod?" I ask the robot.

"Cannot dock with pod. Third-party pod. Unrecognizable."

"Unrecognizable?" I'm confused. "Are you programmed to recognize all staff pods, even prototypes?"

"Yes."

"Do you have a visual?"

"Yes."

"What the hell?" I squint at the computer monitor. "Take me. Let's have a look. Have a robot meet me at the nearest entrance."

This is odd.

A SupplyBot grabs my pod and moves it to an unused airlock latch. I grab an oxygen mask, and a flashlight, and enter the airlock. After fifteen minutes of following a small robot down a long tunnel, we enter a vast room holding row after server row of computers that host the System. I see a few robots adding quantum encryption hardware and replacing redundant components.

We open a new door, and I put on my mask to block the wave of dust. I see robots of various sizes cutting room for the new thorium refinery. Some robots suddenly grow big and lift pieces into place and then shrink small to grab smaller sections. The construction processes is elegant and mesmerizing. *Going smoothly,* I nod.

The small robot leads me to the rear of the refinery construction site.

Several large robots are removing sections of a wall, revealing two and a quarter *massive* flower petals. Each petal is at least two hundred yards wide and silver. Other large robots remove material around a crushed black dome near what appears to be the center of a flower.

I open a map of the Core on my tablet. *None of this is supposed to be here. This space is supposed to be a huge void.* I look around, confused.

"And where's the pod anomaly?" I ask the robot.

"Straight ahead, center," the robot dryly chimes.

"Show me." I nod, holding my air mask tight.

We hike up a large silver petal towards the crushed center. *The craftsmanship is really crude,* I note the silver floor. *Pre-Arbrims? Handmade?* I wonder.

Is this a piece of jewelry?

Huffing and puffing, I catch the robot waiting near the edge of the crushed dome. "Where?" I ask.

"Inside, center," it responds, maneuvering through a four-foot hole on the side of the black dome.

Obsidian? Chipped glass? I note, careful not to cut myself as I duck and enter. I turn on my light.

Before me, lying sideways, is the ten-foot-tall face of a corpse.

"Holy hell! Jesus!" I jump with intense fright. "Fuck! Fuck!" My heart races. I look around. Nearby, I see a thin mummified hand about seven feet tall, holding a giant hammer pointing at the hole I entered.

"Can you identify this person?" I shakily ask the robot.

"Negative. No employee ID located."

"Understood. Holy god! How big is this place?" I stammer and warily walk around the top of the mummy's ten-foot-tall head.

"Approximately 150,000 cubic feet."

"The size of a stadium," I whisper, painting my feeble light over vague shapes. "More illumination please."

The robot blasts light. I see a couch with three thin mummies slouching together, their heads clunked. *Oh god...*

I shakily turn and see loads of boxes with Spanish writing. Scraps of leather. Half-made shoes. In the distance, a row of tables. "What is this place?"

"Unknown," the robot responds.

"Go around, do a count of unidentified employees, and report back."

The robot whirrs away, navigating the inside of the dome.

My blood congeals into ice. *Who are these guys? How'd they get here?*

The robot returns.

"How many?" I angrily shout at it.

"186 unidentified staff members. Would you like me to create HR entries for them?" it plainly asks.

"No!" I shout. "A map? Show me a map? What does this place look like?"

"Yes, area mapped."

"Send it to me!" I angrily wave my tablet.

I open the file to see a layout of the area. Dorms. A kitchen. An assembly area. "This *was* a workshop, from when?" I say to myself.

"Unknown," the robot dutiful adds.

I remember my first day working for Jennifer, when she oddly made me look at her belly ring, before I shrank. My throat tightens dry.

"*This*. This was Jennifer's belly ring?" My shock erupts into fury. I turn my head as panic sinks my spine into ice water. "These guys have *always* been here," I choke. "Before Jen ever came to TempGrace…"

Jennifer is a tomb.

"Oh god," I choke. "We're never going to leave! None of us are going to leave." A panic attack clenches my chest. I feel faint. "I need air," I stammer. I scramble to the exit. *We'll never leave Jen alive. She's intentionally collecting our lives. Cutting them short whenever she wants.* I skid around the giant mummy's head. *We'll never leave Jen alive. I need to escape. We all need to escape.*

I crouch through the opening.

Who do I talk to? My mind sputters. *If only I could contact an independent agency who represent everyone's interests.*

I stand with my hands on my knees outside the black opening, my guts and chest heaving as I overlook Jennifer's refinery melding together section by section.

Jen has unlimited energy. Unlimited power. What have I done? My face drains as I sit against the black dome, aghast.

How can I fight against a monster who only wants to minimize and extract as much as possible, without remorse? I angrily clench my fists. *This is absolutely unacceptable. Jennifer's 'free market paradise' was but an excuse to snare millions of desperate people as hostages to her ambitions, her lust, and her trivial greed.*

And I've given the most powerful human in history a blank check to do whatever she wants. My hands tremble uncontrollably as I stand up, straighten my back, and move forward in fury.

CHAPTER 26—PROFESSIONAL SECRETS

Jennifer. March 2018

Where's Little Antonio today? I smirk, barely hiding my leer as Valentina's awesome figure stretches the thin fabric of her summer dress. We're both dressed to kill tonight at Uncle Ben's birthday party and eager for our final hours at in the prison office to end.

Val's extra radiant today, I sip my usual black coffee. *More glow than normal. I wonder why she's so relaxed and content?* I devilishly muse, distractedly scanning my final emails of the day.

Yesterday, Ant's little face peered from her front-left pocket, but there's no pockets on Valentina's little dress today! *Where's she hiding him? Her bra? Stuffed somewhere kinkier? Or on the couch back home, munching inside a bag of chips watching a movie?*

I need to know but love the mystery.

I bite my lip, frustrated, *I need my men working. I need find a way to mix business and pleasure like that,* I sigh, and return to the amazing memory of the mighty populist leader dwindling to a one-inch-tall *nothing.* Valentina swept him in her hands like a lost mouse.

There was a second when *both* Valentina and Antonio were in firing range. Regrettably, I resisted the whim to shrink each. I simply lingered my hand over the trigger in case he *had* died, and I needed to shrink Val by 'mistake.' *Anything to strengthen my power over a weaker individual, I'm eager to do.* I move my finger into my belly button. *Mmm.*

I'm now officially a State Secret. The General was fascinated we 'just flushed Antonio's body down the toilet.'

"How? How? How?" he asked with glee.

Uncle Greg was furious Ormo had learned the basics about the Gizmo. We spent half the night arguing after he heard the rumor. Eventually I shut him up: "Greg. If you think profit is always good and government regulation are evil, how can you condemn anyone's business practices? Aren't your 'rules' a casual form of regulation? Fuck that. Hypocrite."

What's the point following rules no one cares about? When I see an advantage, I'll take it. I'm no dummy. Innovation, breaking the rules, challenging norms and assumptions—and doing it first— provides the most intense gains. Why should I hold myself back to get smacked by someone who didn't?

Greg is so naive.

Now, most of the time the Red Phone rings, Valentina hands it glaringly to me.

Ha. Take that, Bitch.

"Were you scared back then?" I ask after an hour of long insightful conversation late into the afternoon.

"No. Never," his confident baritone boasts through the Red Phone.

"Really? I'd have been terrified." I make sure to cutely fret, *"God."*

"Hey. Courage little sister. Courage," he affirms. "Sheep are easily freighted. Not so the wolf."

"Rwar. Totally…" I gnash my teeth.

"I was a little worried. At first, my 'violations' of the old laws and norms caused a lot public irritation. But soon life went on as if such violations were normal."

"Sure," I nod. "What's your favorite part, being President? Having so much power?"

"I get asked that a lot," he laughs. "Usually, I say, 'Saving Chile from destruction is the greatest honor of my life,' or something like that. But, Jen, I like you."

Yes, game on! I smirk at the back of Val's head. *One day he'll trust me and she'll be a goner.*

"I'll tell you this: 'The power to hypnotize.'" His voice becomes syrupy as if talking about his favorite dessert. "To declare *my* interests to be 'the people's interests' and have them actually believe me!" he amuses with a few chuckles.

"Huh, really? They do that?" I ask. "Why'd they *not* fight you?" I ask.

"Jen, fear is a 'mind killer,' and the distortion is too confusing."

"How?"

"Easy," Ormo praises. "Many intellectuals were so 'trapped by their own ideas they couldn't open their eyes'. They 'already knew what could and couldn't happen' and only saw what they expected to see. Sure," he continues. "Many rejected the ugly aspects that 'Communists are hiding under your bed, oh no!'" he laughs. "They rejected my 'propaganda facts' but not those impressions. They were disoriented. Couldn't confront it. And their minds disorientate and naturally coordinate with my new authority. Not due to any 'direct terror' from me! My power is simply a wind naturally adjusting everyone's sails."

"I guess that makes sense."

"Actually, Jen, it makes sense to *not* make sense."

"What?" I squint.

"A leader must be intellectually inconsistent, sometimes boldly so. This exposes clear thinkers. The challengers out of line with my authority. Those who I may need to weed out." He sips a beverage.

"Interesting. You're always testing who'll obey you most?"

"Indeed."

"How does that power *feel?*" I ask, my heart beginning to flutter.

"Amazing. Better than drugs. Jen—better than sex."

"'Better than sex?' *Really,* General*?*" I chide.

"Certainly."

"Ha!" I lean into the phone. "Maybe you're having the wrong sex?"

He laughs, "Maybe I am. Maybe I am."

Yes, you are, I imagine the possibilities of playing him.

"People hate chaos more than they love freedom," he adds. "Democracy is chaos. Freedom is chaos. No one knows which way to go or what to do. In moments of stress, people seek homogeneity. Simplicity. Oneness."

"Yeah, makes sense!" I think of Peggy whining she that just wanted food and a job when the TempSchool closed.

The general elaborates, "There's a point when people say 'Enough, it's time for peace and order, leave me alone.' Jen, it doesn't take evil to control a community. Just ordinary desire for security, weak institutions, and short-term thinking from those seeking sheltcr from chaos."

"Is it worth it?" I ask, remaining casual. *Next week I'll ask him over for lunch and we can test the Gizmo so he can have a preview of what it's like to be in the palm of my hand and all the other great things I can do for him.* I imagine rubbing his small body sensually down my neck.

"'Worth it?' Hmmm," the phone is silent as the president ponders. "I don't know. I think, yes? I can't imagine myself anywhere but the top. Honestly, I *love* minimizing those who question the peace I provide. It's the best, Jen. The best. If I even *suspect* they think otherwise, off to prison!" he laughs. "Assuming, we have the space?"

I perk up. "I have tons of room. I need *more* prisoners. ASAP! Orders are crazy. I'm falling behind."

"Really? Jen, that's great. Val always said it's too crowded," he says.

"I organize prisoners differently... I'll give you a first-hand tour." I offer a casual line. "Seriously though. Any reduction in incarcerations will hurt the wonderful growth created by our prison-workshop. I can't have that. The more I look at your justice system, the more waste I see. Prisoners in train cars, blindfolded and bound, but doing nothing? What the hell, General? For what productive result?"

He awkwardly laughs.

"If you *really* want to destroy the old way of politics in Chile, send thousands of troublemakers to me. I'll take all you can find and put them to work," I continue, examining my hair for split ends. "Give *me* $100 million to create a new prison and you can have all prisoners you want. Tens of thousands. Hundreds of thousands." I kick off my prison-crafted stiletto heels to rest my pedicured feet on the desk like the boss I am. "I can even do it for $95 million, if budgets are tight."

I can do it for free but he doesn't need to know that.

Nothing arouses me more than taking more money, taking more control, taking over.

"Really? This is good. Good!" he says. "I can't just kill. We need better solutions. We need reform."

"Reform? Really?" This surprises me. "Why *can't* you kill? You think it's wrong?"

Fucking wimp.

"Lots of times, I've taken lives," he pauses, sounding weary. "I've killed."

"Personally?"

"Yes."

I'm talking to a murder! Hot. I move a finger to my belly button, push, and smile.

"Killing's easy, but it's cheap," he sounds uncomfortable. "I tire of it. We have to be careful. Security. Order. This is what the people crave. The real problem is how violence changes the rules. Changes 'What is acceptable?' Changes 'What is necessary to survive?' People with murdered relatives learn violence is the *only* way to bring wrongs to justice. People then trust no justice but violence. So many close to me, they want more blood. All the time, they want blood. I keep saying, 'No. You guys. It never stops.' Authority cannot be maintained by force alone. I need to persuade others that I have *legitimate* authority. That I'm not just a thug."

"You're confusing. What 'legitimate authority'?"

"I want a Golden Age for Chile, like when the Roman Empire was governed by absolute power under wisdom and virtue. I have a 'Ruler's Calculus.' Mix charisma, confidence, vision, and an insecure population. And ensure the alternatives are worse than following my vision. Easy!"

"Interesting. How do you get charisma?"

"Charisma isn't magic; it's influenced by height and quick wits."

"Height? Really?" I laugh. *I can deal height...*

"Why's that funny?"

"Oh, nothing; it's just such an easy thing," I evade with a delighted smirk. *Height gets those who resist to obey me!*

"Humans are almost programmed to admire and obey taller people. Thankfully, I'm 2.1 meters; it's easier when the king is the tallest guy around. Strangely, it's easier to become a *god-king* than simply a king or president."

"A what?"

"A god-king. Think of the old roman emperors, the Egyptian pharaohs. Think of the rules in old Hawai'i who said Life Forces of the Gods flowed through them as 'manna' into the common people. That without the ruler's connection to heaven, all would die from lack of manna. Their power was orders of magnitude above mine! If a peasant so much as looked at a god-king, they were executed."

"Really? Whoa," I lean back into the chair, intrigued. "How'd they become god-kings?" My heart flutters.

"To become a god-king, I think an upstart needed three things: sit atop the military chain of command, have fanatically loyal followers who obey orders without question and force others to stay in line. I have that. But I'm not a ritual leader who controls the religious hierarchy. I miss that…"

"It's easier to become a god-king than merely a king?" I whisper.

"Yeah, but Chile has no rituals I control. We've been Catholic too long. Can't magically become Pope," he chuckles. "Looks like God-king is off the table for me," he jokes.

But not for me. What's a religion I can find or start that everyone loves?

After a minute of quiet, Ormo adds, "Jen? Anything else?"

"Oh." *How can I give you a good time in bed?* I ask myself, but stammer, "How do you manage the troublemakers?"

"The troublemakers? Oh hell. You wouldn't believe the problems I have with the 'little princes' in my administration. You're lucky. I can't throw my knuckleheads in isolation—their families are too powerful. My hands are tied. I need lieutenants to enforce rules, and their muscle always come at a price."

"I'll make room if you want to get rid of them," I tease.

"If only. Ha. Well, the Administration. I can't cut paychecks *and* organize media notes at the same time. A head of state needs a large staff for the busy work."

Val walks to my desk with a stern hand on her hip and taps a finger on her expensive watch.

"Oh. Mr. President." I note the time. "I've my Uncle's Birthday Party tonight. Sorry to cut off."

"Hey. No problem. Sure, totally understand…"

I hear his smile through the phone.

"So. I'm obviously not invited?" he asks.

"I'm sure you can come. *Come.*" I eagerly rib Val's increasingly darkening glare. "We're at the Richardson vineyard in Maipo. You can *come* anytime you want." I run two dirty fingers between my tits and suggestively sneering at Val.

"No. No. Wish him happy birthday. I have too many meetings," he sighs. "Thanks for talking, Jen."

"You can count on me," I smile.

"I do and will. Bye, thanks," he says and hangs up.

"—Don't fuck with my brother," Val immediately imposes.

I click the phone. "I'll fuck whoever I want," I dismiss. "I'll fuck him. I'll fuck you." I casually gather my things. "And, I'll fuck little Ant so hard you'll need a gynecologist to find him," I smile.

We walk to her waiting limo over cobblestones of stony silence.

Val and I share her limousine for the one-and-a-half-hour ride to Ben's party in the thin air of Alto Maipo wine country as Val sullenly taps her smartphone. I suspect she now regrets her offer to warm our relationship with a carpool. The passing mountains are flame orange with long shadows of the setting sun. Little villages full of little people pass out of reach.

This could all be mine. I thrill at the real possibility. *I could make Ormo love me. Secretly dominate him. By the time I'm 21, I could effectively rule 17 million people and control a $250 billion economy.*

A country where I could be absolute master. No debate. Just me.

I need to be careful not to mess my pants with ideas this scalding hot. Val can probably smell my arousal. *Fuck her,* I smirk.

Under purple twilight and the first speck of stars, Val's driver halts our ice carriage in the backyard of a sprawling estate. The Old Money is throwing Ben a party at their hobby farm in the hills overlooking two thousand acres of grape vines. Val storms towards the reception line leading into the glamorous barn and receives a warm kiss from Uncle Ben. He looks so funny and happy wearing well pressed jean-overalls and a big straw hat!

"Happy Birthday, Uncle Ben!" His grinning face meets mine with a wet sloppy kiss. I wipe his love from my cheek and hand him a hefty ornate envelope. "Open it, open it now," I encourage, wanting to impress the strangers behind me.

"Oh my." He laughs, holding six ounces of solid gold pressed into a three by five inch *"Get Out of Jail Free"* card signed by me. An inside joke. Greg warns that Ben is so cute and sweet he can talk his way out of anything. Ben wraps me in a big hug. "Perfect! Now we can let this party off the hook. Right?"

"Done and done," I cheer, entering the absurdly decorated barn.

Dramatic lighting shadows a timber framework along the ceiling. Large white chandeliers hang from the solid oak beams. Stacked hay bales encircle seating areas as soft straw covers the floor. A "Welcome to Kansas" banner hangs above a professional hoedown conducted by a jug band with a violent fiddle.

"Oh my god. How cute!" I squeal at the baby animals scattered around the party: little goats, baby ducks, and four little lambs trot around. One lamb nips at a lady's long elegant dress to the laughter of many.

I spot Uncle Greg, sulking in a corner. He's lonely friends with a Straw Man, dressed in flannel, grinning on a post.

"Hey, Uncle Greg. Is that your best friend?" I approach.

"Oh, Jen. Thank god you're here. This cuteness is killing me."

He hugs me hard. "Oh. Okay." I tensely accept his surprise affection. "What a great party." I survey the barn. Waiters buzz in tuxedos and stylish mud boots. Women with designer Farm Girl outfits sparkle with the glitter of real diamonds.

"Oh yes, a party." He sloshes his whiskey. "Great," he slurs. "How are you? How've your days been this week?" His eyes are glassy and unfocused.

I grab his arm in amusement. "Let's get you some water…"

How embarrassed would I be if he made a drunk-ass scene? I lead Greg to a side table: a tower of water infused with kiwis and strawberries atop a large ice sculpture that ornately drains a mountain stream through an elaborate village scene chiseled in ice. I quickly pour him a drink, looking warily around as Greg sips.

People know who I am here.

I watch Ben's friends shy away their awkward glances.

A gaggle of thirty baby chickens peck playfully at seeds beneath an orange heat lamp eight feet away. A dozen bimbos coo over how adorable they are; they pick up several chicks and cradle them tenderly next to their thin collar bones and spaghetti string dress straps.

Fucking sluts, I glare. *Modeling. What a mindless distraction.*

I watch a model pull a frumpy seventeen-year-old rich kid into their circle. He obviously plays video games all day and probably will for the rest of his lazy, rich life. *Would never get the time of day from these women unless he was at this party,* I scoff. *At least they're smart enough to suck him dry. Oh god, he can barely talk, this is too painful.* I turn, unable to watch, to Greg, who's fascinated with a spinning miller's wheel in the ice mountain village as he refills a second cup from the stream.

"Chicken skewers, ladies?" A tuxedoed waiter approaches our area.

"Yes. Yes. Snacks!" The bimbos surround the waiter, one of them lovingly cradling a baby chick to her bosom as she bites in and smiles.

"Thanks. Jen," Greg salutes with his glass. "Good idea." He reaches for the last two chicken skewers. "So not free," he groans.

"Oh, yeah?" I laugh.

"Not. Free. At. All." Greg exaggerates with wide drunken eyes. "Ya know, I wanted to charge a $500 cover to help out." He smacks his lips at the party in irritation and shakes his head. "Ben's always so profligate. Parties—what a total scam."

"I think he's having a good time." I watch professional line dancers with cowboy hats drawing timed party guests into a hoedown, with mixed success.

"Of course. A free party? Duh, Jen. Duh, they're having a good time."

"It's Ben's birthday," I say.

"*I* always bought my own birthday cakes. *You* bought your birthday cakes. These 'friends'," his chin juts to the guests, "A blood sucking scam. If I was rational, I shouldn't even do this. I have zero financial incentive." His eyes pool open. "I just really love him. I can only be so rational."

I slowly nod. "It's hard work, being rational. Selfishness takes strength."

"I get stupid and do parties like this," he opens his arms with dismay. "I'll never see this money again and I hate myself for it." He pulls his hair and glares at various attributes of the party: The wine bar. The folk band. "Love is the death of rationality, Jen."

"I hear ya," I say.

"I'm proud of you, Jen. You're clear and focused on what makes money." He gives me an awkward pat on the back. "Nothing else."

"Thanks. I try my best," I say with a curtsey.

"You've challenged me in good ways, too. I think." He nods, "Shown what it means to be ultra rational. Even as I cling to unconscious socialist habits." He touches his heart. "When really, I need to let money do whatever it wants—as long as it makes more money. The serious ass you're kicking is impressive." His bleary eyes squint to focus on me. "How's business?"

"Good. Good. Revenues up another 35% this month," I say, my lips thirsty for wine.

His mouth drops. "35%? 'This month'? Awesome. I'd *love* those numbers. We're so big. I could make $300 million and no one would give three shits," he says. "Stupid. People are stupid. Never let them think for you." He pats my shoulder. "Only trust yourself, Jen. Just yourself."

"Totally," I barely listen as I reach for a glass of red wine from a passing servant. "Hey! Slow the fuck down. Asshole," I glare.

"Sorry, miss!" the waiter jerks to a stop to plead with smile.

I grab his collar, pulling him close. "You need to be my little Wine Bitch tonight." I hold the crystal in the tight space between our faces. "Don't let this glass empty. Keep 'em coming…"

"Of course, miss." His eyes dart with fear.

I reluctantly release him, his timid obedience turning me on. Greg squints but says nothing as the waiter scurries away.

I enjoy a deep sip. "Delicious, Greg. You know a fine vintage!"

"I promise, that's all Ben," an odd distance in his voice acknowledges.

I consume another deep sip. "Wow." I hold my glass to the light. "This must be $300 a bottle?"

Greg winces. "…Parties are such a bad investment," he sighs, shaking his head.

"Holy shit. Baby cows?" I squeal at the sight of two across the barn. I grab Greg's arm and scamper forward in my high heels, demanding we look at the beautiful creatures. The calf we approach has awkward legs and big eyes with funny black and white patches across her skin. I pet her lumpy head.

"Veal, Miss?" another waiter offers our group.

"Oh, yes!" I grab two eager handfuls of veal skewers before anyone else. *Greg needs protein so he lasts the night and won't embarrass me.* I hand him three and bite into one myself.

"Delicious," Greg pats the baby cow on the head. "Oh, there's Marc. Thank god he's here. Later, Jen!" He says over his shoulder, striding to a guy in an expensive suit standing near the entrance.

"Okay," I shrug, feeling abandoned. *I don't want to talk with these other fucking people.* A group of guys and a lady chat nearby. I munch on skewers like an idiot.

"Weren't there *three* baby cows? Where'd the other one go?" someone asks.

"Maybe it was fussy?" another says.

We eat veal and pet the two baby cows until another is led away by a caretaker.

"Cabernet Sauvignon? Miss?" My obedient wine bitch arrives to refill my glass.

"Yes. Duh," I dismiss him.

Someone in an expensive farm suit comments on the music and dancing, "Not sure I feel comfortable with this cultural appropriation. This is what Kansas people do. We shouldn't use their heritage for our amusement."

"Well, it's not *your* birthday. Be nice," a lady offers.

I bite more veal.

"Besides, his husband is from the States, so it's probably okay," another whispers, and they all laugh.

Searching the crowd, I don't immediately see anyone I want to hang with and meander to Ben's circle. Unfortunately, Ben's too damn popular. I back away from his large group of twenty models after four minutes of being ignored on the edge, feeling like a needy fool.

I always got his attention before, I glare, thinking about the fun times we had shopping one-on-one. *But now I'm last in the line?* I sneer. *I don't need Ben.*

I look at my phone for the time. 8:12 p.m. *Ugh.* I look around, bored. *Should I text Ormo photos of the fun? Show him what he's missing?*

—*No no no, not yet.* I slow down the heat. *Stay rational. I get one chance. Don't blow it being needy!* I remember Val saying 'neediness' was a huge turnoff in her circle, enough that she fell in love with her brother's opposition leader. *Ormo has hundreds of women throwing themselves at him all week. Play him smart.*

Wait, where is Val? I walk past the dancers before I see her. *Fuck. She's in the middle-aged bimbo crowd.* None of them smile as

I approach. A lady sends me a soft unwelcome glare as Val pretends not to notice my approach.

Fuck these bitches! I pivot to awkwardly to watch the musicians and the dancers. *I don't need them. I'm fine by myself!*

My wine bitch serves my third glass of satisfaction. *Consuming, that's my fun,* I laugh. The musicians eventually take a break, drink bottles of water, and towel off.

I note more people beyond a large door at the far end of the barn, smoking in the night. I enter the crisp outdoor air. The stars are sharp and sandwiched between dark rolling mountains and the warm glow of Santiago one hundred kilometers to the north. I remember my first night here. The freedom. The possibility. My eyes sting with appreciation of how far I've come.

Hold your head proud, girl.

"Brrr." I chatter my teeth and hug my arms against a sudden breeze. *A chilly summer night? What's the altitude?* I wonder, remembering the swerving drive past grape yards into the hills. *We're in the Andes.* I check an app on my phone. "Ha. 6,400 feet? No wonder Greg was a mess," I say, taking another swig of wine.

Five commandos with machine guns and dogs patrol a hundred meters away. The rich nerdy kid is making out with one of the tall models on a hay bale in the soft light. *Who's playing who?*

My amazement never fails at the impossible things sex and money bring together.

I look back at the warm barn as the band starts their next set. *Why don't I have anyone here I can talk with?* I despise feeling I need someone. *Why can't I find a way to be around people but not really with them? Above them.* I take another sip, wondering who's probably going to hit on me first. *Maybe those guys smoking under the heater?* I glance, making eye contact with the cutest one. *Come to me, bitch,* I silently demand.

Hearty laughter floats around the corner of the barn. *Who are these dudes?* Curious, I walk towards the large silhouettes of a tight old men's club encircling a bonfire. The men smoking cigars suddenly quiet as I approach. I smile and relax, seeing Greg stoke a cigar.

"No wine here, missy. This is the Bourbon Brandy Whiskey Hideout." A heavy guy glares.

"—And scotch," someone adds.

"Yeah. And scotch," the heavy fellow dismisses. "No wine allowed." He puffs a cigar with chubby fingers in the dark glow of the flickering bonfire.

Greg appraises me with a quiet smirk.

"Fine." I chug the last of my wine and toss the glass in the fire with a crystalline crash. "Whiskey me up."

"Atta gal," someone floats over collective laughter.

"You might want bourbon. It's a touch sweeter," the oldest guy suggests. "Amateurs shouldn't start with whiskey." The gray fellow tosses a huge ice cube in a stout glass and pours three ounces of caramel fluid.

I take a sip and evaluate. "Hmm, I dunno. Tastes manly. But small," I scrunch my nose. "Like a tiny $8 billion-dollar market. I think the $100 billion wine market fills my appetite better."

Greg laughs. "This is my niece, Jennifer."

The men's dismissive tone evaporates.

"You're Jen?" a young Indian guy in back stammers.

"Yeah," I sip bourbon. "Who're you?" I look at the group.

"Marc," the guy standing closest to Greg smiles.

"Andrew," the Indian guy eagerly waves.

"Winston," frowns the heavy-set fellow.

"Jim." The oldest man, who offered me the drink, reaches out his hand.

"Jim Jacobson's my boss," Greg smiles. "These are my All Corp co-workers," he salutes with a cigar.

"Just passing through. Thought we'd help rescue Greg's sanity," Winston offers.

"And his open wallet," Marc teases, munching on a chicken kabob.

Cigar smoke rises casually around me in a ring.

"Anyway, Andrew, don't sweat it." Winston scratches his nose, continuing his conversation. "Profit's your only social duty. Whatever wreckage of human lives floats up in the wake of this project is justified under the mantle of business. You get sued. We leave. If you *have* to pay anything and we think it's worth staying— it's a deduction. Don't be afraid to dominate."

"Keep pushing our line," Mr. Jacobson says, sipping his drink. "Been in stickier situations before and they always pass."

"I guess," Andy frowns. "It must be like India then? Our economic growth has been uneven, creating 'islands of California in a sea of sub-Saharan Africa,'" he laughs.

"Yeah, that's the goal!" Winston slaps Andrew on the back.

"Thanks for the water." Greg whispers, sidling next to me.

I lean towards Greg, hoping to soak in Winston's main conversation. "We're a mile up. We're gonna get *smashed.*"

"I know. It's so much cheaper," his face erupts in a grin.

"—And don't worry about the press, Andy," Winston continues. "Deal with public opinion later."

"Opinions are always just a second of wind." Jim Jacobson puffs his cigar.

"And governments are always stupid. It's *impossible* to separate from a globalized economy. They can't keep coddling their people from the truth," Greg shakes his head at Winston.

"What truth?" I interrupt with honest curiosity.

"We're slaves to the Market, Jen. Great and weak alike, she rules us all," Mr. Jacobson adds.

"She?" I smile quietly.

Winston curtly nods at my interruption and returns to Andy. "Asian labor's been killing it for two decades. We need to minimize workers *here* as much as possible. And fast. They're hands down our biggest expense." He runs a chubby pair of thumbs through his suspenders.

"We're in a race to the bottom of labor." Marc forces on Andy, "We have no idea how deep the barrel will go. I'm pissed it's taken so long for reasonable employment regulations in the Americas. But at least we're in the game," Marc says, blowing a big smoky breath at the mountain air. "But that doesn't mean sitting for a break."

"Until Asia cuts *their* rules in response," Winston frowns.

"Again. First one to the bottom of the labor market wins." Marc raises a hand.

"When can I sponsor Asian work camps in the Americas?" Andy asks.

"Maybe soon," Mr. Jacobson nods. "Leasing citizens from India and bringing them to America is the dream. Again, globalization has *three* stages. Moving goods was first, ideas were second; moving *people* is third. The internet started the second stage. We don't know what the third phase will *exactly* look like, but four technologies are key: telepresence, telerobotics, weak migration rules, and the secret."

He shares a quiet glance at Greg and me.

"Lowering the costs of moving people will be the most disruptive phase. It's easier to pick up and move people freely around. Technologies like VR will substitute 'being anywhere' at all." He addresses Andy. "Imagine if someone in India could remote control a cleaning robot in New York for 90% the cost of a US citizen! Services account for 70% of the economy. The third phase will upend far more jobs than the drop of manufacturing did in phase one. That's lots of people hitting those Temp Camps," he smiles, tapping ash off his cigar.

"And the barrel gets a bit deeper. Dropping the cost of labor for us all," Marc toasts.

"Here, here," Winston salutes.

We all raise our glasses and drink.

"Jen has the sweetest deal of all," Greg adds. "She has five hundred *prisoners* working for her, for free."

"*—five thousand.*" I correct with a wink. Greg's face morphs to surprise.

"Already spoiled rotten?" Marc laughs incredulously. "Holy hell."

"What a deal! Can we have some?" Winston smiles.

I love this. Even Mr. Jacobson is envious. I casually shrug. "I'll have more soon. Send proposals. I'll think on them."

"No wonder the prison deal with Ormo is stalling," Marc irritably scratches his chin. "But if only prisons could scale. That's the problem. I wish more countries were willing to lock their people away. To Ormo!" Marc cheers and the circle clinks glasses again.

"A great position, Jen," Winston applauds. "Brilliant part of the 13th amendment was the loophole for slavery. Slavery is illegal, except as a punishment for duly convicted crimes. Then prisons are allowed to put prisoners to work and take the profit."

Andy smirks. "And funny how 'crime' is becoming more common these days, eh?"

"Hell, in a *truly* free society," Marc adds, "people could work without pay if they want! Worship hard work just for the sake of it, if that's what they believe."

"—or are made to believe." Winston grins.

Marc nods, "As compensation, they'll earn invaluable experience and the satisfaction of hard work."

"A fine dream," Winston chimes. "That's the frontier for sure. Bummer that prisons aren't usually full of the brightest folks." His chubby cheeks frown.

"Actually, I have lots of students and professors." I smile, drawing heat from the fire into my fingers.

"Really? Wow, perfect!"

"How much do you make?" Mr. Jacobson asks.

"Personally? Um, about $1.1 million a month," I sip.

"Psshst," Winston complains. "In revenue?"

"No. Profit." I smirk.

"Oh, my god."

Yes, I'm one of those. I bless the group.

"Well," Marc offers, raising his glass again. "To the Frontier, the forefront of civilization!" he slurs.

We raise a toast to my prisoners with expensive whiskey.

"Yeah," Winston says. "To the frontier. The subjugation of the brutes; those who worship each other, rather than themselves."

"Can you handle the Frontier, Jen?" Mr. Jacobson asks, his face stern.

"Sorry. Handle what?"

"Enforcing civilization? Are you *actually* comfortable with inequality? The real world doesn't work like a prison," he laughs. "Can you squeeze and humiliate labor *without* a State serving them to you on a gold platter? That's the test of character, Jen. Holding true to your ideals no matter what." Mr. Jacobson finishes with a dismissive sip.

I look firmly at the silent group, drop my glass to the ground, and stormily walk away.

They laugh at my departure.

Ten feet away, I snap my fingers and shout, "Wine bitch!" at my server who is assisting a couple under the heat lamps forty feet away. "Serve me!" I shout, opening my arms expectantly.

He tilts his head at my voice in a terrified glance, apologizes to the couple, and hurries over. "More wine miss?"

"No fucking shit." I say at his approach.

Hands trembling, he starts to pour a glass of Cabernet. "No. Kneel." I mutter, fighting the urge to bite my lip.

"Huh?" he quizzically asks.

"Kneel as you pour!"

He kneels, his face level with my crotch. I drunkenly run fingers through his hair. *God, this is nice.* The whole yard is silent, staring, as he timidly offers a glass.

"Good bitch." I sip.

He moves to stand and enforce his will.

"No. Stay." I force a hand in his hair, chug a huge mouthful of wine, yank his hair back, and slowly spit a ruby stream on his face.

"Hey," he complains, struggling to remove his face from my humiliation.

I shake a gentle '*No*' as my mouth empties. My fingers clench his hair tighter.

"More." I drunkenly move my glass to his soggy figure. He refills.

I drench him again with a second shower of mouth-wine, resisting as best I can the burning urge of my crotch to eat his face alive. *Too many people watching,* I despair, fighting back arousal.

I hear guys laughing.

"Okay, enough alcohol abuse," Marc chimes.

I kick my wine bitch onto his back. "You're pointless without me," I scoff and return to the fire pit with a red wine soaked smile.

Everyone's laughing, except Greg, who hides behind an awkward nip of whiskey.

"Nice," Winston nods.

"Okay," Mr. Jacobson tenderly pats my back. "Point taken. I *believe* you're capable of labor practices we might enjoy." He clears his throat. "We're a global network experimenting with totally self-regulating markets—totally free from the restricted movement of ideas, goods, labor, and people."

"Really?" I ask.

"Even if it destroys traditional ways of life or nation states," Winston says.

Mr. Jacobson nods at the group. "We're policy entrepreneurs. We do infrastructure deals. International trade partnerships and agreements. We pour billions into international educational machines composed of think tanks, bloggers, temp agencies, and fake citizens' groups to portray the interests of billionaires as the interests of the common people—which is true, because inequality is so important to the economy." He swirls his drink, ice clinking in the glass. "We wage war on trade unions, public education, and all attempts to regulate businesses or tax the ultra-rich. Now, Jen, our machine is shaping governments across the world, leveraging of money to protect money."

"But we keep this quiet. Ya, hear?" Winston puffs. "We must counter any vocal and sustained will of the people, unless their 'wills' shape to our interests."

"We still need to think bigger, I bet," Marc adds with an open shrug. "Think 'religion.' Industriousness has been America's unofficial religion since its founding. Religions glue diverse groups into multi-ethnic empires, reducing stupid 'us' versus 'them' problems that slow business. The Market is our higher power. Issuing judgment. Rewarding good behavior."

The Market is our religion. Partly the alcohol, but mostly the heady conversation makes my knees weak. *Money is spiritual essence of the free market. The more money I have, the more godlike I am. The poor are without money, are dirty and full of sin.* I quietly murmur.

Mr. Jacobson nods, "Let's talk more, Jen."

I'm drunk, in the barn, when I finally see Val leaving for the bathroom.

I follow, wait, and sneak behind her as she leaves.

"Where is he?" I whisper, groping her tits. She spins to glare as I pat her ass. "Is he here?"

"Jen. Stop," she angrily pushes away my hand.

"No. Is he here…" I drunkenly run my other hand down her belly.

"—Jen. No." Val grabs my wrist with fury. "Stop asking. Now."

"Ha." I burp, "I can't." With glassy eyes, I stumble away; the floor already spinning.

I drink some water and pick off several of the small buildings from the mountain scene to use as ice cubes. *Yum.*

I dance sloppily with a duo of gay cowboys through the last songs of the night.

"What? Val left without saying goodbye??" I stammer at the valet desk guy. "What a bitch. Fuuuck herrr!" I slur, lips trembling.

I find Greg with a $100 bill to buy a ride home.

"Jen. Sssure," he mutters, leaning drunkenly on me as harsh house lights blink on. "Sorry you got ditched. We're going in thirty minutes." He wobbly offers an open hand. "Can you wait? Just a bit more?" he squints at me.

"Surrre. Fine. Thanks." I sit on a hay bale outside to slow my spins and wait, hardly able to keep my eyes open.

I watch the last of the party loudly stumble away. Two guests leave arm in arm. "I just loved those cute baby animals. Oh, honey—let's a get farm?" A fancy lady asks her man.

"Whatever you need, babe," he kisses her.

Gross. I openly gag at their affection and receive a sour look.

I watch the cleaning crew suck the last of the baby chickens into large shop vacuum.

I sigh. *If only I could suck people up like that...* I grin. *When Ormo's mine, I'll snort prisoners like cocaine!*

I envision a hundred inmates in line for execution. They're blindfolded, thinking they're about to die before firing squad. Their heads hang. They've no idea where or how huge I am. I loom over their specks of lives like a celestial deity, plug a nostril and snort them in. *Oh, god, that'd be so hot.* I grind my knees in lustful pressure at the mere thought of inhaling those lives. *Ugh.* I rub the imaginary bliss of that nose candy. *If only I had more useless prisoners. I'd snort some right now. Fuck!*

I look at my phone. *Maybe I just play with a few of them? Snuff the laziest workers?* The thoughts of the productivity gains, due to my terror, makes me wet. *Oh my god,* I grind my knees together even tighter.

I call Juan to see if he'll take me to work after Greg and Ben drop me off. No, answer.

"Asshole! It's only 2:30 a.m.! What better things do you really have? Seriously." I blast into his voice mail.

The limo delivers us home at 4:00 a.m.

I feel empty in my room. A buzzing hum angrily rattles my ears through the oppressive silence. I can't sleep.

I'm without my prisoners. I hate this loneliness. I need my connection. Why can't I have a connection that's permanent?

CHAPTER 27—REBELLION

Eddie. November 2027

I've only eaten only two bags of Jen's Humiliation Spinach this week. Five bags of goop wait in my freezer as emergency rations. I rub my chin, feeling more cheekbone than before. *I've lost five pounds.* I'm starving myself on principle. *Jennifer's artificial food crisis is insane, a crime.* An email this morning smeared a new layer of creamy shit on Jen's amoral pie:

"Supply chain disruption: Due to labor collectivization beyond Jennifer's control, a permanent 30% surcharge is placed on all food purchases. Sorry!"

"Is she starving us deeper into submission?" I ask Jen's three-inch wide belly jewelry on my desk. *Silver pedals outside, a black heart inside. A perfect fit for Jen. Ornate beauty camouflaging a dark oppressive heart.*

From what little news I dare sneak through the firewall, I know there's no 'Labor Collectivization' anywhere inside or outside Jennifer. She's rationally seizing an opportunity to price gouge innocent hardworking employees. *Squeeze us tighter, smaller.*

With a hand under my chin, I tenderly spin the silver flower. *The graves of my predecessors are on my desk...* The Bots needed to move it out of the way and dispose of it. I volunteered to take it, as evidence. As motivation.

I scan HR files with intense focus, looking for dissidents from each section, employees who might have interest in some "Networking Conversations." Research is slow. Painfully slow. I need to be ridiculously careful as I splice the search into my other work. She's drilled fantastically deep wells of executive omniscience into our corporate system. Jennifer can see my screen, read my emails, and largely forbids employees communicating with one another about what they're working on, unless it's absolutely relevant.

We've fallen so deep, we're an extension of Jennifer's ego, just another part of her.

I also pace my effort because I know the fate of previous dissidents: Instant Flushing or worse.

Jennifer once had a group of rebels who naively thought the System couldn't possibly keep track of millions of employees. So they tried to gather enough pods into Jen's brain to attempt an aneurysm. Jen's Mechanical AutoImmune system noticed the effort immediately and tore their pods to pieces right then and there. I was only notified after the fact, reading Jennifer's AutoImmune quarterly report.

I look at Jen's jewelry.

Who am I looking for? I check my paper matrix. *High IQ. High independent thought. Low System Scores™. Creative aspirations. I have only four names: Thomas. Sara. Alex. Rachelle. What can only five people do?!* I rub my temples. *Assuming they're even interested to meet and make plans?*

I remember Jen's conversation in those TempGrace cubes. "This is what happens, Ed, when you work to change things." Her long hair tousled around her beautiful face, the seduction of her vicious smile was intensified with dark lipstick. "First, they think you're crazy, then they fight you, and then, all of a sudden, you change the world."

Can I beat her at her own game? Fight back the doubts. Innovate. Change the world.

Her work was her life. She rarely left the office; only went home to sleep. Zero social attachment.

Maybe?

My doubts collapse on me. *I fell fast and hard. My life is her work too! Shit...* My blood boils again with thoughts I've burned into the ceiling the past few nights: *If only I'd known back then she already had over a hundred slaves locked away.* I was unaware of so much when we first spoke. Unaware what it really meant to fulfill the bottomless cravings of one individual's greed and lust. Unaware of the impending death of whole social systems, balances of power, and the total denial of the basic human conventions that have evolved to balance societies over thousands of years.

Fucked up, I chew my pen, walking to the edge of my pod. *Can rational self-interest, with the right justification, enable wholesale slavery?* But then I suddenly worry, *how do you emancipate someone who's not technically a slave? We're not technically slaves, though practical circumstances define that we are.*

I've turned off the gorgeous simulations of an imaginary outside world so I can better see the truth. I power the external lights to see what Jen's gallbladder cell wall looks like today. *If we're all vassals to the head, shouldn't rational self-interest ultimately expand the self beyond 'the self?' And include mandatory respect for the system and infrastructure that delivered Jennifer's success? I'm part of Jennifer's success. My co-workers are part of Jennifer's success. The city of San Antonio was part of Jennifer's success.*

Where's our share?! I touch the warm walls, watching the pulse of Jen's intensely far away heart vibrate the flesh that entombs me.

How did Jen so narrowly define herself, and forget about the health of the superorganism that supports her?

Did Jen's self-empowerment philosophy easily morph into the raging excuses of a closet psychopath? Or was she always fucked up?

I hear my computer beep with an instant message from Sara: *"Yes TH night works. Let's have cocktails and talk life. Kari's Bistro in New Pangue?"*

"excellent," I lean forward. *"8pm?"*

"sure," my conspirator responds.

I smile. *"the others are good to meet as well,"* I type. *"perfect!"*

Sara's dark skin, confident smile, and lit attitude have been non-stop for an hour.

"I've no time off, no rest. Even when I'm trying to eat, she'd call me: 'You are not here to rest. I'm paying a lot of money for you.' To her, I'm a slave. Not human." She shakes her head, complaining about her TempWork as a marketing director for one of Jennifer's clients, a high-end fashion line.

I eagerly nod. *I'm connecting with another person, and it feels so right.* I'm having fun. *Why haven't I gotten out more?* I sober, *until the $300 drink bill and $500 shuttle fee hits my bank account. But I don't care,* I brush off the worry. *We're finding a way out of Jennifer, no matter what it costs.*

"Then I realized," Sara waves her glass at Thomas, the old P&L Analyst contracted to an oil giant. "*Predatory behavior* is the sin. Bosses, corporations, markets, collectives, governments…are all tools! It's when those in power choose to abuse those without, to benefit themselves—that things sour. Labels are a distraction."

"Agreed," I add, looking at the group. "I've darkly realized, recently, some people—certainly Jen," I whisper, lowering my chin. "Actually, *lust* to abuse others. Seriously." I eye the table. "They *want* to inflict pain. Stay on top no matter what. That craving drives them, drives their reasoning. And it's so deep you'll never counter it. If you're in the way, and weaker, so long." I dismiss with a swat of my hand.

"No one can be 'totally free' to 'do whatever they want,'" adds Alex, from Inner Nano Engineering. "We've forgotten there *have* to be restraints. Limits on power. Or society will become permanently trapped in a godless goddess of greed," his hands points outside the bar room, "and it happened because people trusted *greed* to solve their problems more than their community could. Trusting that 'greed is always healthy, no matter what'? Utter foolishness!"

Thomas leans forward conspiratorially. "I'll tell you," the grey-haired man adds. "The greatest achievement of the Temp doctrinal system has been to divert public anger from the corporate sector to the government. The governments were at least *somewhat* under popular influence—unlike corporations," he nods around to Jennifer. "Businesses have plenty of rational interest to destroy the 'crazy idea' that government could be a tool of popular will; of, by, and for the people."

"Yeah. Thanks, Thomas," I add. "Anyone else?" I ask.

We sit quietly.

Rachelle scratches her arm. "We're alive, but not living," she sighs. "I feel that everywhere. I can't sleep. I'm done with this. All of it," she tensely looks at the dim bar across her seat. "I just want to give up and get a free lunch for once. Tonight, is basically my vacation," she says, throwing up her hands. "Before, Outside, we could take weekends off and hit the beach. Now, a night like this costs *the same* as a week-long vacation!" She points to her drink. "When I was unemployed I could at least work on my own things. Spend time with friends. Collectively work on things," she eyes us suspiciously.

"Here's what worries me," Alex turns heavy. "It's going to get worse. Worse than this. Sooner or later, we'll run out of jobs. We already have, when you look Outside." He points behind his shoulder and through the hundreds of miles Jennifer's flesh to the world beyond. "Even Inside, Jennifer's nano-automation is getting better each year. I've seen the process improvement simulations we run in Robotics." He looks sternly, "And they're *bad* for many of our co-workers. Now that Jennifer acquired all System developers, she can introduce physical robotic *and* software combinations Inside and Outside to businesses across the economy. We owe it to ourselves tonight to think about what society will look like *without* universal employment. The days 'everyone who wants a job, can have one' are long gone. We need to nudge Jennifer toward better outcomes for workers. Question is, Eddie, how?"

"Totally, Alex. Thank you." The table looks at me. I shift uncomfortably. "None of you speak directly with her. My influence is actually really small," I deflate. "As small as all of yours. Honestly, she's *impossible* to have a conversation with unless she's humiliating you or telling you what to do. She's not interested in fact. She warps whole realities to feed her bottomless emotional and psychological needs. It's Jennifer first, and always."

Sara sighs, "We'll never 'win' an argument with someone so extreme; those types are never open to counterargument."

I nod. *This is getting bleak.* We sit quietly.

I speak, "With a future of abundance, I hoped we'd never need worry about basics like food, never like we have this past week." I look at Sara, "Did you know seventy-two thousand coworkers got knocked into Storage this week because they couldn't afford higher food prices?" I snap my fingers. "Just like that." The fact genuinely surprises everyone. "Did you also know that Jennifer makes $87 million a *day* in profit? And our incomes all had a 30% food tax?"

If that doesn't radicalize them, nothing will. Beyond learning the fates of our predecessors. Need to sit on that bombshell, for now.

Alex is upset. "I value hard work and profit, sure. But not at the cost of people's lives. *No,* " he clenches his fist. "Some profits shouldn't be made."

"Well, it's not our place to say what profits a corporation can and can't make though. That's a *regulation,* " Rachelle's face turns sour.

"But I've no motivation!" Sara's anger boils. "Jennifer's so exploitive. I don't give a shit about her profits. She's hundreds of thousands of times richer than us. How can we live consumed by such inequality? She's consumed our lives," she pats her belly. "We need to protect those who are just starting out so they don't stumble blindly under the feet of gods."

Splendid, I smile.

Thomas frowns, "Intense wealth inequalities rapidly corrode cooperation. The more people know the true scale of how much Jennifer makes above her workers—the more we'll lose our ability to cooperate." He laughs. "I was a history professor, before TempColleges took over," he brushes off the past. "There's a pattern in history. When a empire expands to becomes successfully dominant, common survival of the people becomes less and less a goal; the selfishness of the elites and special interests consume the political process. The spirit 'we're all in the same boat' is strangled by a 'winner take all' mindset among elites who cannibalize each other, enriching themselves as everyone else becomes increasingly impoverished. Soon, a formerly great empire becomes so dysfunctional that more cohesive neighbors can tear it apart."

"And eventually cooperation drops to where even barbarians can easily strike at the heart of capitol?" Sara asks.

Thomas nods.

"We can be those barbarians," I say.

"Might not even need the war paint." Thomas frowns, "Arnold Toynbee once said, 'great civilizations are not murdered— they die by suicide.'"

"Okay. We wait," Rachelle says. "Jennifer will eventually commit suicide—economically."

"And where will *we* be when that happens?" Sara asks. "Locked in a corpse?"

"No. Of course not. She'd never allow that," Alex says.

"Yes. She would," I say, my head low. "Might even prefer it."

"Prefer it? No way," Rachelle scowls. "Who'd be that weird? Come on. Let's just wait for the IPO, get rich, and retire," she shrugs.

A few others nod.

"An IPO is a reasonable approach," Thomas agrees. "Sharing the wealth. Ensuring co-workers have a stake improves collaboration. We have to be wary of violence. Inequality increases violence. Getting shares kept me here. Everyone will win big and we'll be more equal. This inequality is only temporary."

I shake my head. "What if the IPO's a lie?" I ask.

"Wow." Thomas raises his eyebrows. "You have proof it's a lie?"

"Not directly," I frown, feeling uneasy.

"Then we need to get the facts from Jennifer," Thomas nods. "Not your speculation."

My jaw clenches as my mind flashes to the tomb of our predecessors hidden in the Core. I can't share my suspicion that Jennifer has no desire to ever let us be independent. That we're permanently trapped unless *our group* finds a way out. I'd cause mass panic. A mass flushing. "We need to make plans. Get organized," is all I offer.

"But how do we fix this?" Sara asks. "How do we get our lives back?"

"Let's appeal to her greed?" Rachelle asks. "Use it? The more greed, the better."

Sara adds, "We could make it easier for employees to start their own, small, part-time businesses! Jennifer can own a small percent of the success and we build a network of business incubators across the System. *Inclusive* capitalism could create more shared prosperity. I dunno." She cutely bites a fingernail.

I nod.

"Liberated people are ingenious. They create profitable inventions," Thomas says. "Serfs, slaves, subordinated women, people locked in someone else's world—are not. They don't care. They don't collaborate."

"Jennifer won't listen to facts unless they directly boost *her power,*" I say. "Economics. Creativity. Development. None of these matter to her; only *power* matters. She'll never want us paid well, because then we might follow our own dreams and not be consumed by hers."

"Well, we can't quit. She'll Flush us," Rachelle says. "I'm not going to have three years of 24/7 hard work having me fight my way out of the sewer *again.* No, sir." She shakes her head.

"She'll Store us or Flush us whenever she wants," I counter. "It's in our contracts, encoded in the System. Our size too." I think for a bit. "It's all arbitrary."

"How do you know that?" Alex asks.

"I'm the System Admin. Jennifer approves System implementations, but I have root access. I can make changes to the roots of our operations. But it'll send any change alerts directly to her."

"Really?" Sara leans forward. "How?" she asks.

"In the Core, where the System hardware is, a few hundred miles from here," I point vaguely in a direction.

"You've been there?" Alex asks.

"Several times," I darkly snort. "Actually, I'm the only employee who ever has."

"Hm, that's something real," Alex responds, a bit flustered. He sits stunned and conflicted.

"I could go to the root. Barricade myself in and adjust the entire System. There'd be no way she could shut me down without destroying herself."

Sara nods.

"What adjustments?" Thomas carefully asks, his eyes tight.

"I dunno yet. Basic things? Like cheaper food. Free information. Lift the firewall around everyone's minds."

"What firewall?" Rachelle asks, confused.

I look at her. "Um, the firewall Jennifer ropes around the company. She filters all information we get from Outside. Even *I* don't really know what's going on."

"Ha, guess I hadn't noticed," Rachelle shrugs.

I swallow my nerves. Only Sara looks engaged. Thomas is suspicious. Alex seems lost in a daze.

"Hey, I'm open to ideas," I say. "We're a community." I note Alex cringe at the word. "I could reprogram the bots to ensure there's no Flushing. Free those in Storage to work Outside. Ensure wages reflect our effort and the market value of our work. We could invert our System approvals—employees could manage and approve *their* managers activities and decisions!" I laugh.

"There's lots of changes in the System Core we can make that would protect workers' rights and self-determination, even if we never protect particular jobs. I get it," I look at Alex, "technology makes jobs irrelevant—like the Nano department does all the time. But why not give workers the confidence and space to relearn? Not cling to 'how things used to be.' None of this is technically hard, we

306

know what levers to pull, we just need to do it. It's Jennifer's *power* that blocks us," I frown.

"And our fear. Who's to say *you* won't steal Jennifer's accounts and property for yourself?" Thomas suspiciously asks.

"Seriously?" I ask flustered, as my head tilts. "I'm risking my career, my *life* here."

"Seems like a rational opportunity to replace Jennifer, Inc. with 'Eddie, Inc.' Only you'd steal what Jennifer's worked so hard building," Thomas accuses.

"No! Guys, I mean, that's not why I'm here. Maybe I could? Come on," I stammer. "I'm trying to collaborate here."

"Look. It's hard for us to assume you won't take an opportunity to steal profits," Rachelle layers her own doubts. "If *all* that money is lying on a table in the Core, like you say, it seems rational to me that you'd take it all and run."

"Wait. No, these are *our* profits. Our work that's been taken from our teams," I stab my heart with an angry thumb.

"Redistribution isn't the answer," Rachelle dismisses. "That's been proven by TempScience." She blinks several times. "You have to work harder if you want more money. Ed. It's that simple," she collects her things to leave.

"Jesus, guys!" I tensely grip the lounge chair arm. "This is *our* work. Jennifer is profiting from *us*. The value you earn ought to be yours. Jennifer, Inc. can't *totally* be just about Jennifer! There has to be more," I shout, wringing my hands in frustration.

"Well." Thomas folds his napkin. "Let's meet same time and place next month, Eddie," he says and glances suspiciously around. "We'll hear your specific ideas and exactly how you'll implement them." He looks hard at everyone. "You all can share your ideas too. The more concrete, the better."

"Sure," Alex nods, looking sad.

"I'm fine with that," Rachelle thinly smiles with a twinkle in her eye.

"Okay, I'll have more details then. Fine." I shrug. "Sara. What do you think? You've been quiet."

"I dunno man, it's so over my head. I'll have to think long and hard on this stuff," Sara says, three fingers rubbing her temples.

"Okay, sure," I relax.

Everyone stands. Only Sara looks me in the eye as we shake hands. Our enormous tabs are reluctantly paid with groans.

"Oh, Sara." I interrupt her shocked review of a $438.39 bill, as the others depart.

Gosh, she's cute...

"Yeah?" Her smile brightens the dark room.

"What'd you *really* think?" I ask with a hand on my chin.

"Great meeting. *Lots* of ideas," she smiles.

"Um, hey. I know it's a lot today. I get it," I rub my arm. "I take for granted a lot I've seen. So, um, if you want. I have an info dump here you could take a look at in your spare time?" I reach in my pocket for a small flash drive and hand it to her. "It's a summary of the shitty things Jennifer's done to us with the raw data. At least what's well documented. We're not allowed to share any of this this," I whisper. "Keep it close." I close her hands around it.

"Gosh, Eddie. Wow." A nervous smile crosses her face as she looks to the door.

"Read my notes. Look at the reports. The System's wrecked, Sara. *Wrecked.* We need to fix it so the pains are shared by more than just us, and gains are shared by more than just Jennifer." We walk to the exit. "And if you get confused by anything, give me a call. Or we could meet up again, maybe you and I?"

"Okay," she says and gives me a quick, shallow hug. "Hey. Gotta catch my shuttle." She looks at her smart phone. "Lots to think about."

"Totally! Yeah." I squeeze into her again. The curves of her chest and hips brush against me.

"Oh," she backs away, awkwardly smiling again, "Okay, 'Bye,'" and walks into the crowded street.

"Sara, what did you think of my note?" I instant message her two weeks later. *"You never responded to my draft :)"*

"oh hey," she responds three days later. *"been busy sorry! i quick looked. pretty intense. are you sure you wanted to share this with me?"*

"Yes! I do! please keep reading," I eagerly type. *"I want it to hit the greater world one day..."*

A warning jumps into my mind: "Violating the confidentiality agreement will result in Termination."

"ok" she types.

There are so many things I want to tell Sara but can't under Jennifer's omniscience.

Sara, I want to hack the System at the core. Share my story. Share Jen's stolen wealth and destroy these invisible chains she's tightened around our necks! I want Jennifer to collapse. I want Jennifer to end so all employees may live a free and self-directed life.

Sara, I think you're pretty. I think you're smart.

Sara, I'd like to buy you a trip to a park or a one-way return ticket to the world of natural light. I'll take you to dinner on a beach, ask about your hobbies. Maybe you're good at softball. Maybe you like to sing crappy pop tunes. I want to know. I want to love you. Start a life.

Sara, please read the files. Find my note.

"Does that plan make sense?" I look at the sour faces of Alex, Rachelle, and Thomas around our dark Kari's Bistro table.

I'm disappointed Sara had a last-minute project from her boss this week—but I can no longer delay justice.

I miss her smile.

She makes my purpose seem real. Greater than myself.

"The plan's not going to work," Rachelle says with a stony face.

"Why?" I ask, noting her rude tone.

She reaches into her coat pocket. "Because you three are officially sanctioned as Collectivists and In Breach of Contract! You're all off to Storage!" she says, raising her Inspector badge.

"What?" I blink in shocked disbelief. "An Inspector? When did that start?"

"Two years ago, moron. All of you, up!" She waves her fingers forward.

Thomas starts laughing. "I'm a Special Agent for area A132!" He reaches into his pocket to reveal his own special identity card. "I'm investigating Eddie, too. Sorry, it looks like you *two* are gonna have a bad day," he grins at Alex and I. "Conspiracy for Community and Anti-Privatization is added to your charges."

My heart pounds, my legs unable to move. "No, no, no. I'm sorry. Alex," I blink tears at him.

Thank god Sara didn't come! Thank god Sara didn't come!

Alex looks at me with dead eyes, "Well," He says and reluctantly stands. "I'm sorry too. It's only *you*, Eddie." He displays his Special Agent ID as Thomas and Rachelle burst into hysterics.

"I've seven MechGuards here to arrest you for the unauthorized theft and use of CEO property."

"No. What?!" I bury my head in my palms, fury burning through my chest.

Alex's tone softens after he pushes a button on his phone. "You have interesting comments, Eddie, truly, but it's not right to take other people's property for yourself. That's violence, Eddie. And stealing Jen's jewelry? That's weird, man," he disproves with a scowl.

Seven MechGuards storm into the bar lounge, creating a wave of unexpected gasps among patrons jumping from their seats. A mechanical circle forms around me and slowly tightens.

"No. No. No. How are you doing this?!" I glare at the three. "You're defending a monster who's consumed us all? Jen's committed *murder!*" I shout at Alex.

"So you say," Thomas demeans.

"Hey, I'm getting a $5,000 bonus for this," Rachelle adds without apology. "Can't argue with half a year's salary! I *work* for my money, Eddie," she types on her smart pad with a smirk. "Too bad you can't learn that."

The guards close on me. "Admin Override. Stop all functions." I order the guards to halt and shutdown. I stand and run outside.

"Shit!" Rachelle reacts in panic.

"How do we contain the Admin?" Alex stammers.

"I don't know," she yells, chasing after me. "Get him!"

I run through crowded streets, through an artificial park to the nearest Terminal ticket kiosk. Fingers trembling, I order an emergency direct ride, key in my home Pod ID, accepting the 3000% surcharge.

"Sorry," the mechanical kiosk voice blurts at me, "The destination: Pod A0001-A0001 does not exist. Are you sure you typed correctly?"

"Yes!" I slam the wall and retype my home address.

"Sorry. Pod does not exist."

My heart rate skyrockets. I thrash looks of terror, searching for pursuit.

I type a new destination, any place close to the Core I can find.

"Sorry. Traveler ID A0001-A0001 does not exist."

An icy chill fills my veins. "What? Why?" I choke.

"No record and no authorization found for User. Try a new User ID."

I look frantically behind me. *No sign of my pursuers.* I close my eyes, trying to relax, thinking what to do next.

An angry red alert bursts on all digital billboards nearby: "Danger! Collectivist in area. Stop with all means."

"Fuck, fuck, fuck!" I retreat to an isolated area of the park with fewer pedestrians.

I crouch, clutch my phone, trembling like a trapped animal, and call Sara.

"Sorry this number is blocked," the System voice informs me.

"No," I cry as tears burst down my face. I nearly throw my phone to the concrete floor, angrily flailing my arms in frustrated rage. I breathe heavy and hard, my arms bracing my knees for support.

I look at an artificial tree. An artificial pond. The thin walkway through the small park. A child and his parents play with a ball in artificial grass.

Could I hide and live in the private park?

—No. Panhandlers are instantly thrown into Storage... I sigh heavily and sit my doomed ass on the sidewalk.

At least I'll get some rest in the dark oblivion of Storage. And I'll be alive. Technically.

Wait. I look at my phone again, my thumb hesitating over "Jen." *Do I have a choice?* I dial. The line connects.

"Hello, Eddie," she chirps. "How's your day?"

"Um. Something's wrong with my credentials," I thinly say, hoping she doesn't suspect anything.

"Yeah. I know," I hear her bite into an apple. "You've been naughty!"

My world crashes. I pinch my eyes. "Fuck." A sob tumbles from my mouth. *End of the road.* "Hey, can we negotiate?" I ask. "Jen? Please?" I cry.

"No, you've lost my trust," she says pleasantly.

"Oh, God," I explode with a harsh sigh. I look at the artificial ceiling, the artificial blue sky and artificial white clouds floating in the imaginary beyond. "Please forgive me? Please, Jen?"

"No," She says.

I swallow hard and calm the trembling in my voice. "Those guys in your jewelry. How long were they working for you?" I ask.

"Who?" she genuinely wonders.

"Those guys in your old belly button ring! Who I found in the Core." I rub my forehead, sadly looking around. "The ring with the silver petals and black center." Tears stain my face.

"Oh, yeah." She casually remembers. "Um, I dunno. A long time? Over ten years? They eventually got ideas like you, thought they could be independent from Me. No, Ed. No one leaves Me," she says. "Not now, not ever. Hey. Millions of workers are just fine with only Me. I don't know what to say." She sounds disappointed, "It's a bummer you can't be on board with that."

"Over a hundred-people died in there!" I scream.

"Only a hundred?" she asks. "Wonder where the rest went. Hey, so look," her tone shifts. "I've got a meeting. I've *finally* announced the secret to my success: In-Sourcing you all. And *everyone* wants in! All Corp shareholders are about to sign a huge contract with me," she reports as a grin radiates through her voice. "Don't have time for you dragging this out. Bye."

Click.

"Wait! What'll happen to me?" I ask her silence. I stare at my dark, trembling smartphone. "Oh god. Oh god. Storage for me, huh?" I look with vivid clarity at the concrete sidewalk and small scraps of trash next to me. I touch one. *Storage?*

Not me. It's supposed to be later or never. Not now. I melt into a human puddle of sorrow next to a few discarded candy wrappers. *I always knew we had an end date. But 'the end' is always supposed to happen to someone else. Not me.* A wrapper touches my hand and I look at it, my lip trembling. "Looks like someone ate the best parts of you too, and you're thrown away." I address my discarded brother.

The red wanted signs around the park suddenly blink back to advertisements.

My heart skyrockets. "What?" I wipe the tears off my face. "Jen canceled the search?" I wobble to my feet with a timid smile.

The red sign returns with an additional picture of my face and "$10,000 Reward!"

I feel a blow strike my side as I'm instantly tackled.

"Got him! Here's the Collectivist!" the man shouts.

I awkwardly struggle and wrestle with I have no idea who, nearly breaking free from his grip on my leg as a mob of once calm park-goers descends on me.

"No! Stop! What are you doing?" I shout, pulling away.

"How dare you take my hard work, mister!" A guy punches me.

Blows pound my chest and face. I feel my clothing rip.

"We *need* these jobs, ass. How dare you threaten them with your lazy sins!" A guy savagely kicks me.

I laugh through swollen eyes. *No one in this mob are types I'd even remotely consider would violently assault someone. An old man. A frumpy lady. A trio of teenagers. Am I this pathetic?*

A sharp pain sears my head as someone rips out a tuft of my hair. "How dare you be lazy. Fucking scum," a lady shouts, spitting in my face.

"*I* got him first! *I* was first!" A screaming between co-workers morphs into a secondary brawl between two men fighting over my reward.

Through the angry tangle of feet, I see MechGuards charging fast to facilitate order and my capture.

My protective curl pries open as I'm pushed flat on my bruised back by a dozen people pinning me down. I look through the blood in my eyes. I look at their hatred, their anger, their ignorance looming over me greater than Jennifer ever did.

"You're a disgrace to corporate generosity. You don't deserve Storage. That privilege is *our* afterlife!"

I see the bottom of a boot rise high and race towards my eyes.

The world explodes in permanent darkness.

CHAPTER 28—LIBERATION

Jennifer. September 2018

Time to check operations, my heart glimmers. I shut the laptop and nearly skip down the hallway with the giddy click-click of my stylish knee-high boots. After running numbers this morning, I discovered profits have *tripled* since removing dozens of wasteful steps from workshop operations last quarter.

Tripled!

Rather than waste *My* time shrinking and unshrinking materials and supplies and being in the middle of all that headache; a few months ago I entirely redesigned storage and product component flow. Store rooms and their parts are now *directly* accessible to all critical points of my assembly line.

Now the guards enjoy their own recreation and media areas, a small spa, a video game arcade—all perks for staying loyal. Ormo taught me to always keep the muscle happy.

And we don't need to build a new prison at all. Ormo sent the biggest check of My life as a 22nd birthday present. My mood sours thinking about him. *He's getting scared. Or cold feet?* I've no idea. He frustratingly refuses to meet me in Valparaíso. All we do is send dirty texts! *Coward.*

Get over here and let Me crush you. I clench my thighs in frustration.

Whatever, I dismiss, leaning into the retinal scanner. The workshop door lock unclicks. *I have all the men I need.*

My heart jitters with joy as I walk into the Operations room. All prisoners stop what they're doing and stand at attention as my footsteps thunder their earth. I think how often women internalize the message it's better for us to be smaller. *No, fuck that. I'm a Titaness made real!*

"Relax, boys. Back to work," I tell them. I permit their attention to return to their jobs only after they wave and shout their love up to me. Even Giorgio offers his admiration.

I sigh, relax into my comfortable administrator chair high above operations, and watch my workers' toil; radiating a powerful affection over them. I spend two hours a day simply watching the sprawling complex of clear plastic hamster cages that imprison my five thousand workers. The colorful plastic tubes twist and turn from the factory room to the packaging area, storage, dorms, recreation room, and a kitchen. The standard hamster palaces were hilariously too large for my half-inch men. I nearly died laughing when realized I needed to make the cages 75% *smaller* to match the scale of my employees!

And an added benefit of minimizing operations? I list, *No one disobeys Me when they're half-an-inch tall. I have all the respect, attention, and obedience I've always deserved.*

What a marvel, I smile with a hand on my chin. *My little civilization.* I relax, having fun thinking about how much money I make each second, while sitting and being magnificent.

How the hell is All Corp dragging their feet on this? I frown at their incompetence. *They must be totally delusional to not see the opportunities. Good thing I'm here to take the technology to the next level. Libertarians can't organize for shit. I'll have to breathe life into their Free Market dream, by force. Which I suppose is how Free Markets evolve anyway. Assholes.*

Force, and fear of force, allows me to finally own souls.

I take good care of those who are worthy, and train workers to do anything to keep me happy while expecting nothing in return. I can be firm and ruthless, or caring and generous when needed. If I'm feeling generous, someone might get rewarded or assigned a special task. I've trained my workers to love it all, no matter what.

My thoughts wander.

I'm My workers only link between their workshop prison and the market. I'm their sole source of life and sustenance. I grin, thinking bigger. *Manna—the spiritual energy necessary for society to thrive, came only from Hawaiian god-kings. Hawaiians were convinced the whole world would fall without the king's Manna connecting the world of gods to men.* I look at the colorful tubes full of miniature men hard at work. *I hold their whole world together. I'm their world. Their deity.*

The thrill surging through my veins becomes too intense. *Today, I need My fix!*

"Worship break!" I shout and stand imposingly. "Bow, losers," I demand. All of the prisoners stop what they're doing and lower their faces to the cold plastic cage floor, aligning with me as their Mecca.

"It's funny." I laugh down at the workers. "I suspect humans are way more intensely hierarchical than we think. If they don't have an actual god," I open my arms suggestively to Myself, "they make one up." I point to the ceiling. I sigh into a comfortable warm glow. *Why do I only do this three times a day? This is all so sweet.* I marvel at their puny kneeling bodies as excitement churns inside me.

I open the top of my warehouse, the largest hamster cage, to enjoy a closer look. I note someone looking bored, moving his head around.

"Naughty! You know the rules," I say, brushing my hair behind an ear. "You're only supposed to focus on *Me*." I lower my right thumb and squish his distracted defiance into a pool of goo and blood. No one else moves, and I spare his neighbors the same judgment.

Murder gives me a high unlike any other. It feels unreal! *Absolutely fantastic. I'm so proud of Myself!*

The occasional execution also minimizes any unbelievers stupid enough to actually demonstrate a lack of belief in Me; like being too slow to prostrate before his god-queen, or doubting a product direction or compensation package I offer. Operations work smoothly, and thus more profitably, when people fully internalize the social norm that I am their Absolute. They don't stop and think. They don't waste time with questions. There's no option for defiance, only obedience to Me.

Ideal market efficiency!

Ormo says none of these guys will see the light of day anyway, so I can do whatever I want.

Finally. Pure freedom!

"Thank you, gentlemen," I stand and smooth my expensive dress. "Brought you a treat today." I reach into my purse for a cookie wrapped in a napkin. "Like chocolate chip?"

They jump and cheer.

"Perfect! Make room. I'm coming in." I jab the cookie at the center of the cafeteria area and slowly step one foot at a time through the open hatch of the largest cage. My boots tower two-hundred feet above them. I'm beyond caring whether their insignificant eyes look past my tight knee length skirt. *Enjoy the view, if you dare, boys. It can kill.*

I eat, allowing my crumbs to tumble to the slaves at my feet. "Damn, this is a good cookie," I chew. "Have at it."

Workers dash through the rain of crumbs to grab whatever they can, while trying to avoid the larger pieces. I've crushed more than a few skulls doing this. *It's their fault for not paying attention.* I lean over the work yard, enjoying massive bites as a sensual smile spreads across my lips. Crumbs shower through the clear plastic ceiling openings. I watch fights break out over receiving the honor of My Manna. *Only My crumbs feed you.* I devilishly wiggle my toes in my sexy boots. *Who knew trickle-down economics was so steamy?*

I stand tall, my relative eight-hundred feet figure shadowing the plastic prison I've built around them. "You're nothing. No longer even human. Just an extension of Me."

I adore being in charge. I feel powerful, sexy, sensual. I swear these work sessions are like getting high on drugs. *If so, then fuck me, I'm hooked!* I feel warmth between my legs, watching them flinch at my mere presence. *Total bliss...*

Playfully, I hover my left heel over their yard. The workers jump and scatter as I laugh, "Hey, look. This is the W88 model from last week. Check out the beauty of your hard work." I show the amazing craftsmanship of their boot on my foot and lower it mere inches above a dozen men. "Ha. Wouldn't it be funny if your own work killed you?" I laugh. "I'd love that. Keep up the hard work," I coo, slowly lowering my foot over the men, who scatter away in time. I laugh and place the other foot outside the hamster palace and return to my throne.

I sit in my chair and watch.

Beautiful. "Guys. I want to speak honestly here." I adore with a hand on my chin. "Scrape all thoughts from your mind that you'll ever be equal. That's never been even a remote possibility." I scoot my chair closer. "No. The truth is that you'll look at me with a face of fear, but mostly an expression of awe, of worshipful wonder, and a dose of lust. You'll beg to offer yourselves to me, but it won't be necessary. I already know what you want, and you're going to get even more than you hoped." I lean intimately forward. "All because I noticed a glimmer in your eyes before you dwindled away. I know, secretly, deep in your hearts, buried so deep you don't even know...

You want this." I point to the vast difference between My Glory and their patheticness.

"You *want* to be pushed around. Minimized as much as possible. You tell Me to stop, but I know that's the last thing you want. Before this fiscal quarter is over, I'm going to make you admit how *hot* all of this oppression makes you feel." I raise an excited eyebrow. "Then the fun *really* begins, and we'll become something special."

A week later, the riots start on my drive to work.

I wouldn't have come if I knew about this mess, I fume at the fucked traffic of downtown Valparaíso. *Could've worked from home. My pets don't* really *need to eat.* "Why didn't Val tell me this shit?" I check my phone again for any response to a what-the-hell's-happening text.

Nothing.

The driver honks at an unmoving horde of people in the street and apologizes for my mounting irritation.

Over an hour later, I storm into Val's office, asking what the fuck's going on. When I enter, it looks more empty than normal. Her photos, artwork, and fashion magazines are gone. A few cabinets have turned into outlines of dust on the wall. Other cabinets hang open with empty drawers. Her desk is clear, except for an envelope. I approach and see it is marked "Jen."

I open the letter to read a mass Death Warrant with a note: *"It's over, Bitch. Execute them all and run."*

"'It's over'?! Fuck, fuck, fuck." My throat tightens and mouth dries. "The regime's over? How? Is Ormo dead!?" My heart plummets as I reach for the Red Phone. The line's silent. *Damn it!* I slam the phone on the desk once, then twice, and then several times, shattering it to pieces.

"No! It was so perfect!" I growl through shallow and fast breaths. "I'm not done yet! God damn it." I scream at the empty room.

Is everything I've worked for over? I call Uncle Greg on my cell phone, pacing across the room three times before he connects. "How long for a helicopter out?" I blurt, "Yeah, I know. Shit's fucked. The prison roof? Forty-five minutes?" I look at the clock. "10:15? Sure. No, I don't care how much it fucking costs. *Jesus!* Hurry. Yes, I'm fine. Gotta clean up. Bye."

I use the black phone to call all remaining guards to protect the doors. *Half of them didn't show today!* "Shoot to kill, if needed. Defend this place at all costs." I demand their lives from them. "Protect Me."

The chief shouts his praise and his honor.

Yeah, yeah, I end the phone call.

"My prisoners. Shit." *No one can know about my operations.* I haven't even told Uncle Greg about my new and improved processes. *Didn't wanna risk that bombshell,* I worry. *I love and respect the man, but it's obvious that he can't be trusted with his own medicine.*

I jog to the war locker, grabbing some grenades. Running to my operations room, I realize as I enter: Dead men still speak.

Can't have tiny corpses lying around, that'll look bad.

My slaves obediently fall to the floor in prostration as I enter.

The beautiful sight pains my heart all the more. "Gosh. All this hard work!" I sigh. "You're all so perfect." I bitterly slump on my throne and savor the last seconds of the immense beauty at my feet.

"It's been fun, guys. It really has," I slowly kneel on the floor, soaking them in, wanting us to be as close as possible. "We've come so far. I'm happy with so many of you. I really am." I caress the plastic tubes with a sad smile at My five thousand men. I moan in frustration, then stand, unsure exactly what to do next. "Let's at least get organized," I huff. "Okay, on your feet. Line up. Office relocation time."

They comply in hesitant confusion.

I dump a bulk box of packaged cookies on the floor, lift the access hatch to my worker's cage and lay the box on its side near the main work yard.

"In the box. Now," I say.

They obediently march in.

"Careful now," I warn as the last few enter, and gently tilt the two-foot by two-foot box upright, tenderly cradling it in my arms. They tumble and adjust. "I love rocking your world," I coo at them, my hair streaming past the box rim.

Five thousand men feel so light. So nothing.

I carefully set the box aside and pile all the supplies and evidence I can see on the Agravity pad, and shrink it to nothing. I stomp on a few spots to make sure of its destruction.

I look at my phone. *Twenty minutes.* I sit next to the box and peer in. All their tiny faces look at me in unison as I approach. They're standing around as if packed in a popular concert hall waiting for the next show to start.

"Guys. I really, *really* wish there was a way to keep you working…" I watch their confusion turn into intense concern.

Can I save some, tuck them away? I look at the basic supplies on the shelf and spot an untouched hamster ball in its packaging.

"Yes!" I grab the plastic ball, joyfully spinning it in my hands a few times before opening it.

"Hey, Section Leaders," I announce over the box. "Raise your hands." About seventy workers obey. "All of you, to this corner." I point.

They walk and cluster. Other prisoners shuffle aside.

"Raise your hands again." I see most everyone is where they should be and reach in, scooping them in the hamster ball. Three handfuls work for all seventy.

I shut the ball door and hold it to my face. "Perfect," I laugh at their worried faces on the walk to the Agravity pad and shrink the ball to smaller than a BB. I pick it up.

"Where to hide you?" I think, gently rolling the tiny ball between my fingers, greatly enjoying the chaos and terror I'm causing the men. "Oh! I know." I open the office supply cabinet for a roll of packing tape and lift my shirt. "Guys. Make good friends with My belly button lint." I lift my silver and obsidian flower belly piercing, and push the ball deep into my navel, sealing them in with a short piece of tape. "Here's some air," I say, gently poking at the tape with the point of a scissors. "There." I drop my shirt and pleasantly rub my belly. "That feels really nice, actually." I nod in satisfaction as a deep glow spreads from between my legs to every inch of my body. *Mmm...*

"What do I do with you?" I look at the box. "Whatever I want, I guess?" I answer with a smirk. *Oooh, I know.*

My breath quickens as I kneel next to the box. I pick a random guy, hold him in my hand, and compare him to a dark red fingernail. "Did you know, in old times," I caress him, "images of rulers 'eating' poor people show up across history?"

He shakes his head, no.

"In ancient India, the king was called, *vishamatta*, 'the devourer of peasants.' Cool, eh?"

He looks confused.

"Eh," I shrug and my gaping maw consumes him whole.

An explosion of feeling erupts on my tongue. His terror. His warmth. His soul. His whole life locked behind my lips.

The best part is the idea that his entire life led to this point! I simmer at the thrill. *Everything he's ever done. Every struggle. Every dark day was not to make him a stronger person. Just a better meal for Me. I imagine all his dreams and expectations on how his life will go—shattering to dust right now on the tip of My tongue.* I slowly play my tongue over his thrashing limbs, reminding him how small he is. How cruel life really is.

My darkness is his darkness. Forever. I tilt my chin slightly and swallow him alive.

I feel a flutter in my stomach as he enters and struggles.

Oh my god. Oh my god. My hands clench the fabric of my dress shirt. *Oh my god.* I sit overwhelmed by the surge of pleasure flooding all prior dams of restraint. *He feels amazing. I love him so much.* I almost cry with joy, savoring his every twitch and jump. I memorize our togetherness. *A whole person is inside Me! A whole person is becoming Me!*

The tenderness of our love entwines in the purity of our permanent connection.

I eventually feel his activities drown.

More.

I move to the cookie box like a greedy child and grab another love to consume. Swallow. Grab another. Swallow. I grab another not even seeing who it is. Swallow. My frenzy stuffs thirty snacks down my throat before I begin to ache.

"Ugh. Too many already?" I frown, feeling disappointed and bloated. "I'm never going to eat *all* of you fast enough." I look at the time, feeling nauseous but amazing. I pause with my hands on my knees. "*Ugh.*" I burp, the back of my hand covering my mouth. *Better not puke. Better not puke.* I look at my food baby and gently massage my children. "I'll remember you forever," I sigh with a pat.

The room contracts.

"Oh no," laying my hands on the concrete floor. *Something inside doesn't feel right.* Despite how amazing it feels, is a fundamental part of me is rejecting this? I lean forward, arms trembling, and puke up half my men—many of them still alive.

"Gross." I scowl, watching the few without broken legs struggle to their feet.

I can do this. I can do this, I chant, scooping the mess of ten men in my hand before the ones who can run get too far on their little limbs. One even bolts two feet before I toss him in the box, to the intense screams of horror from others.

"Sorry guys, I'm full!" I frown, oblivious to the terror below. "We'll have to do this the quick way." I move the box to the Agravity pad to make my prisoners smaller. *Much smaller.*

Examining the now one inch box, I'm barely able to view the seething faces. "My eyeball is bigger than all of you!" I laugh at what is essentially a small stadium in My fingers. "In you go."

I shoot them in my mouth like a college girl would a tequila shot, and crumple the box in my pocket. I've no water to chase them and have to make do with a slow, dry swallow. Five thousand grains of human sand tickle my throat, mouth, lips, and tongue.

I love how insignificant My workers are.

I hear gunfire echo down the hallway. "Fuck." My heart quickens. "Guys," I inform anyone alive. "Those assholes will *never* find their friends and families. *Never.* You don't even exist anymore." I grin. "You're in your permanent prison. Your permanent home. Me."

I savor the omnipotent glow, slowly appraising the room.

"Shit. The Gizmo." I note the revolutionary contraption and move to stack it and the computer on the pad, bringing them to a micro-sized toy—using a broom handle to trigger the ignition. "I'll borrow another Gizmo later." I carefully wrap the quarter-inch Gizmo in tissue, and tuck it into a makeup container in my purse.

I stop. *No dummy, what if someone steals your purse?*

I remove the small Gizmo from my purse, lift up my shirt and gently peel back the tape across My belly. "Ouch. Fucking hairs," I complain, stomping a foot. I carefully tuck the wrapped Gizmo into my belly button next to the ball of men, sealing the tape again. *Now all My workers are safe and secure.* I smile, gently stroking the contents of my belly.

I peek out the door. Not seeing anyone, I adjust my hair and fix my outfit in the mirror. *Wonder what the five thousand workers struggling for life on My tongue and in My throat are feeling?* I lick my lips, wondering if anyone is stuck on them. I remove a dark cherry lipstick from the purse, apply another coat, and casually toss three grenades behind me. My soulless operations room explodes once I'm safely down the hallway.

"If anyone asks," I say in a cute little girl voice to my workers, drowning in my spit, "'I'm just the secretary. Val ran out, I'm not sure where. You know she's the General's sister?'" I laugh.

On the rooftop garden, I sprawl across a reclining chair as smoke billows across the seething city. The sun's hot and warm. I smile as gunshots echo across the city; my tongue explores little grains of human sand stuck in my teeth. *My little secret,* I smirk.

Noting that it's 10:10 a.m., I walk to the edge of building. *What the fuck's happening out there?* I muse with disinterest. An unwashed horde of thousands mobs the street. Burning cars. Smashing windows.

Destroying other peoples' hard work! I tisk, waving my hands over them for perspective, minimizing the chaos as much as I can.

"I'm the Gemini Giant this time, you fucks! I'll eat all you ants. You'll know only Me—your deity—whether you accept Me or not," I growl.

A wack-wack-wack thuds low on the horizon as five attack helicopters cut through the city. Four hover at each corner of the building, their guns menacing the neighborhood. The central craft lowers to the roof; seven black commandos jump out to secure the chaotic swirl of flowers, plants, and garden patio furniture with their assault rifles.

I'm waved forward.

"Thanks, boys," I shout, grabbing the nearest hand into the chopper. We lift into the sky, the city's failures disappearing behind as tall pillars of smoke.

Greg's estate is a fortress. Jeeps with machine guns patrol the perimeter. Heavily armed guards control all access points. Work crews install flood lights and heavy-duty command tents.

"What the hell happened?" I burst into Greg's hectic office, interrupting him with few senior militant dudes.

"Jen. That evacuation cost $180,000. These guys need payment *now*," he says.

The commando team looks intently at me.

"Fine," I roll and reach into my purse for the check book. "Who do I make it out to?

"Omni Security," nods a muscular gruff guy.

"—Sure," I say, scribbling.

"Mission number…" he references a clipboard. "Uh. Add this mission number in the memo line please," he looks at me. "Alpha 17 Charlie 84 Hector Delta Foxtrot."

"Huh?" I ask.

"For the accountants. A17C84HDF."

"—HDF?" I clarify

"Yeah," he nods.

"There. Thanks." I hand him the check.

"This better not bounce," the commando leader smirks as he leaves, with dark tones of rape in his final look.

"Ha. It won't." I drily laugh at his pathetic show of strength. *He doesn't need to know I'm worth $160 million. I'm just a dumb girl. Right?* The value of precious gems has gone *way* up with all the global instability. "Anyway, what the hell's going on?" I demand of the room.

"Ormo was assassinated. Seven o'clock this morning," Greg says.

"Oh." I try imagining one of my prisoners assassinating Me. *Never could happen. They're too weak.* I gently tap my belly. *Smart.*

"Who did it?" I ask.

"One of his favorite lieutenants, ironically," a lead commando offers.

"Yikes. Well," I shrug. "That's the price of sharing power. The moron was soft."

Greg narrowly looks at me. "Jen, it's going to cost an *extra* $40,000 a month to live under private militia protection," he says, nodding to the guys around him. "And that's just basic expenses. Food. Water. Travel. Everything will be more expensive too."

"Fine. Whatever," I say.

Greg tenses his lips. "You're okay paying $62,000 a month to stay?" he asks, awkwardly scratching his chin.

I call his financial bluff with a shrug. "I suppose. I can afford whatever security and comfort I want." I eye an apple in a fruit basket on the snack table.

The casualness surprises him. "Um, oh. Well, actually, Jen," he suddenly becomes less diplomatic. "I want you out. And I want the Gizmo back."

"Can't. Destroyed the Gizmo." I grab an apple, then put it down for a better one.

"You destroyed the Gizmo?" His jaw drops in tense anger.

"Yeah. No evidence," I lie, cleaning the apple with a sleeve.

"Jesus. Jen, why didn't you take it with?!" Greg rages, a hand tugging his hair.

Is anyone still alive, stuck in My lipstick, to witness this conversation? I darkly muse. "Um, capture? What if some crazy political party got a hold of the technology and had no morals. We'd all be goners, jeez!" I roll a pair of eyes and take a bite of apple, distractedly wondering how many lives the simple action ended. An intense surge of warmth drips from my heart, down.

Greg points to the fruit. "The Gizmo doesn't work on organics. What's the threat? Fine. Whatever. That sucks, Jen," he sneers. "Expect a $25 million invoice coming your way. And you better fucking pay it. Find a way."

"Whatever. Sure," I take another apple bite. *Yum.*

"Jen." Greg continues with his fucking lecture. "I've heard rumors about your prison the past few weeks. Dark fucking rumors. Suddenly, all the prisoners have disappeared? And not even the guards know where they are. All Corp loses the new prison contract. Thousands are arrested by Ormo. Thousands are sent to jail and never seen again? What the hell happened?" he glares coldly at me.

"Val, she had things really locked down." I enjoy another bite. "Couldn't trust the guards. Not sure what she did." I chew. "Remember her saying 'we should just the shoot the fuckers' the past few months. I was in administration, focused on the workshop."

"Yeah? Really? Well no one talked about Val. They talked about you. About 'The Empty Goddess.'"

"Ha!" I laugh. "Really? I'm not empty. Promise that," I say. *I'm full of thousands of people.*

"Jen. Honestly, I don't feel comfortable with you here. At this point, your liabilities outweigh your potential returns. You make this place a *huge* target. I'm about making money, not politics. Honestly, I think you're a lot more like Grandpa than I first worried. I've noticed things. How you treat servants. Your attitude. Gave me chills… Thank god you're a woman, and only men can be bad guys. You're not violent, just antisocial."

I feel workers churning in my stomach. *Probably struggling to use bites of apple, bites of My manna,* I correct, *as life rafts.*

Struggling for last chances at life only I can provide, yet choose to deny. I smile, feeling light. At peace. I've never been happier.

"Fine. I get it," I nod pleasantly. "Okay. Bye, Greg. Thanks for getting me here. I'll be packed and out in a few hours." I wander away. I grab a bottle of wine on the way upstairs to finish Myself and the rest of my prisoners off.

I pack two suitcases, keeping only my favorite shoes and dresses. "Only the things that give you joy," I drunkenly remind myself debating a purple and black dress.

I open a large jewelry case and drool at so much money. An intense amount. My fingers tenderly worship my wealth and simultaneously I finger the belly button tape. Giddy bolts of energy rocket through my veins.

This must be what heaven feels like!

I'll look poor. Pretend to be poor, invest this money. *Buy a small army or a navy? Use the Gizmo to set up My own workshop.* I push the tape and the trapped men deeper into my soft flesh. *Oh god that feels amazing. An office hidden in a belly piercing?!* I shudder in pleasure and anticipation at the glimmers of distant dreams clicking into place. *Put the Gizmo on a turret to fire at anything or one I want?*

I caress My stomach. *I'll have My workers' souls so close. My only wish for the ones inside me already is that their suffering didn't end so quick, that they could last longer.* I throw more unwanted clothing onto the leftover pile.

One day, I can take American TempCamps to the next level. Help millions of people know the immense peace of My ownership and rearrange the entire socioeconomic landscape of the earth. To be more free.

More Me.

I shut the suitcase and lug it out the door. *Become the next Mr. Jacobson? One day I'll eat him alive too. Everyone alive will rot in My guts. Where they belong.* I reach under my shirt to caress the seventy hidden souls, and smile.

Whoever can live will live only as Jennifer.

The End.